MARVEL LEGENDS
BLACK PANTHER

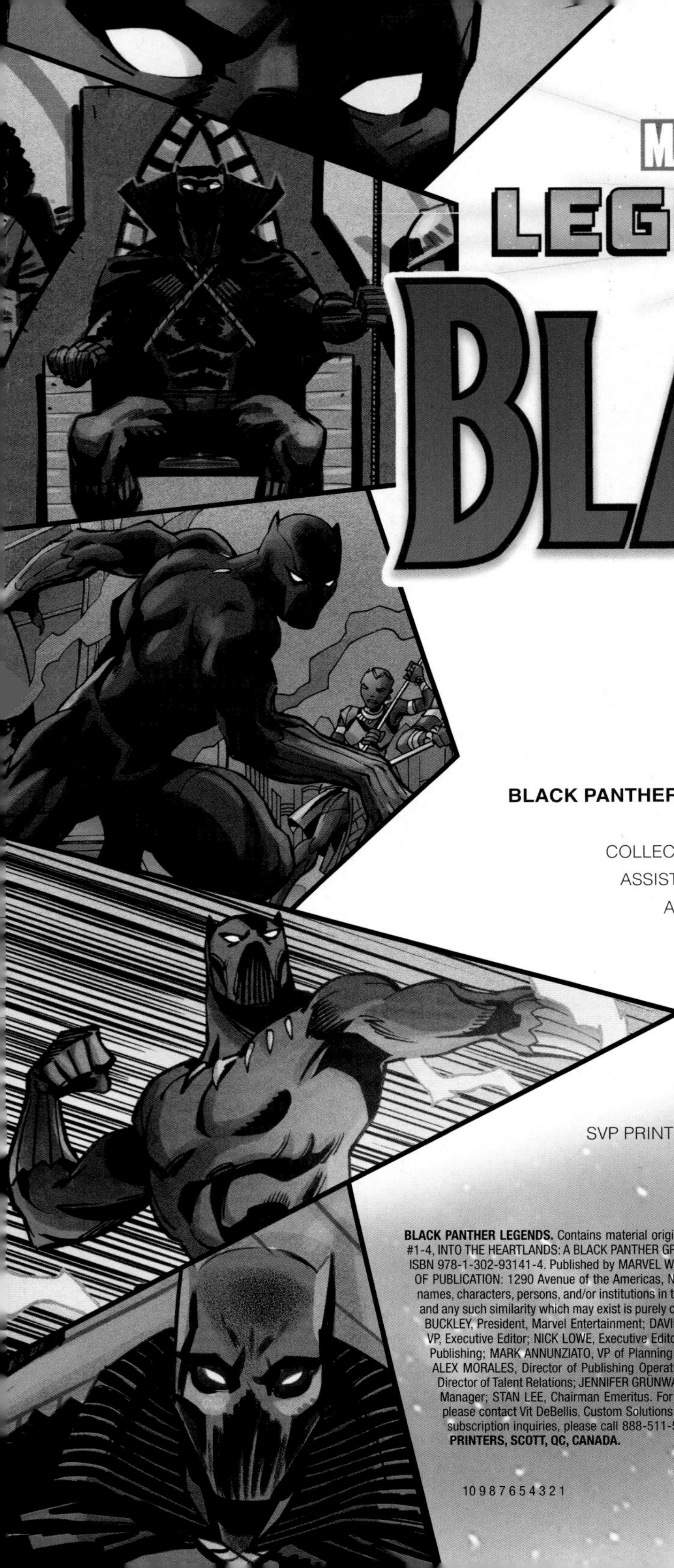

MARVEL

LEGENDS

BLACK

BLACK PANTHER CREATED BY **STAN LEE** & **JACK KIR**

COLLECTION EDITOR **JENNIFER GRÜNWAL**
ASSISTANT EDITOR **DANIEL KIRCHHOFFE**
ASSISTANT MANAGING EDITOR **MAIA LO**
ASSOCIATE MANAGER, TALENT RELATIO
LISA MONTALBAN
VP PRODUCTION & SPECIAL PROJEC
JEFF YOUNGQUIS
BOOK DESIGN
SARAH SPADACCI
SENIOR DESIGNER **JAY BOWE**
SVP PRINT, SALES & MARKETING **DAVID GABRIE**
EDITOR IN CHIEF **C.B. CEBULS**

BLACK PANTHER LEGENDS. Contains material originally published in magazine form as BLACK PANTHER LEGENDS (2 #1-4, INTO THE HEARTLANDS: A BLACK PANTHER GRAPHIC NOVEL and SHURI: A BLACK PANTHER NOVEL. First printing 2 ISBN 978-1-302-93141-4. Published by MARVEL WORLDWIDE, INC., a subsidiary of MARVEL ENTERTAINMENT, LLC. OF OF PUBLICATION: 1290 Avenue of the Americas, New York, NY 10104. © 2022 MARVEL No similarity between any o names, characters, persons, and/or institutions in this book with those of any living or dead person or institution is inten and any such similarity which may exist is purely coincidental. **Printed in Canada.** KEVIN FEIGE, Chief Creative Officer; BUCKLEY, President, Marvel Entertainment; DAVID BOGART, Associate Publisher & SVP of Talent Affairs; TOM BREVO VP, Executive Editor; NICK LOWE, Executive Editor, VP of Content, Digital Publishing; DAVID GABRIEL, VP of Print & Di Publishing; MARK ANNUNZIATO, VP of Planning & Forecasting; JEFF YOUNGQUIST, VP of Production & Special Proj ALEX MORALES, Director of Publishing Operations; DAN EDINGTON, Director of Editorial Operations; RICKEY PUR Director of Talent Relations; JENNIFER GRÜNWALD, Director of Production & Special Projects; SUSAN CRESPI, Produ Manager; STAN LEE, Chairman Emeritus. For information regarding advertising in Marvel Comics or on Marvel. please contact Vit DeBellis, Custom Solutions & Integrated Advertising Manager, at vdebellis@marvel.com. For Ma subscription inquiries, please call 888-511-5480. **Manufactured between 7/22/2022 and 8/23/2022 by SOLI PRINTERS, SCOTT, QC, CANADA.**

10 9 8 7 6 5 4 3 2 1

PANTHER

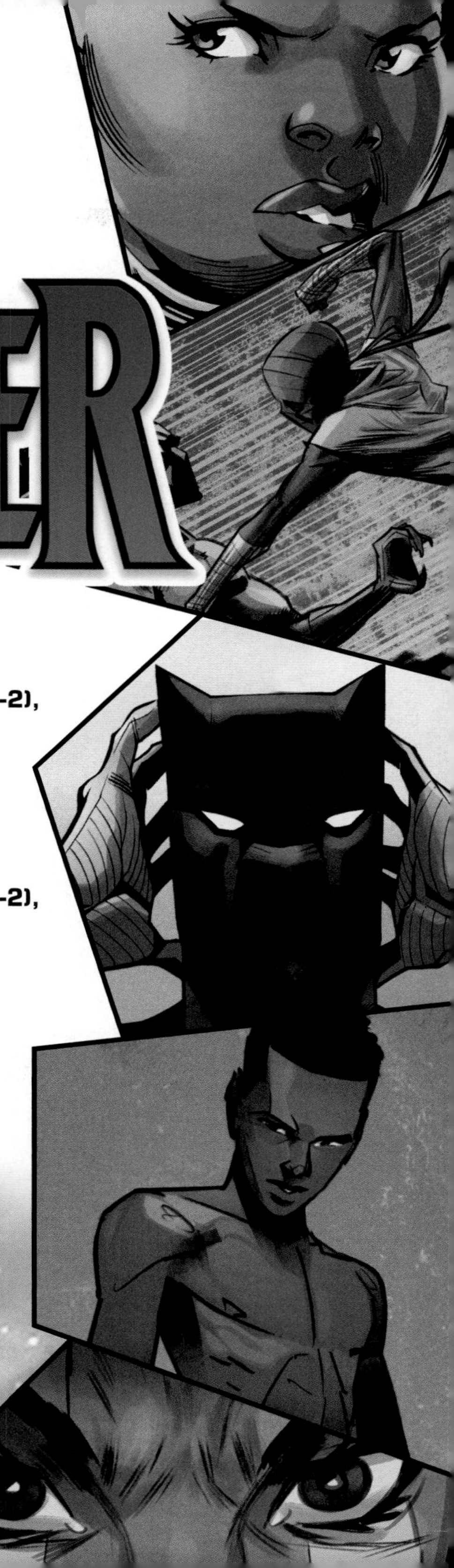

RITER TOCHI ONYEBUCHI

ENCILERS SETOR FIADZIGBEY (#1-2), FRAN GALÁN (#2-3), ENID BALÁM (#4) & RAMÓN F. BACHS (#4)

KERS SETOR FIADZIGBEY (#1-2), FRAN GALÁN (#2-3), ROBERTO POGGI (#4), OREN JUNIOR (#4) & RAMÓN F. BACHS (#4)

OLOR RTISTS PARIS ALLEYNE (#1-2) & IAN HERRING (#2-4)

ETTERER VC'S JOE SABINO

OVER RT SETOR FIADZIGBEY (#1-2) & JAHNOY LINDSAY (#3-4)

SSOCIATE DITOR CAITLIN O'CONNELL

DITOR LAUREN BISOM

ONSULTING DITOR WIL MOSS

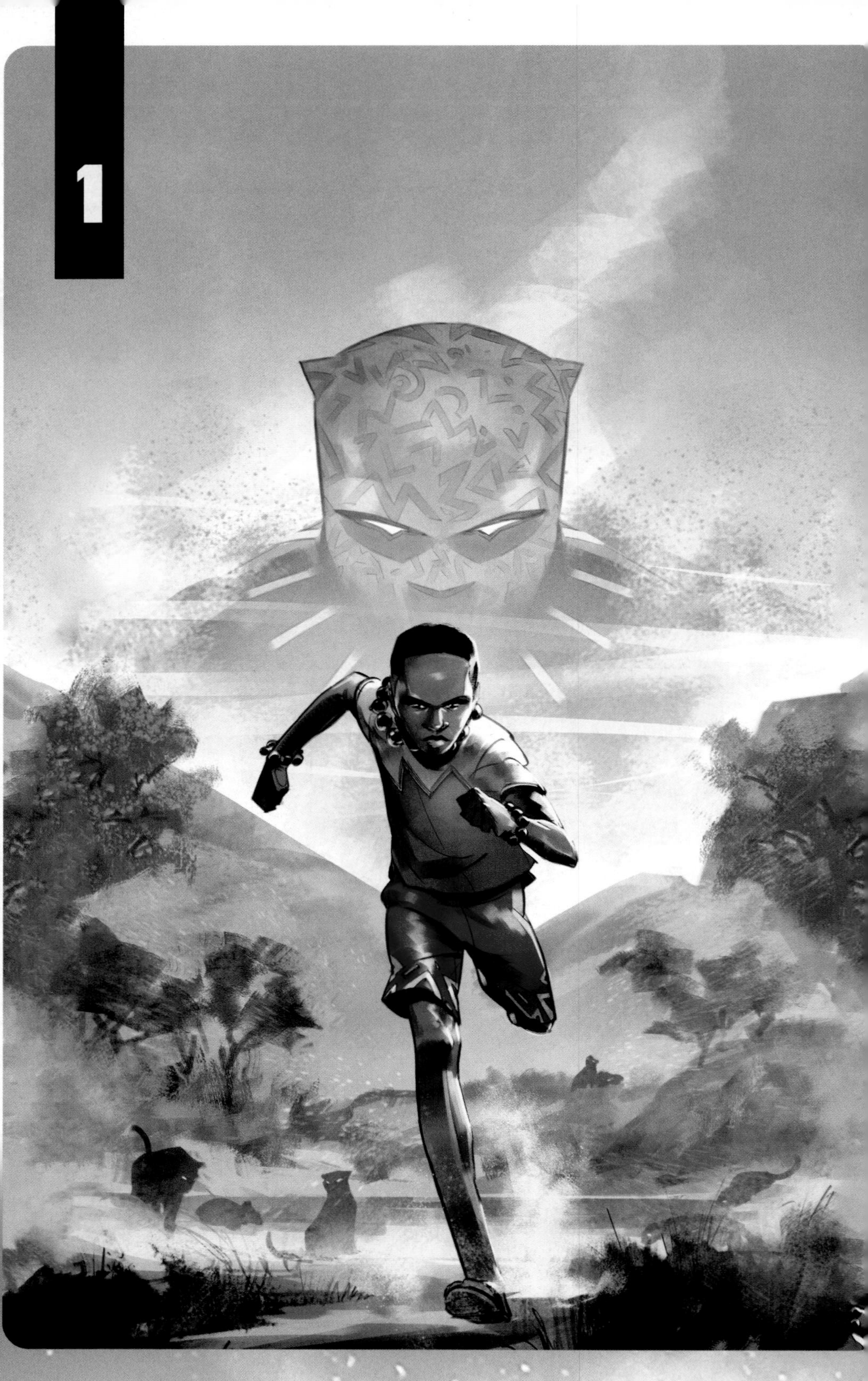
1

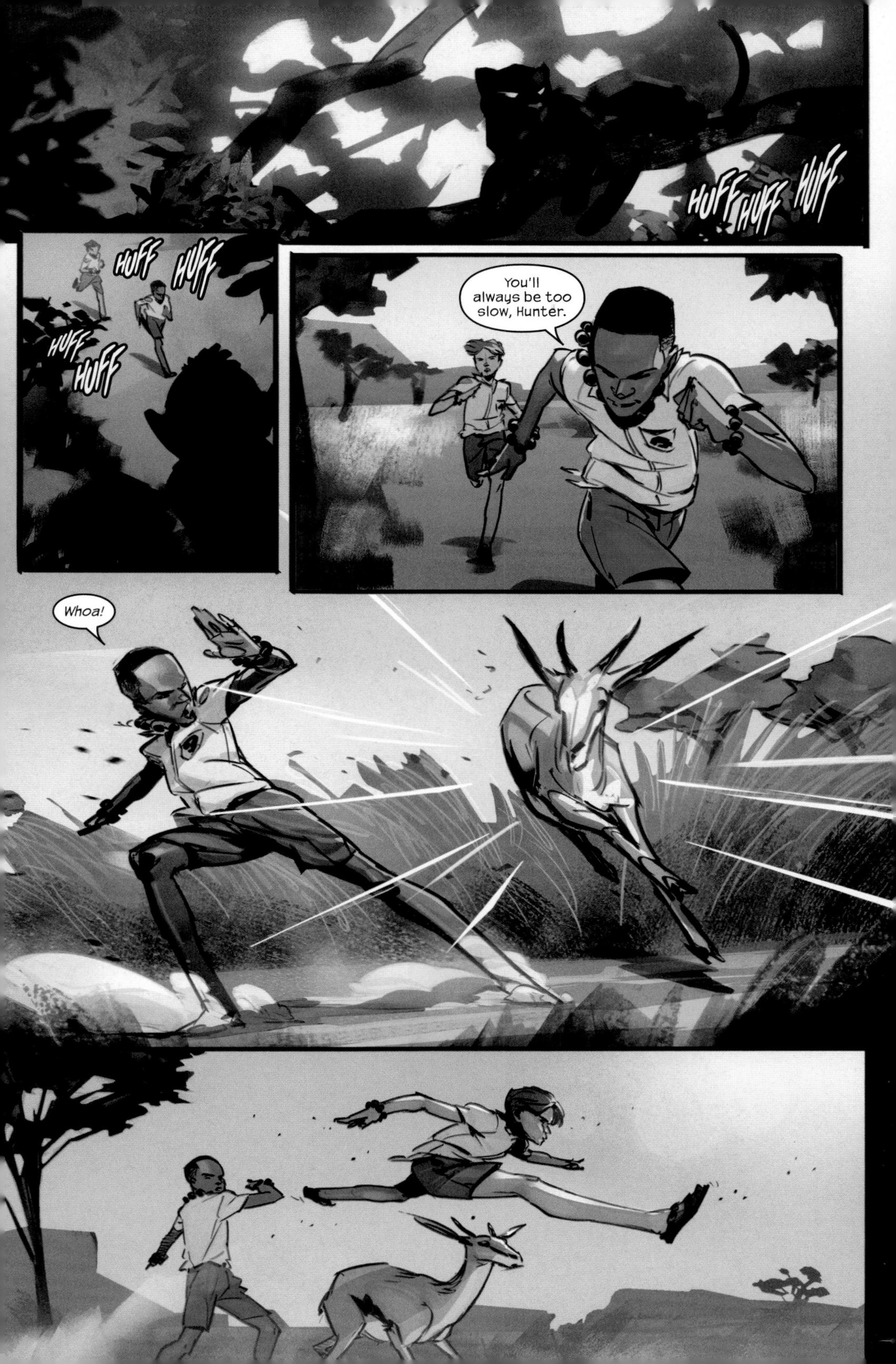
HUFF HUFF HUFF
HUFF HUFF
HUFF HUFF
You'll always be too slow, Hunter.
Whoa!

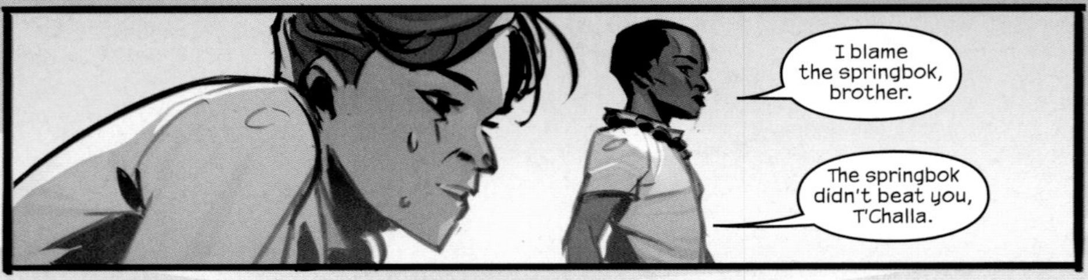
I blame the springbok, brother.
The springbok didn't beat you, T'Challa.

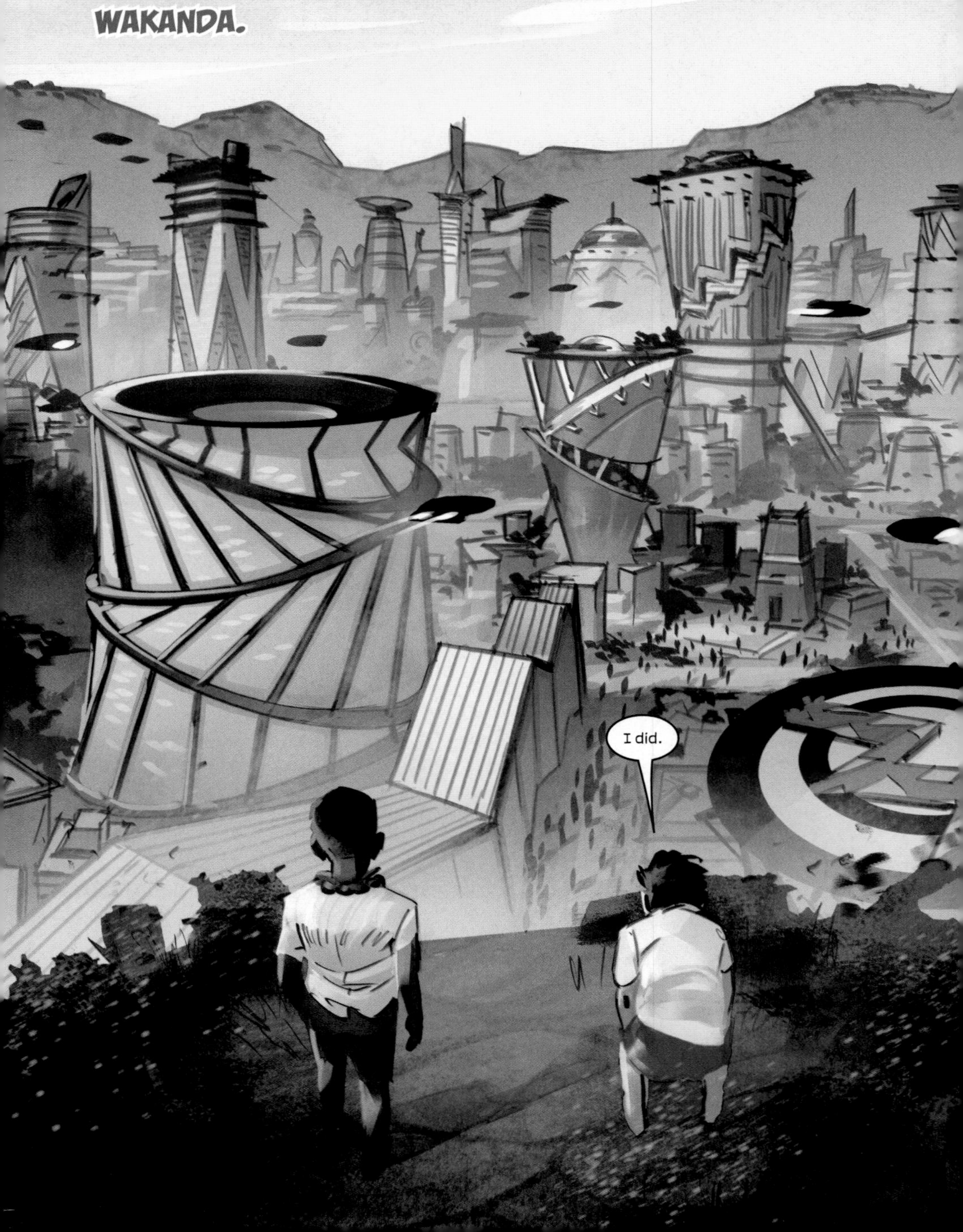
WAKANDA.
I did.

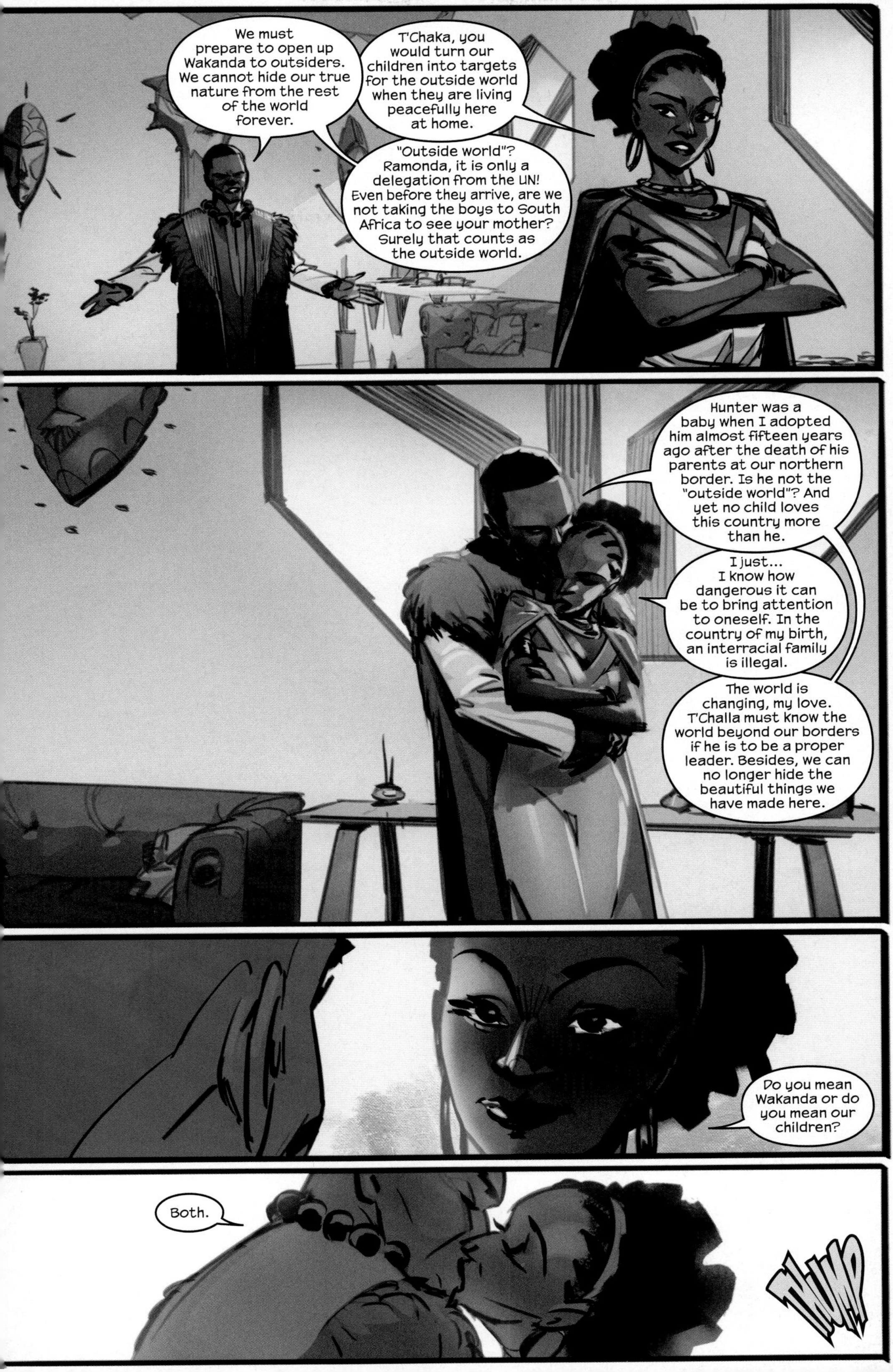
We must prepare to open up Wakanda to outsiders. We cannot hide our true nature from the rest of the world forever.
T'Chaka, you would turn our children into targets for the outside world when they are living peacefully here at home.
"Outside world"? Ramonda, it is only a delegation from the UN! Even before they arrive, are we not taking the boys to South Africa to see your mother? Surely that counts as the outside world.
Hunter was a baby when I adopted him almost fifteen years ago after the death of his parents at our northern border. Is he not the "outside world"? And yet no child loves this country more than he.
I just... I know how dangerous it can be to bring attention to oneself. In the country of my birth, an interracial family is illegal.
The world is changing, my love. T'Challa must know the world beyond our borders if he is to be a proper leader. Besides, we can no longer hide the beautiful things we have made here.
Do you mean Wakanda or do you mean our children?
Both.
THUMP

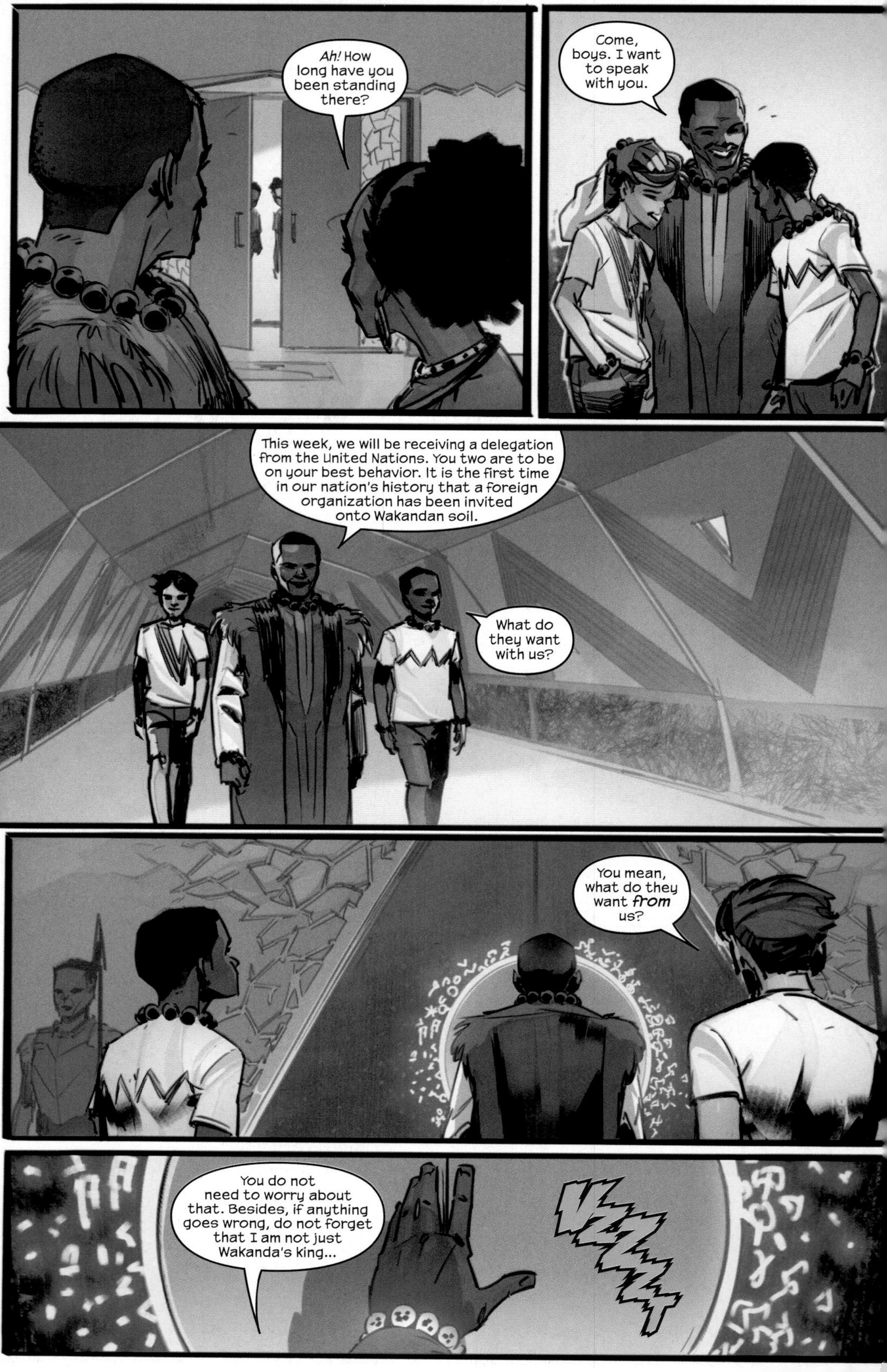
Ah! How long have you been standing there?
Come, boys. I want to speak with you.
This week, we will be receiving a delegation from the United Nations. You two are to be on your best behavior. It is the first time in our nation's history that a foreign organization has been invited onto Wakandan soil.
What do they want with us?
You mean, what do they want from us?
You do not need to worry about that. Besides, if anything goes wrong, do not forget that I am not just Wakanda's king...
VZZZT

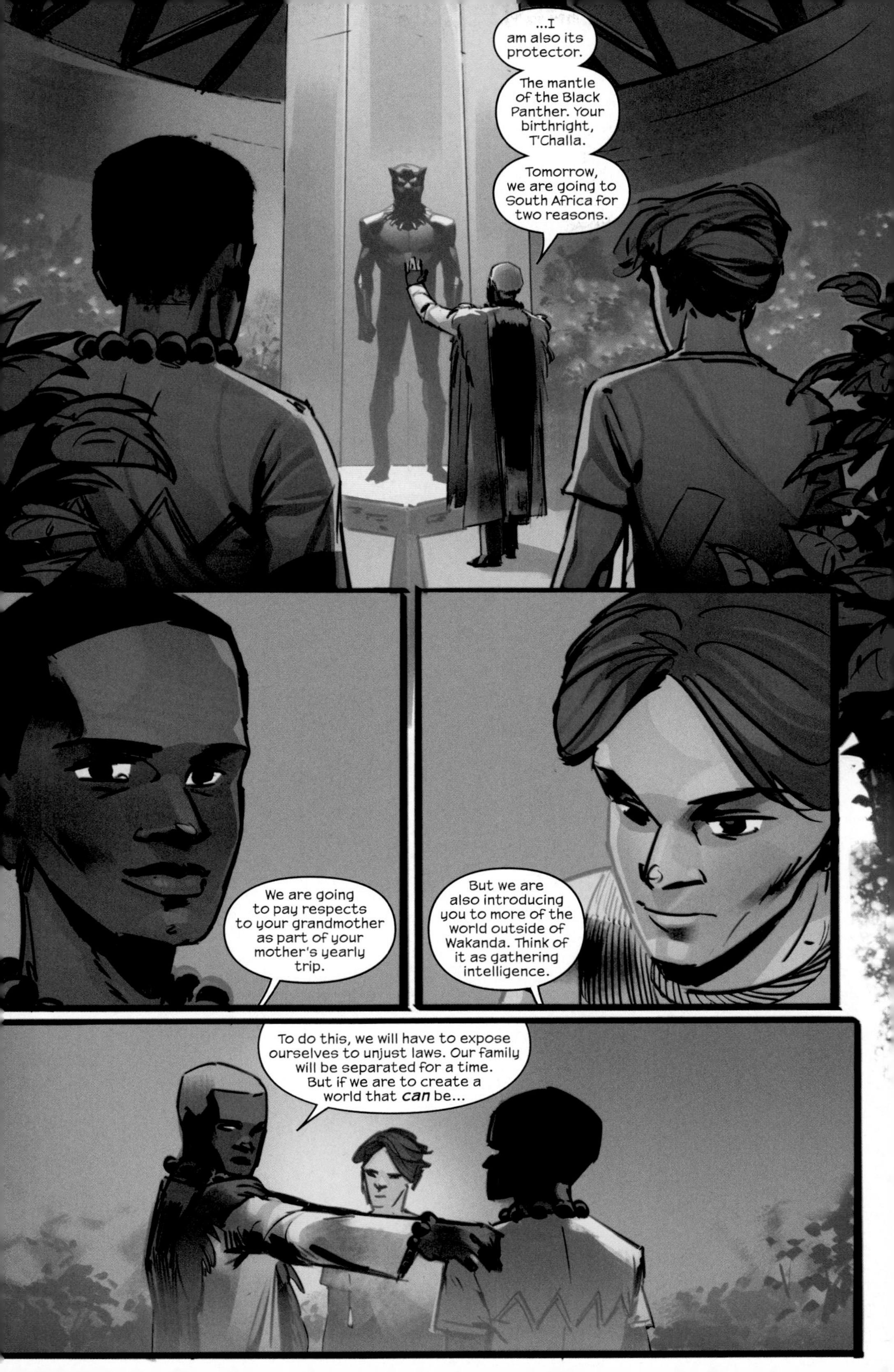
...I am also its protector.
The mantle of the Black Panther. Your birthright, T'Challa.
Tomorrow, we are going to South Africa for two reasons.
We are going to pay respects to your grandmother as part of your mother's yearly trip.
But we are also introducing you to more of the world outside of Wakanda. Think of it as gathering intelligence.
To do this, we will have to expose ourselves to unjust laws. Our family will be separated for a time. But if we are to create a world that *can* be...

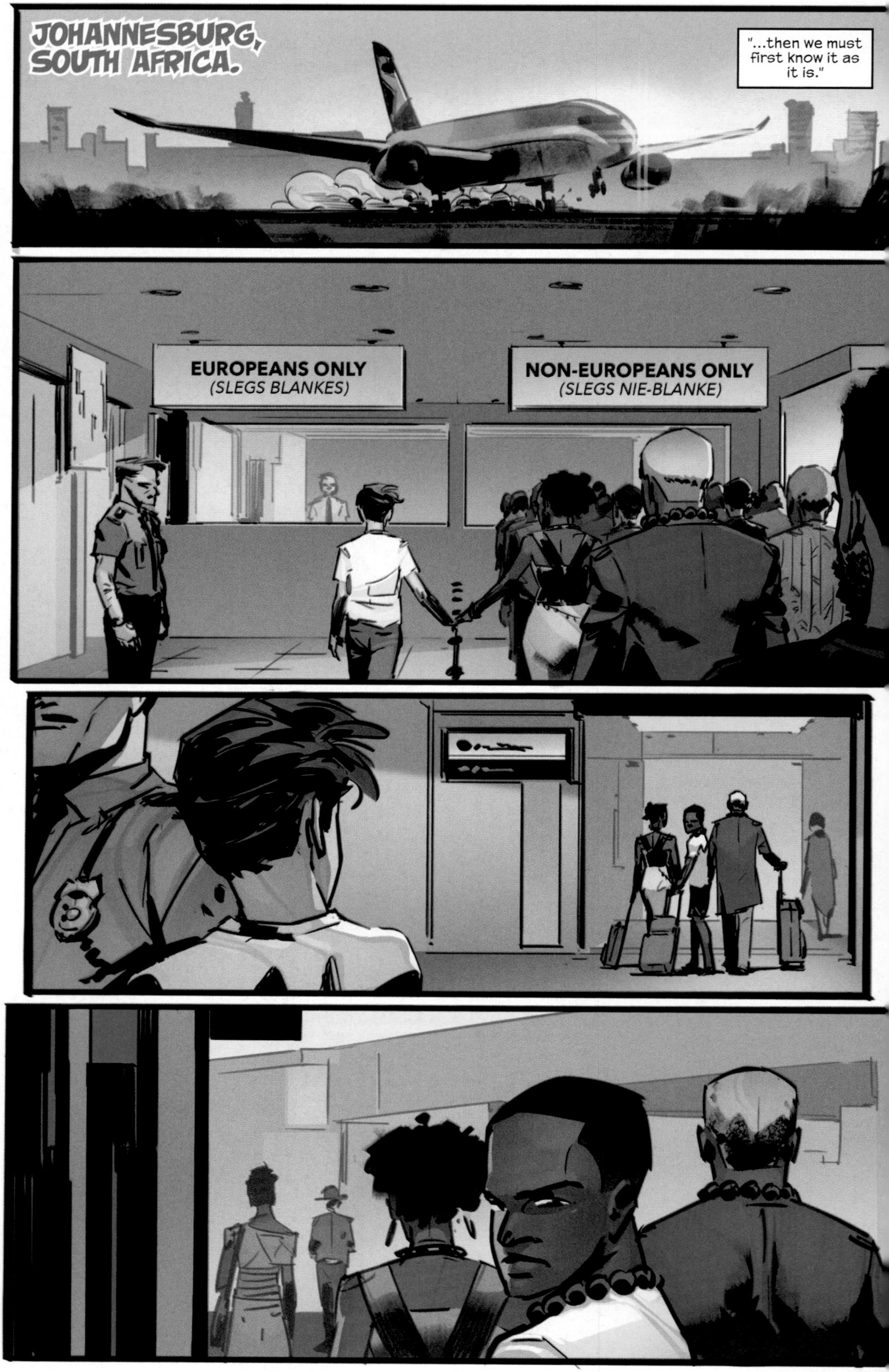
JOHANNESBURG, SOUTH AFRICA.
"...then we must first know it as it is."
EUROPEANS ONLY
(SLEGS BLANKES)
NON-EUROPEANS ONLY
(SLEGS NIE-BLANKE)

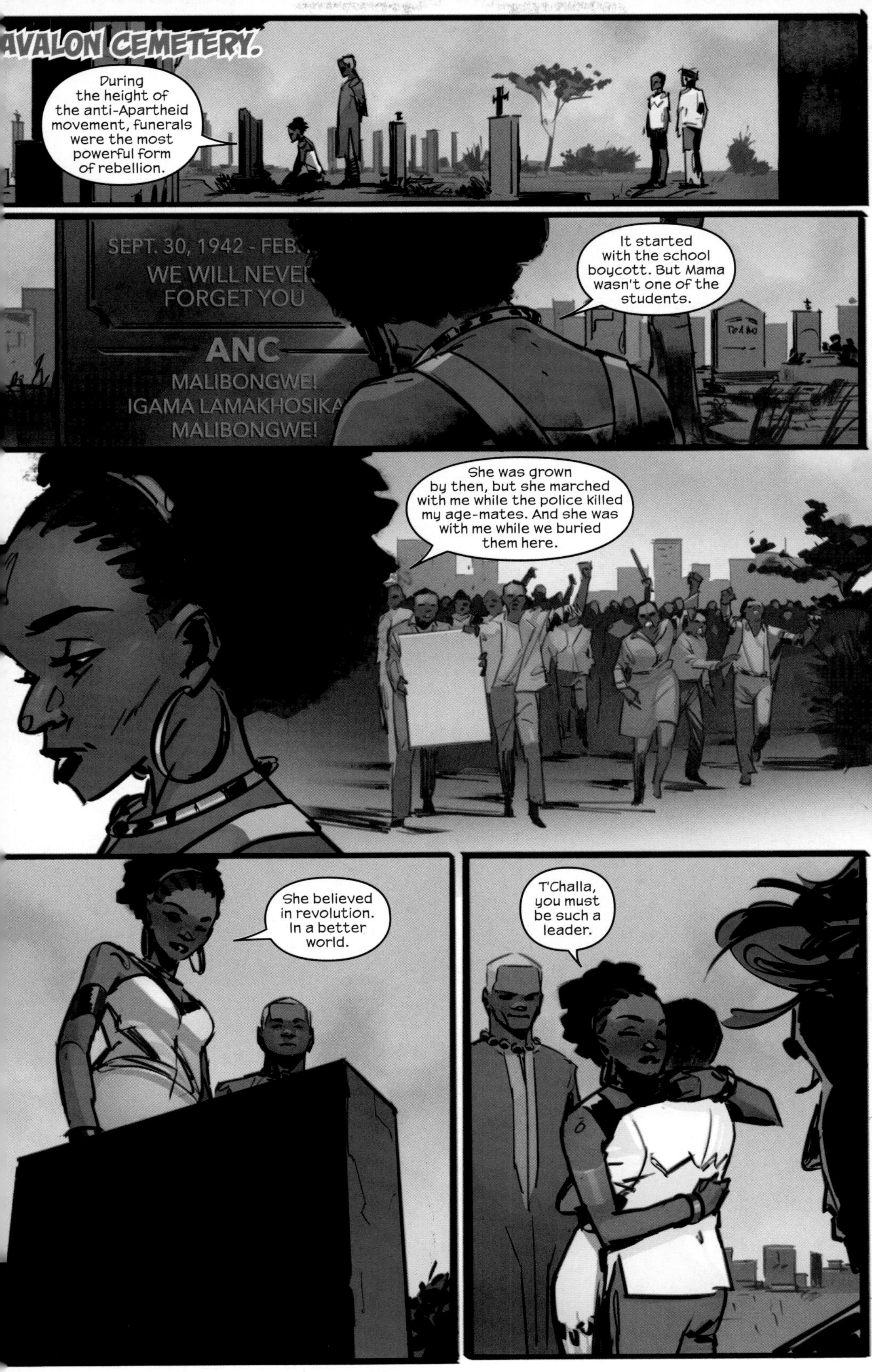
AVALON CEMETERY.
During the height of the anti-Apartheid movement, funerals were the most powerful form of rebellion.
SEPT. 30, 1942 - FEB.
WE WILL NEVE
FORGET YOU
ANC
MALIBONGWE!
IGAMA LAMAKHOSIKA
MALIBONGWE!
It started with the school boycott. But Mama wasn't one of the students.
She was grown by then, but she marched with me while the police killed my age-mates. And she was with me while we buried them here.
She believed in revolution. In a better world.
T'Challa, you must be such a leader.

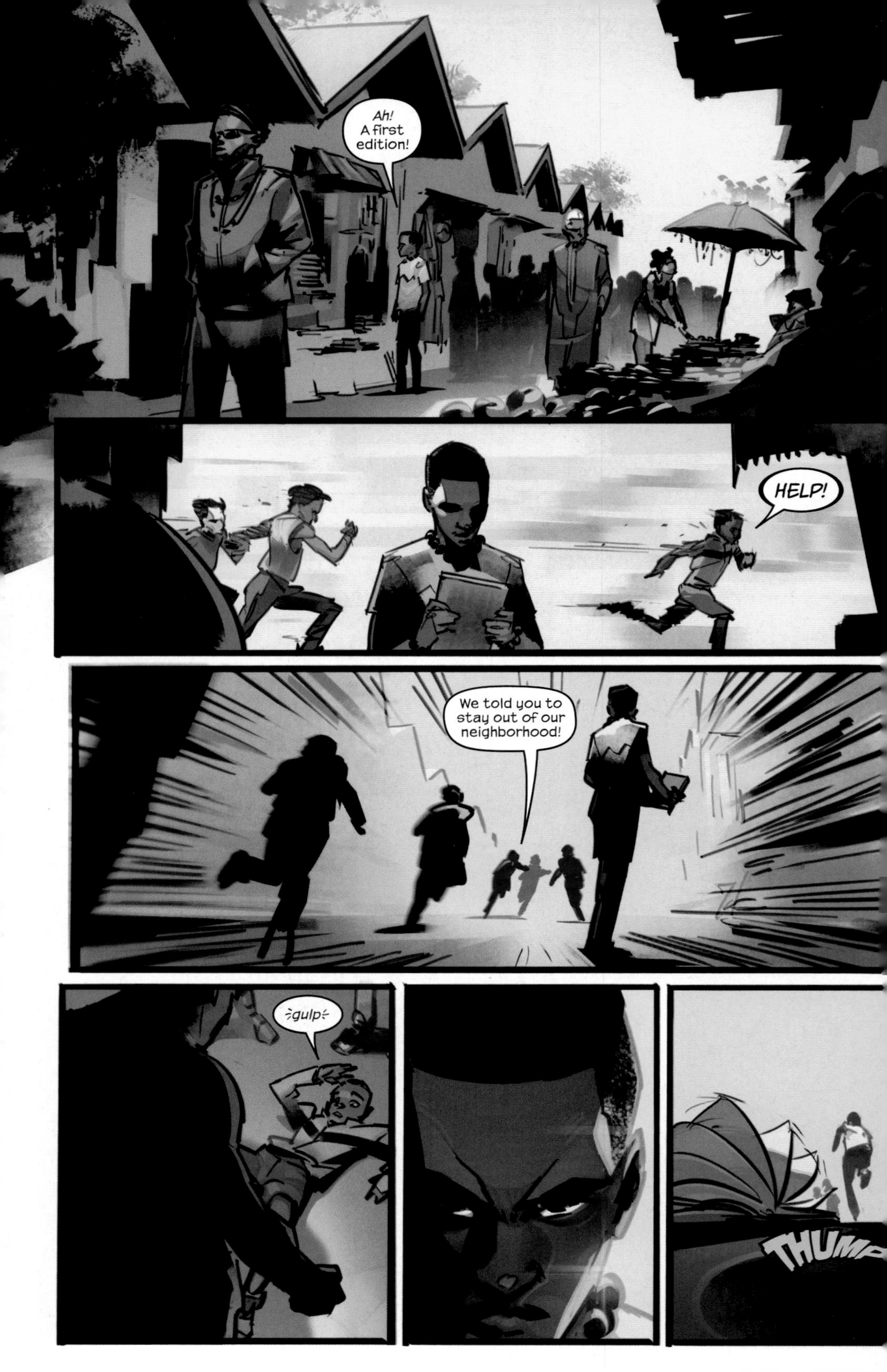
Ah! A first edition!
HELP!
We told you to stay out of our neighborhood!
gulp
THUMP

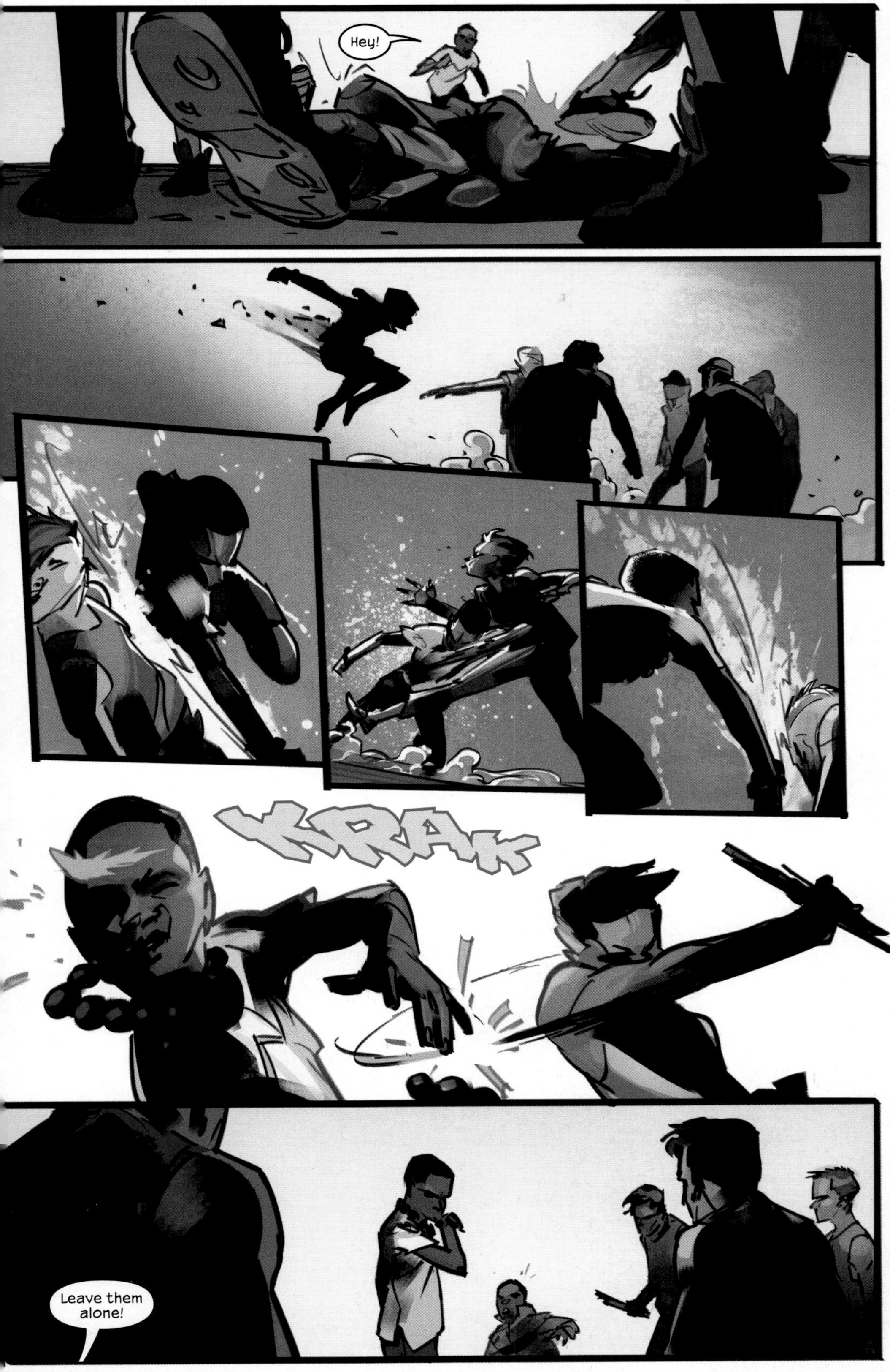
Hey!
KRAK
Leave them alone!

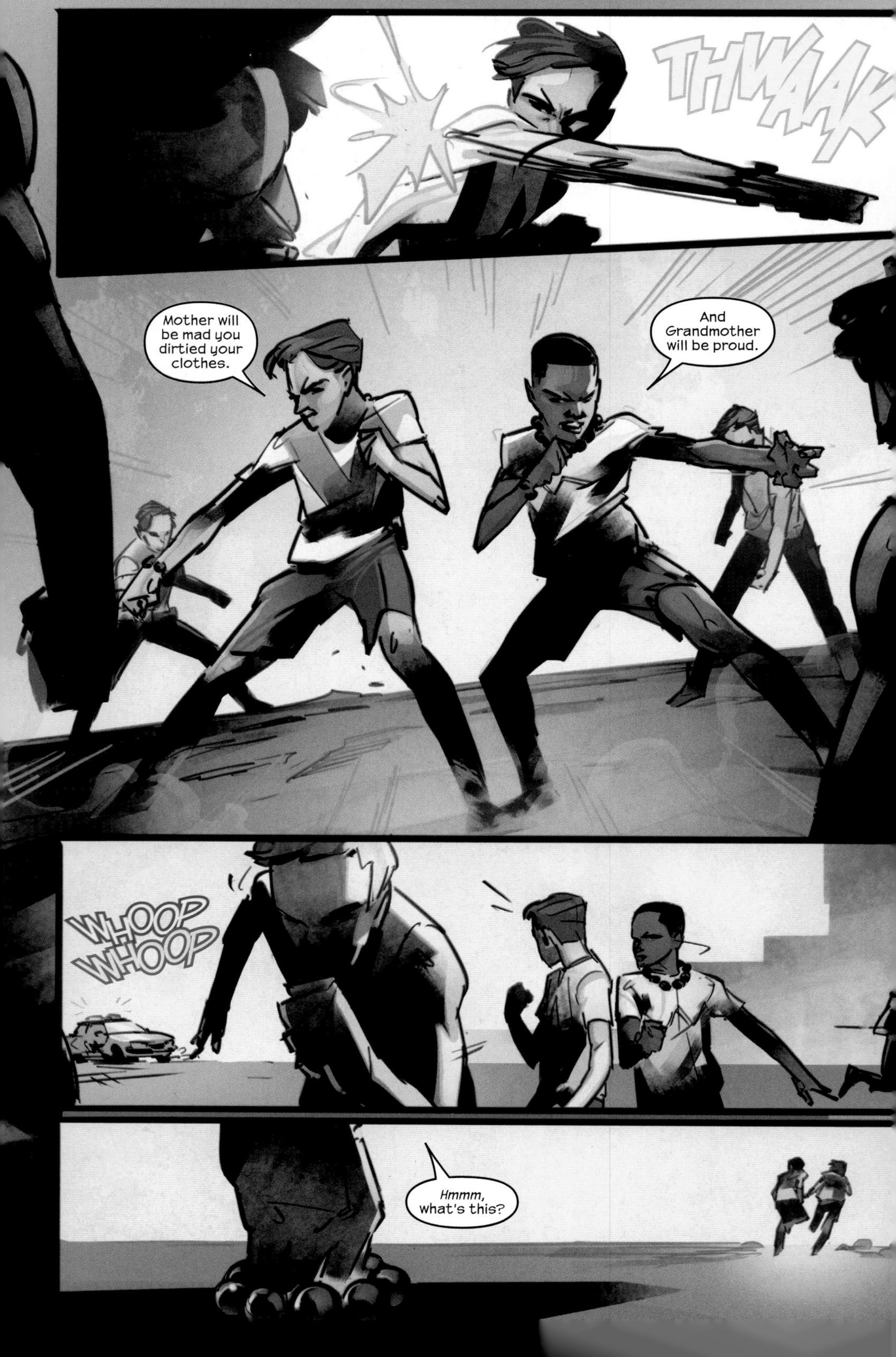
THWAAK
Mother will be mad you dirtied your clothes.
And Grandmother will be proud.
WHOOP WHOOP
Hmmm, what's this?

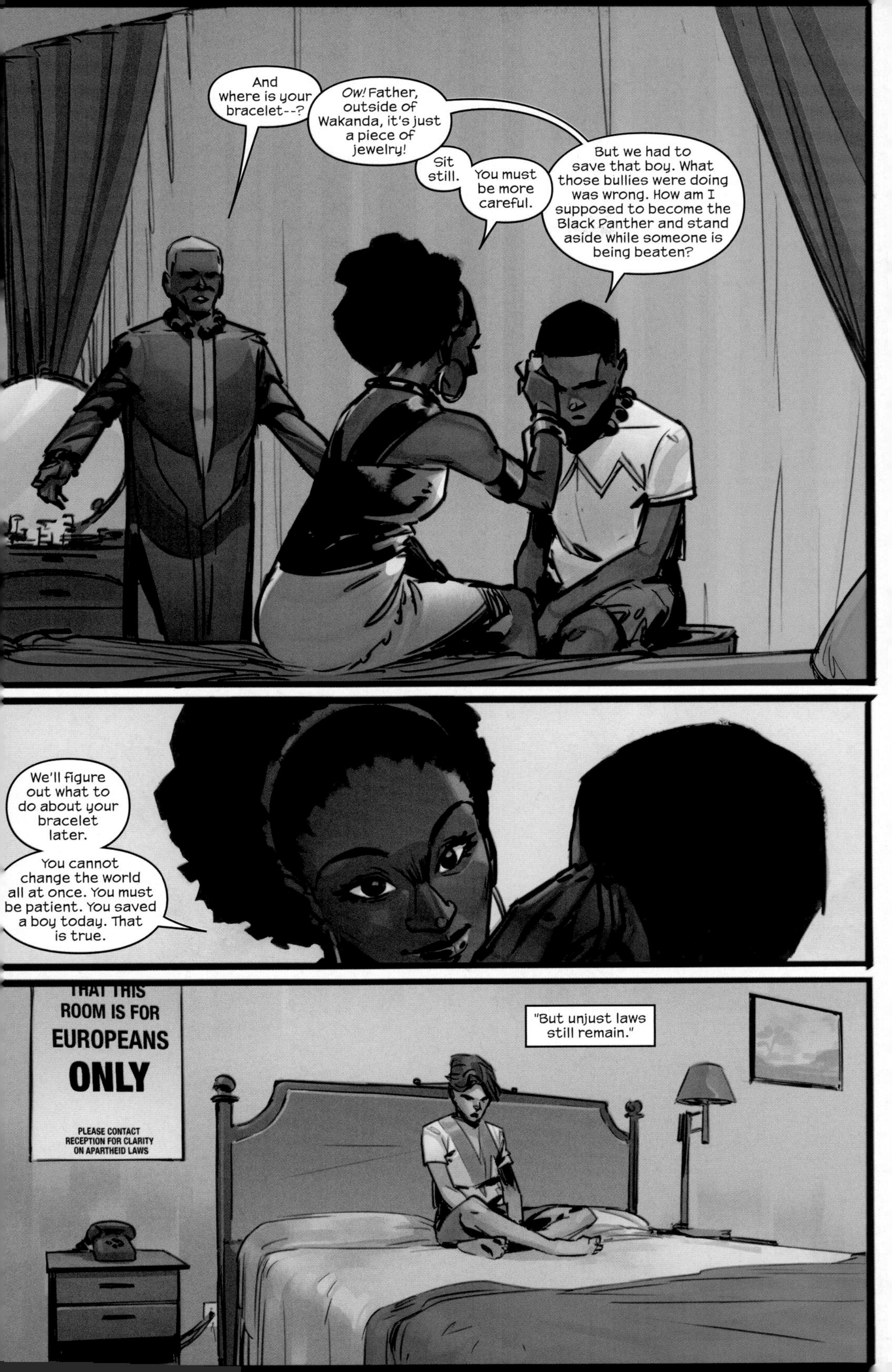

And where is your bracelet--?
Ow! Father, outside of Wakanda, it's just a piece of jewelry!
But we had to save that boy. What those bullies were doing was wrong. How am I supposed to become the Black Panther and stand aside while someone is being beaten?
Sit still.
You must be more careful.
We'll figure out what to do about your bracelet later.
You cannot change the world all at once. You must be patient. You saved a boy today. That is true.
THAT THIS ROOM IS FOR EUROPEANS ONLY
PLEASE CONTACT RECEPTION FOR CLARITY ON APARTHEID LAWS
"But unjust laws still remain."

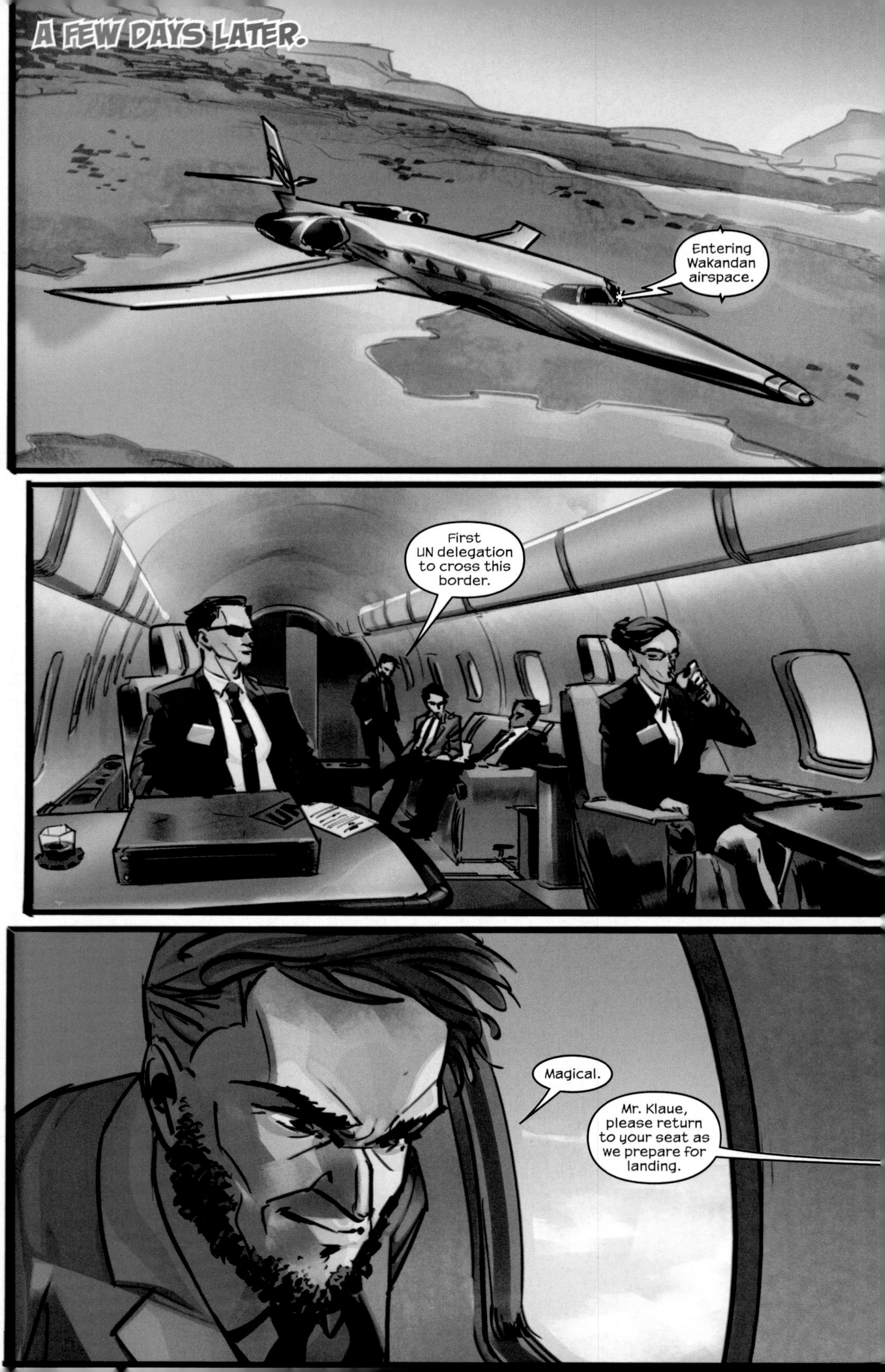
A FEW DAYS LATER.
Entering Wakandan airspace.
First UN delegation to cross this border.
UN
Magical.
Mr. Klaue, please return to your seat as we prepare for landing.

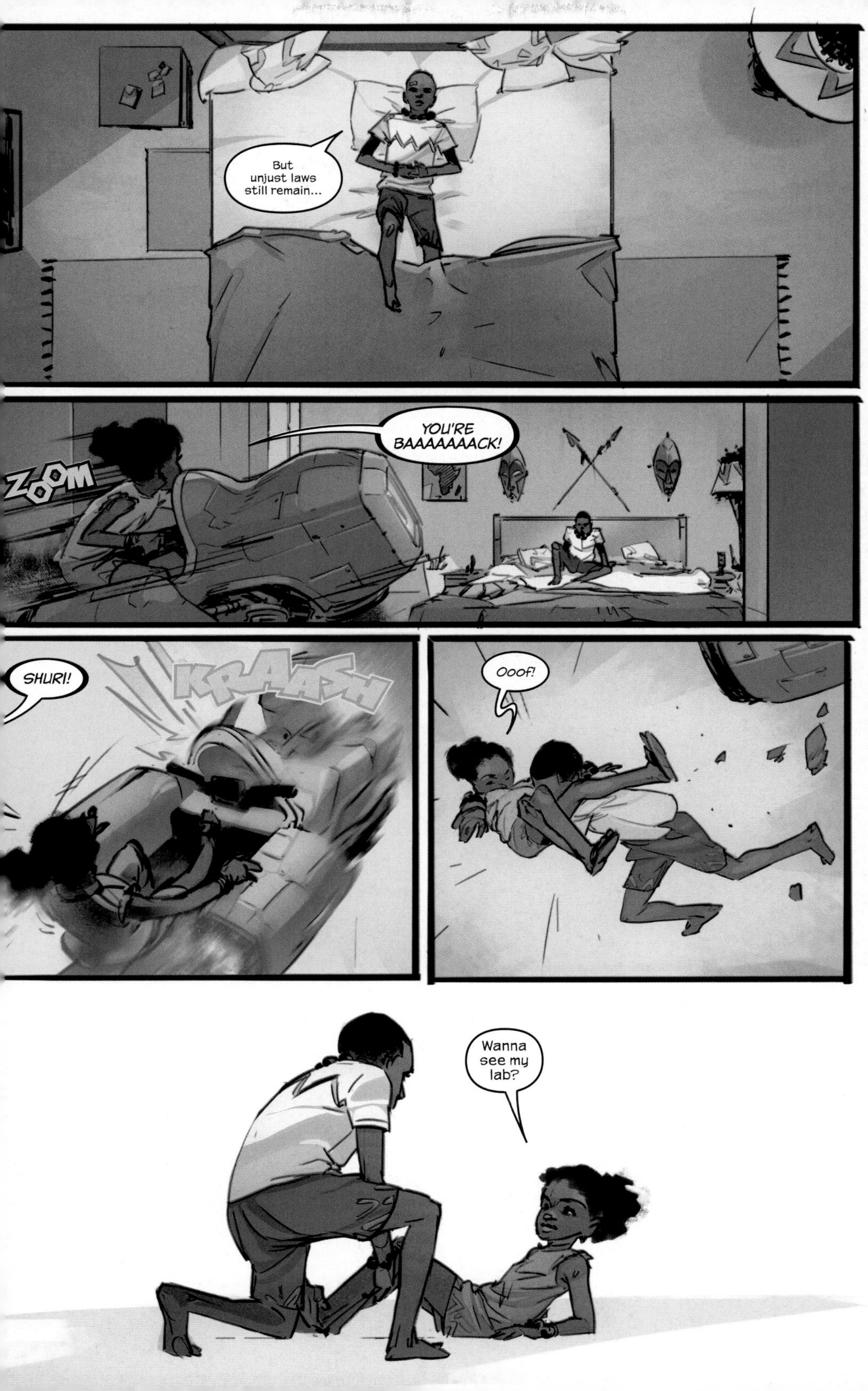
But unjust laws still remain...
ZOOM
YOU'RE BAAAAAAACK!
SHURI!
KRAASH
Ooof!
Wanna see my lab?

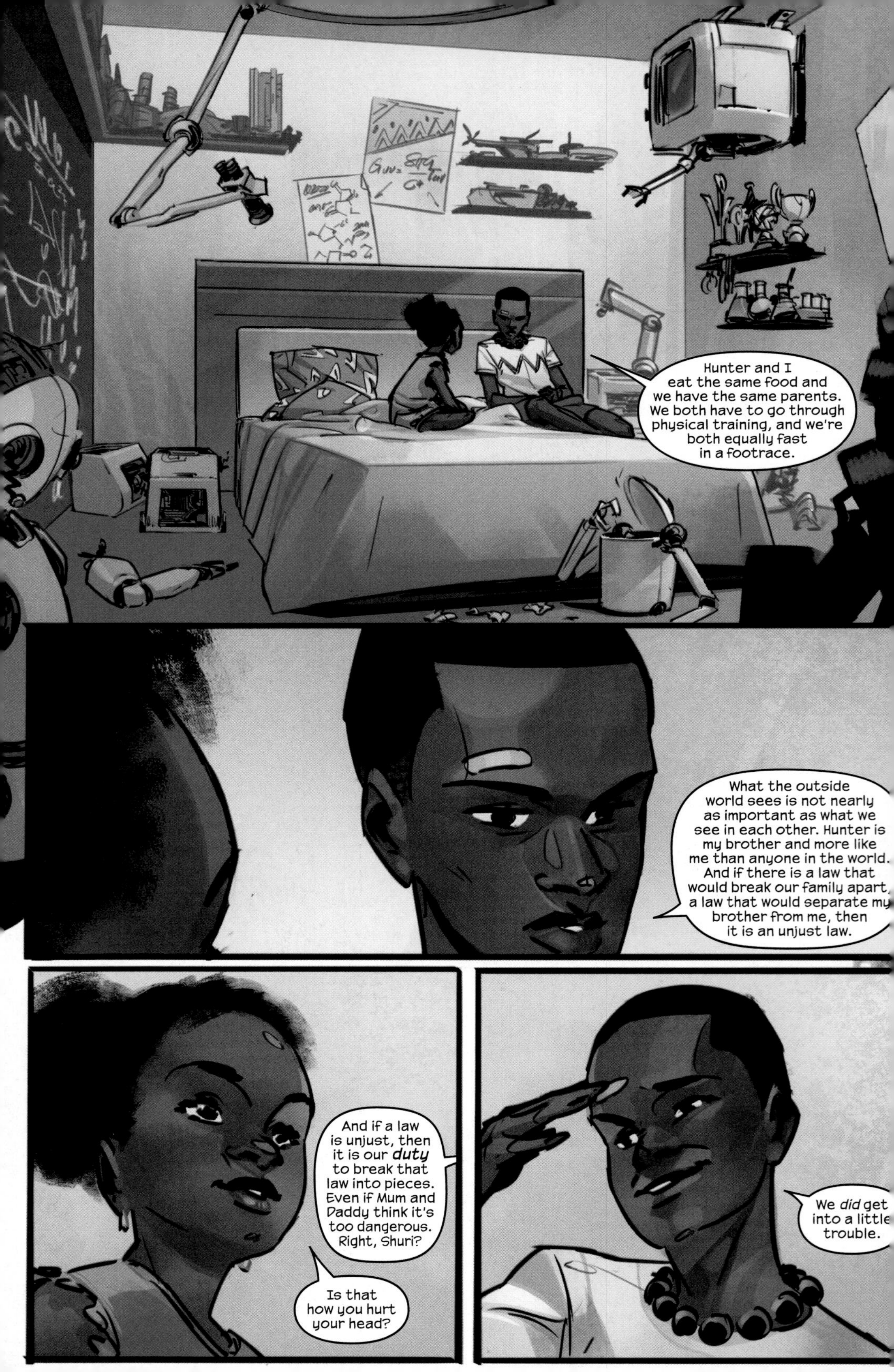
Hunter and I eat the same food and we have the same parents. We both have to go through physical training, and we're both equally fast in a footrace.
What the outside world sees is not nearly as important as what we see in each other. Hunter is my brother and more like me than anyone in the world. And if there is a law that would break our family apart, a law that would separate my brother from me, then it is an unjust law.
And if a law is unjust, then it is our *duty* to break that law into pieces. Even if Mum and Daddy think it's too dangerous. Right, Shuri?
Is that how you hurt your head?
We *did* get into a little trouble.

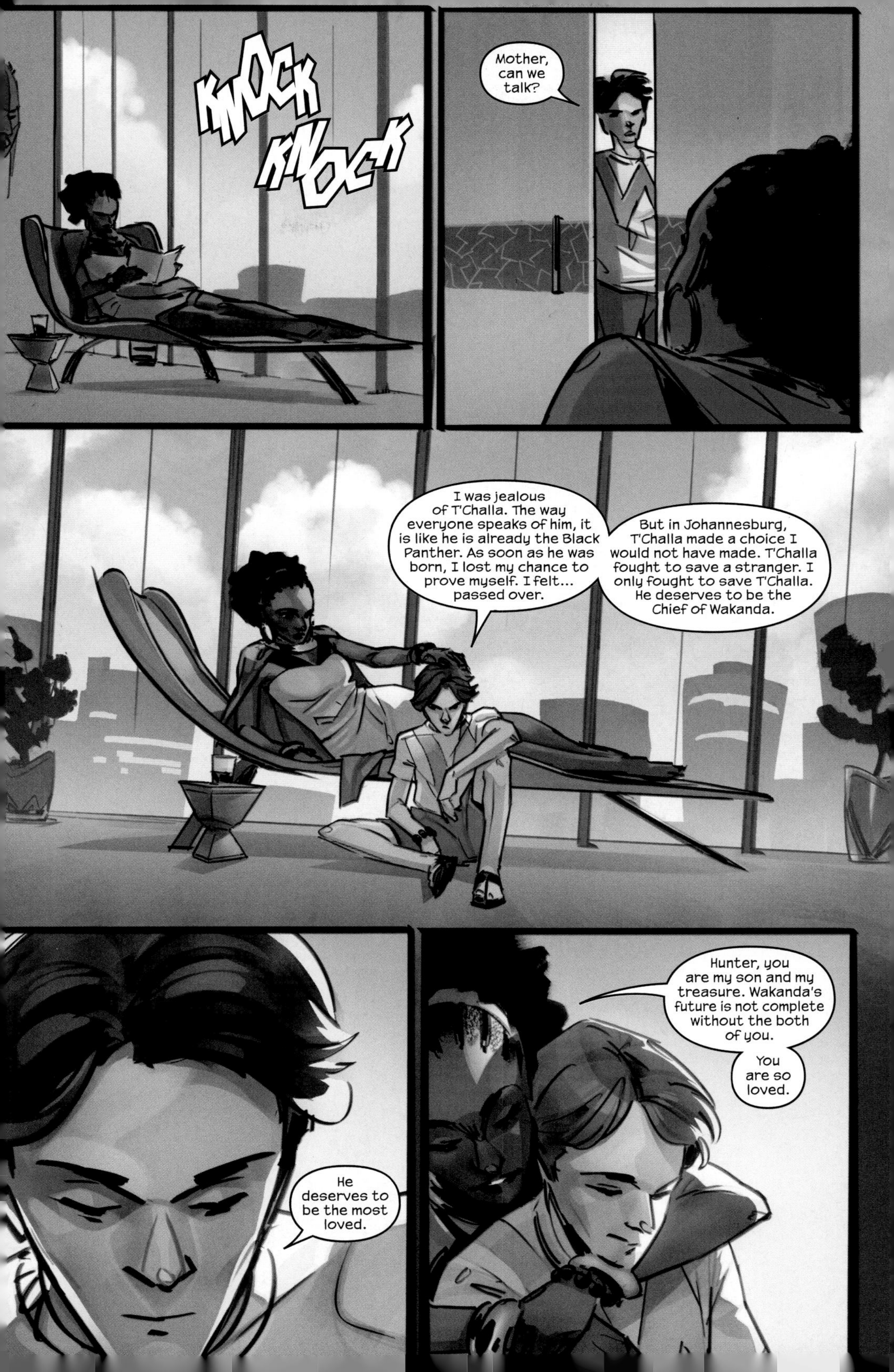
KNOCK KNOCK
Mother, can we talk?
I was jealous of T'Challa. The way everyone speaks of him, it is like he is already the Black Panther. As soon as he was born, I lost my chance to prove myself. I felt... passed over.
But in Johannesburg, T'Challa made a choice I would not have made. T'Challa fought to save a stranger. I only fought to save T'Challa. He deserves to be the Chief of Wakanda.
He deserves to be the most loved.
Hunter, you are my son and my treasure. Wakanda's future is not complete without the both of you.
You are so loved.

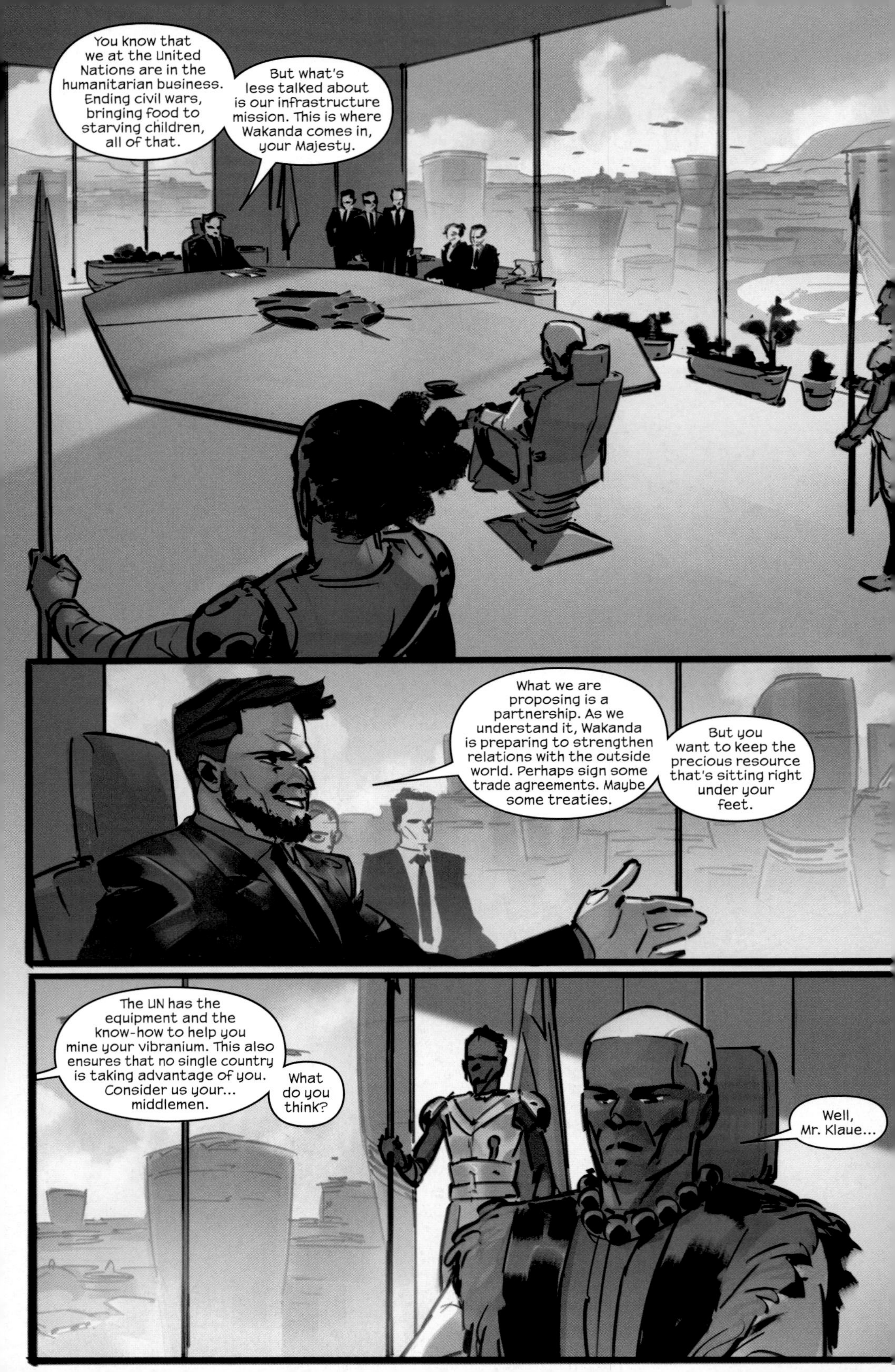

You know that we at the United Nations are in the humanitarian business. Ending civil wars, bringing food to starving children, all of that.
But what's less talked about is our infrastructure mission. This is where Wakanda comes in, your Majesty.
What we are proposing is a partnership. As we understand it, Wakanda is preparing to strengthen relations with the outside world. Perhaps sign some trade agreements. Maybe some treaties.
But you want to keep the precious resource that's sitting right under your feet.
The UN has the equipment and the know-how to help you mine your vibranium. This also ensures that no single country is taking advantage of you. Consider us your... middlemen.
What do you think?
Well, Mr. Klaue...

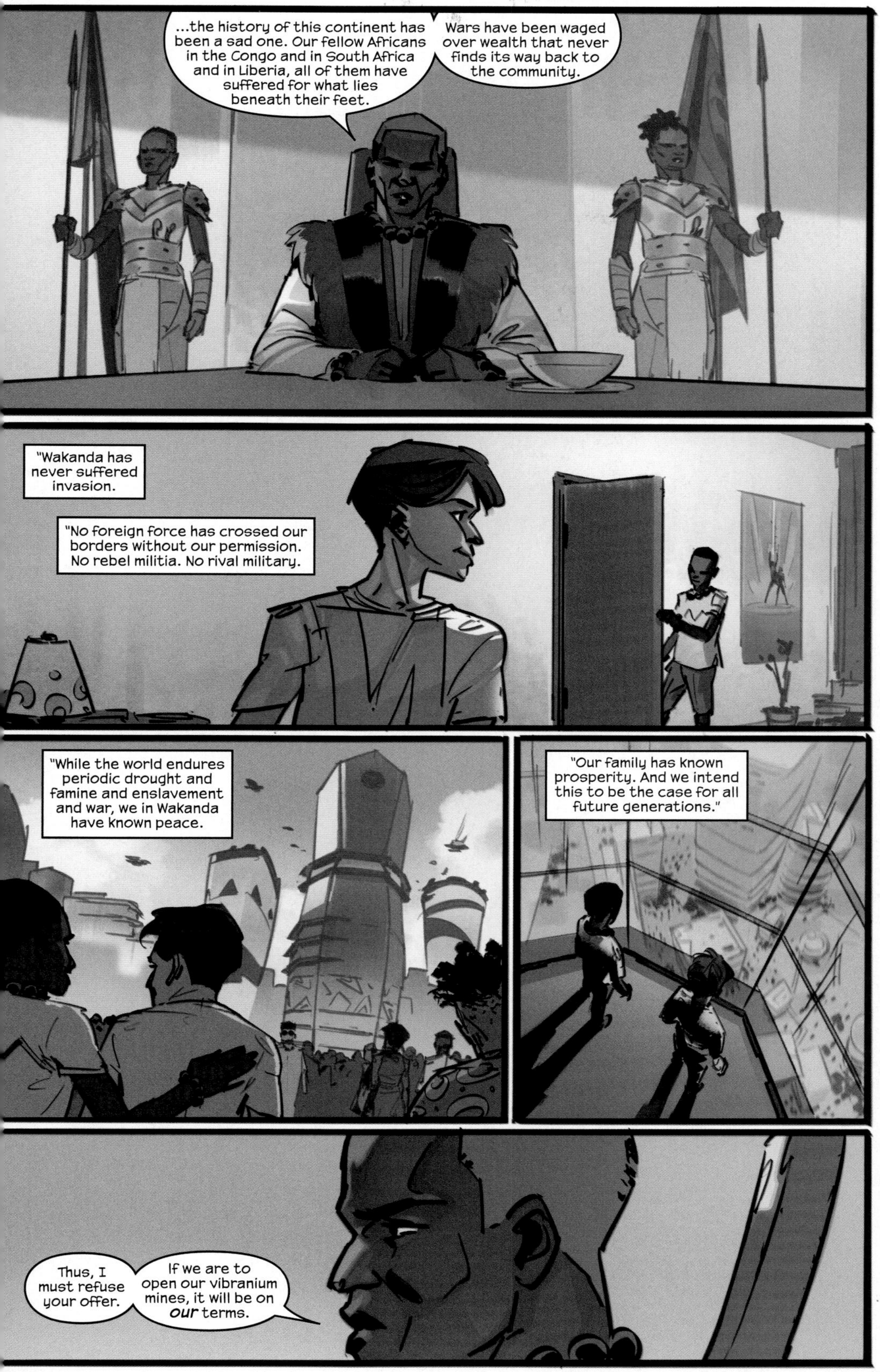
...the history of this continent has been a sad one. Our fellow Africans in the Congo and in South Africa and in Liberia, all of them have suffered for what lies beneath their feet.
Wars have been waged over wealth that never finds its way back to the community.
"Wakanda has never suffered invasion.
"No foreign force has crossed our borders without our permission. No rebel militia. No rival military.
"While the world endures periodic drought and famine and enslavement and war, we in Wakanda have known peace.
"Our family has known prosperity. And we intend this to be the case for all future generations."
Thus, I must refuse your offer.
If we are to open our vibranium mines, it will be on *our* terms.

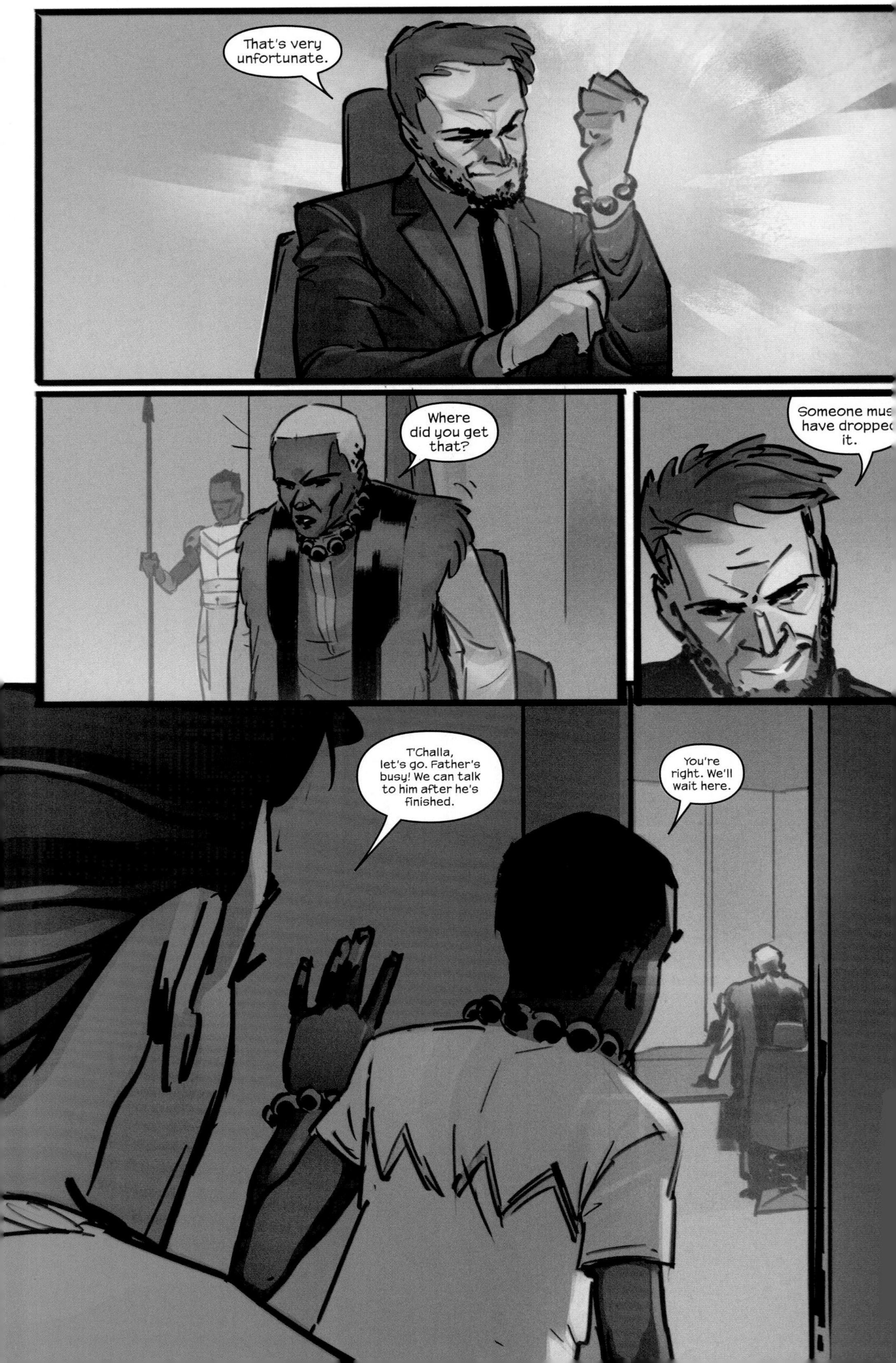

That's very unfortunate.
Where did you get that?
Someone mus have droppe it.
T'Challa, let's go. Father's busy! We can talk to him after he's finished.
You're right. We'll wait here.

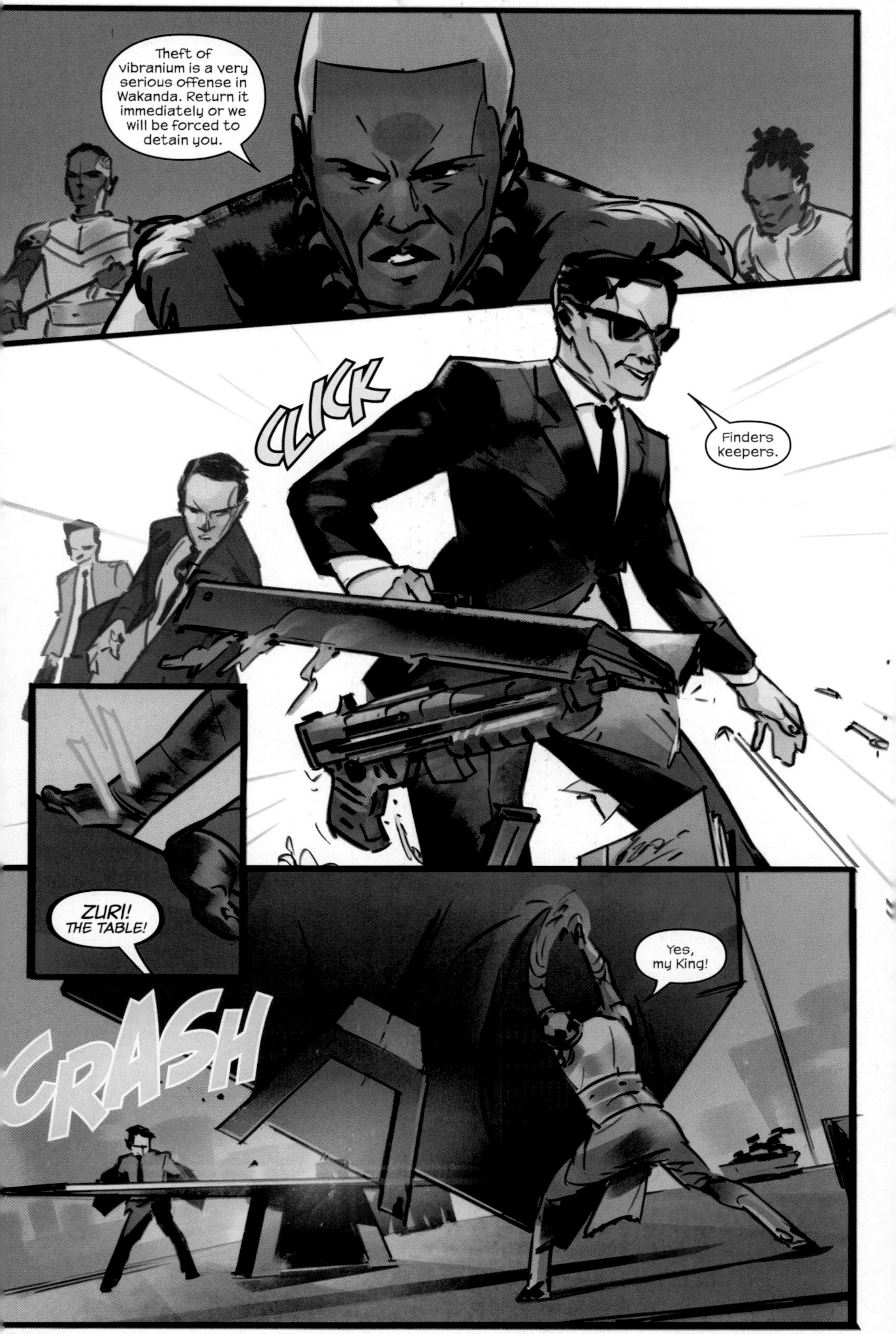

Theft of vibranium is a very serious offense in Wakanda. Return it immediately or we will be forced to detain you.
CLICK
Finders keepers.
ZURI! THE TABLE!
Yes, my King!
CRASH

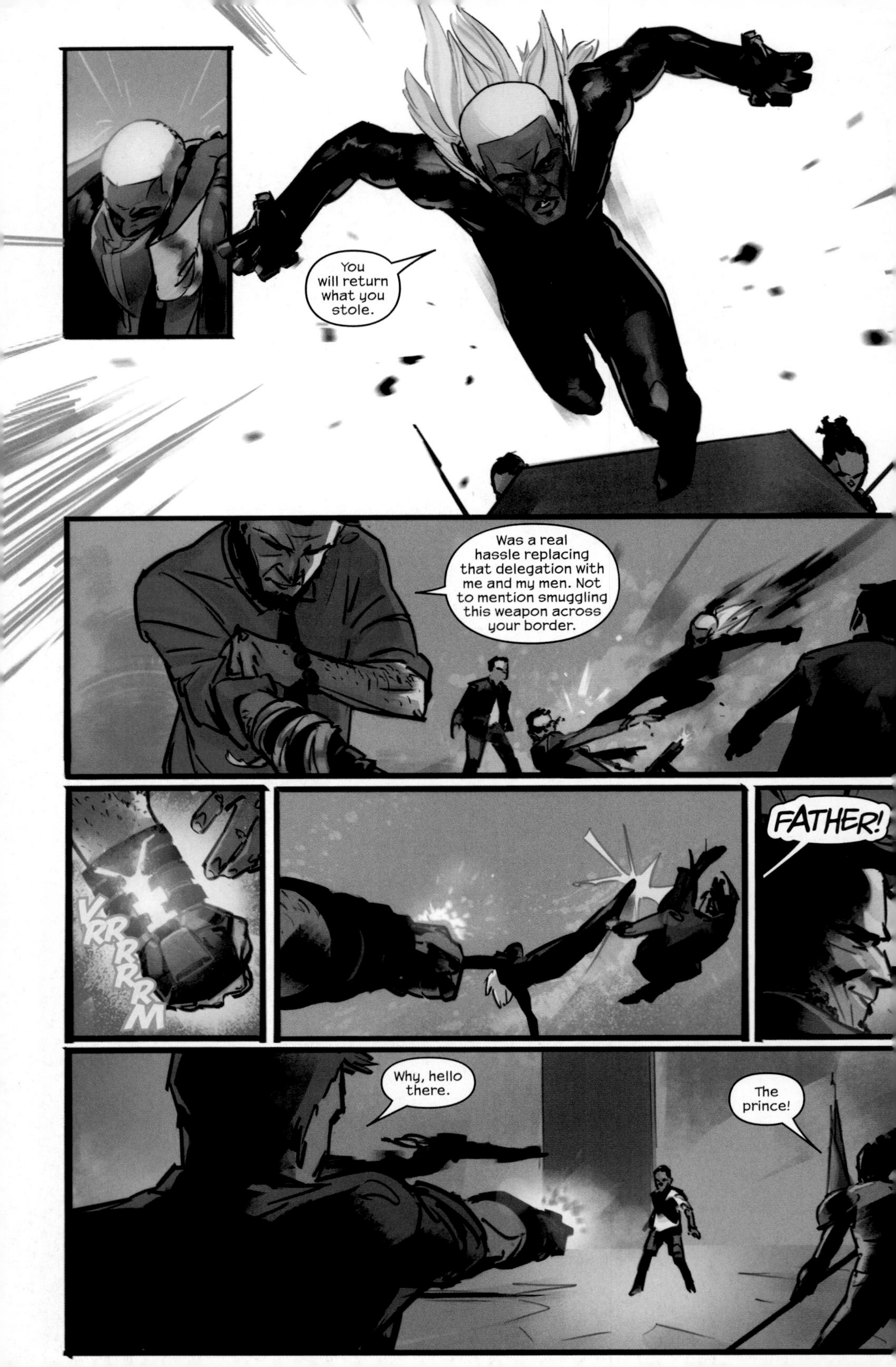
You will return what you stole.
Was a real hassle replacing that delegation with me and my men. Not to mention smuggling this weapon across your border.
VRRRRRRM
FATHER!
Why, hello there.
The prince!

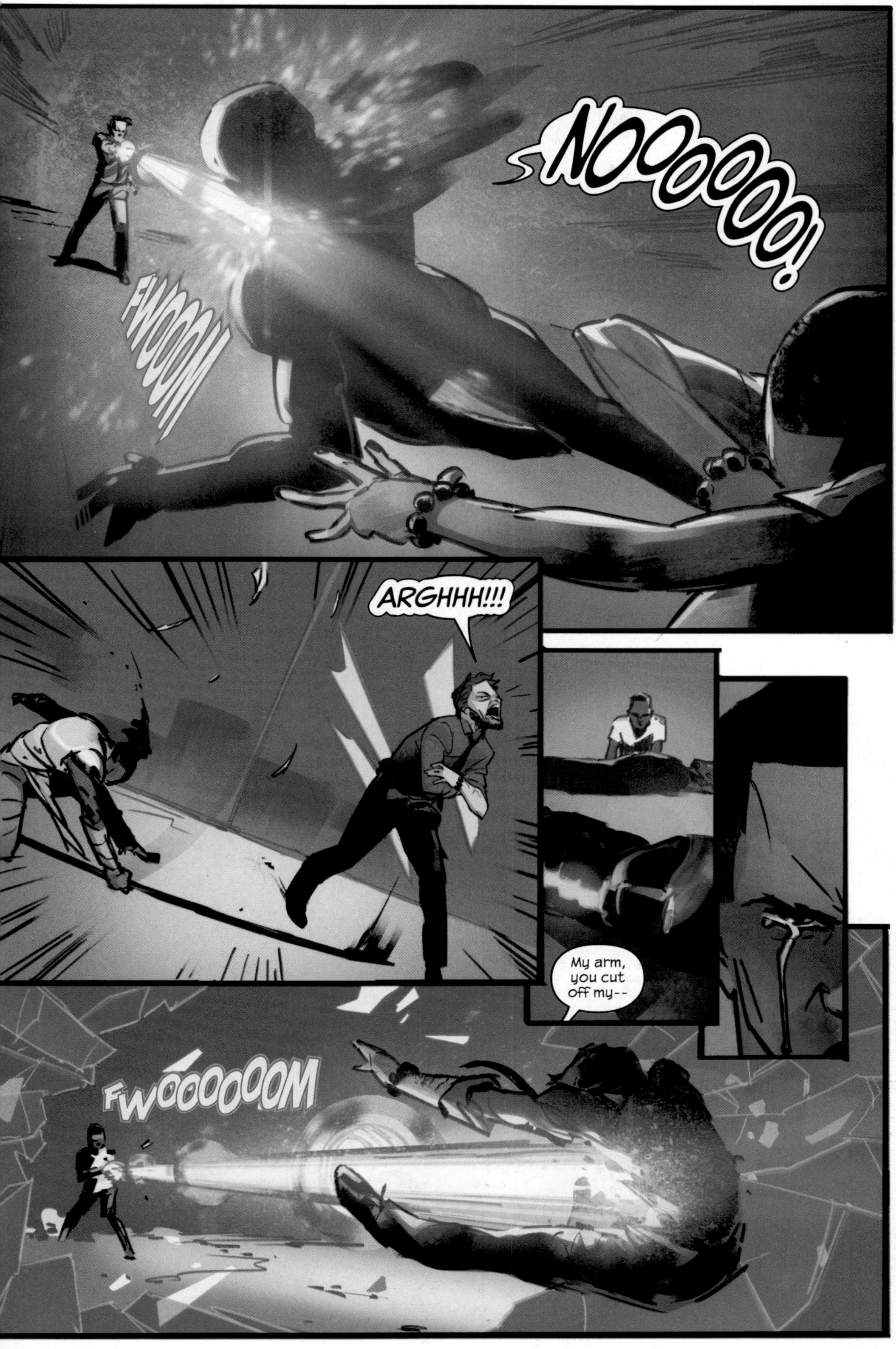
NOOOOOO!
FWOOOM
ARGHHH!!!
My arm, you cut off my--
FWOOOOOOM

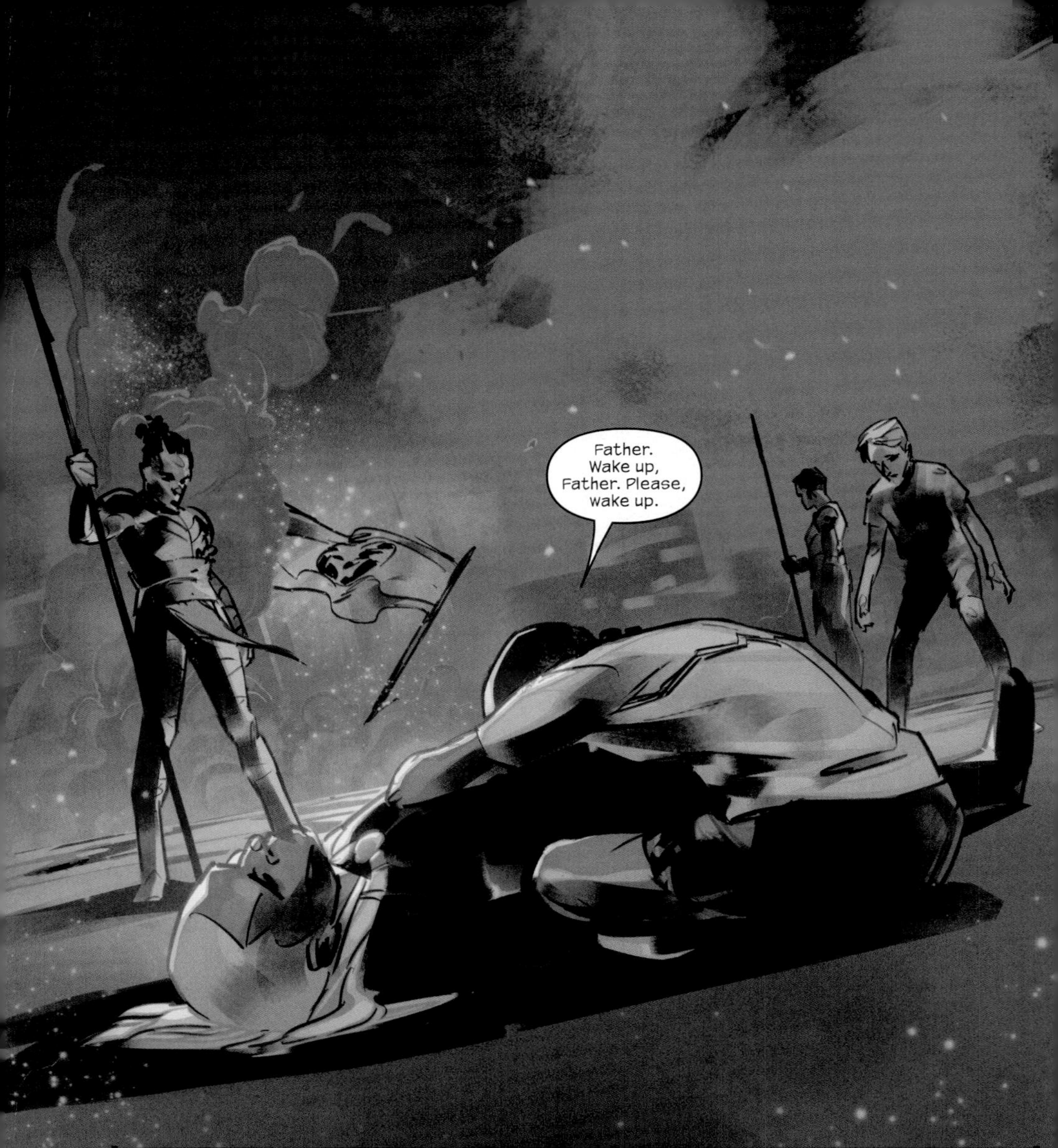
Father. Wake up, Father. Please, wake up.
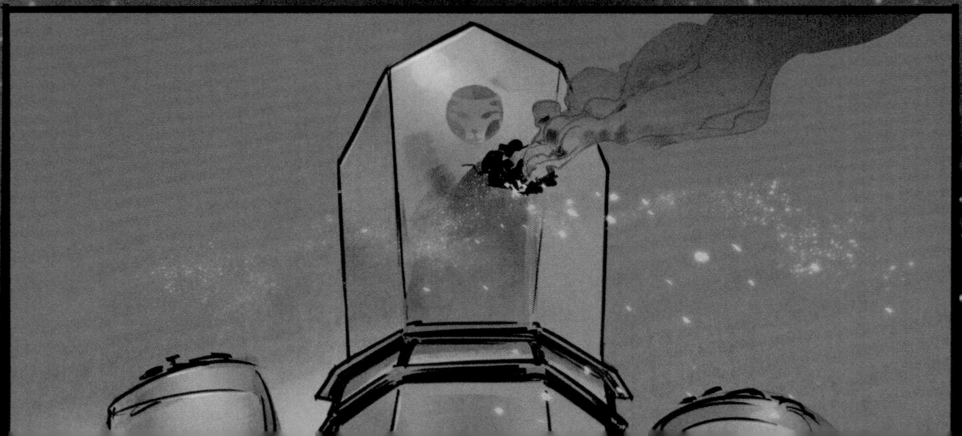

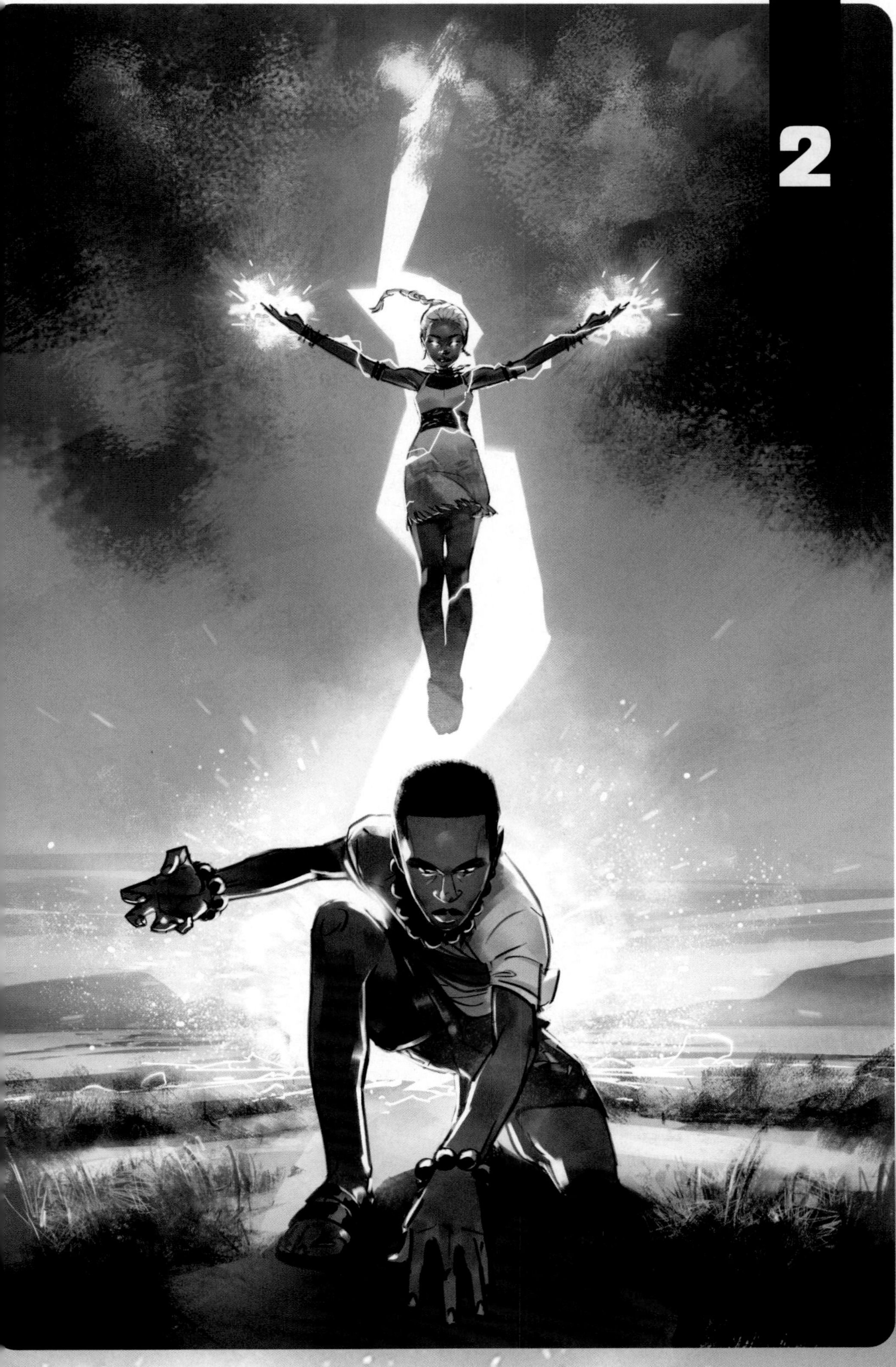

2

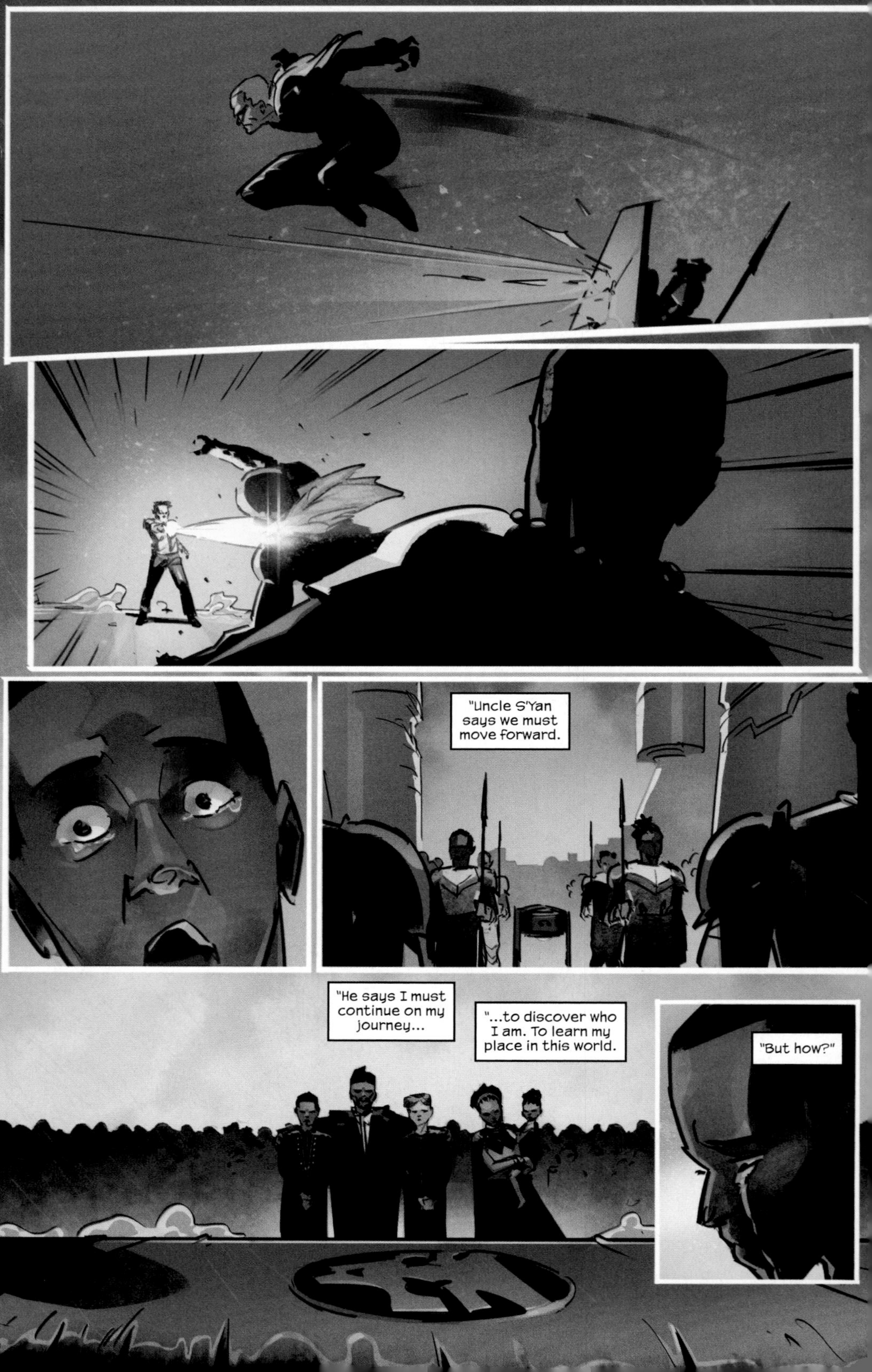
"Uncle S'Yan says we must move forward.
"He says I must continue on my journey...
"...to discover who I am. To learn my place in this world.
"But how?"

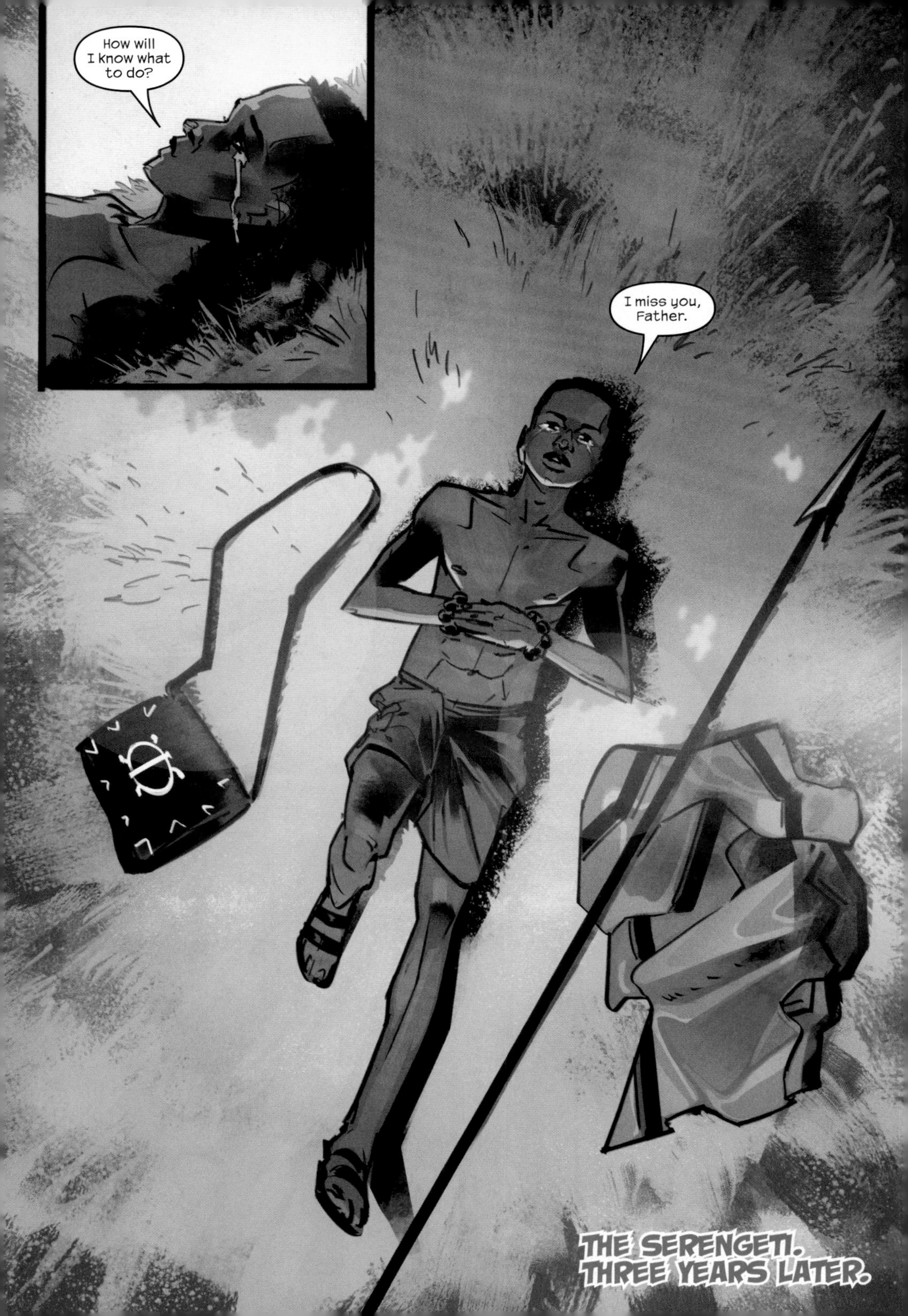
How will I know what to do?
I miss you, Father.
THE SERENGETI. THREE YEARS LATER.

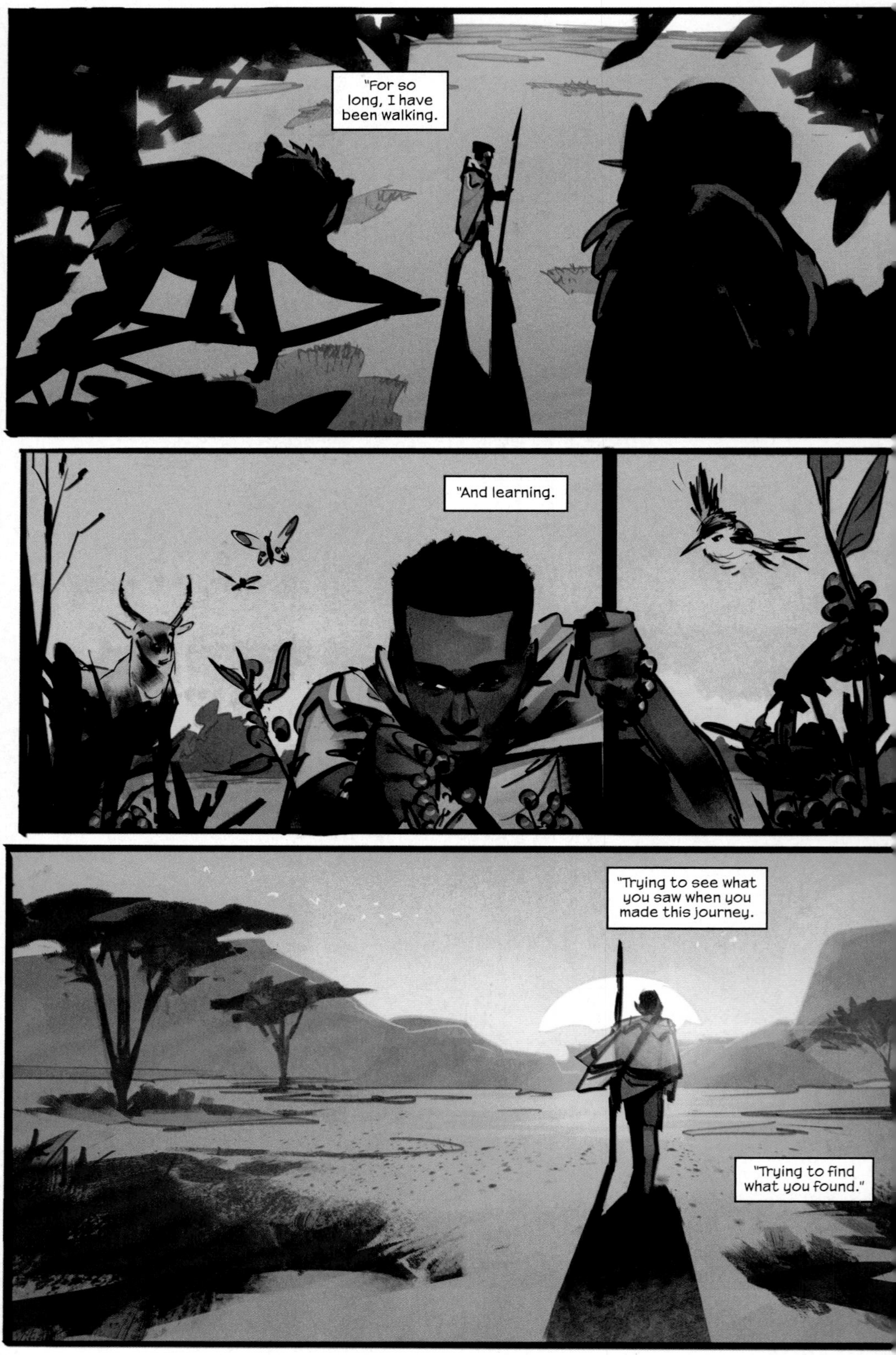
"For so long, I have been walking.
"And learning.
"Trying to see what you saw when you made this journey.
"Trying to find what you found."

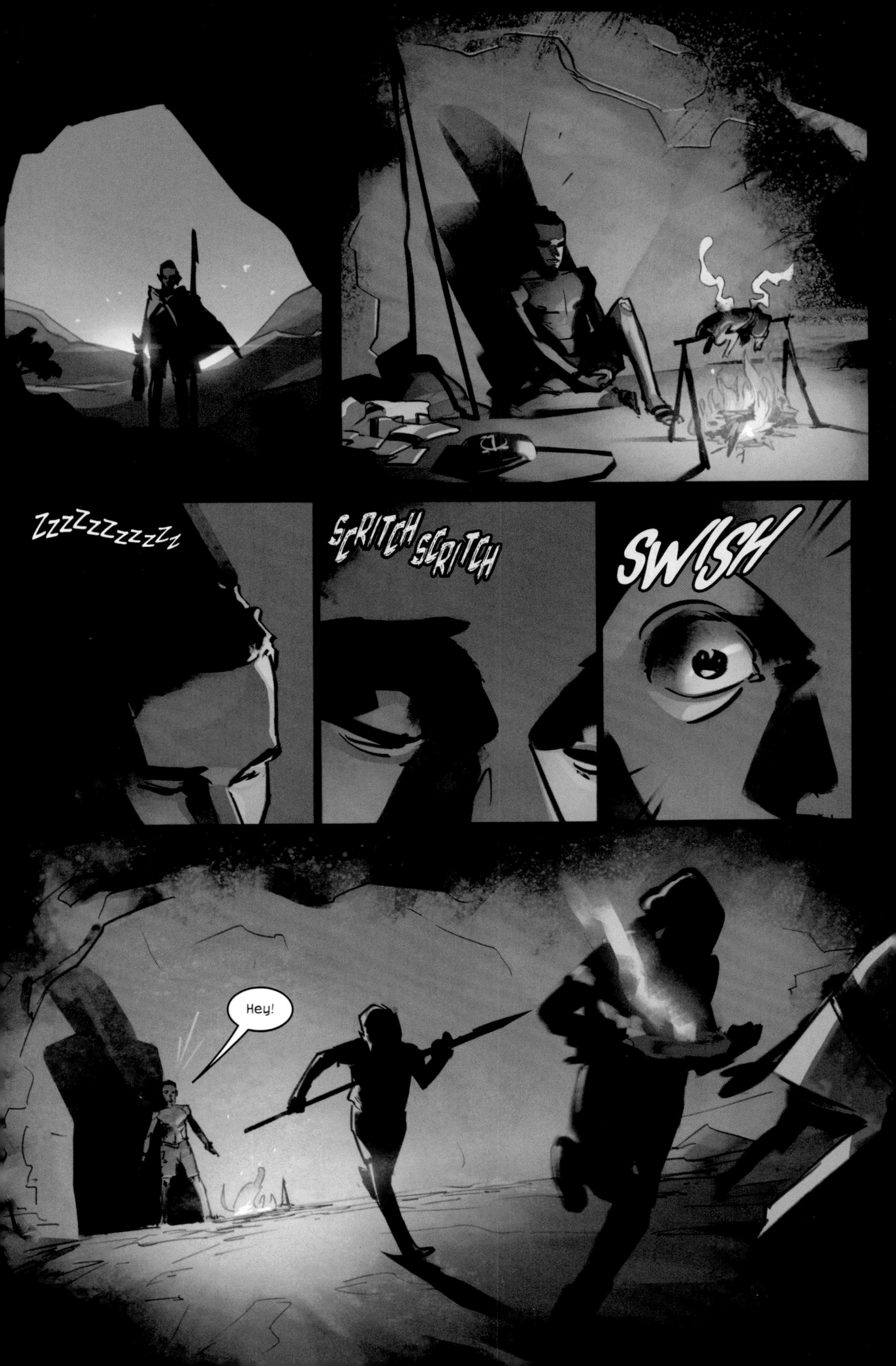
ZZZZZZZZZZZZ
SCRITCH SCRITCH
SWISH
Hey!

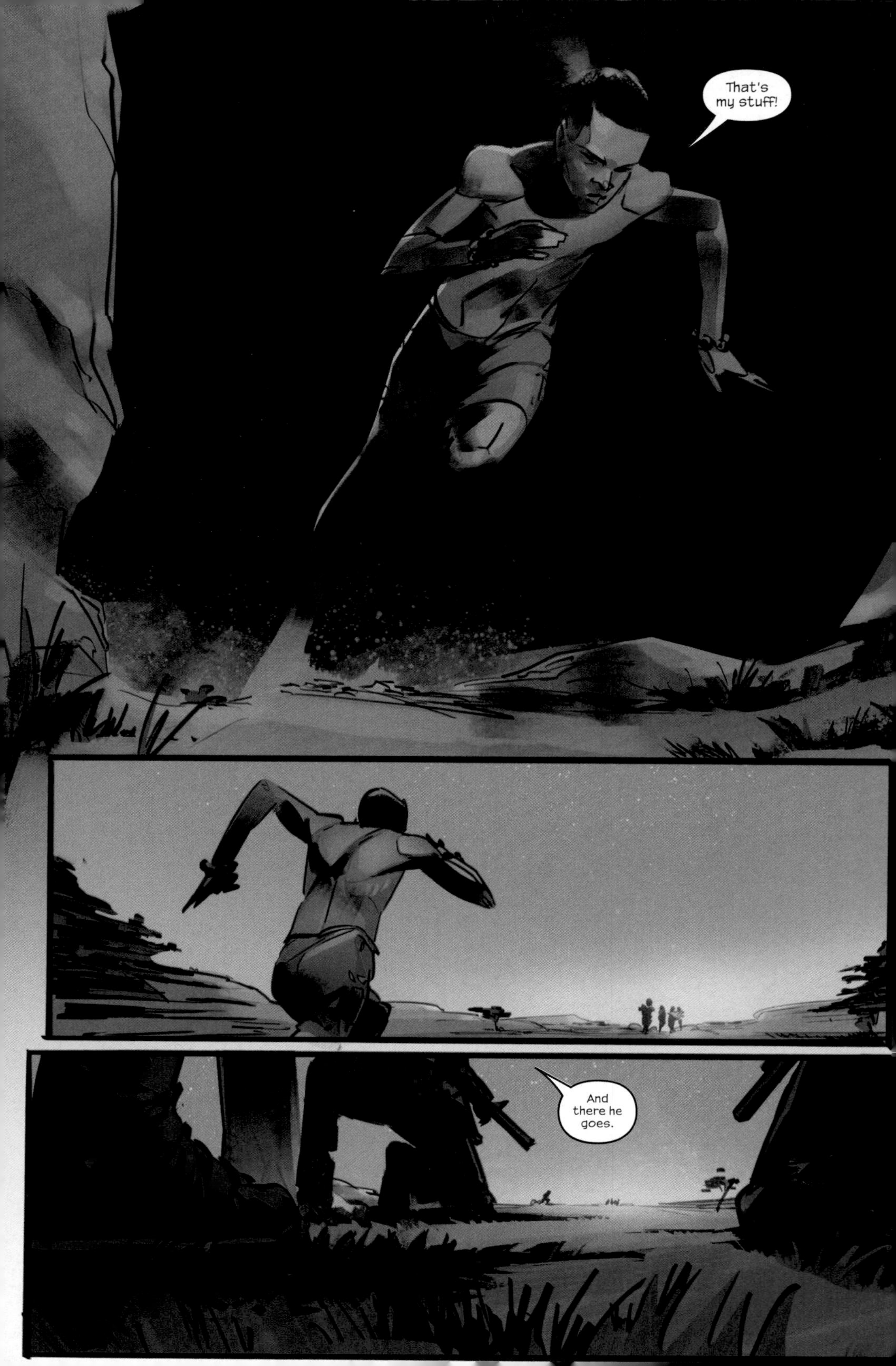
That's my stuff!
And there he goes.

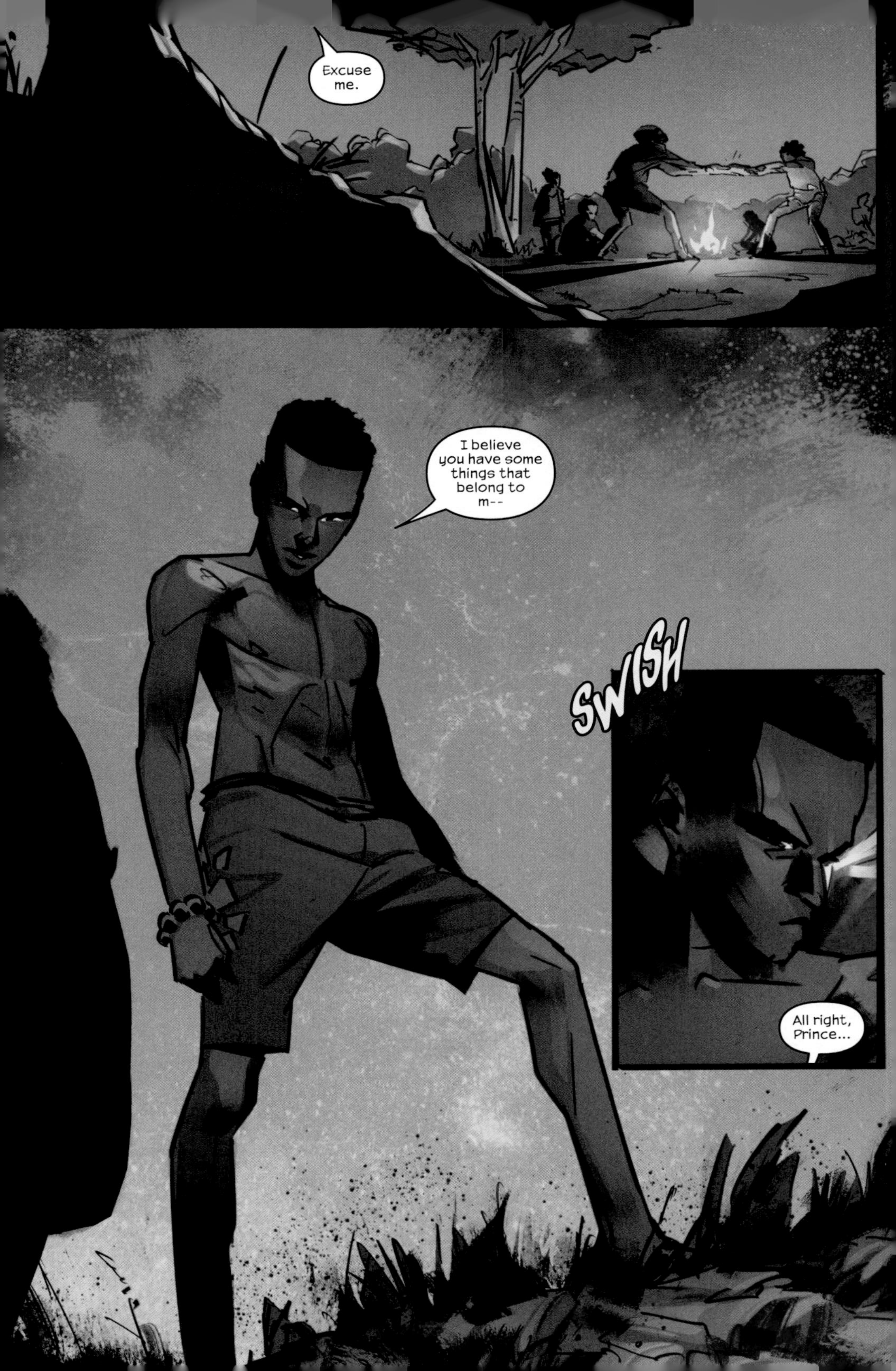
Excuse me.
I believe you have some things that belong to m--
SWISH
All right, Prince...

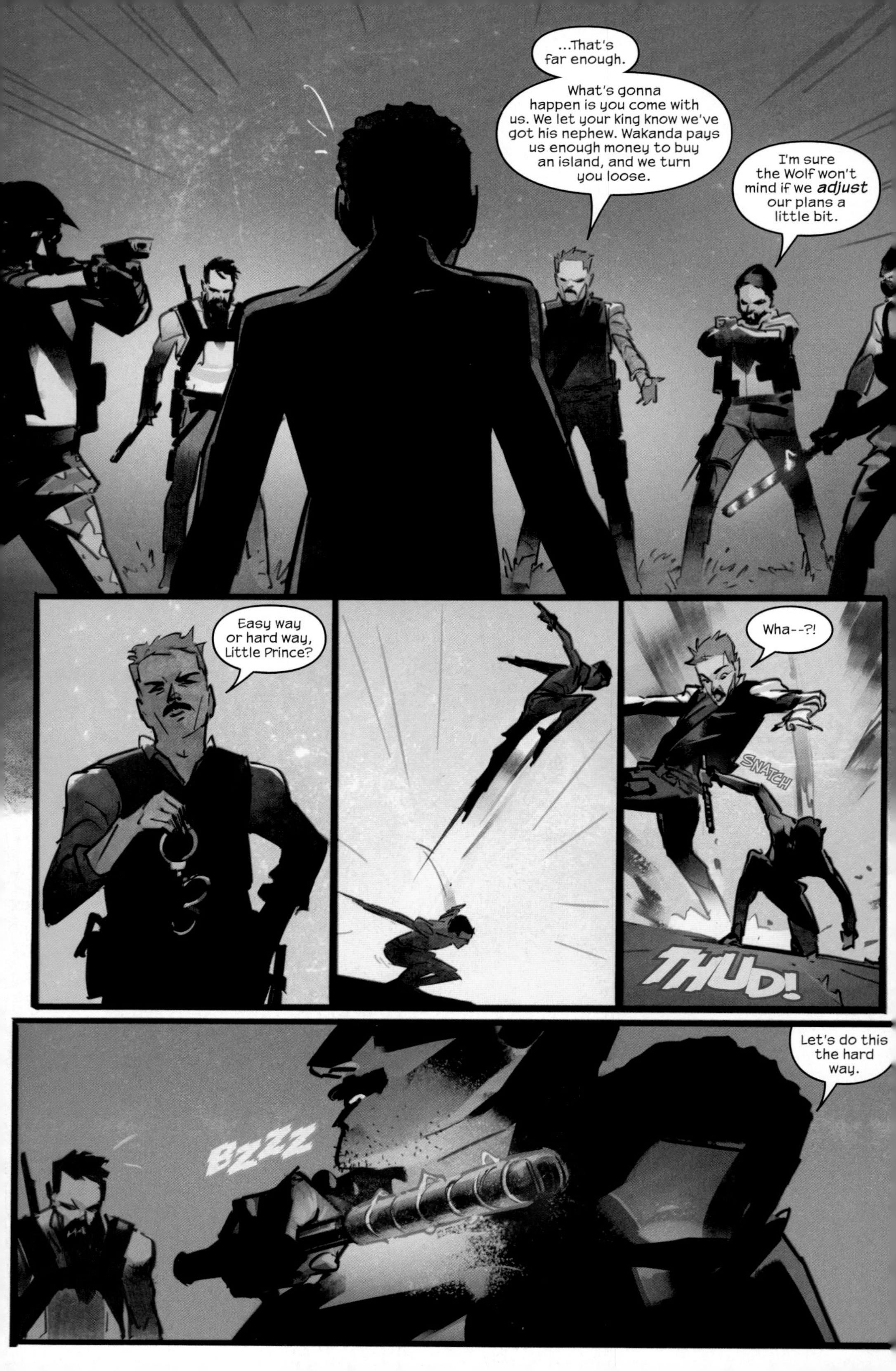
...That's far enough.
What's gonna happen is you come with us. We let your king know we've got his nephew. Wakanda pays us enough money to buy an island, and we turn you loose.
I'm sure the Wolf won't mind if we *adjust* our plans a little bit.
Easy way or hard way, Little Prince?
Wha--?!
SNATCH
THUD!
BZZZ
Let's do this the hard way.

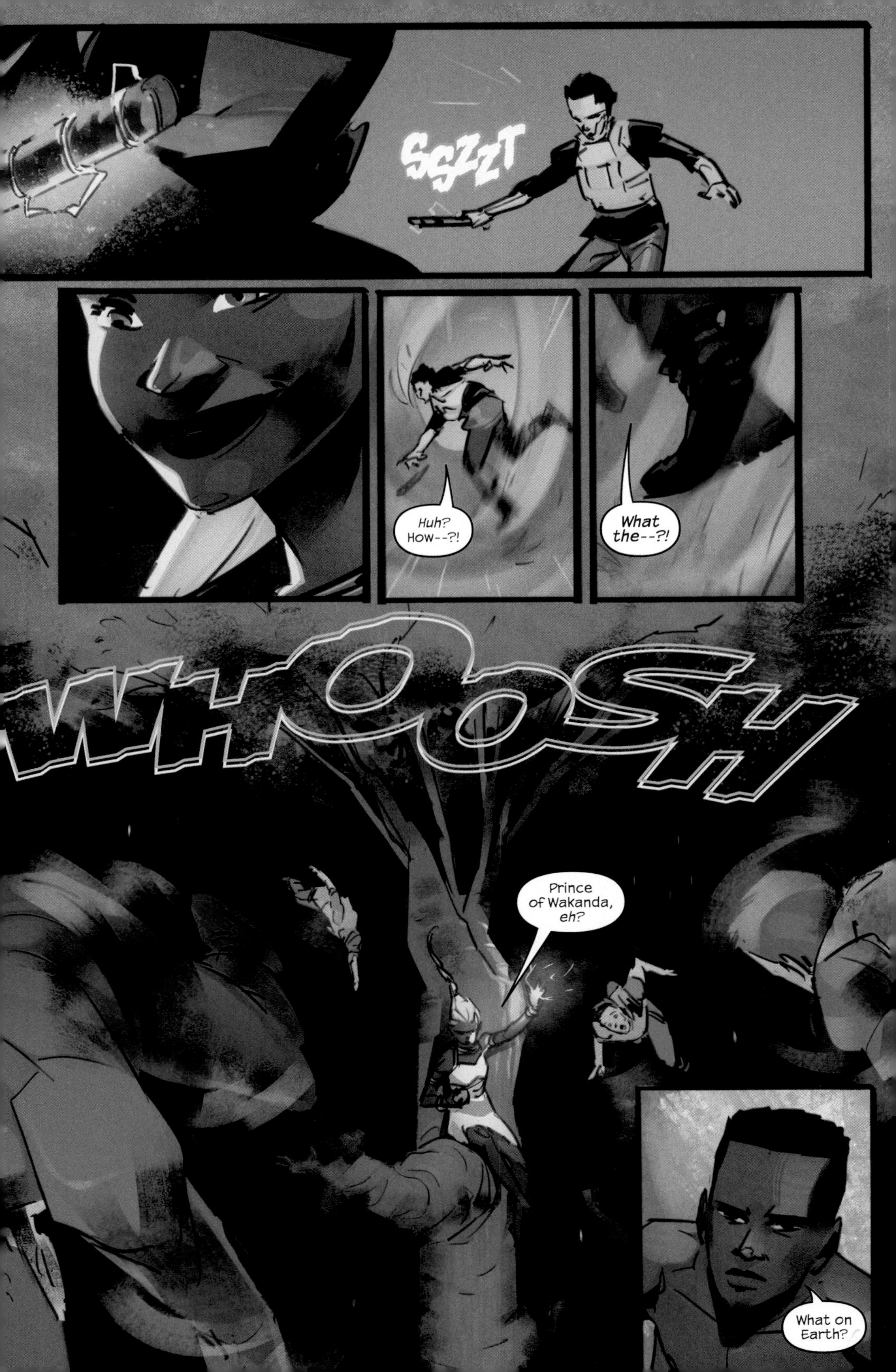
SGZZT
Huh? How--?!
What the--?!
WHOOSH
Prince of Wakanda, eh?
What on Earth?

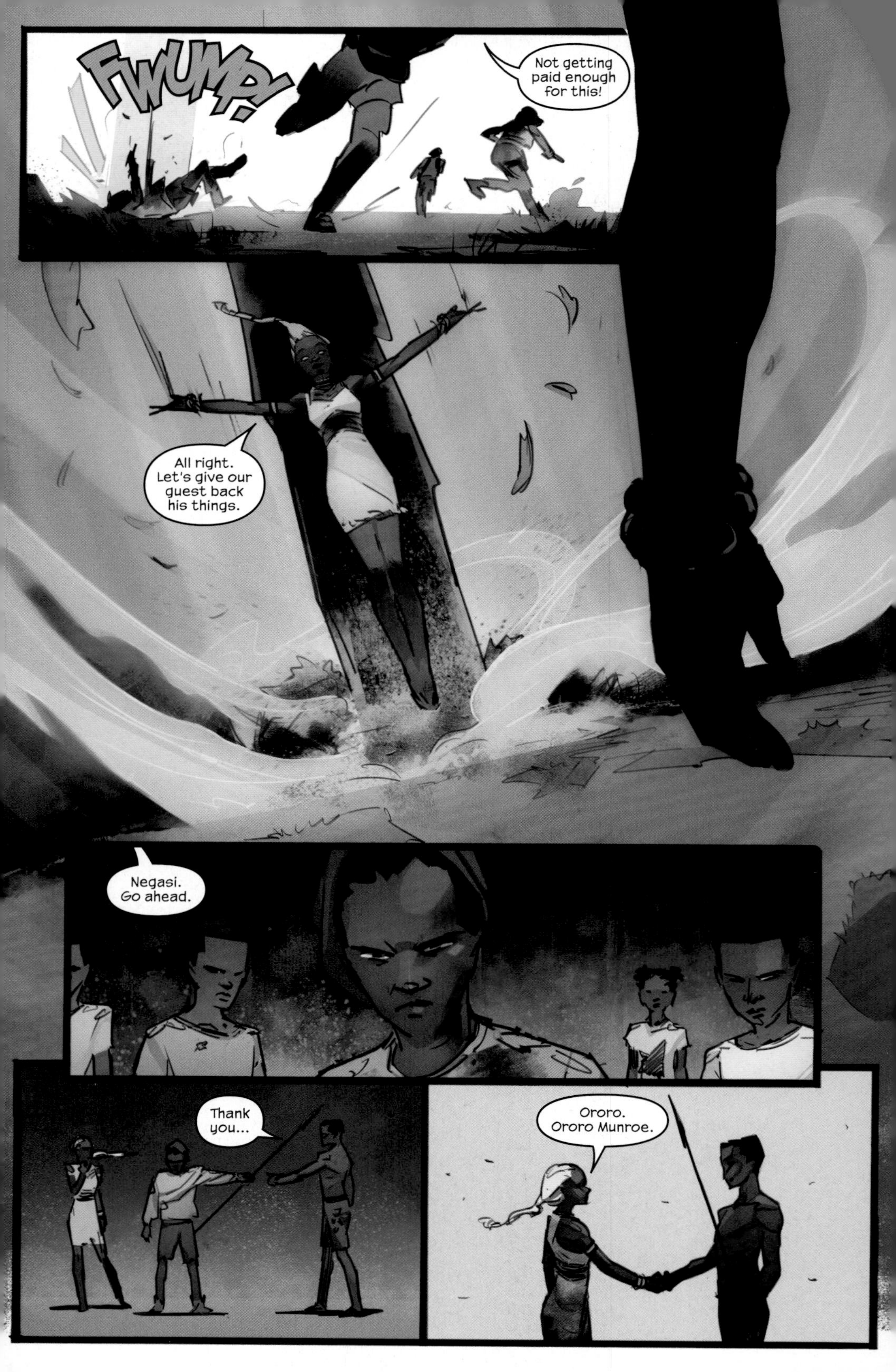
FWUMP!
Not getting paid enough for this!
All right. Let's give our guest back his things.
Negasi. Go ahead.
Thank you...
Ororo. Ororo Munroe.

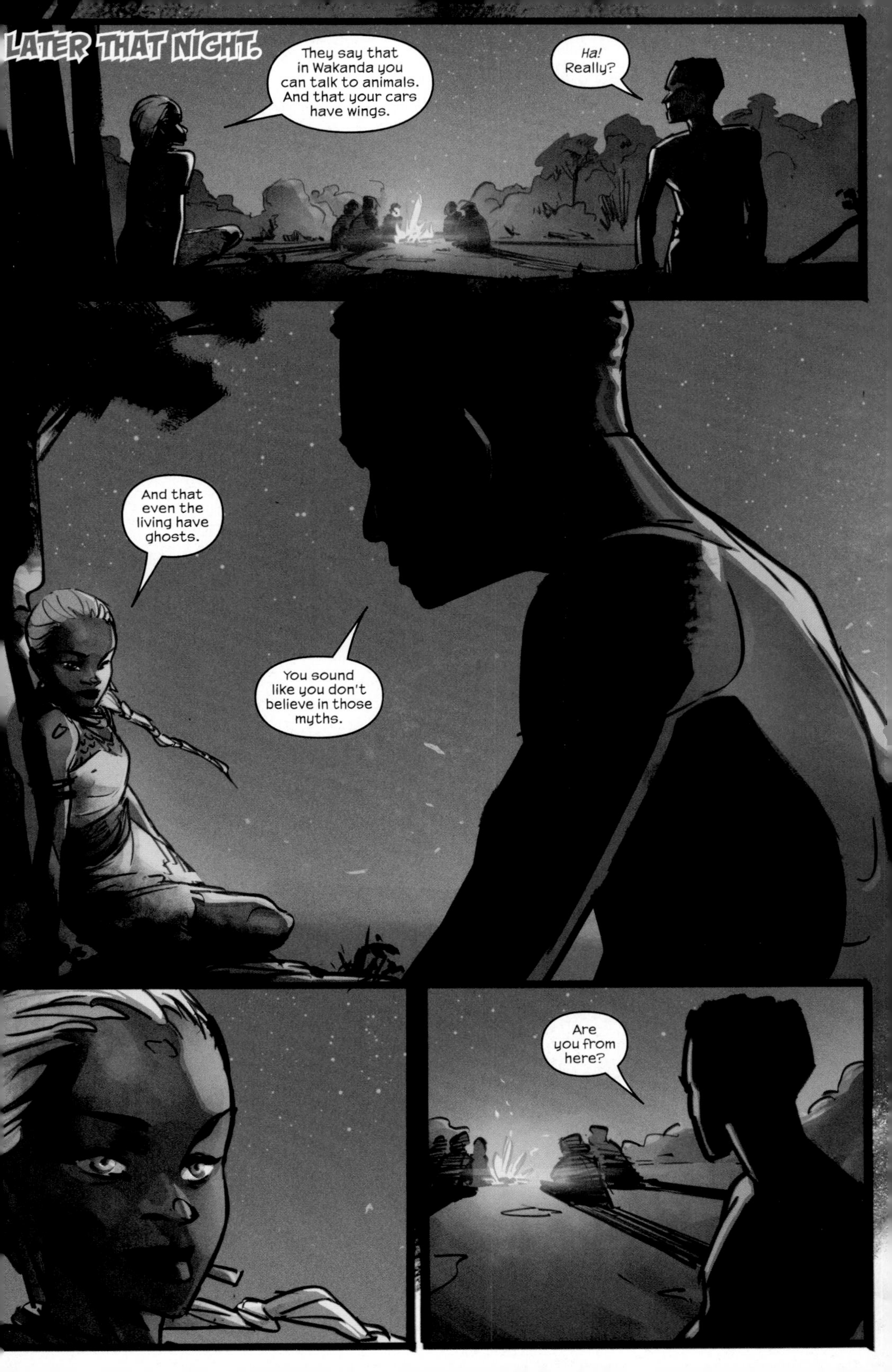
LATER THAT NIGHT.
They say that in Wakanda you can talk to animals. And that your cars have wings.
Ha! Really?
And that even the living have ghosts.
You sound like you don't believe in those myths.
Are you from here?

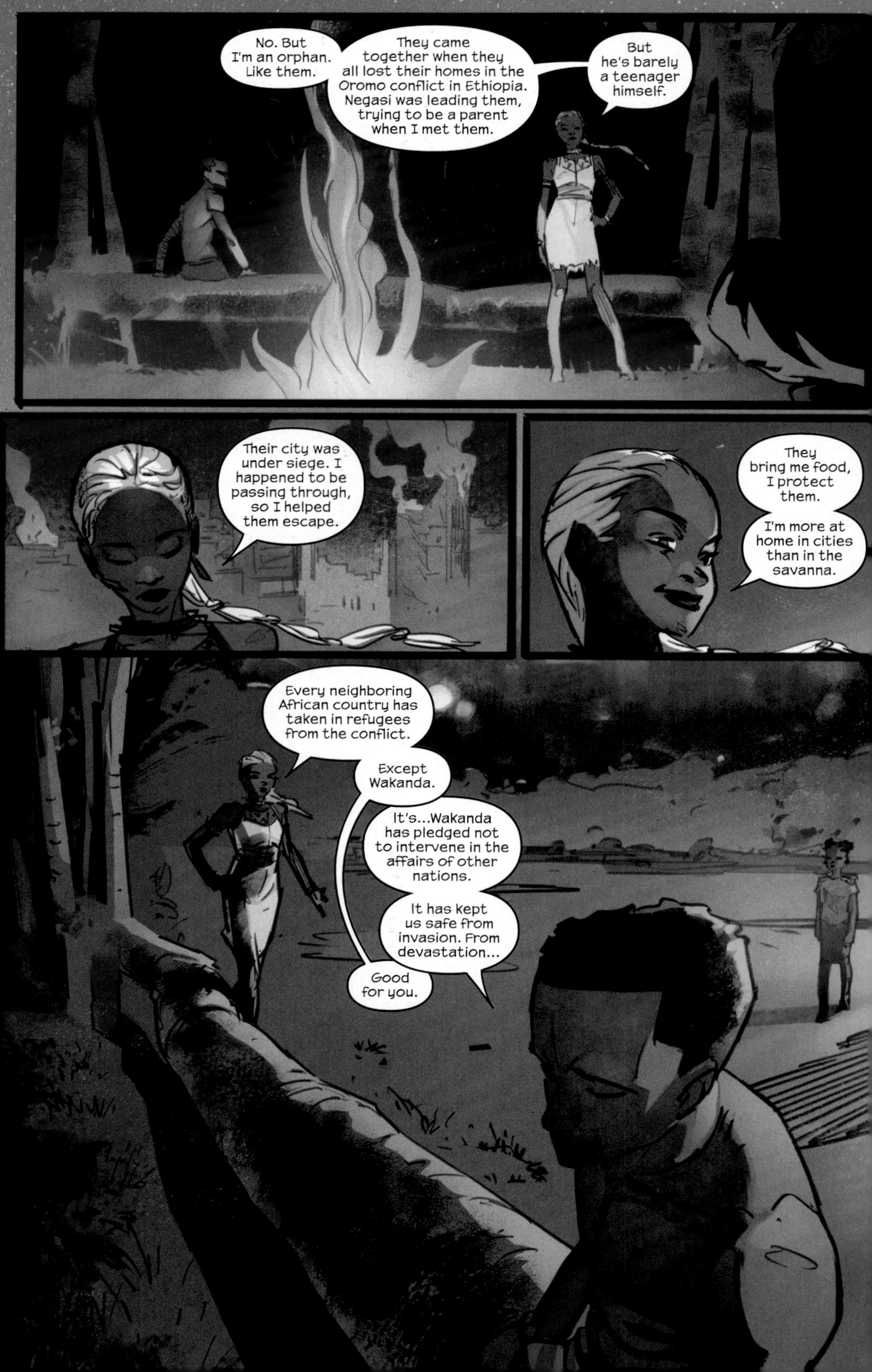
No. But I'm an orphan. Like them.
They came together when they all lost their homes in the Oromo conflict in Ethiopia. Negasi was leading them, trying to be a parent when I met them.
But he's barely a teenager himself.
Their city was under siege. I happened to be passing through, so I helped them escape.
They bring me food, I protect them.
I'm more at home in cities than in the savanna.
Every neighboring African country has taken in refugees from the conflict.
Except Wakanda.
It's...Wakanda has pledged not to intervene in the affairs of other nations.
It has kept us safe from invasion. From devastation...
Good for you.

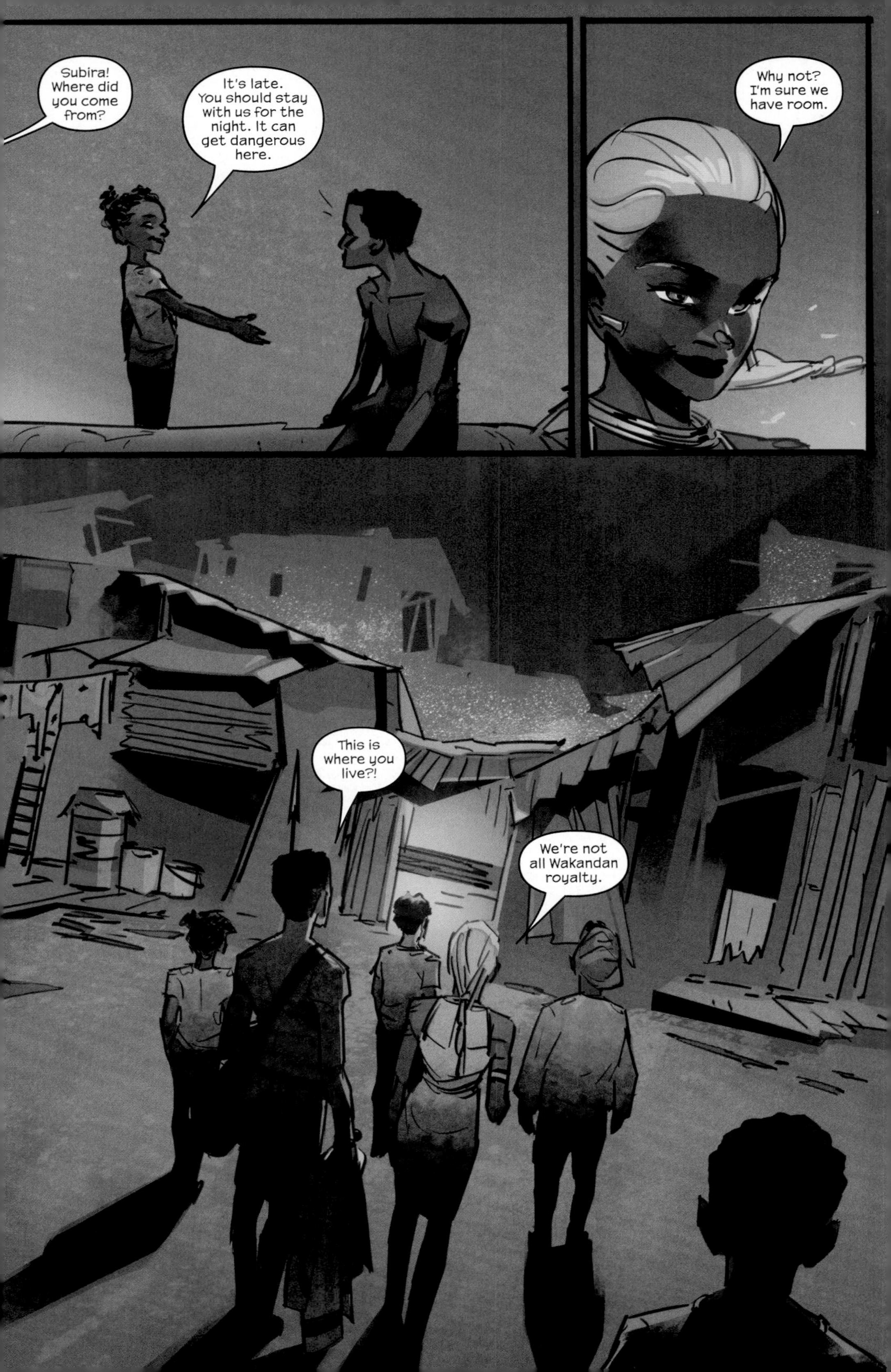
Subira! Where did you come from?
It's late. You should stay with us for the night. It can get dangerous here.
Why not? I'm sure we have room.
This is where you live?!
We're not all Wakandan royalty.

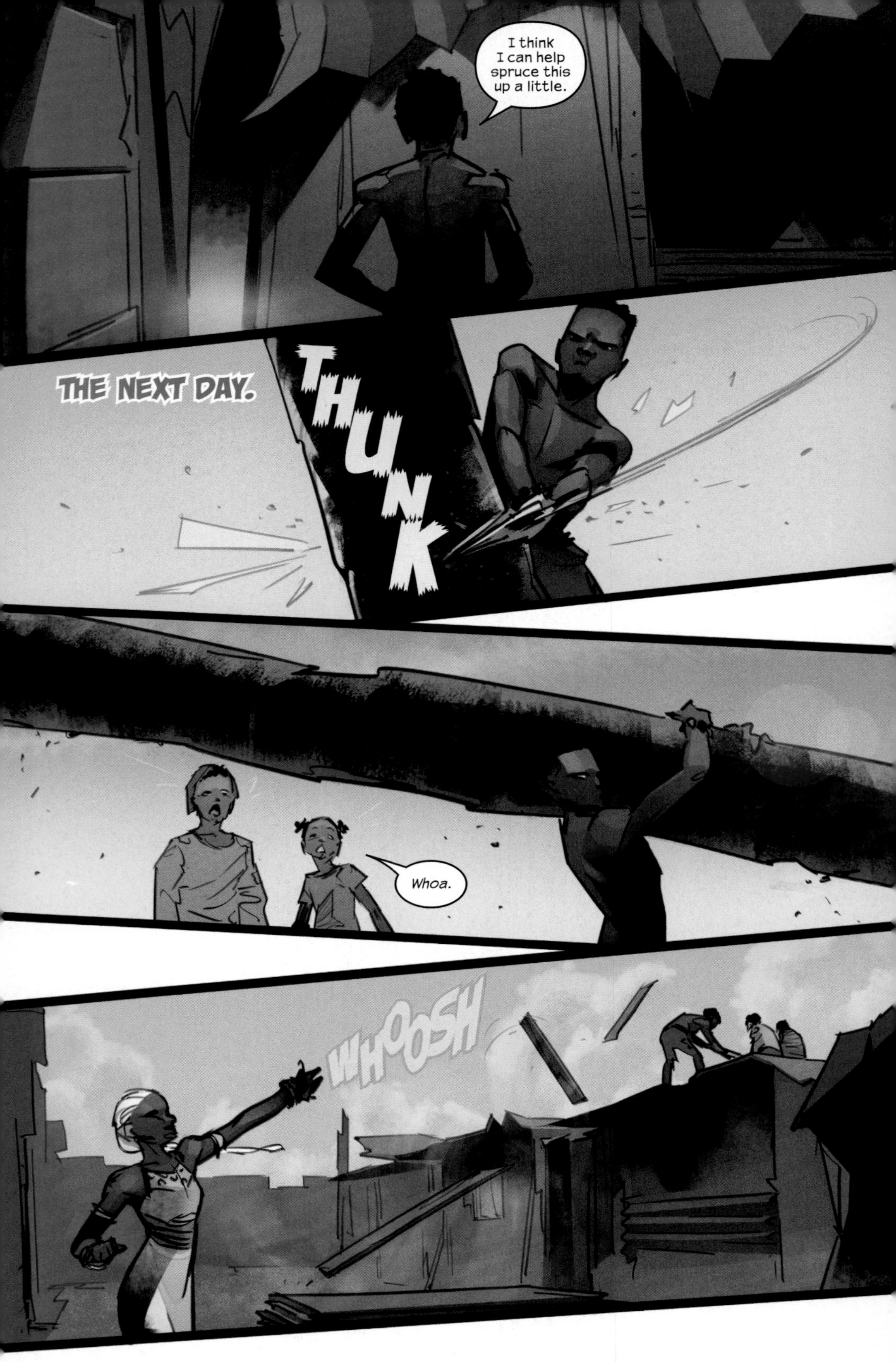
I think I can help spruce this up a little.
THE NEXT DAY.
THUNK
Whoa.
WHOOSH

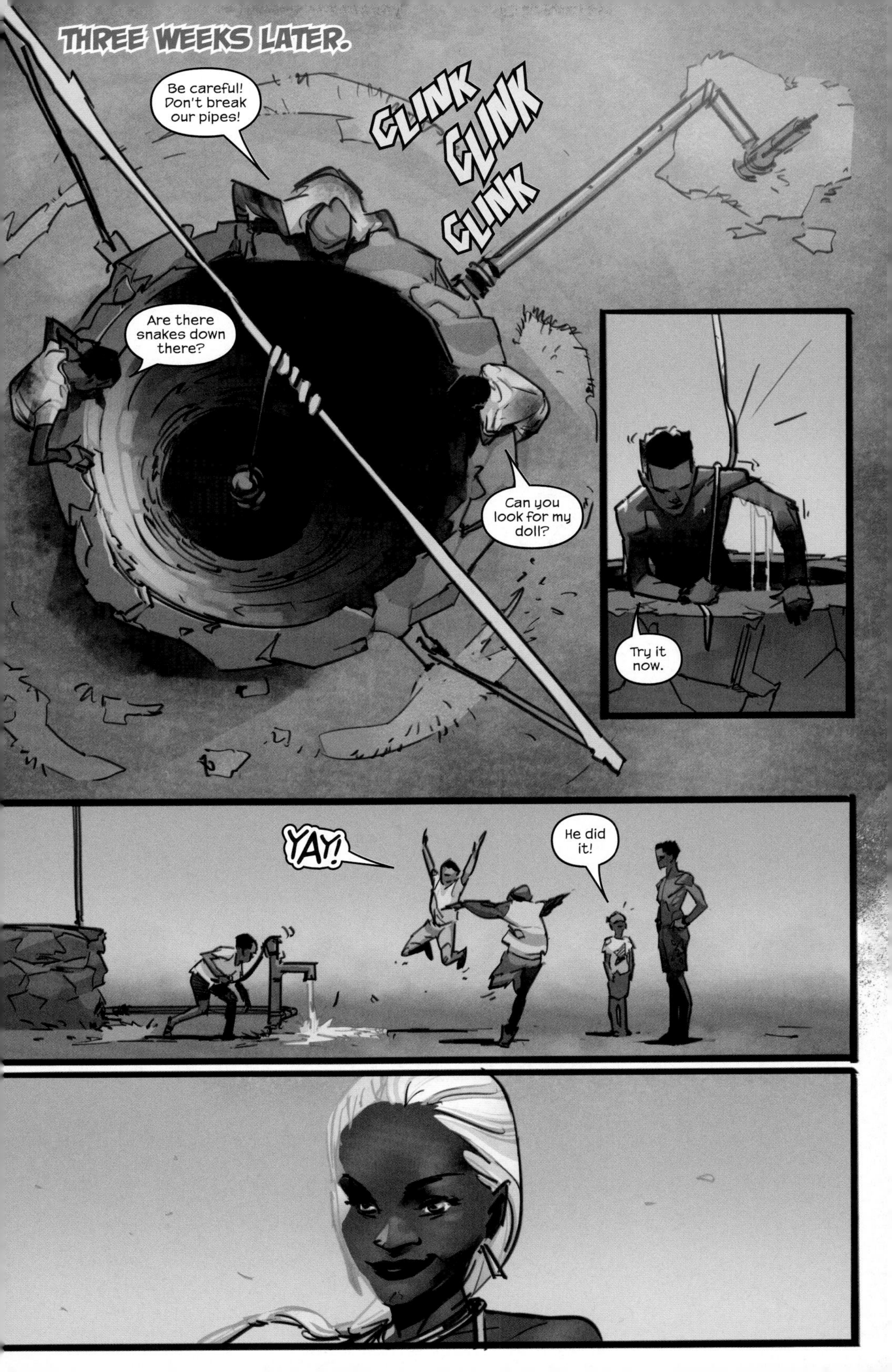
THREE WEEKS LATER.
Be careful! Don't break our pipes!
CLINK CLINK CLINK
Are there snakes down there?
Can you look for my doll?
Try it now.
YAY!
He did it!

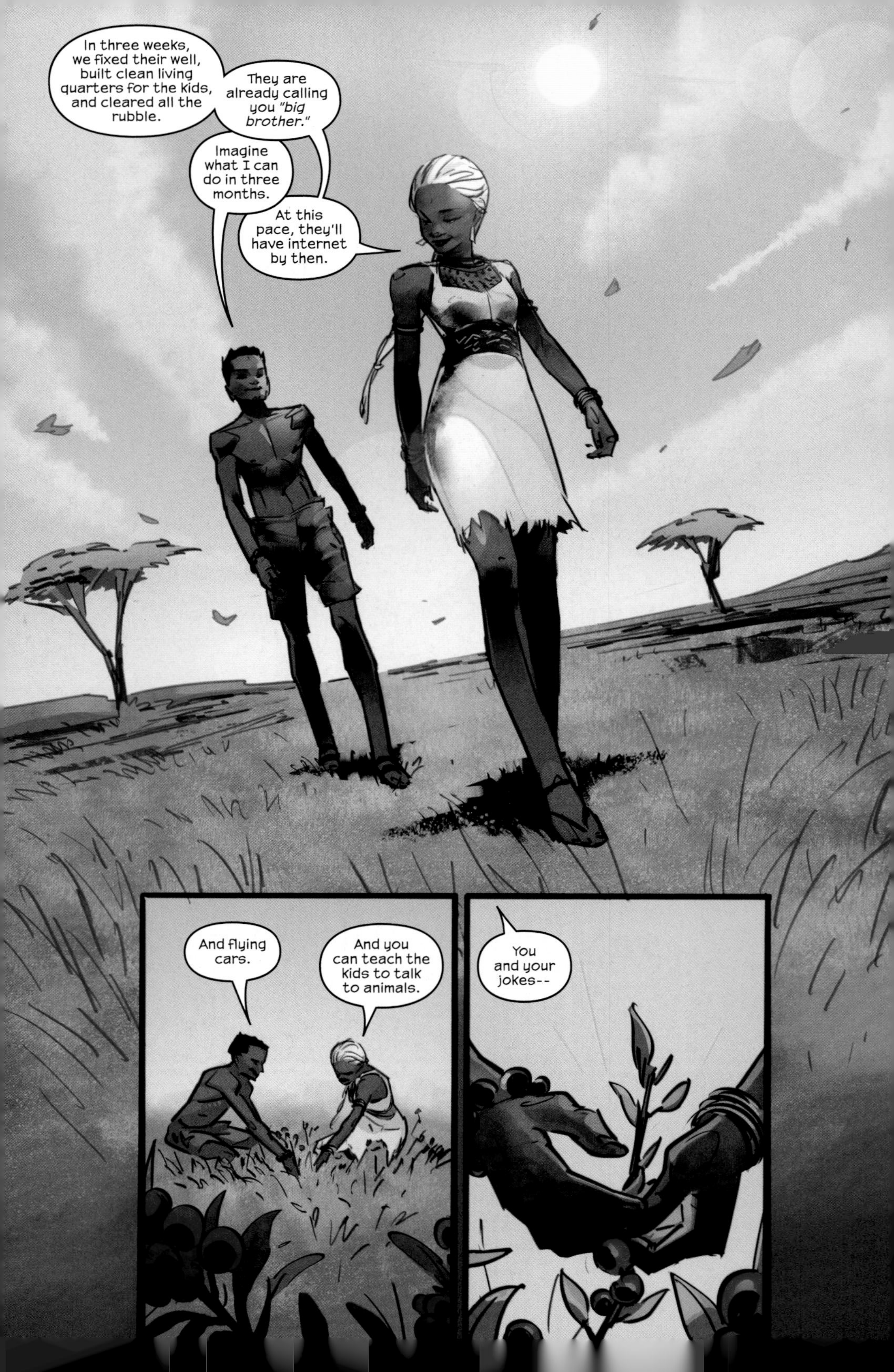
In three weeks, we fixed their well, built clean living quarters for the kids, and cleared all the rubble.
They are already calling you *"big brother."*
Imagine what I can do in three months.
At this pace, they'll have internet by then.
And flying cars.
And you can teach the kids to talk to animals.
You and your jokes--

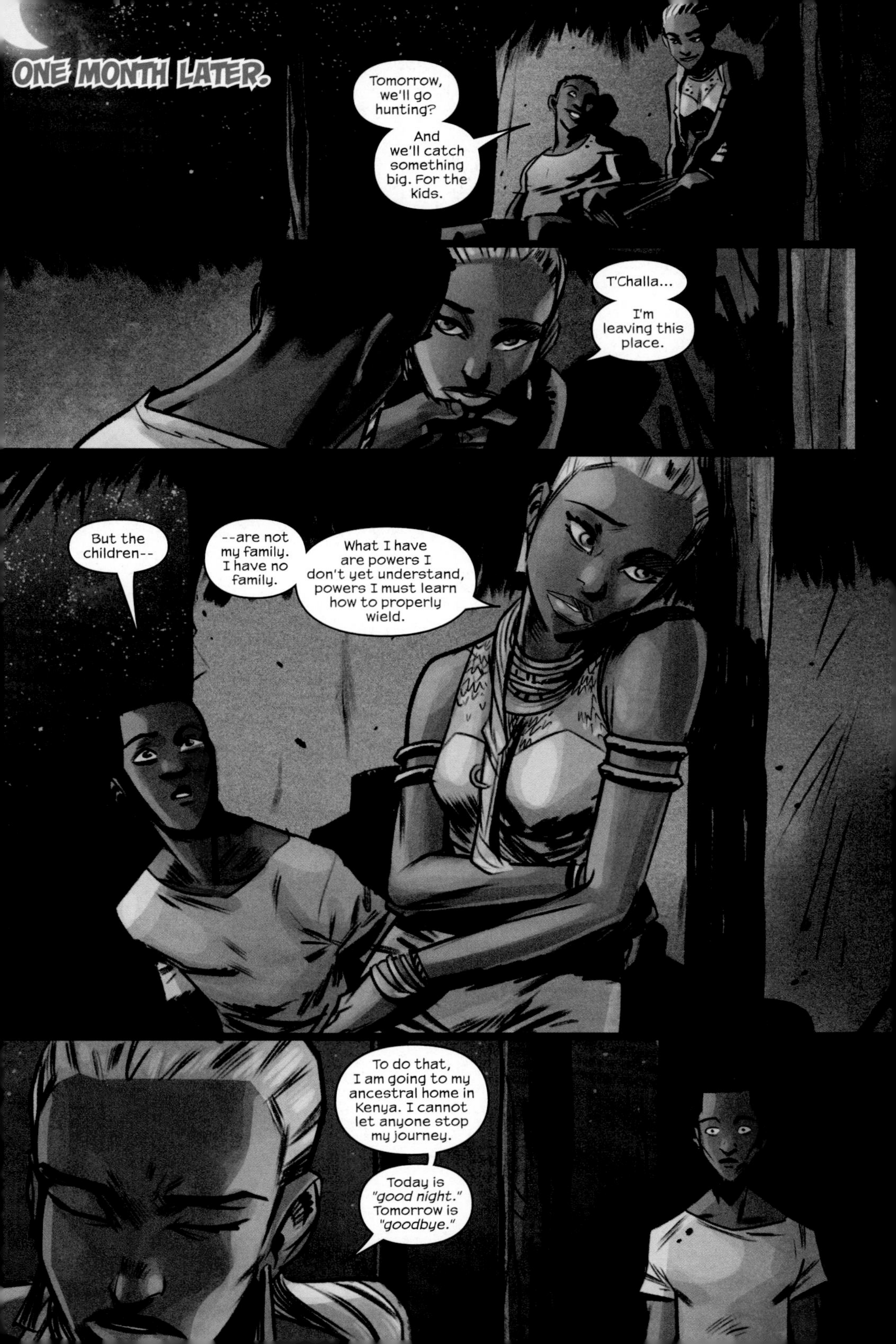
ONE MONTH LATER.
Tomorrow, we'll go hunting?
And we'll catch something big. For the kids.
T'Challa...
I'm leaving this place.
But the children--
--are not my family. I have no family.
What I have are powers I don't yet understand, powers I must learn how to properly wield.
To do that, I am going to my ancestral home in Kenya. I cannot let anyone stop my journey.
Today is "good night." Tomorrow is "goodbye."

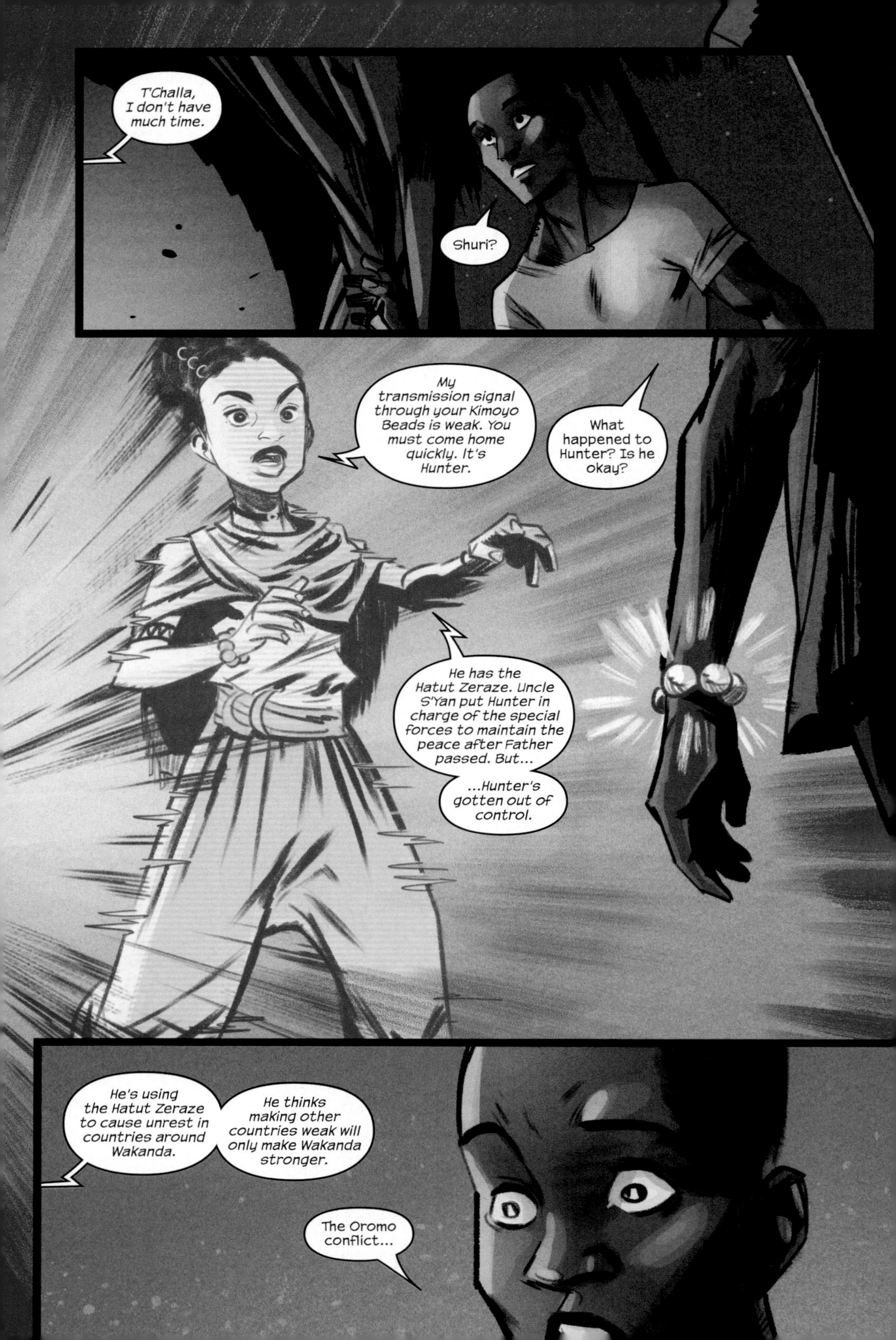
T'Challa, I don't have much time.
Shuri?
My transmission signal through your Kimoyo Beads is weak. You must come home quickly. It's Hunter.
What happened to Hunter? Is he okay?
He has the Hatut Zeraze. Uncle S'Yan put Hunter in charge of the special forces to maintain the peace after Father passed. But...
...Hunter's gotten out of control.
He's using the Hatut Zeraze to cause unrest in countries around Wakanda.
He thinks making other countries weak will only make Wakanda stronger.
The Oromo conflict...

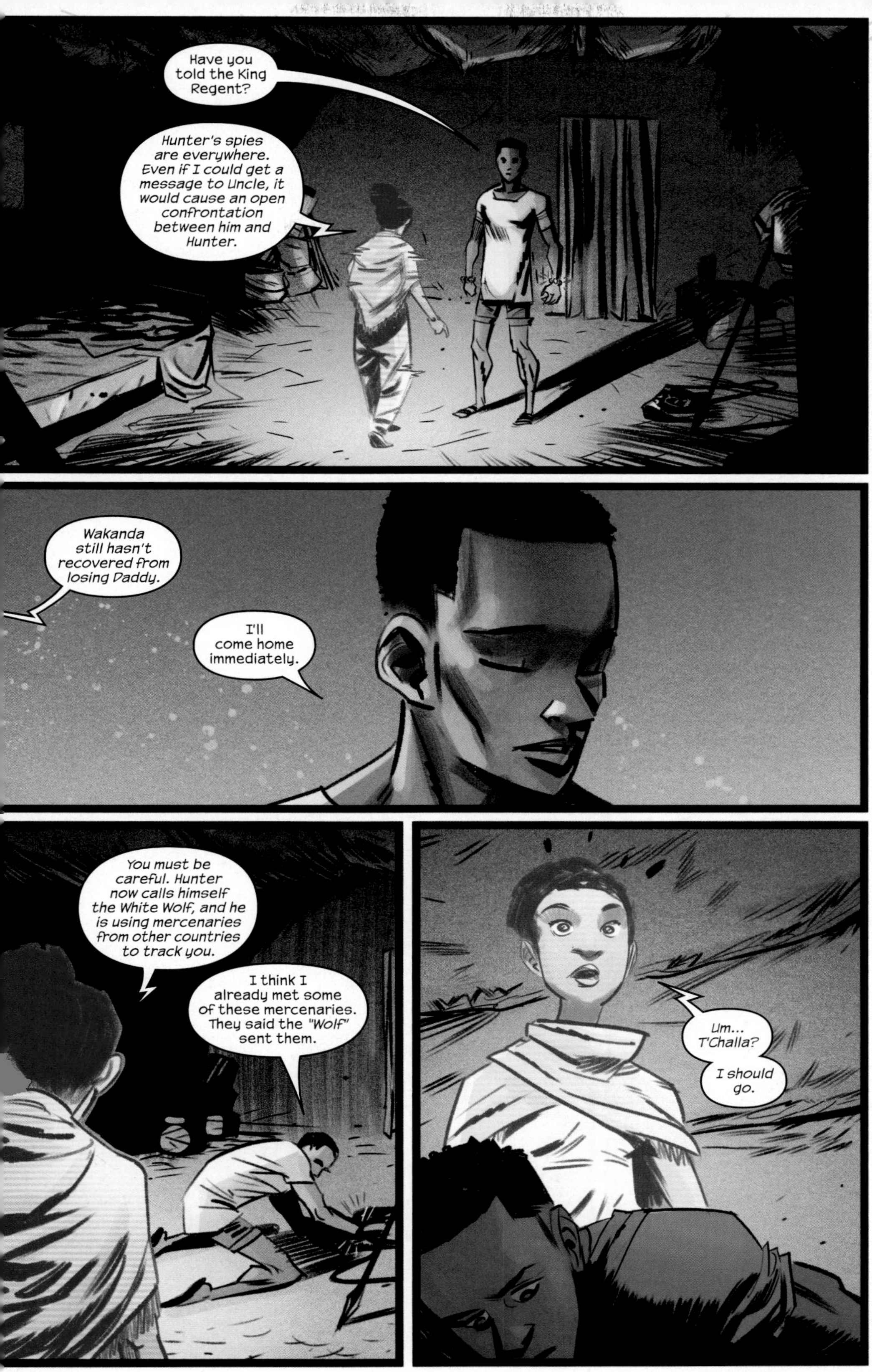
Have you told the King Regent?
Hunter's spies are everywhere. Even if I could get a message to Uncle, it would cause an open confrontation between him and Hunter.
Wakanda still hasn't recovered from losing Daddy.
I'll come home immediately.
You must be careful. Hunter now calls himself the White Wolf, and he is using mercenaries from other countries to track you.
I think I already met some of these mercenaries. They said the "Wolf" sent them.
Um... T'Challa?
I should go.

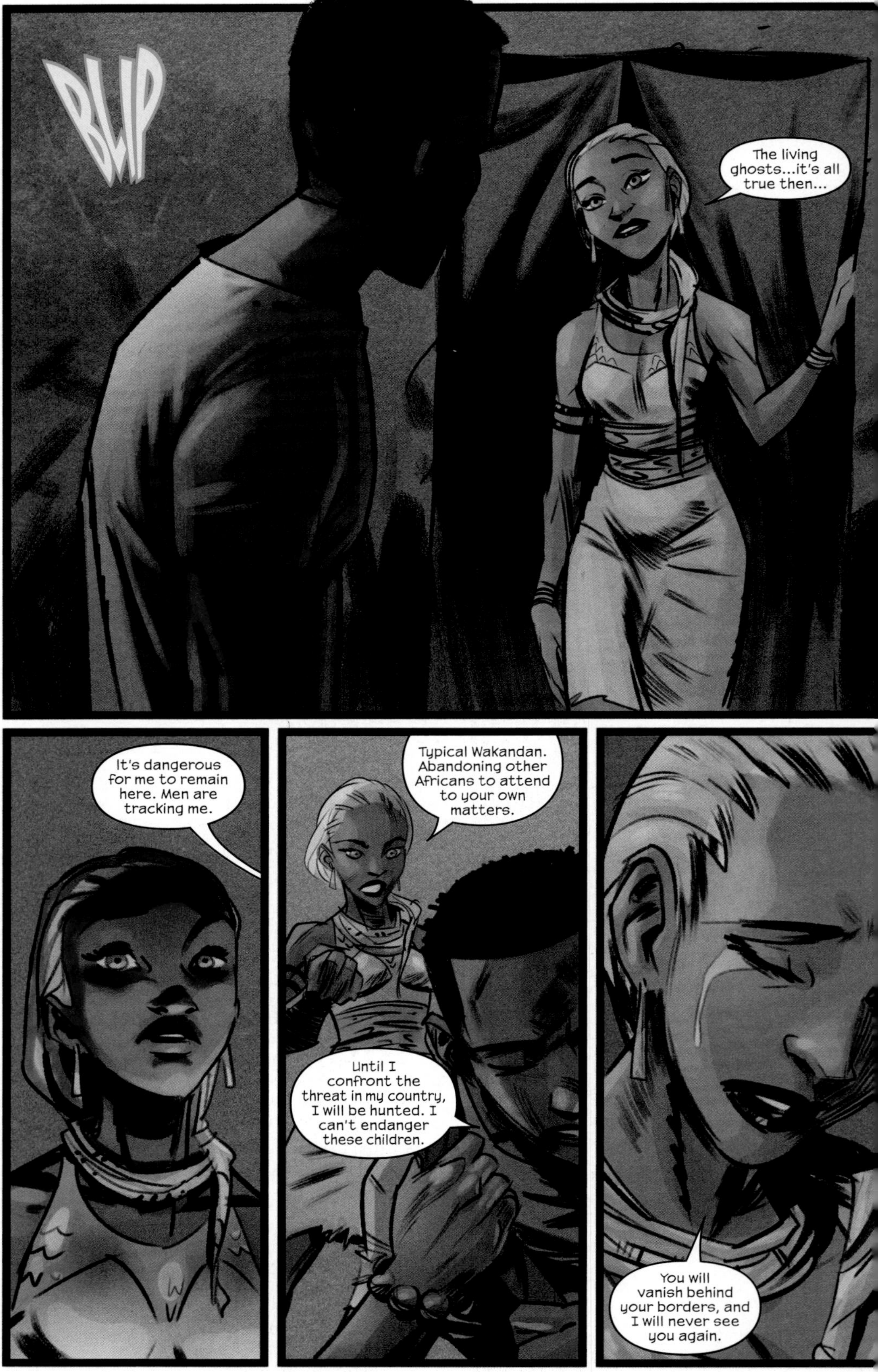
BLIP
The living ghosts...it's all true then...
It's dangerous for me to remain here. Men are tracking me.
Typical Wakandan. Abandoning other Africans to attend to your own matters.
Until I confront the threat in my country, I will be hunted. I can't endanger these children.
You will vanish behind your borders, and I will never see you again.

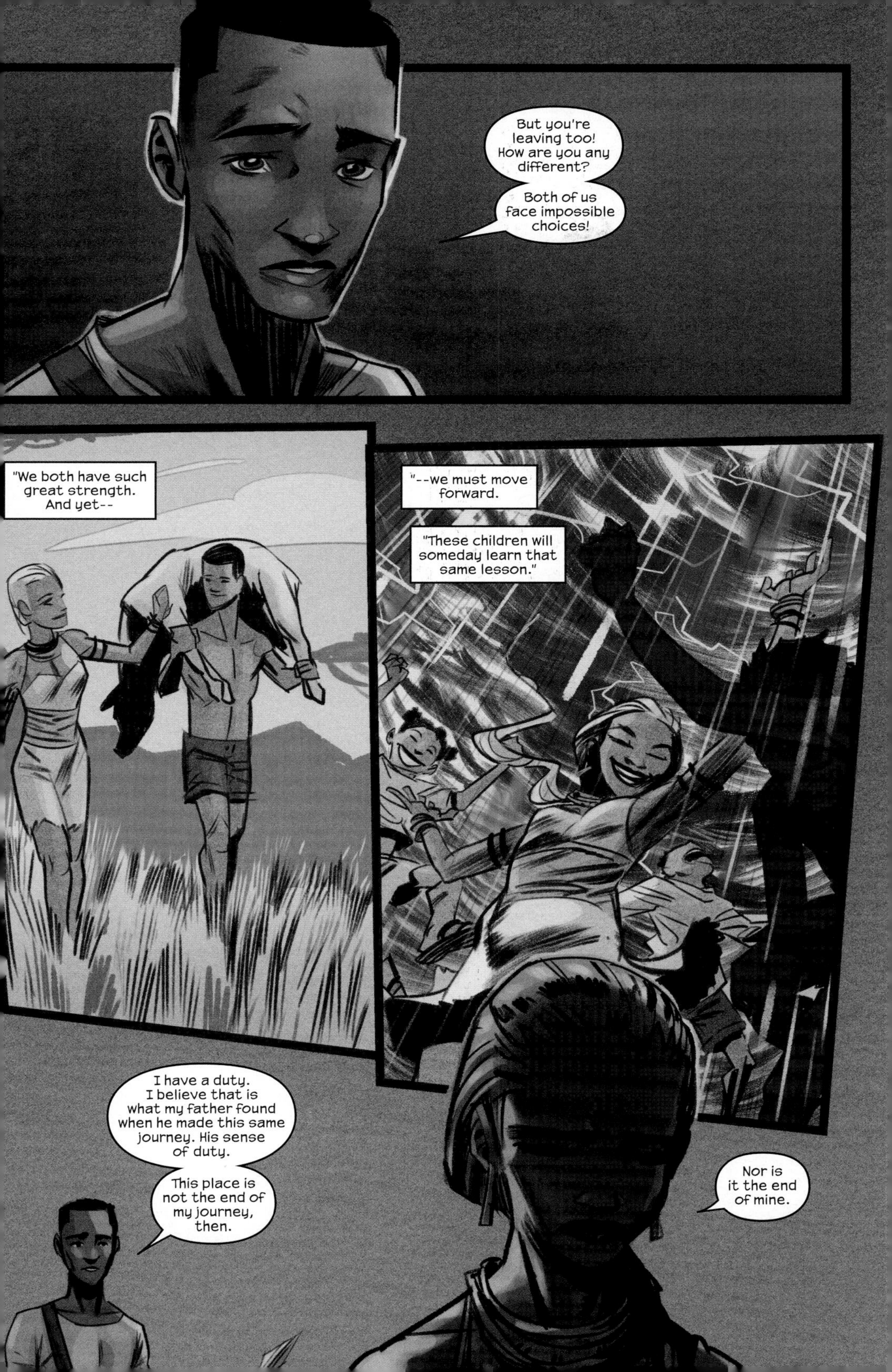

But you're leaving too! How are you any different?
Both of us face impossible choices!
"We both have such great strength. And yet--
"--we must move forward.
"These children will someday learn that same lesson."
I have a duty. I believe that is what my father found when he made this same journey. His sense of duty.
This place is not the end of my journey, then.
Nor is it the end of mine.

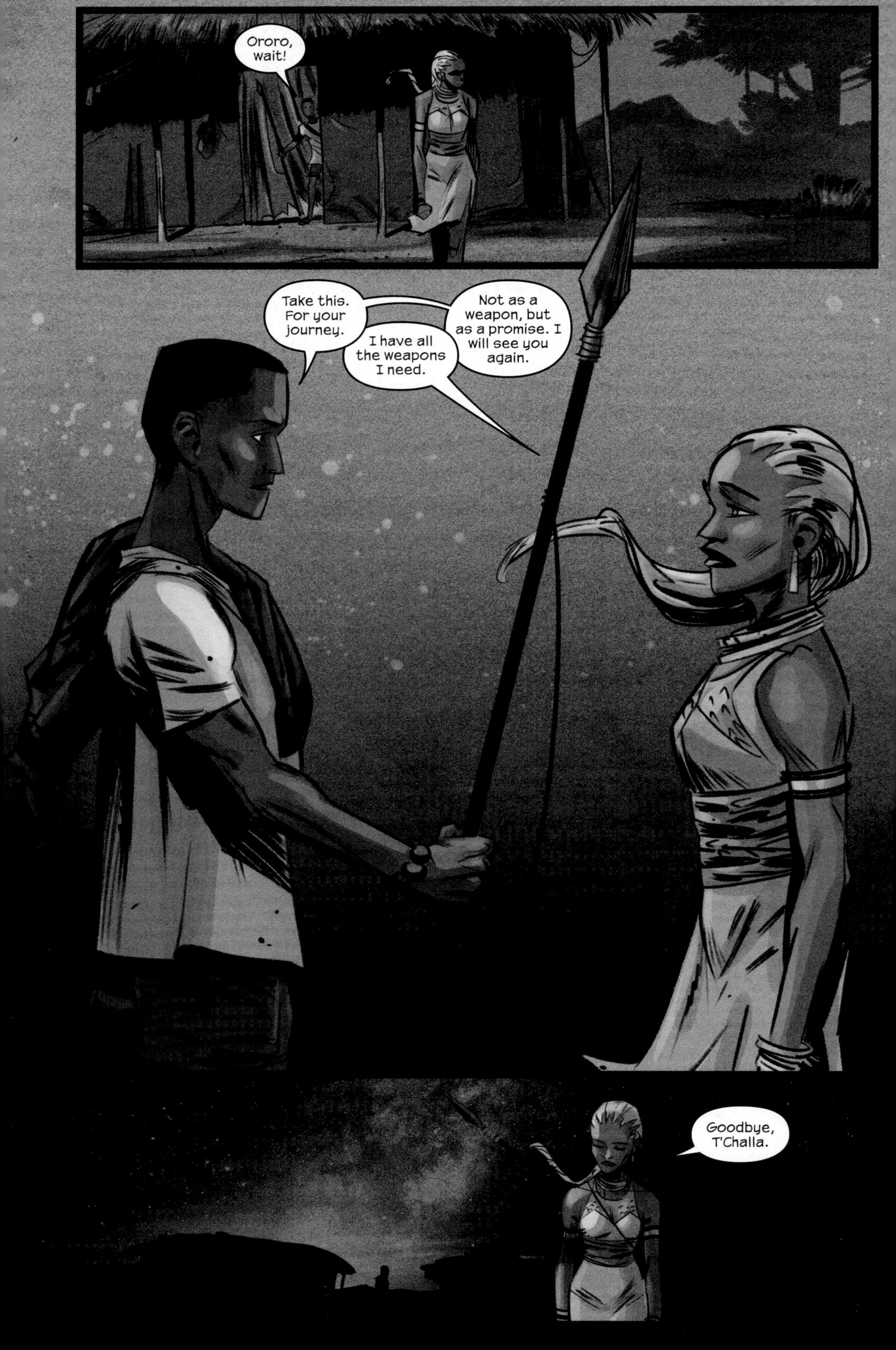
Ororo, wait!
Take this. For your journey.
I have all the weapons I need.
Not as a weapon, but as a promise. I will see you again.
Goodbye, T'Challa.

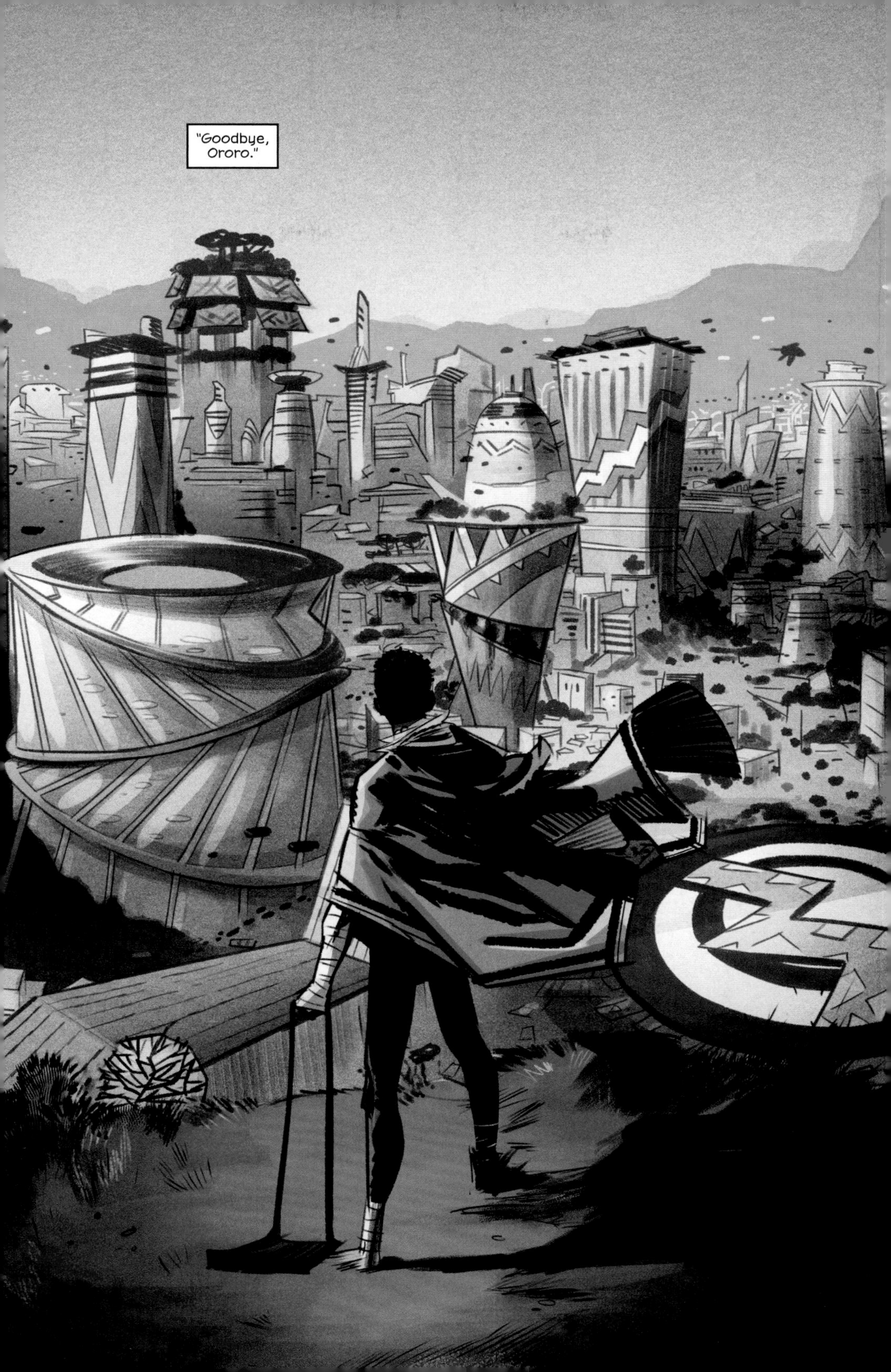
"Goodbye, Ororo."

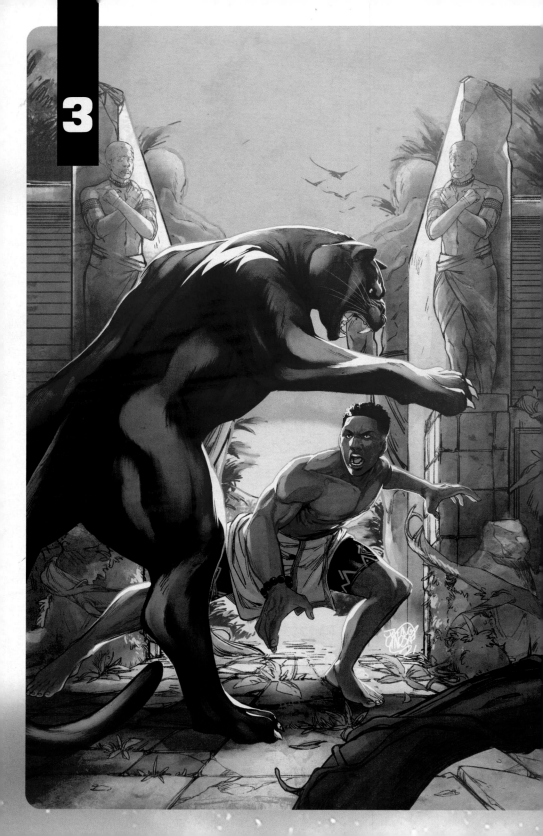

3

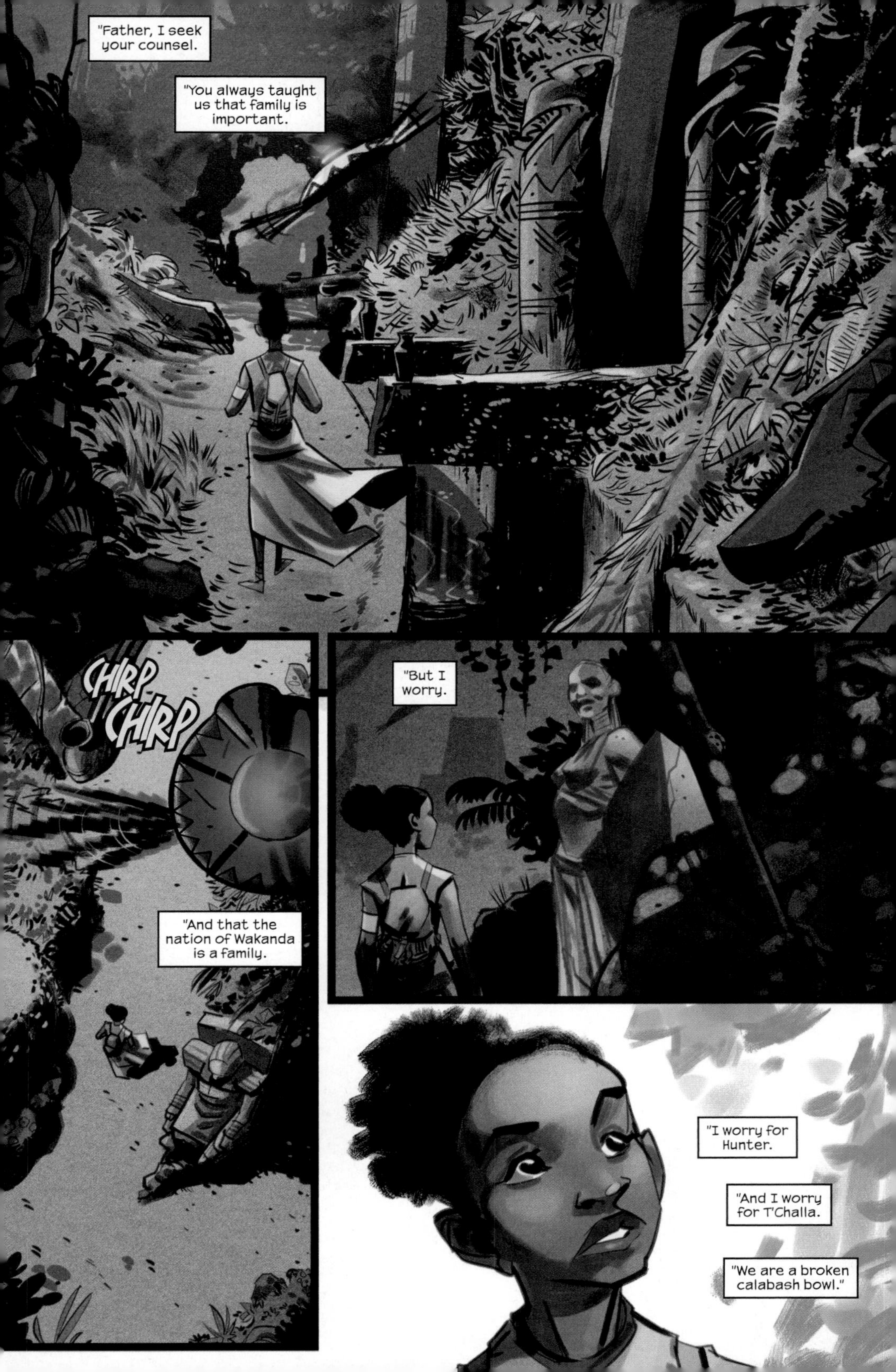

"Father, I seek your counsel.
"You always taught us that family is important.
CHIRP CHIRP
"And that the nation of Wakanda is a family.
"But I worry.
"I worry for Hunter.
"And I worry for T'Challa.
"We are a broken calabash bowl."

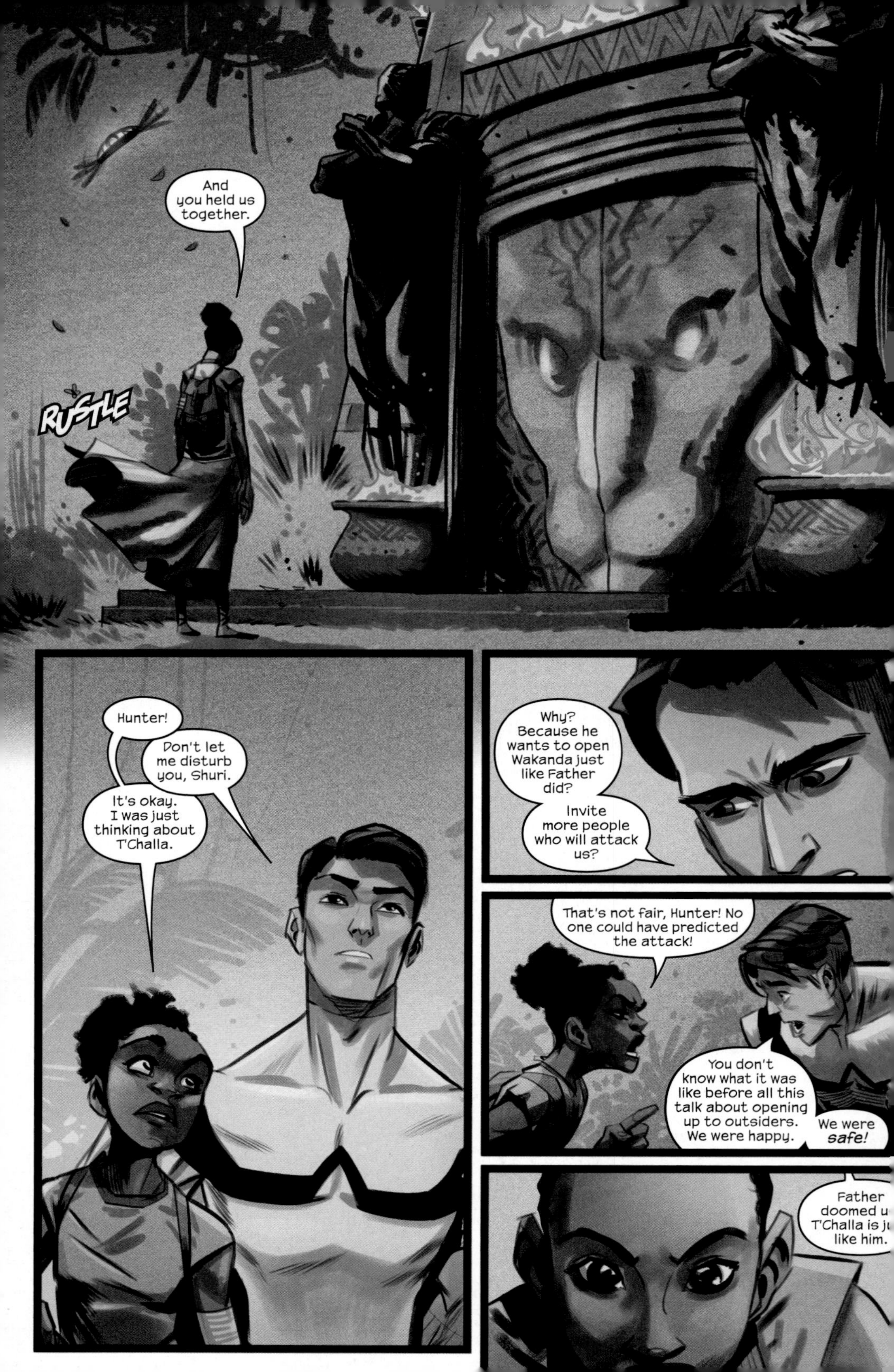
And you held us together.
RUSTLE
Hunter!
Don't let me disturb you, Shuri.
It's okay. I was just thinking about T'Challa.
Why? Because he wants to open Wakanda just like Father did?
Invite more people who will attack us?
That's not fair, Hunter! No one could have predicted the attack!
You don't know what it was like before all this talk about opening up to outsiders. We were happy.
We were safe!

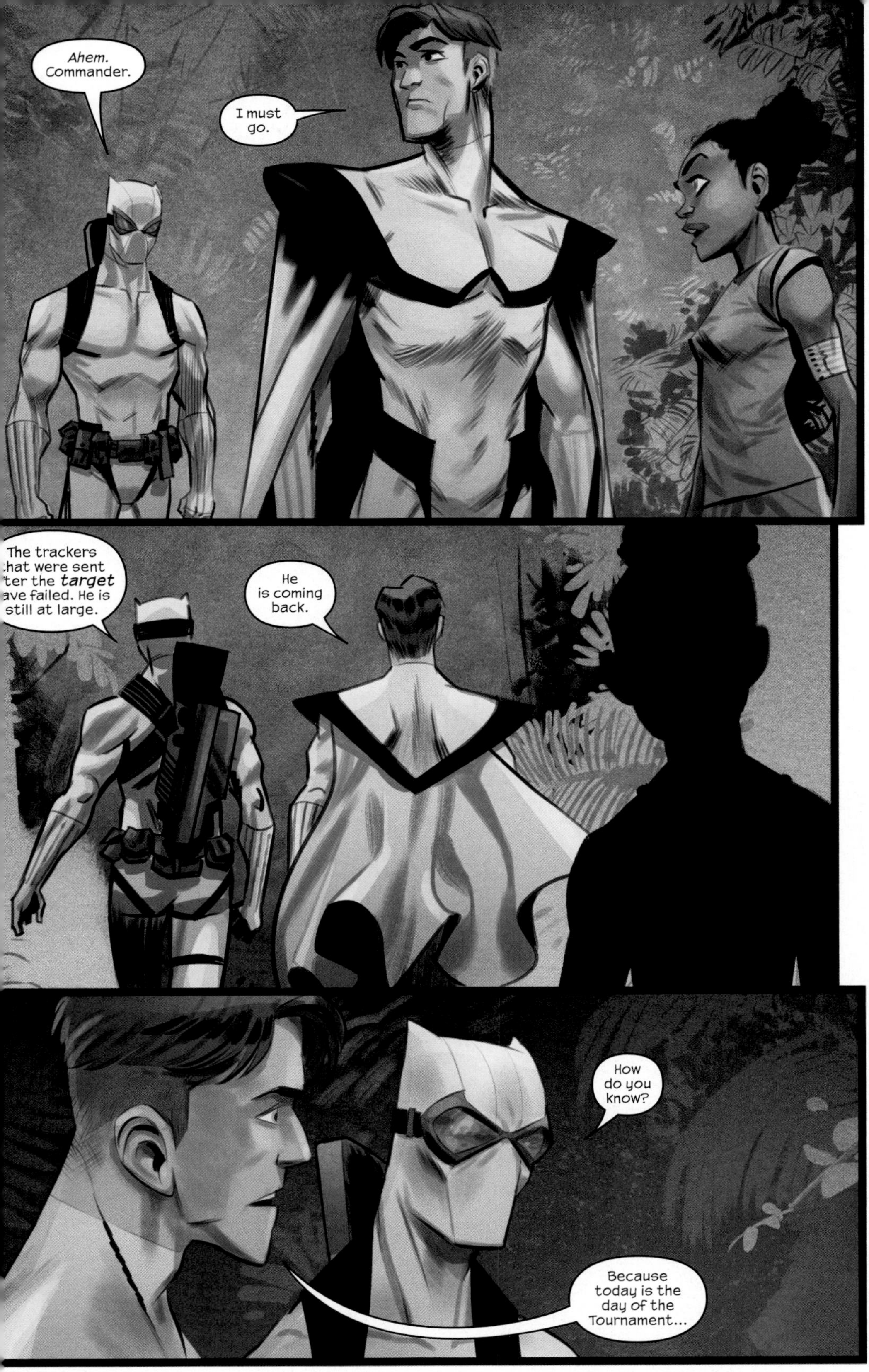

Ahem. Commander.
I must go.
The trackers that were sent ter the *target* ave failed. He is still at large.
He is coming back.
How do you know?
Because today is the day of the Tournament...

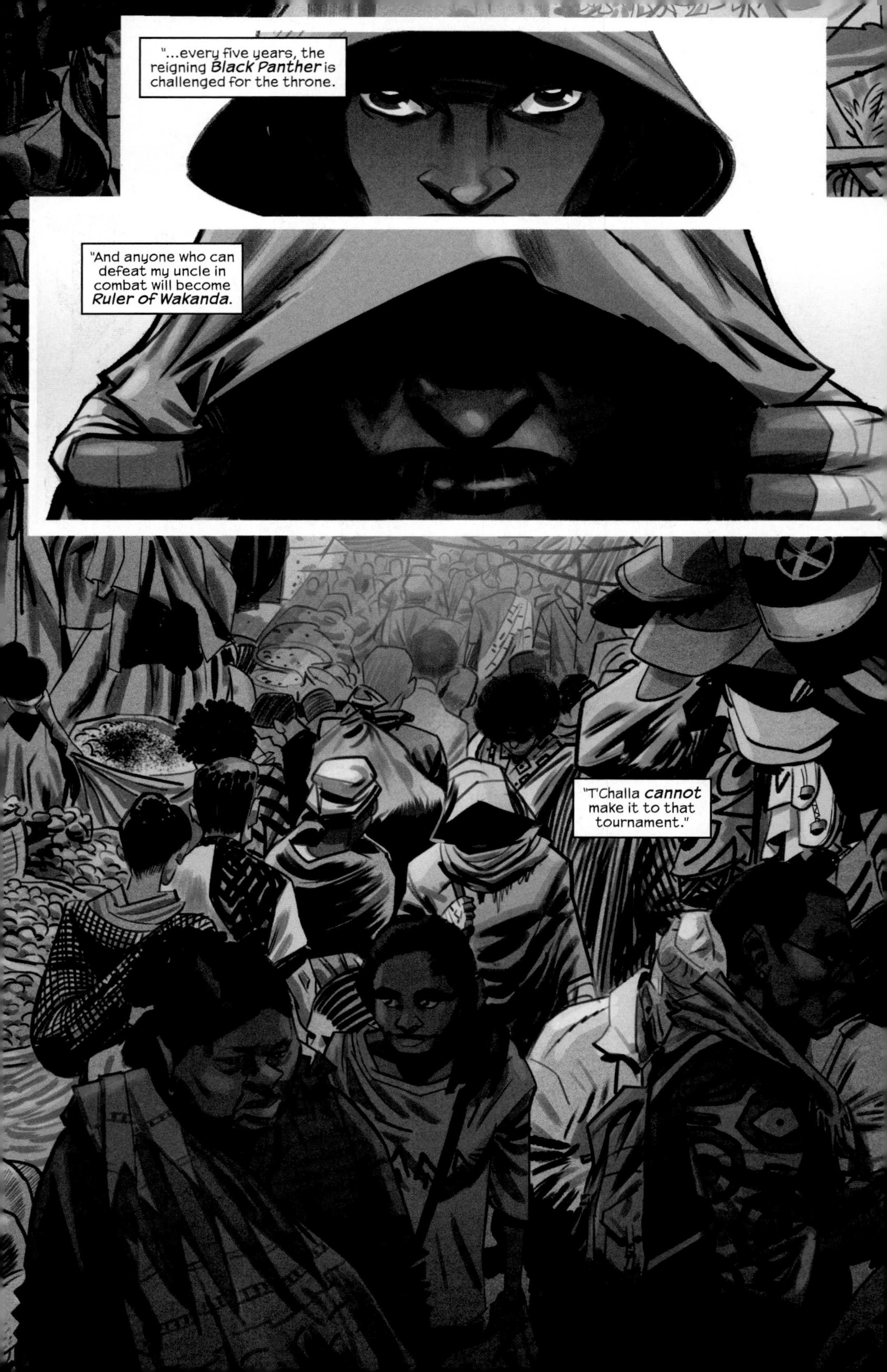
"...every five years, the reigning *Black Panther* is challenged for the throne.
"And anyone who can defeat my uncle in combat will become *Ruler of Wakanda*.
"T'Challa *cannot* make it to that tournament."

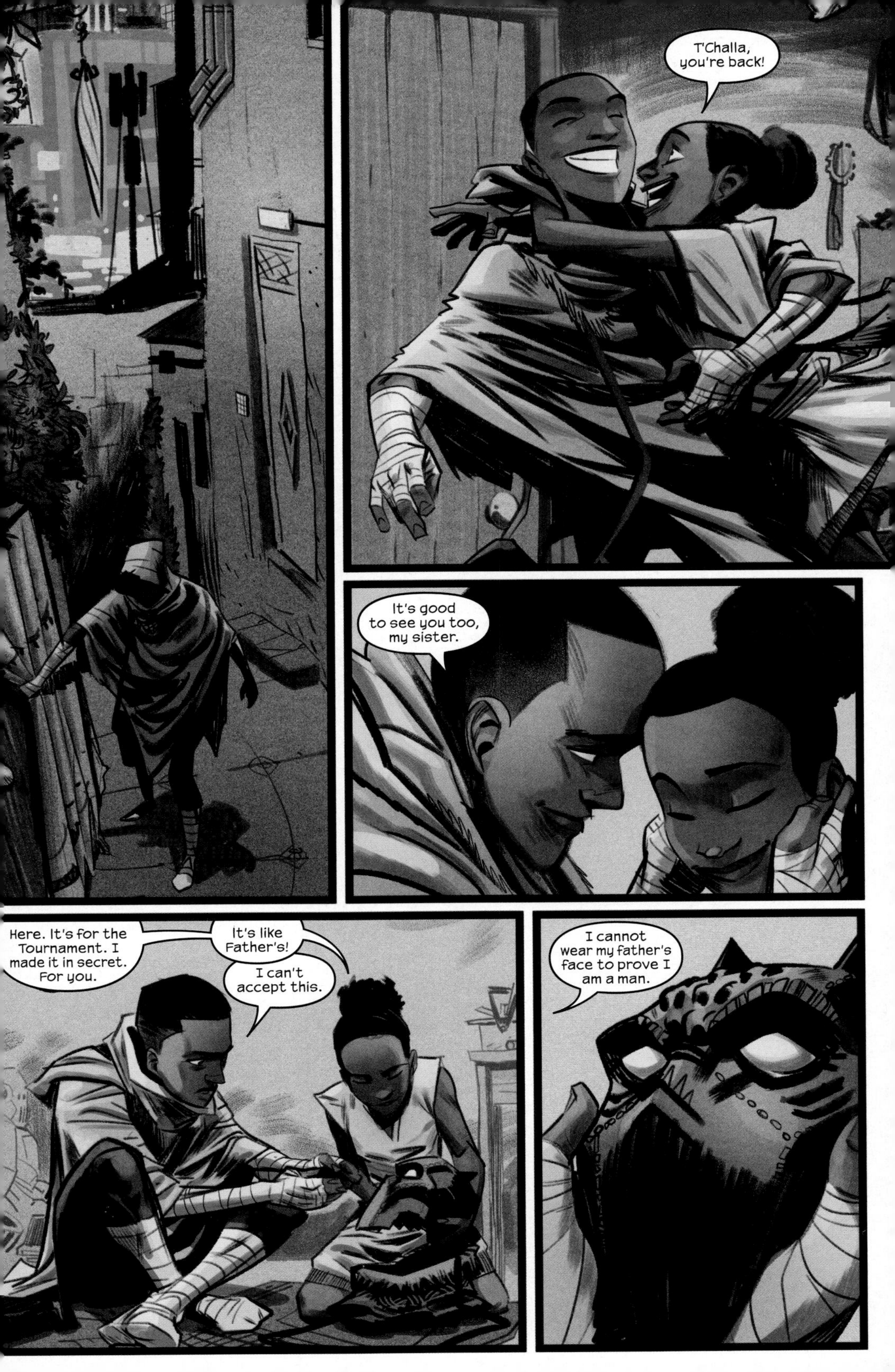
T'Challa, you're back!
It's good to see you too, my sister.
Here. It's for the Tournament. I made it in secret. For you.
It's like Father's!
I can't accept this.
I cannot wear my father's face to prove I am a man.

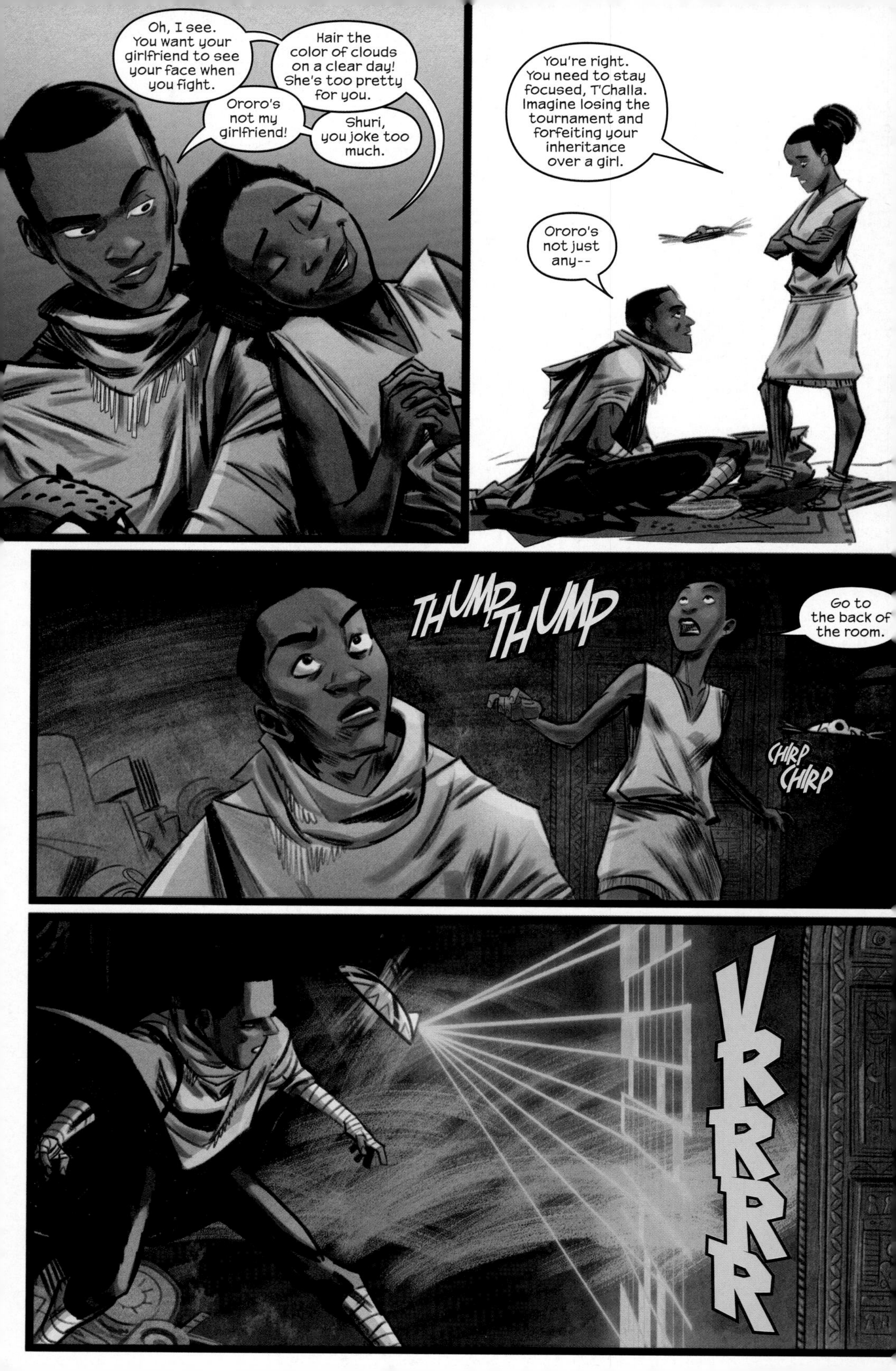
Oh, I see. You want your girlfriend to see your face when you fight.
Hair the color of clouds on a clear day! She's too pretty for you.
Ororo's not my girlfriend!
Shuri, you joke too much.
You're right. You need to stay focused, T'Challa. Imagine losing the tournament and forfeiting your inheritance over a girl.
Ororo's not just any--
THUMP THUMP
Go to the back of the room.
CHIRP CHIRP
VRRRR

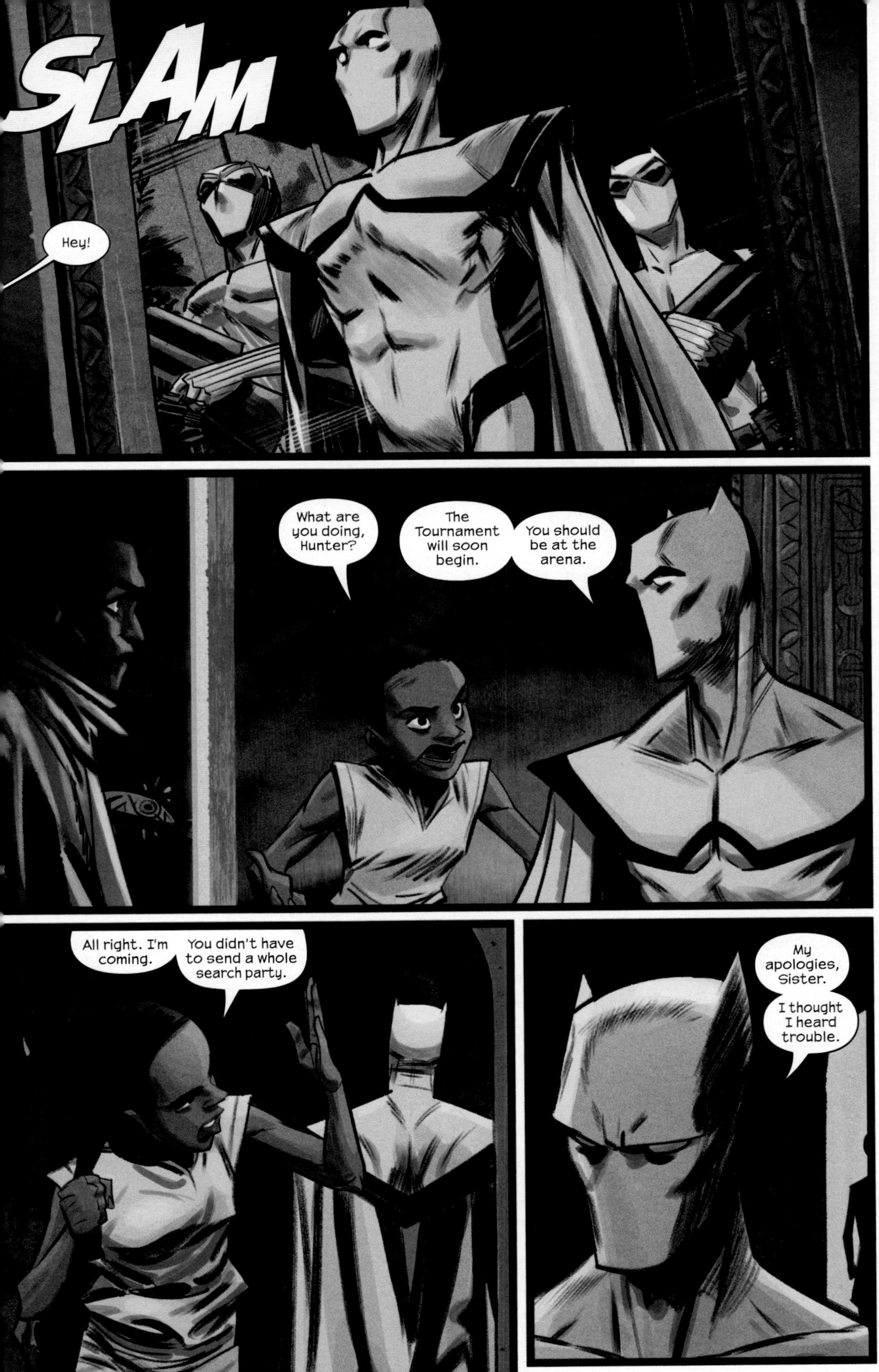
SLAM
Hey!
What are you doing, Hunter?
The Tournament will soon begin.
You should be at the arena.
All right. I'm coming.
You didn't have to send a whole search party.
My apologies, Sister.
I thought I heard trouble.

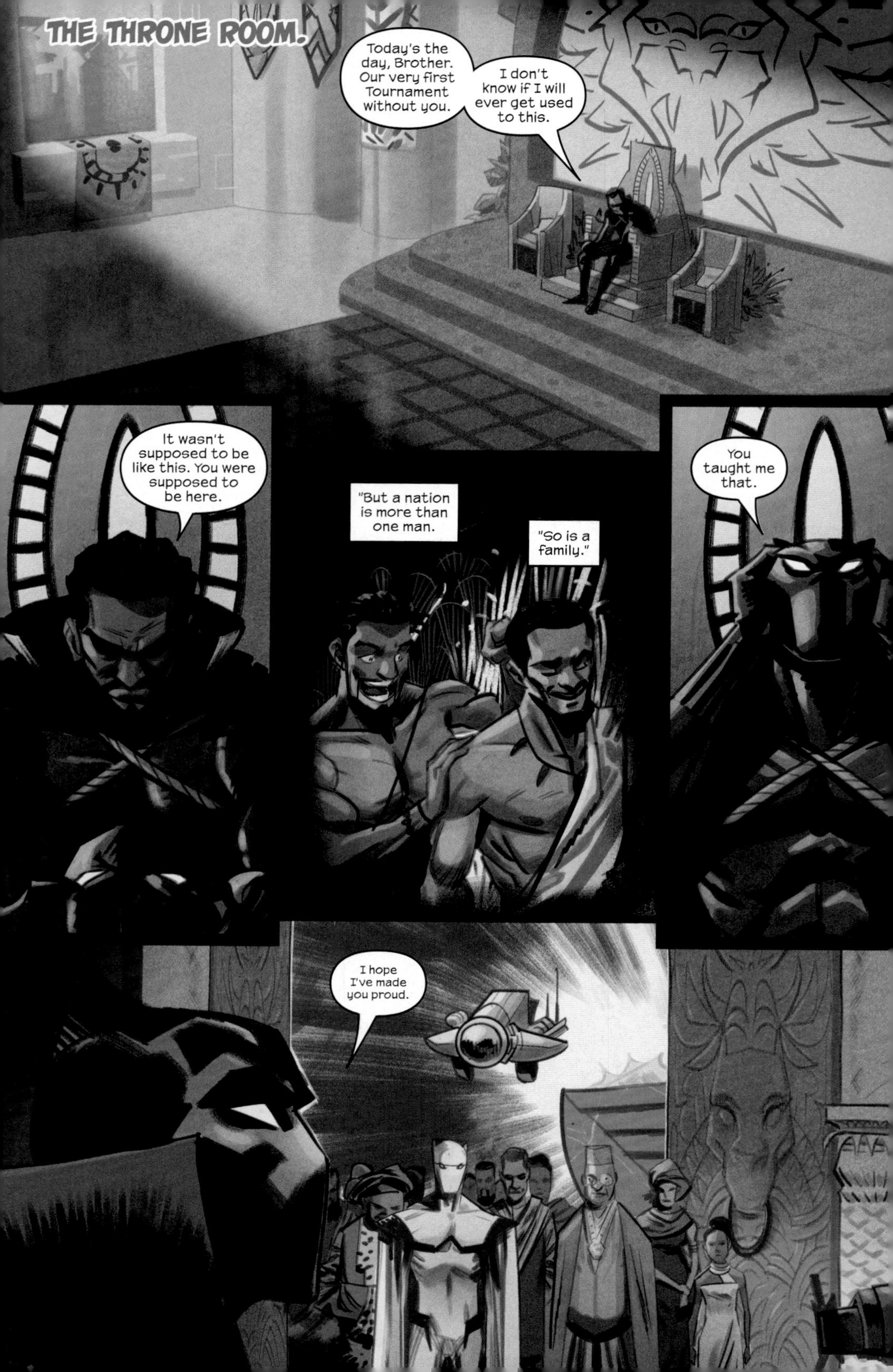
THE THRONE ROOM.
Today's the day, Brother. Our very first Tournament without you.
I don't know if I will ever get used to this.
It wasn't supposed to be like this. You were supposed to be here.
"But a nation is more than one man.
"So is a family."
You taught me that.
I hope I've made you proud.

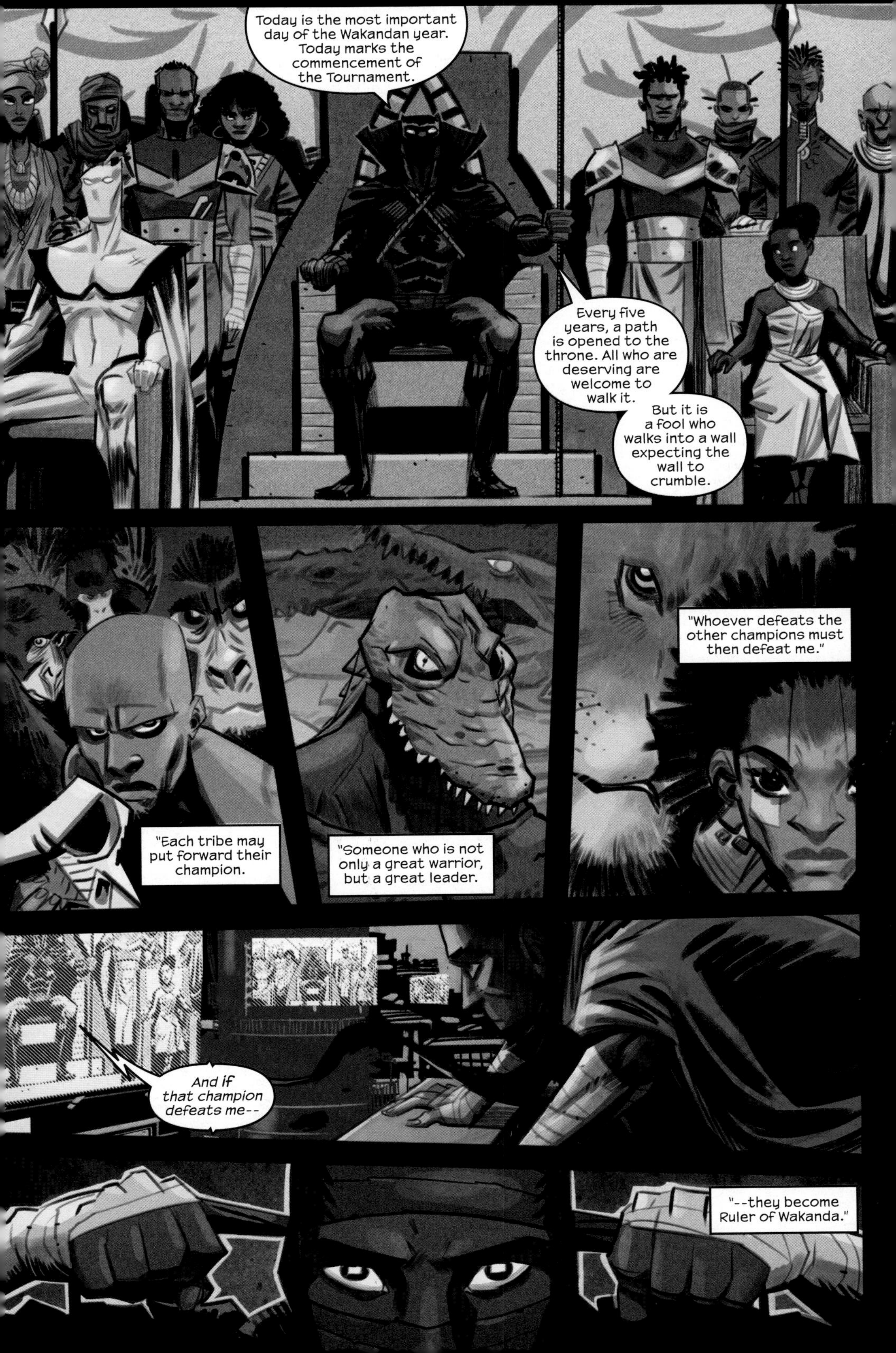
Today is the most important day of the Wakandan year. Today marks the commencement of the Tournament.
Every five years, a path is opened to the throne. All who are deserving are welcome to walk it.
But it is a fool who walks into a wall expecting the wall to crumble.
"Each tribe may put forward their champion.
"Someone who is not only a great warrior, but a great leader.
"Whoever defeats the other champions must then defeat me."
And if that champion defeats me--
"--they become Ruler of Wakanda."

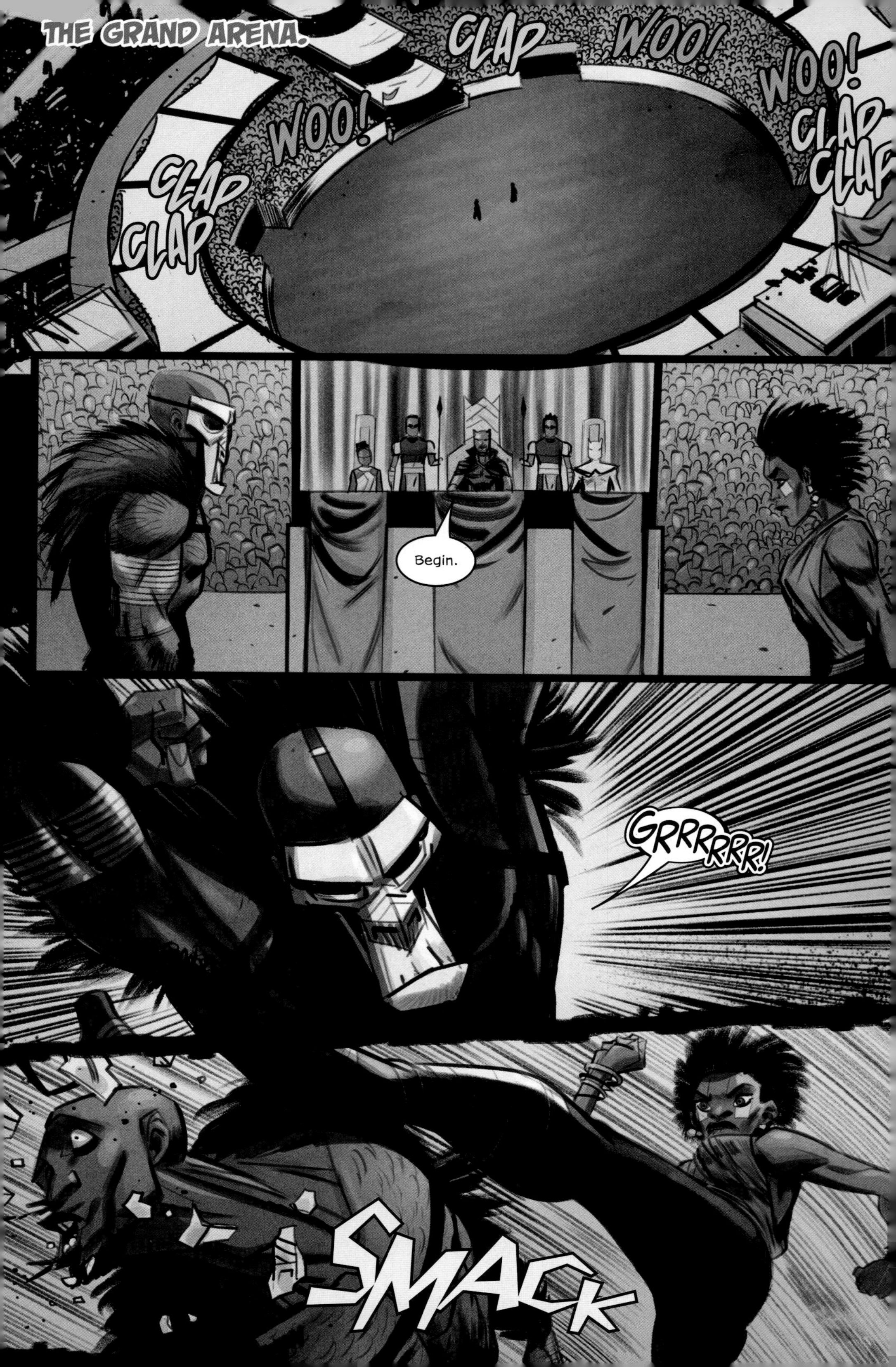
THE GRAND ARENA.
CLAP CLAP
WOO!
CLAP
WOO!
WOO!
CLAP CLAP
Begin.
GRRRRRR!
SMACK

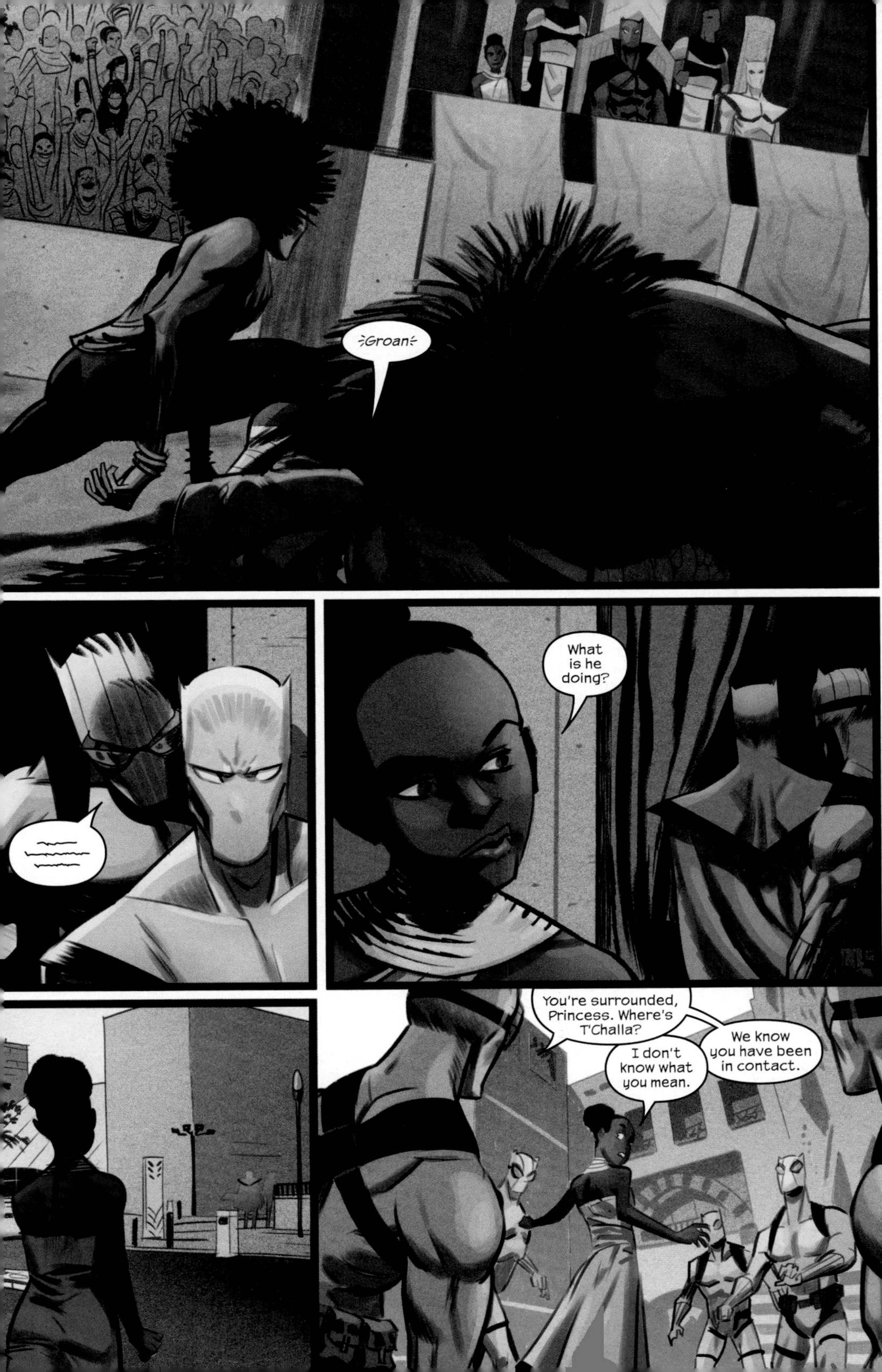
Groan
What is he doing?
You're surrounded, Princess. Where's T'Challa?
I don't know what you mean.
We know you have been in contact.

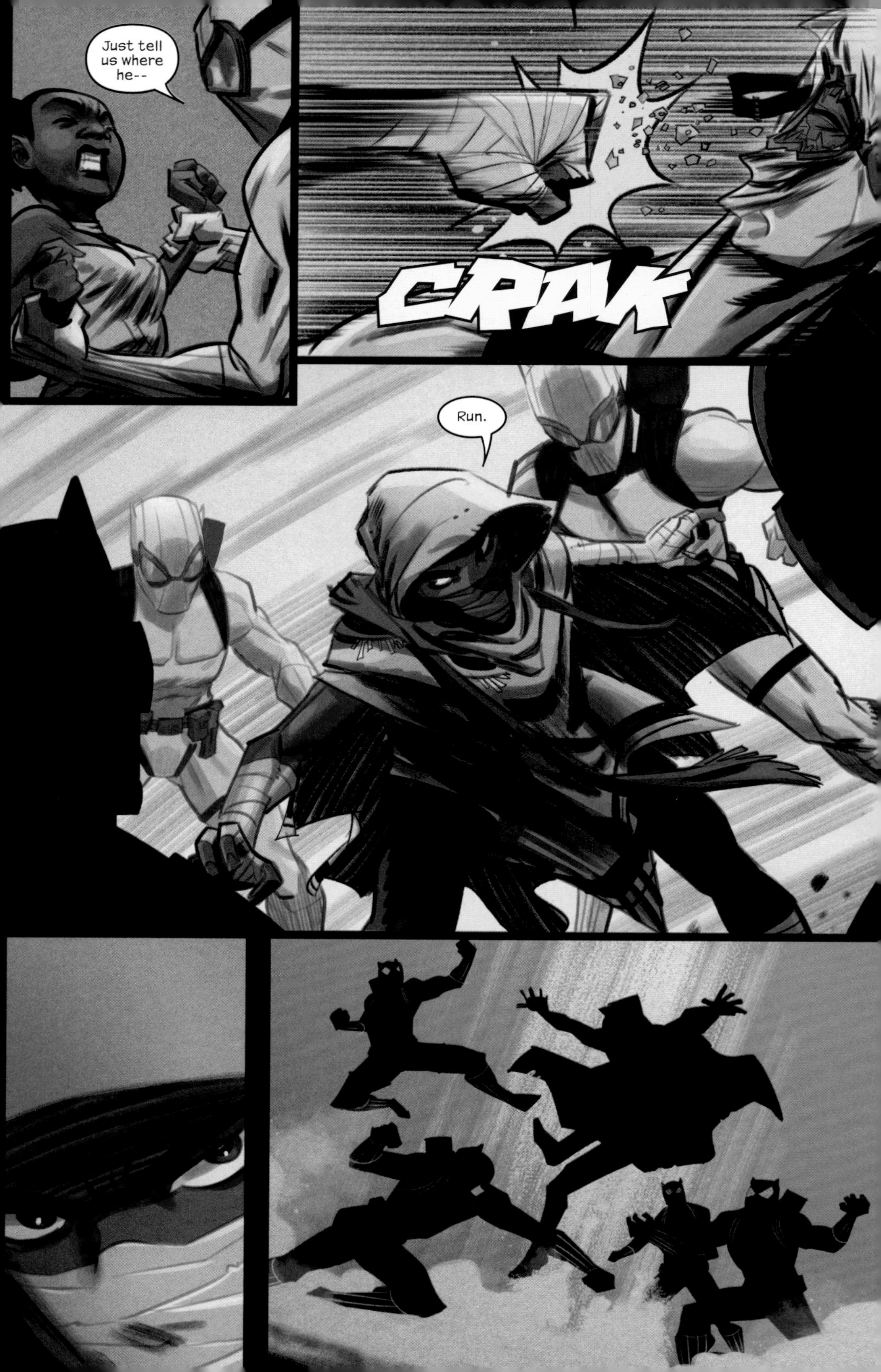

Just tell us where he--
CRAK
Run.

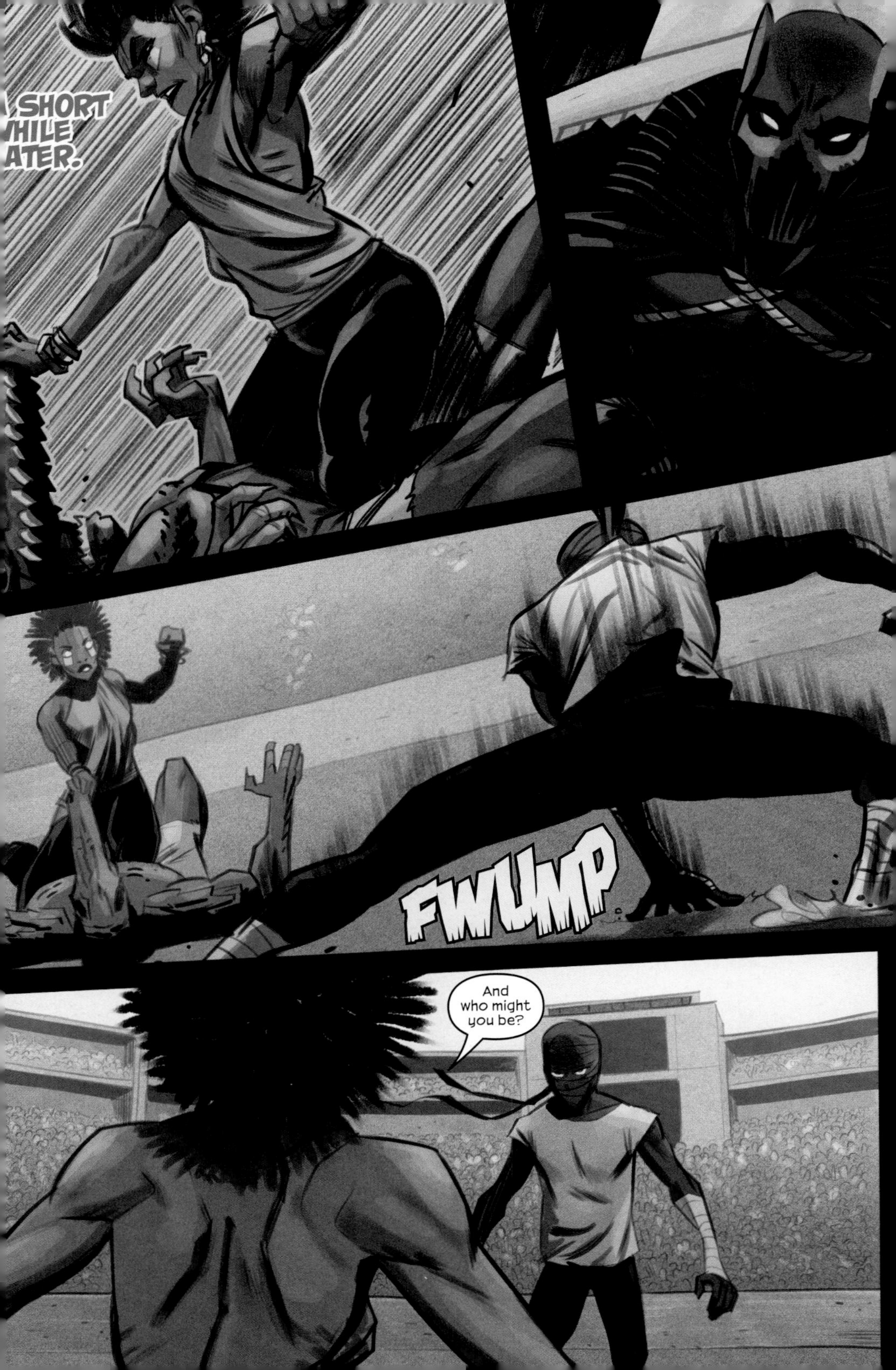
A SHORT WHILE LATER.
FWUMP
And who might you be?

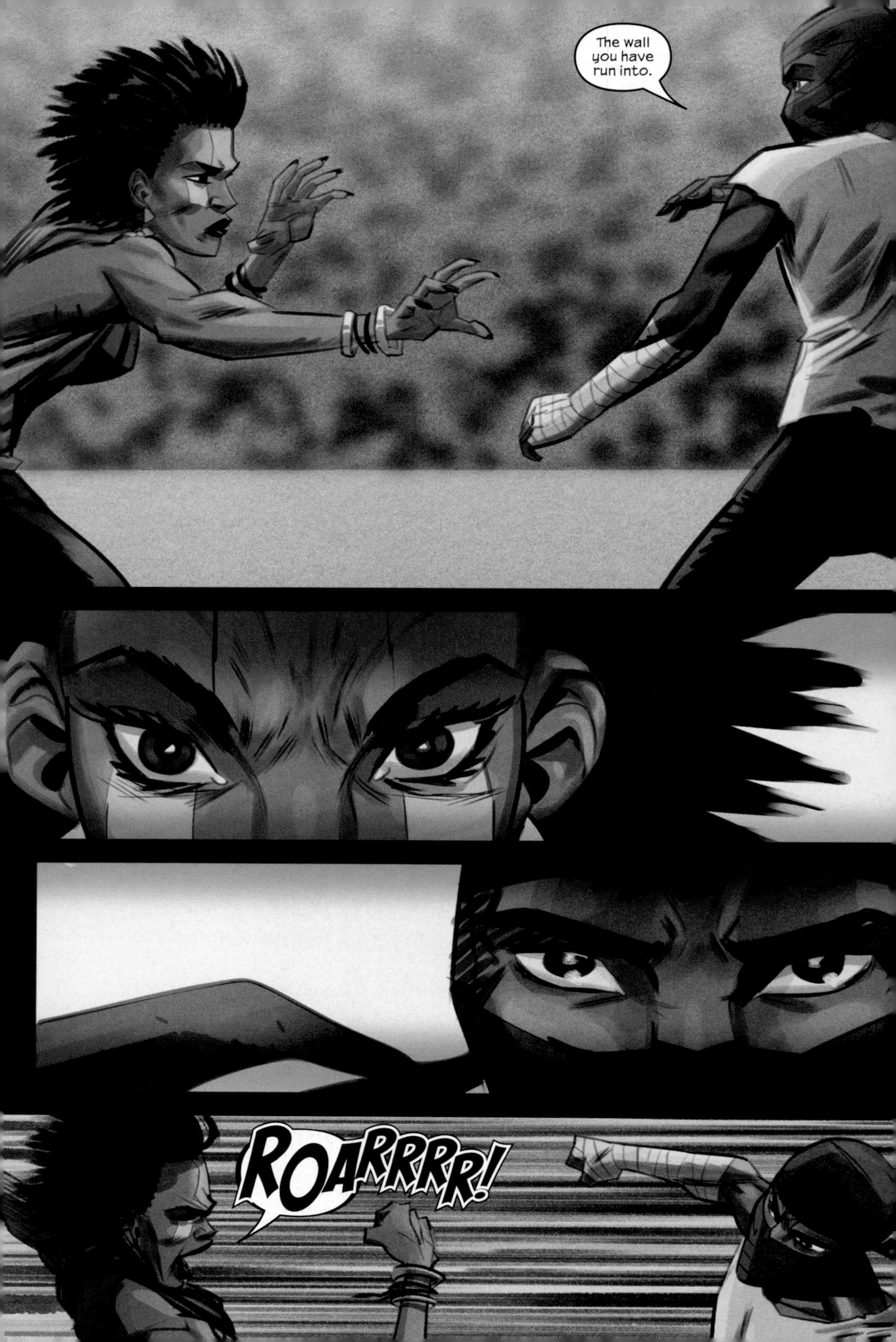
The wall you have run into.
ROARRRRR!

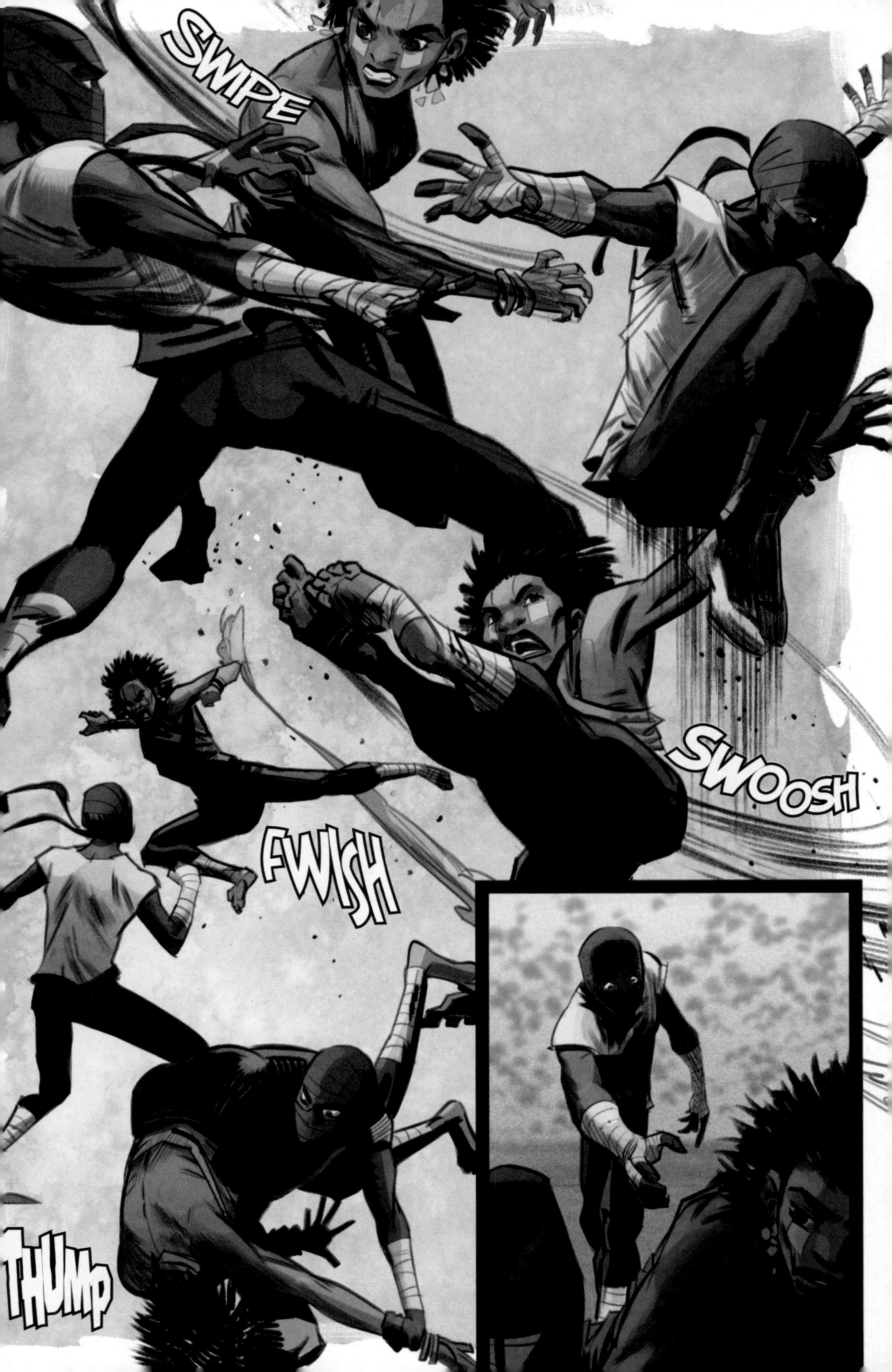
SWIPE
SWOOSH
FWISH
THUMP

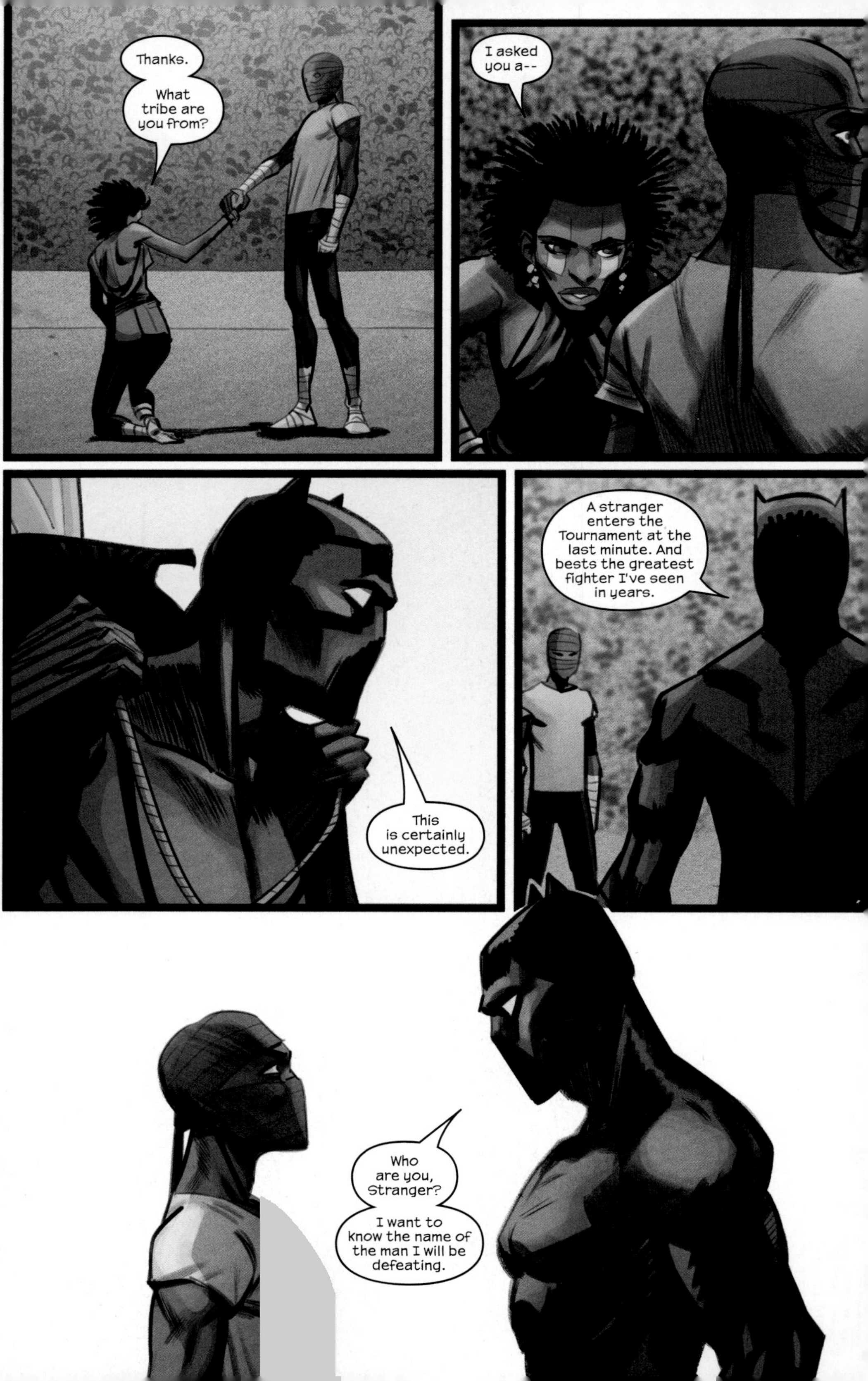
Thanks.
What tribe are you from?
I asked you a--
This is certainly unexpected.
A stranger enters the Tournament at the last minute. And bests the greatest fighter I've seen in years.
Who are you, Stranger?
I want to know the name of the man I will be defeating.

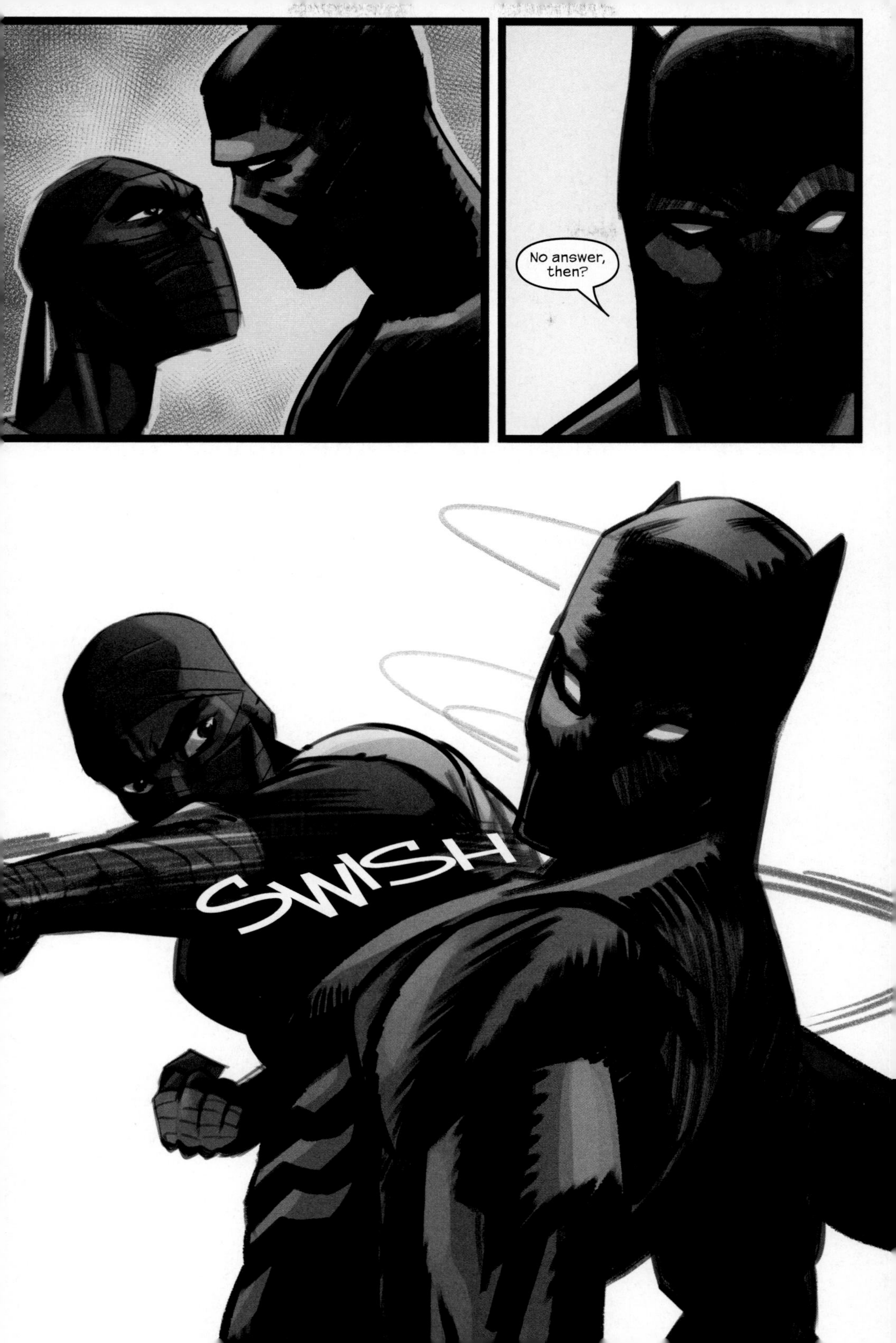
No answer, then?
SWISH

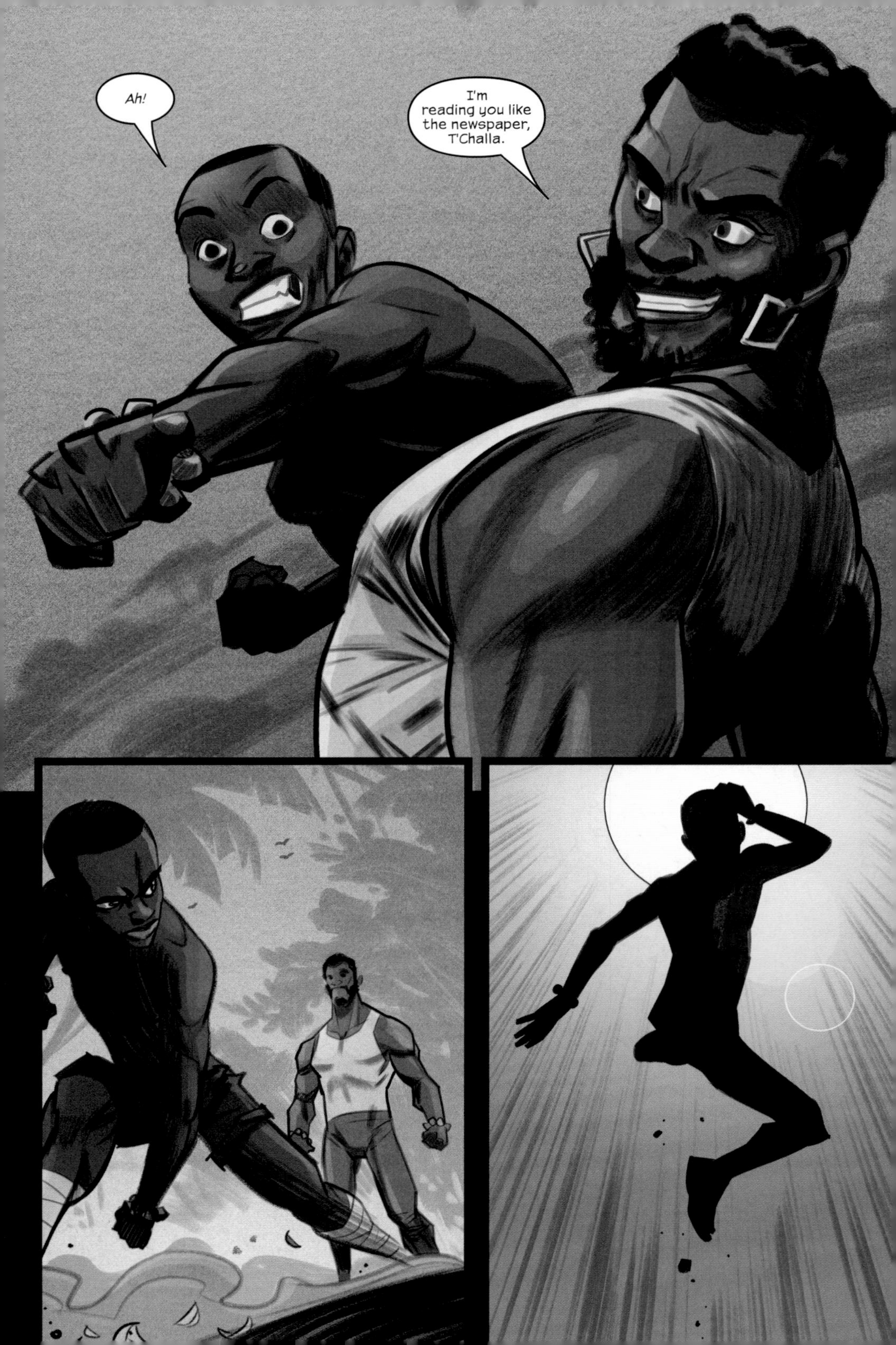
Ah!
I'm reading you like the newspaper, T'Challa.

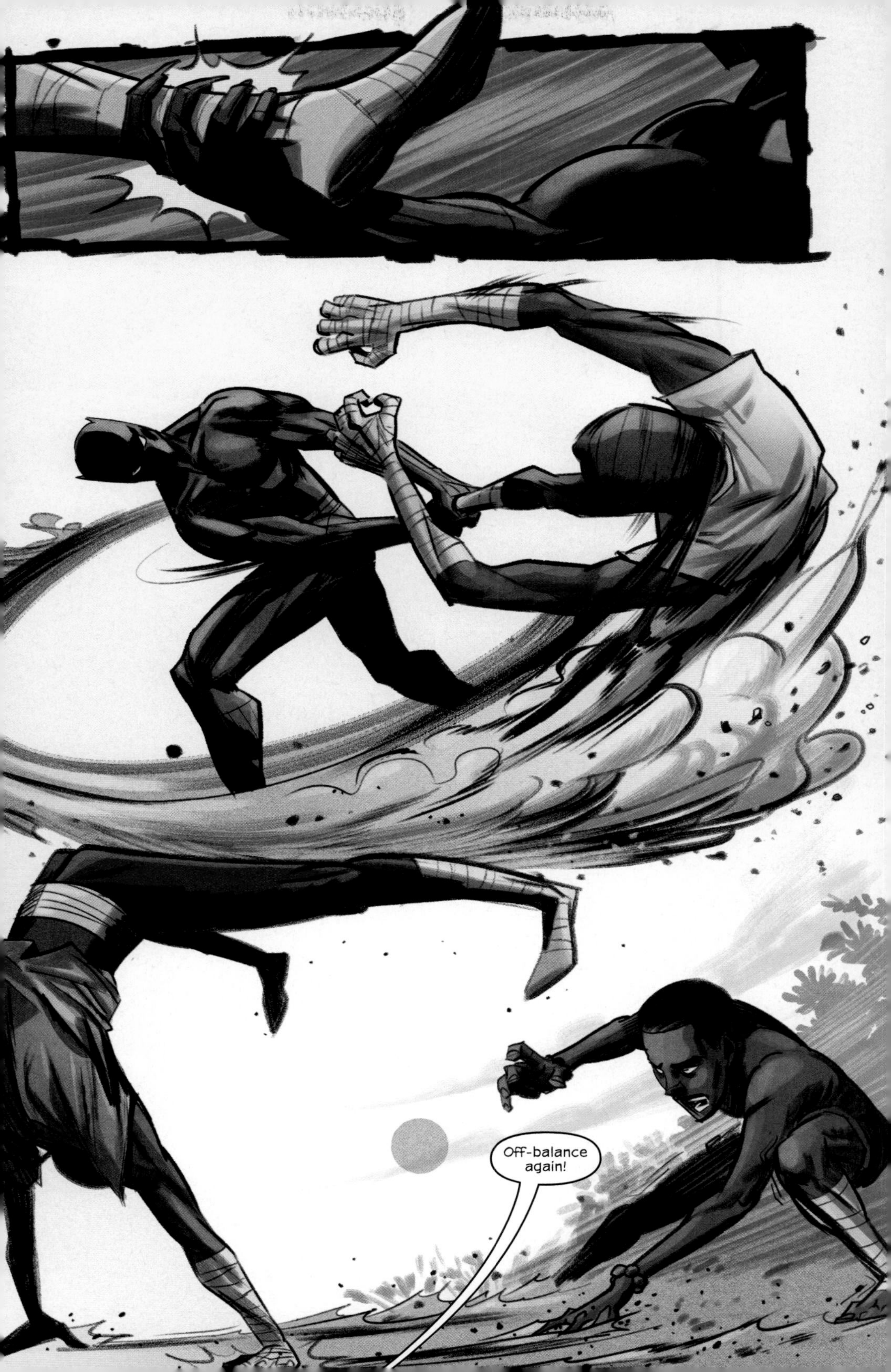
Off-balance again!

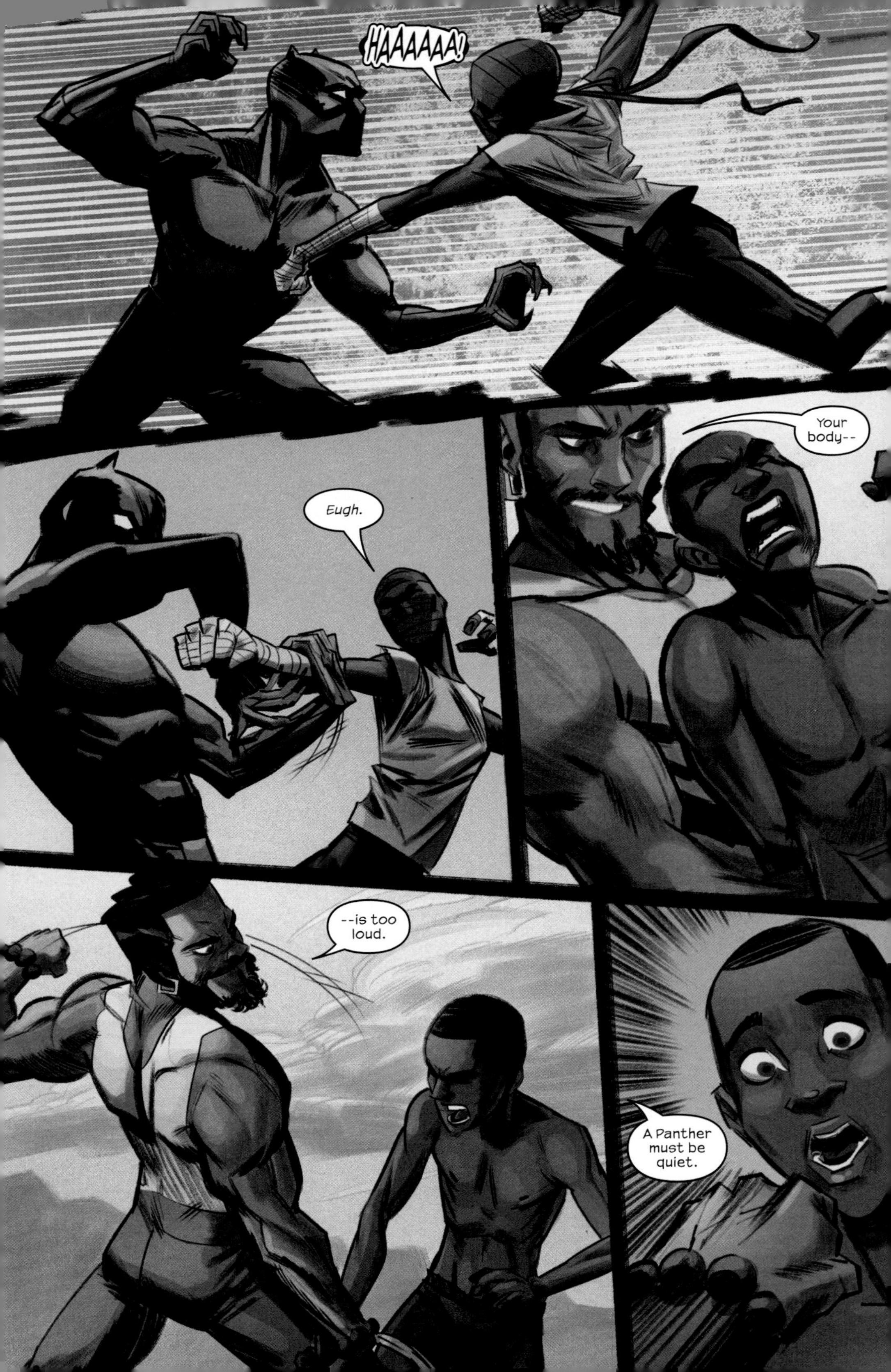
HAAAAAA!
Eugh.
Your body--
--is too loud.
A Panther must be quiet.

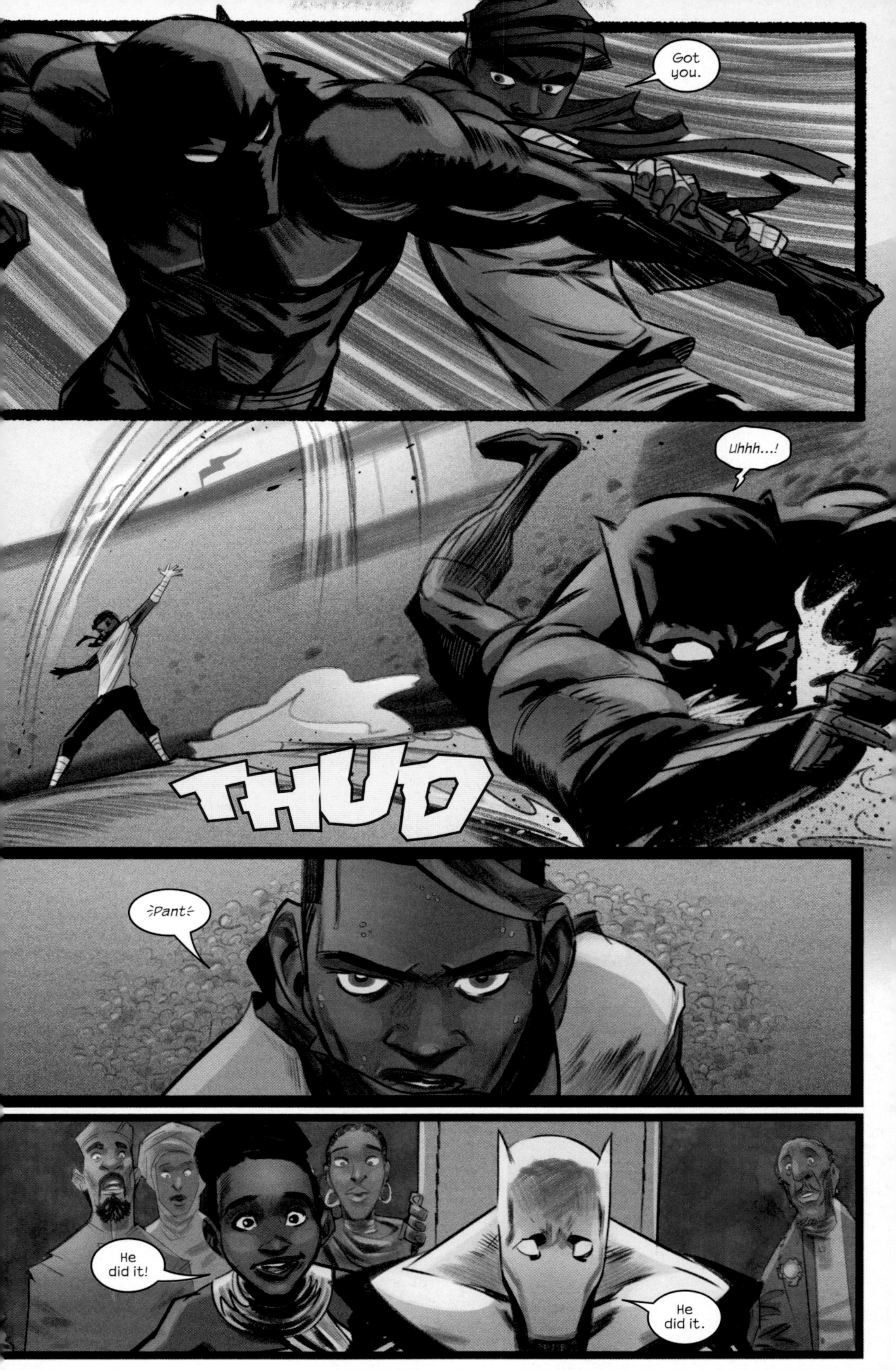
Got you.
Uhhh...!
THUD
Pant
He did it!
He did it.

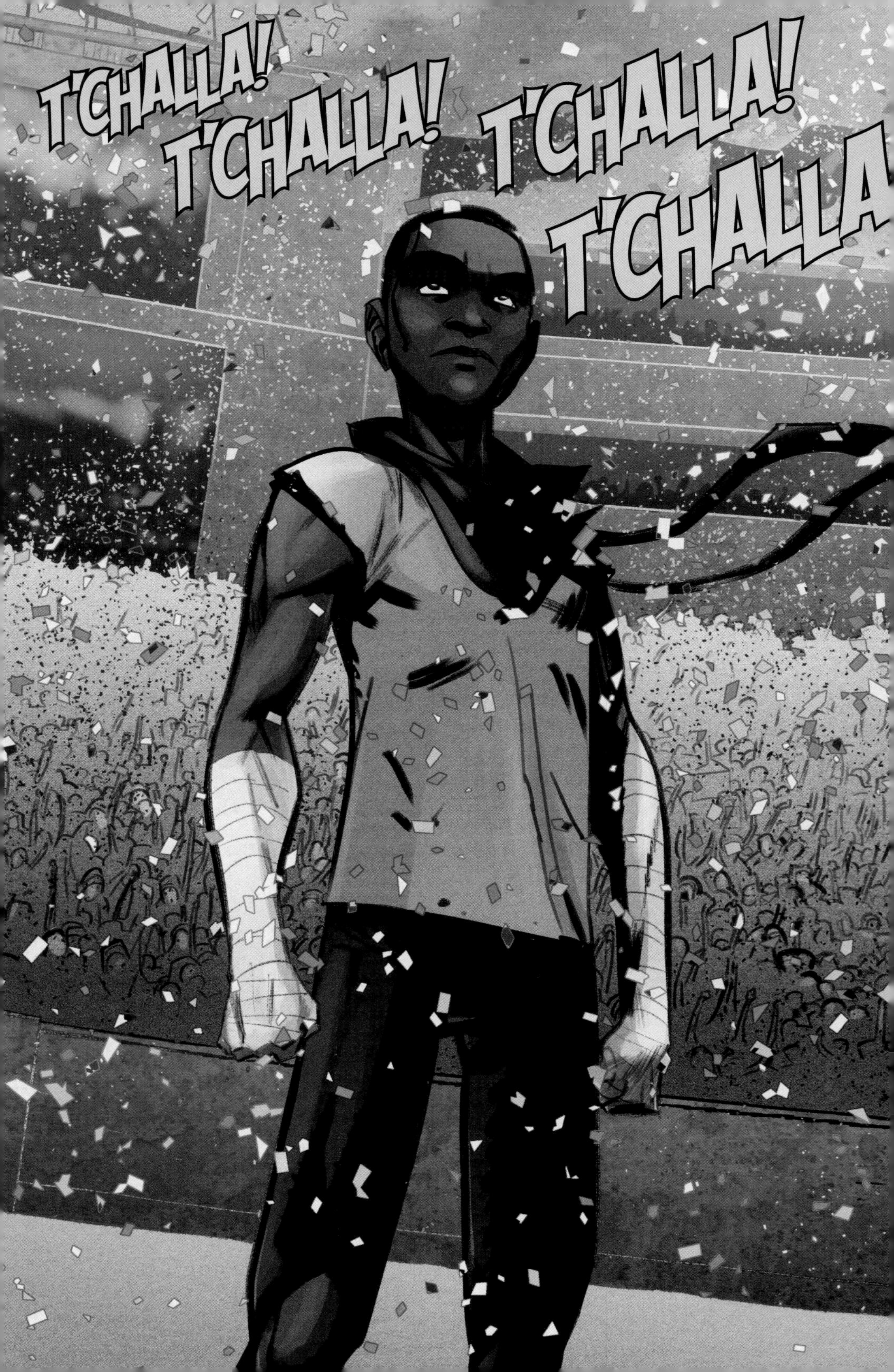
T'CHALLA!
T'CHALLA!
T'CHALLA!
T'CHALLA

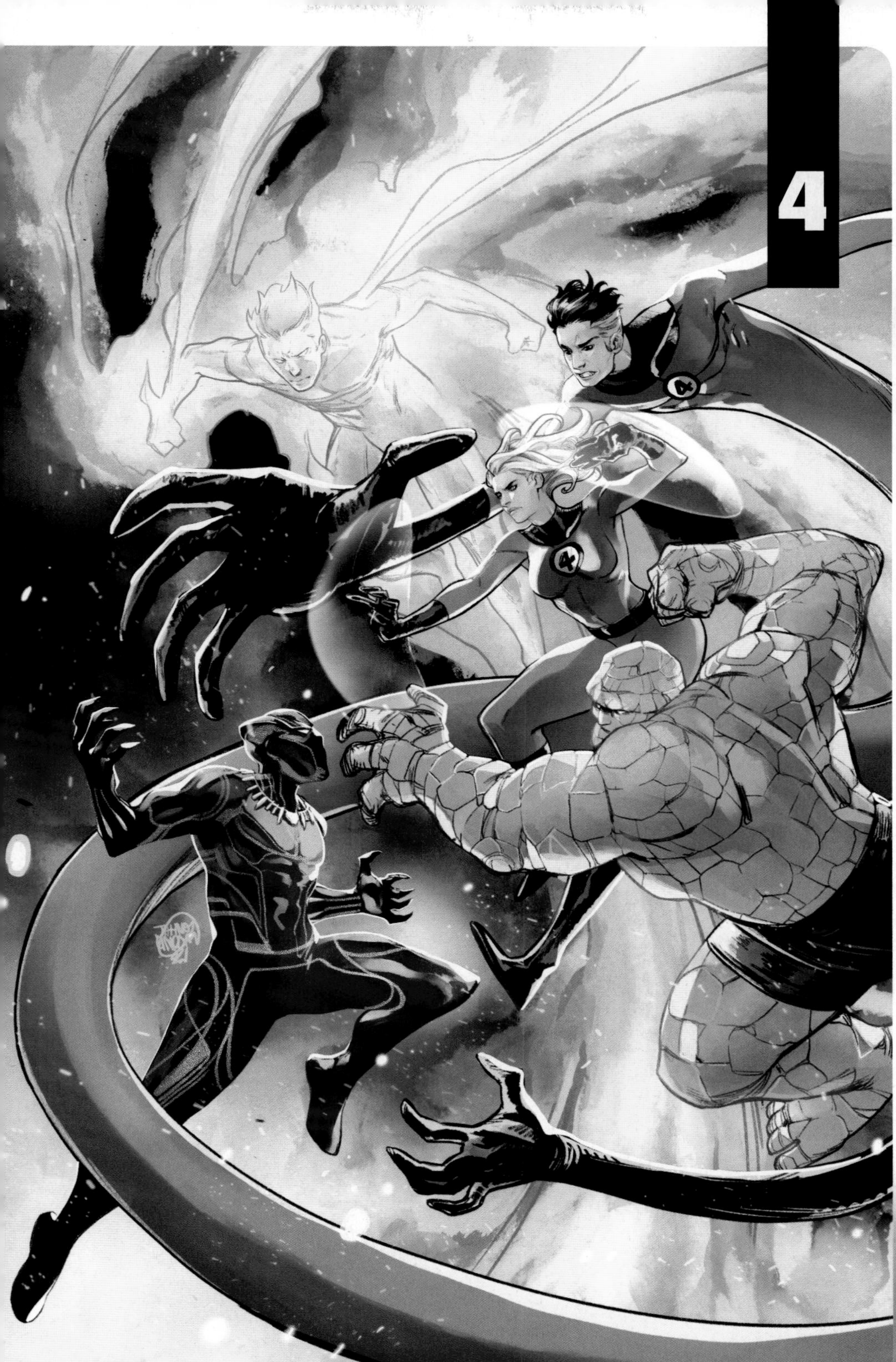
4

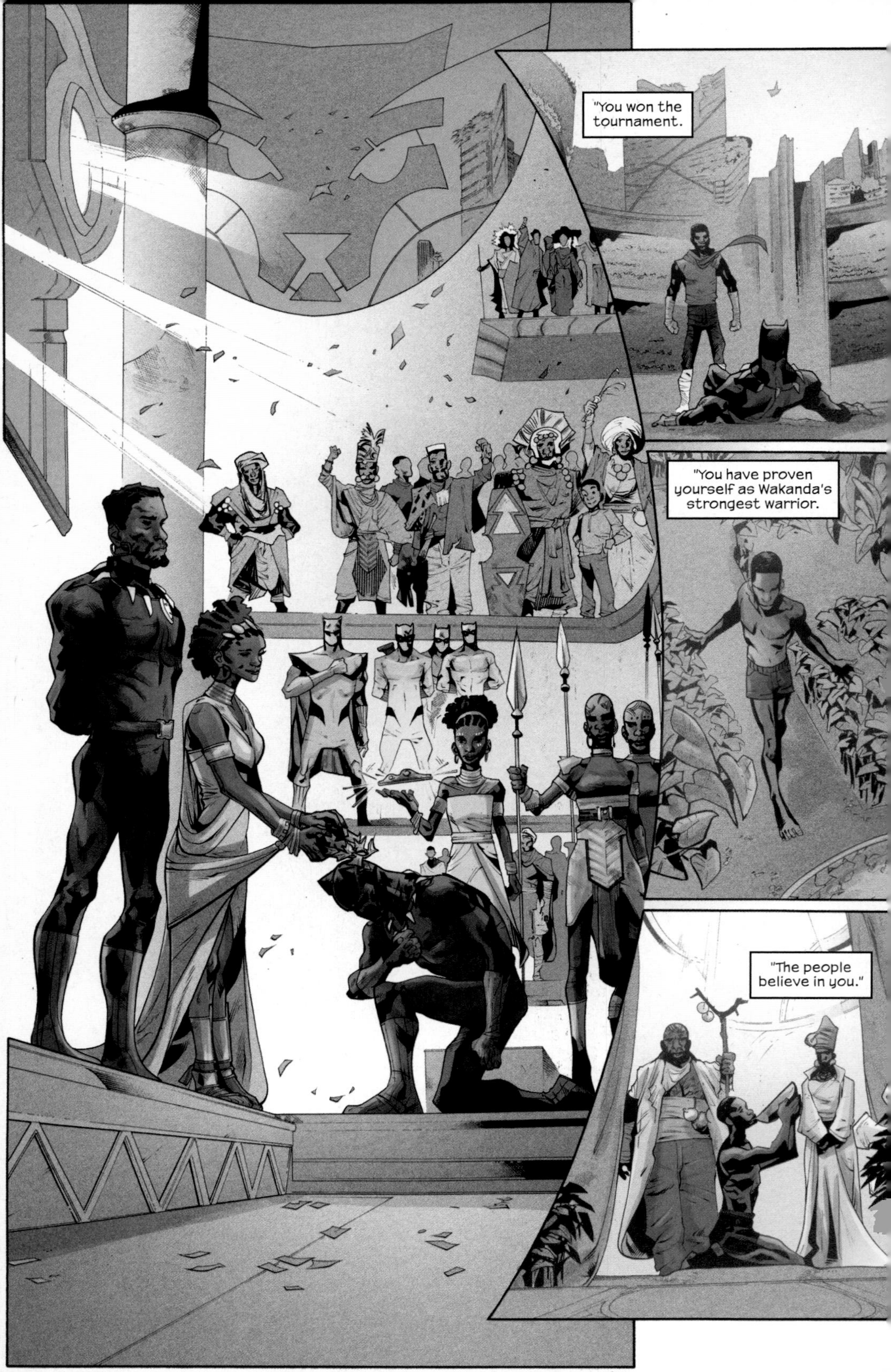
"You won the tournament.
"You have proven yourself as Wakanda's strongest warrior.
"The people believe in you."

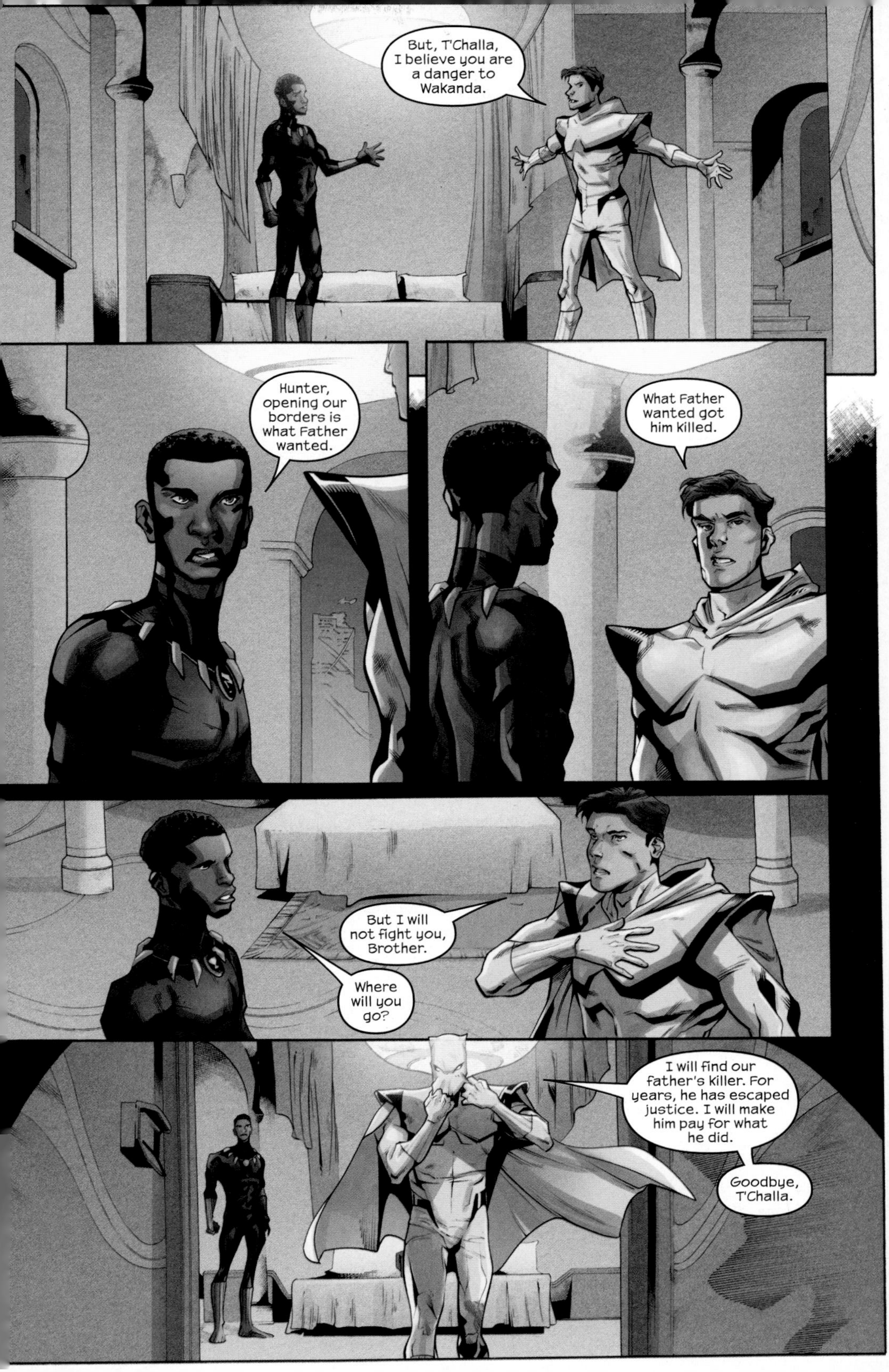
But, T'Challa, I believe you are a danger to Wakanda.
Hunter, opening our borders is what Father wanted.
What Father wanted got him killed.
But I will not fight you, Brother.
Where will you go?
I will find our father's killer. For years, he has escaped justice. I will make him pay for what he did.
Goodbye, T'Challa.

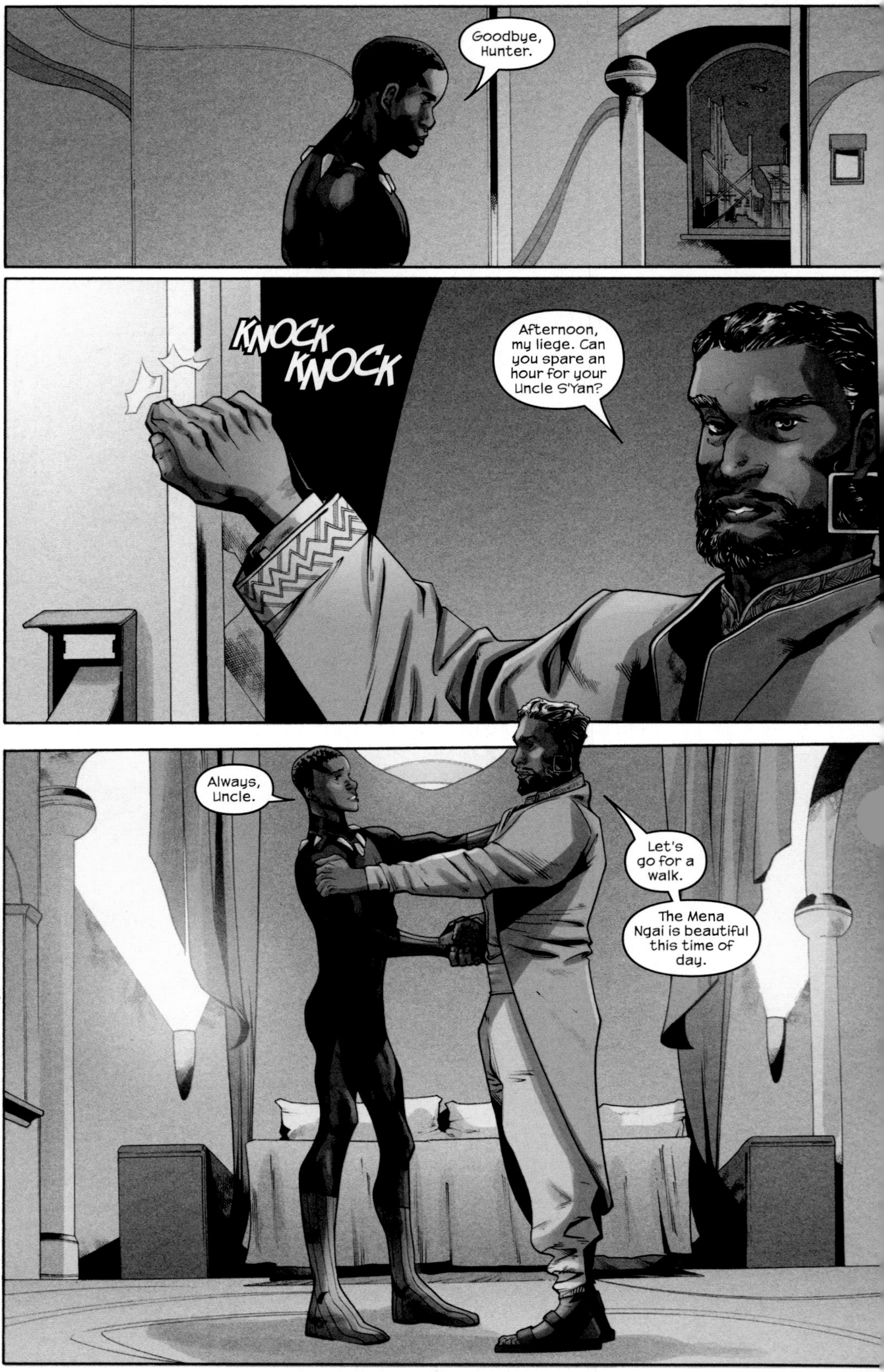

Goodbye, Hunter.
KNOCK KNOCK
Afternoon, my liege. Can you spare an hour for your Uncle S'Yan?
Always, Uncle.
Let's go for a walk.
The Mena Ngai is beautiful this time of day.

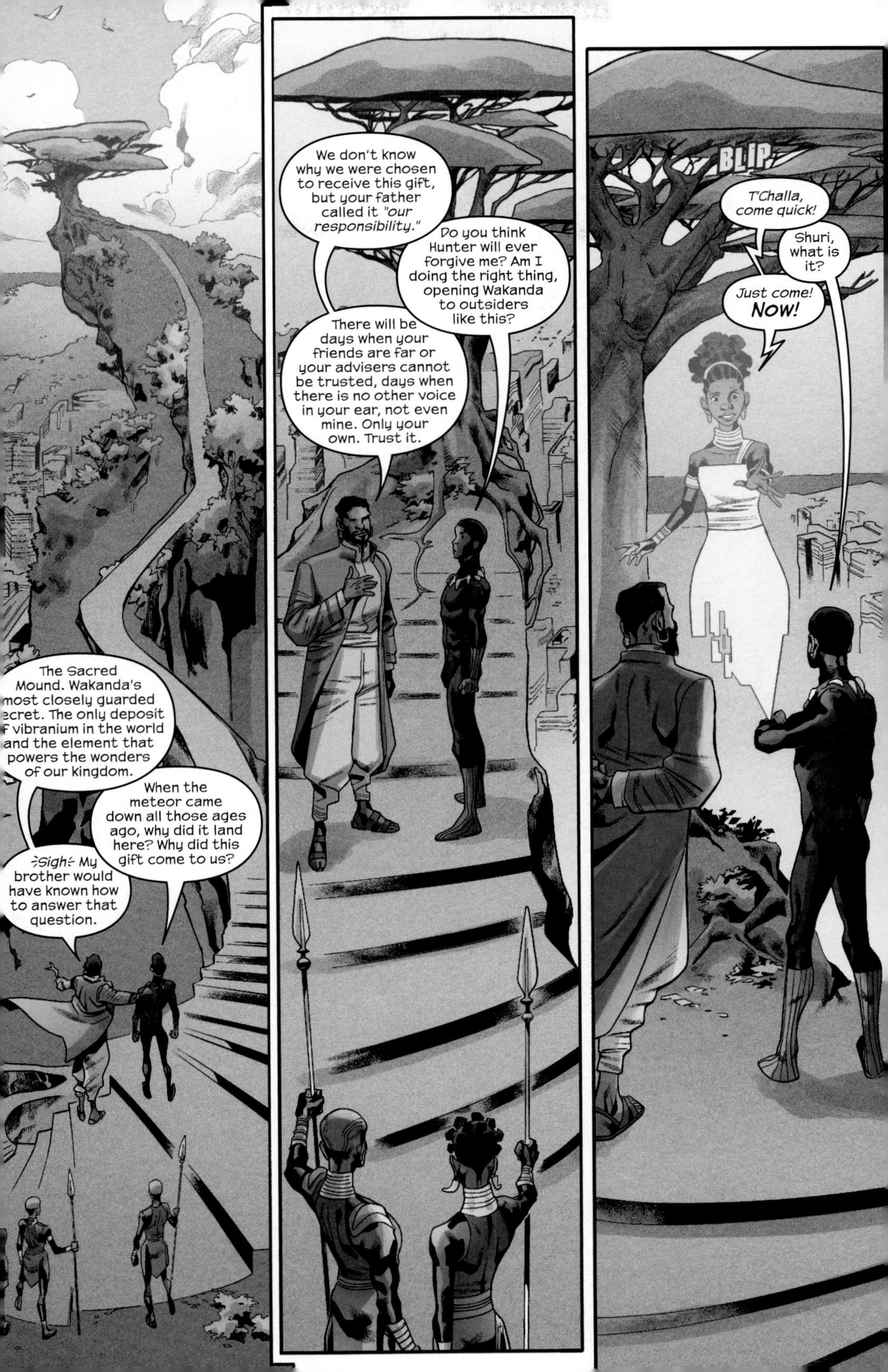

The Sacred Mound. Wakanda's most closely guarded secret. The only deposit of vibranium in the world and the element that powers the wonders of our kingdom.
When the meteor came down all those ages ago, why did it land here? Why did this gift come to us?
Sigh My brother would have known how to answer that question.
We don't know why we were chosen to receive this gift, but your father called it "our responsibility."
Do you think Hunter will ever forgive me? Am I doing the right thing, opening Wakanda to outsiders like this?
There will be days when your friends are far or your advisers cannot be trusted, days when there is no other voice in your ear, not even mine. Only your own. Trust it.
BLIP
T'Challa, come quick!
Shuri, what is it?
Just come! NOW!

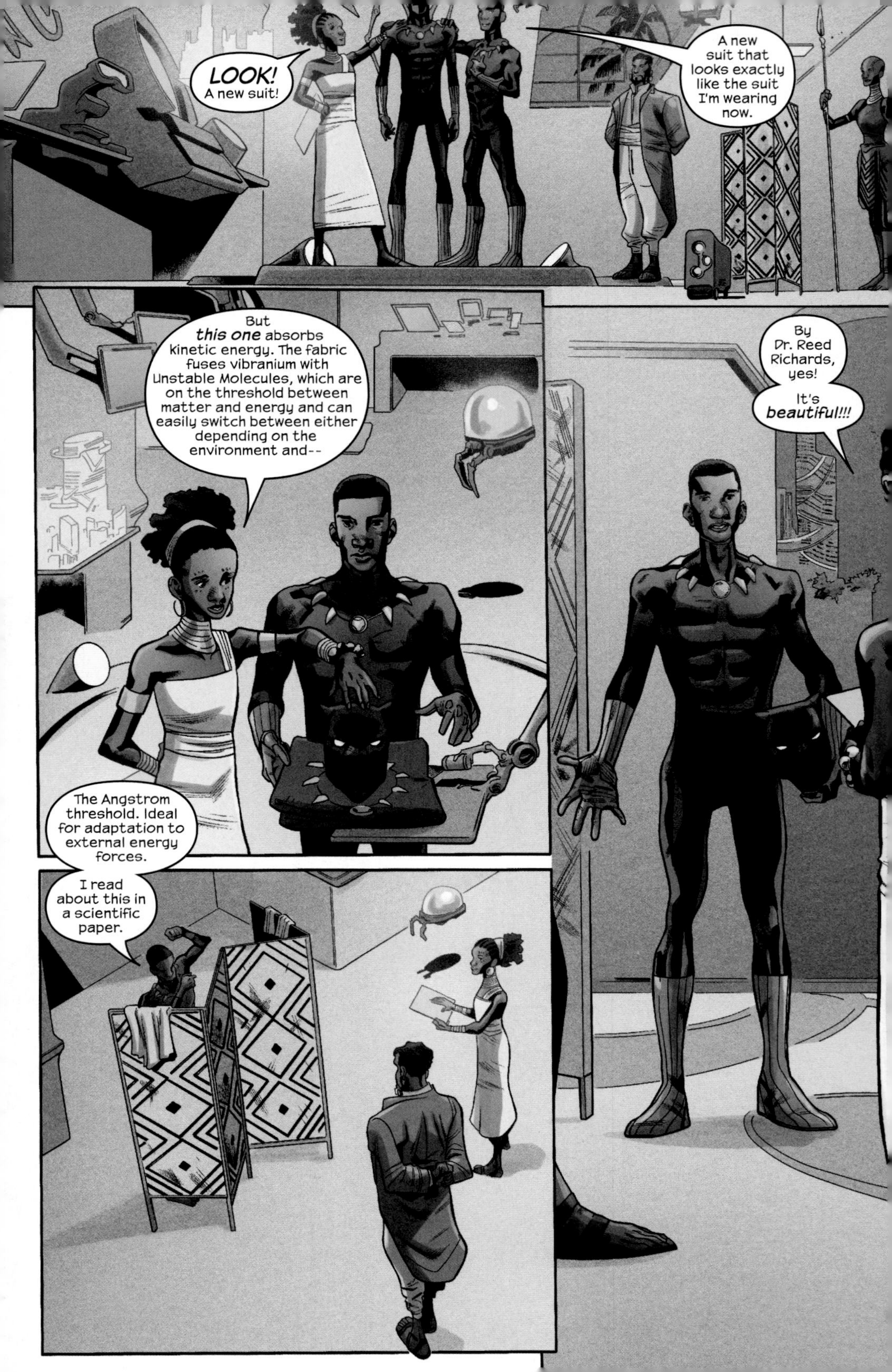
LOOK! A new suit!
A new suit that looks exactly like the suit I'm wearing now.
But this one absorbs kinetic energy. The fabric fuses vibranium with Unstable Molecules, which are on the threshold between matter and energy and can easily switch between either depending on the environment and--
By Dr. Reed Richards, yes!
It's beautiful!!!
The Angstrom threshold. Ideal for adaptation to external energy forces.
I read about this in a scientific paper.

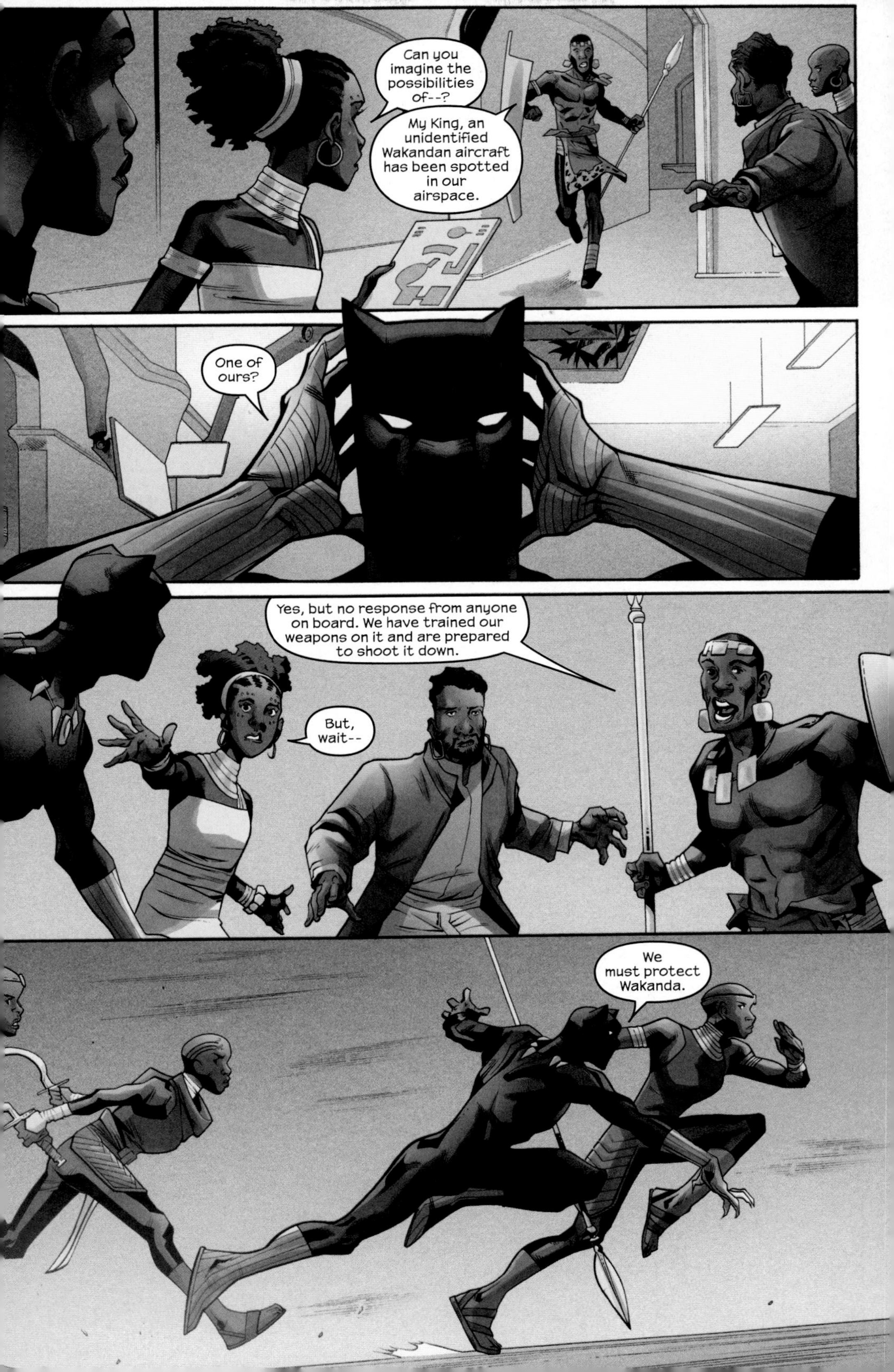
Can you imagine the possibilities of--?
My King, an unidentified Wakandan aircraft has been spotted in our airspace.
One of ours?
Yes, but no response from anyone on board. We have trained our weapons on it and are prepared to shoot it down.
But, wait--
We must protect Wakanda.

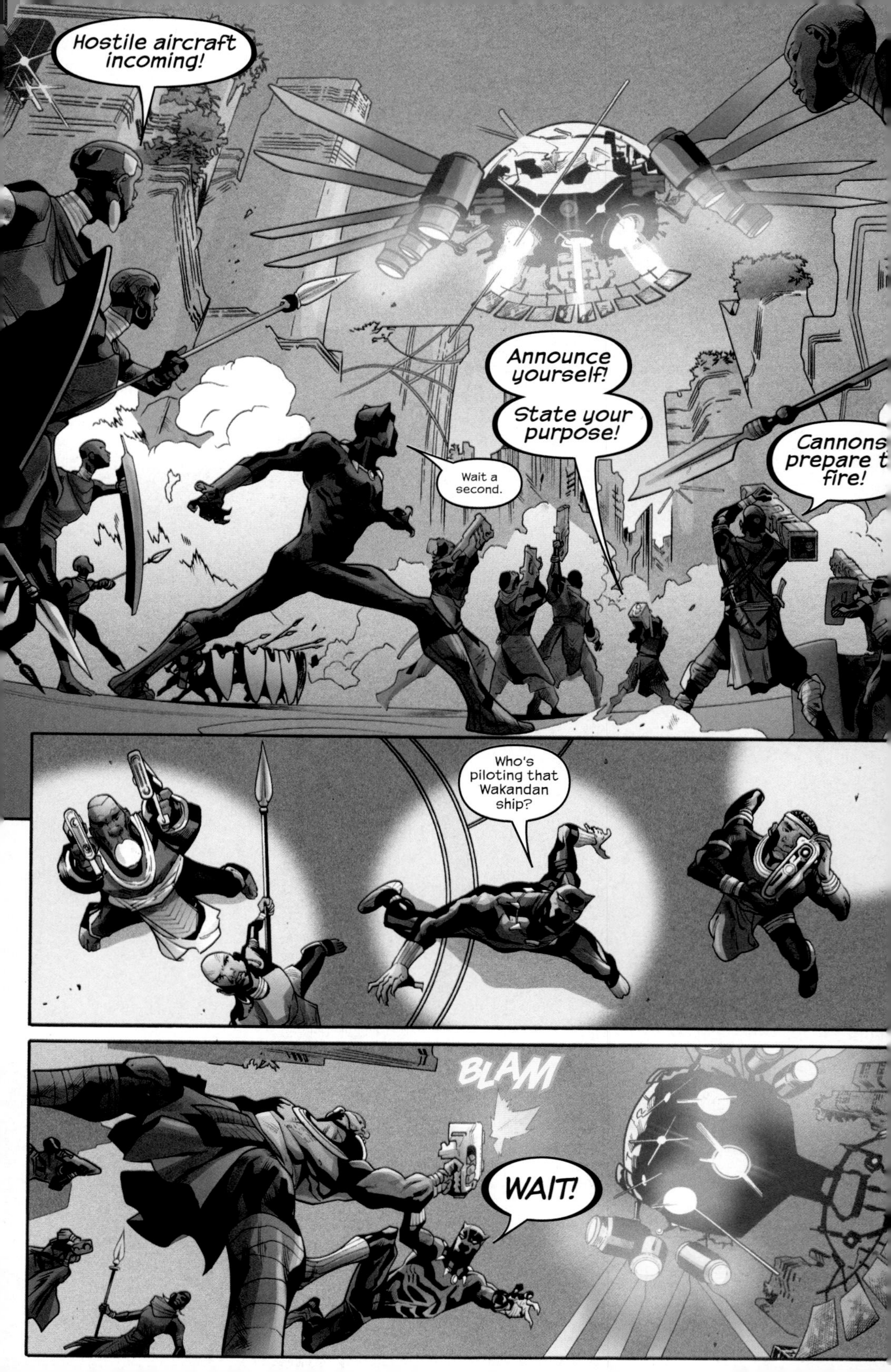
Hostile aircraft incoming!
Announce yourself!
State your purpose!
Wait a second.
Cannons prepare t fire!
Who's piloting that Wakandan ship?
BLAM
WAIT!

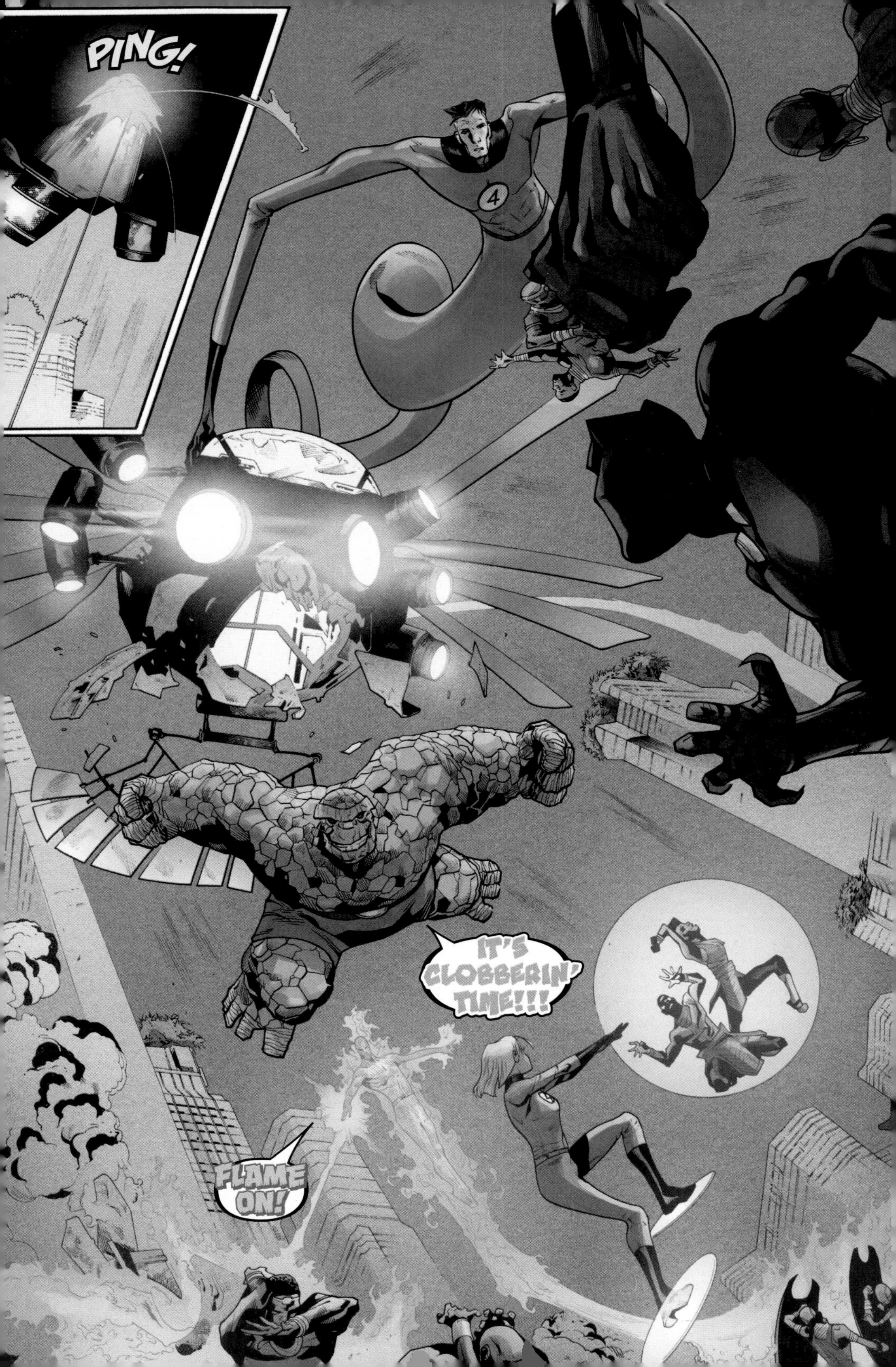
PING!
IT'S CLOBBERIN' TIME!!!
FLAME ON!

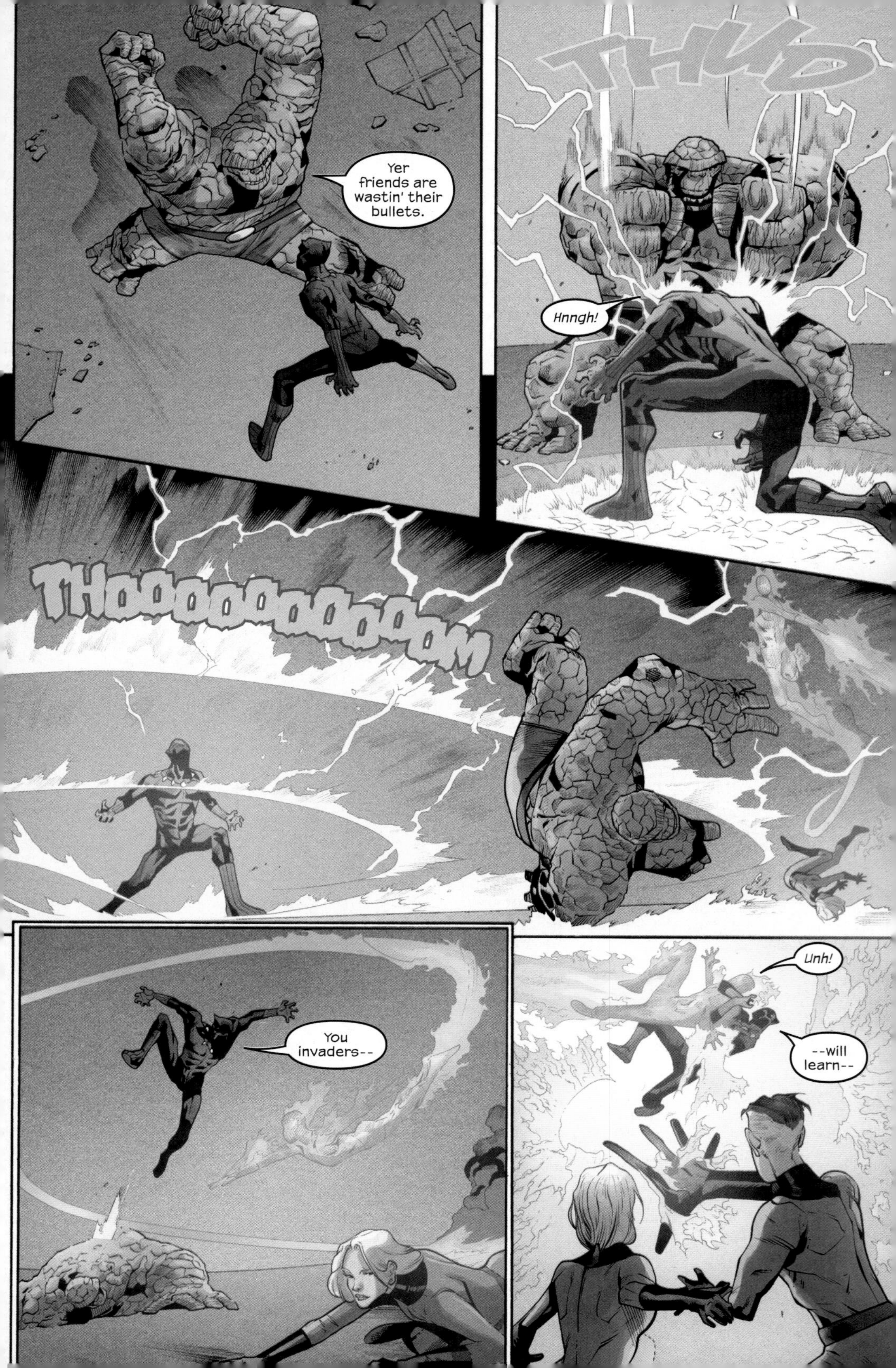
Yer friends are wastin' their bullets.
THUD
Hnngh!
THOOOOOOOOOOOM
You invaders--
Unh!
--will learn--

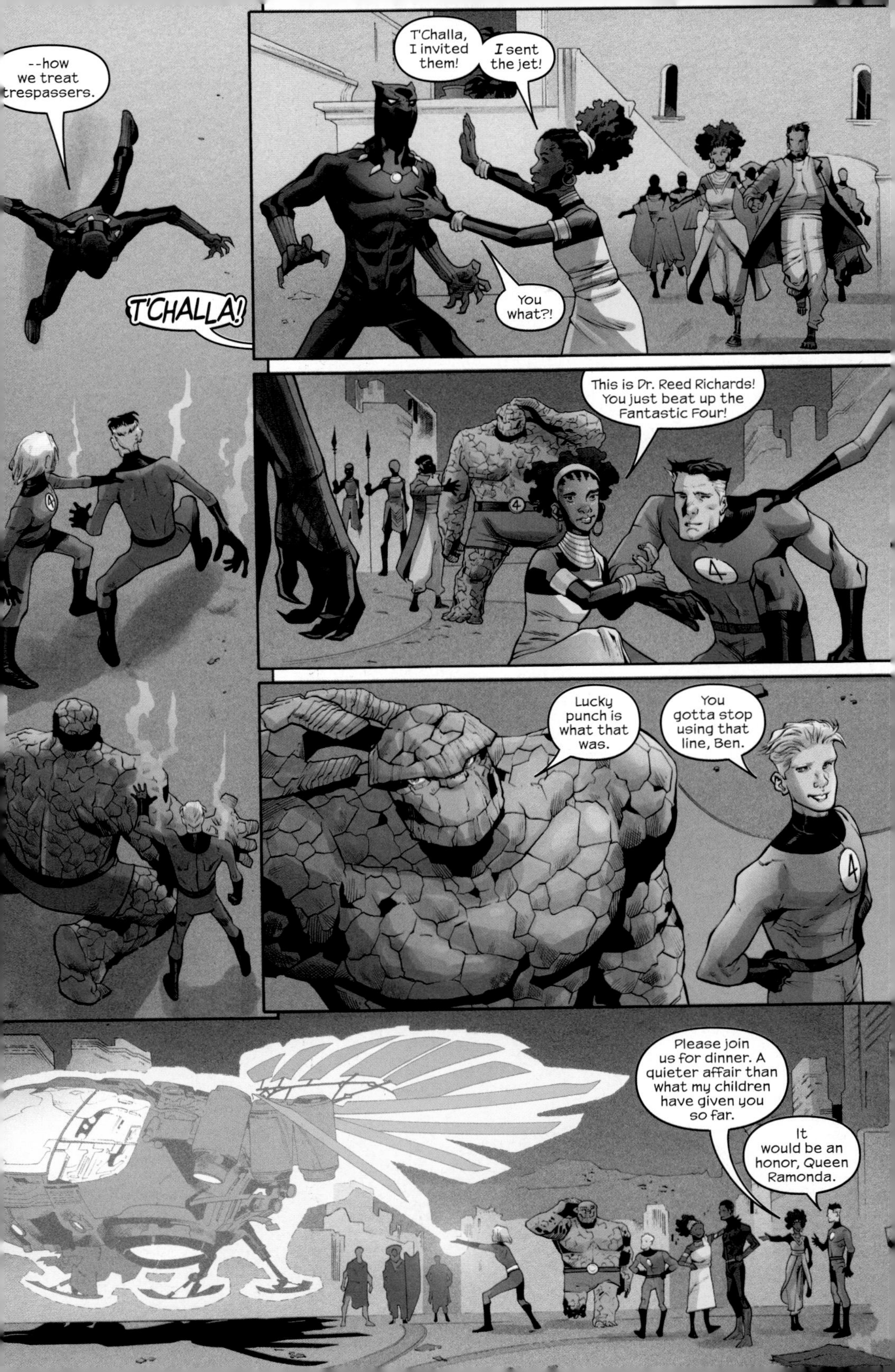
--how we treat trespassers.
T'CHALLA!
T'Challa, I invited them!
I sent the jet!
You what?!
This is Dr. Reed Richards! You just beat up the Fantastic Four!
Lucky punch is what that was.
You gotta stop using that line, Ben.
Please join us for dinner. A quieter affair than what my children have given you so far.
It would be an honor, Queen Ramonda.

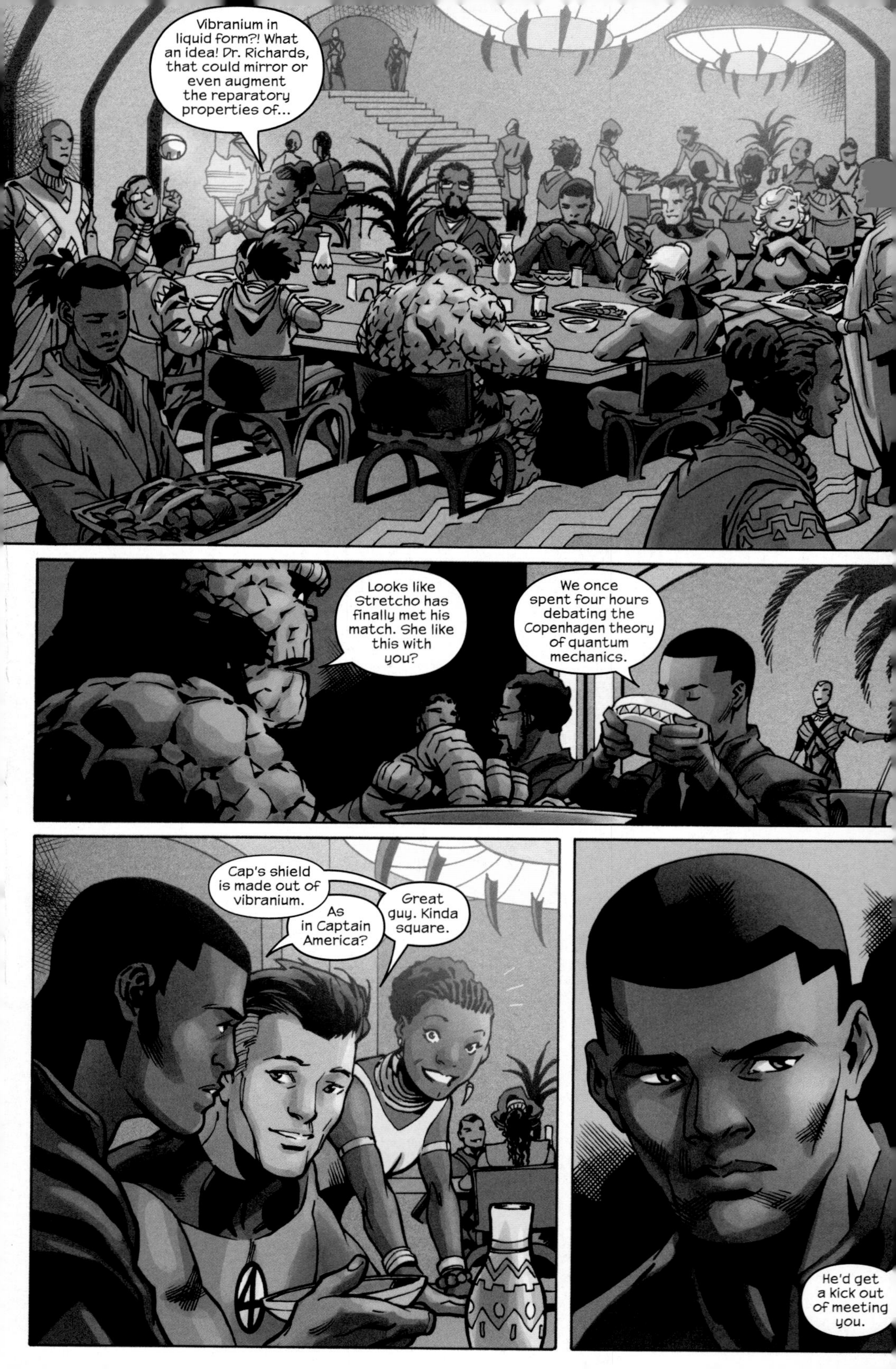
Vibranium in liquid form?! What an idea! Dr. Richards, that could mirror or even augment the reparatory properties of...
Looks like Stretcho has finally met his match. She like this with you?
We once spent four hours debating the Copenhagen theory of quantum mechanics.
Cap's shield is made out of vibranium.
As in Captain America?
Great guy. Kinda square.
He'd get a kick out of meeting you.

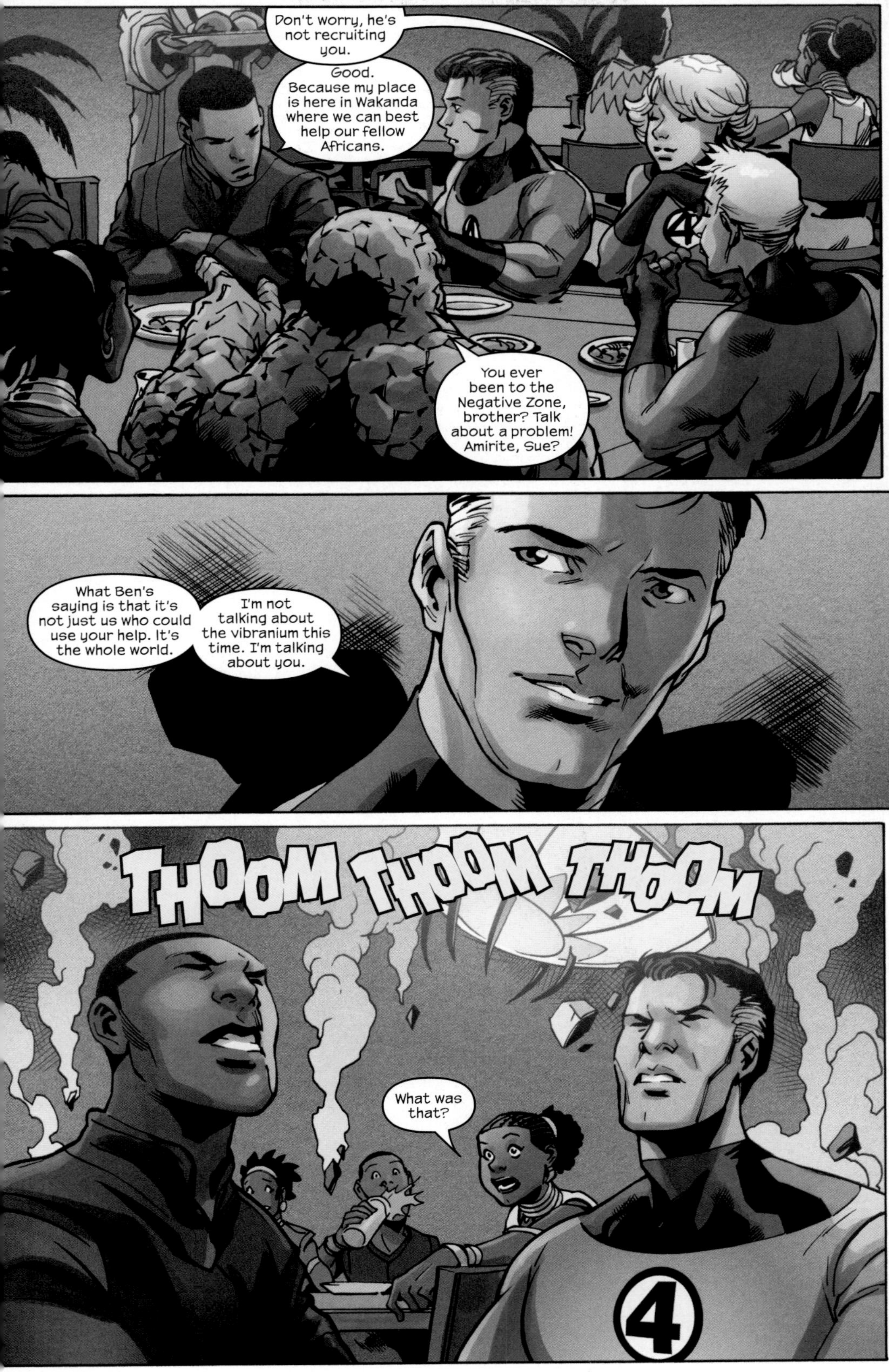
Don't worry, he's not recruiting you.
Good. Because my place is here in Wakanda where we can best help our fellow Africans.
You ever been to the Negative Zone, brother? Talk about a problem! Amirite, Sue?
What Ben's saying is that it's not just us who could use your help. It's the whole world.
I'm not talking about the vibranium this time. I'm talking about you.
THOOM THOOM THOOM
What was that?

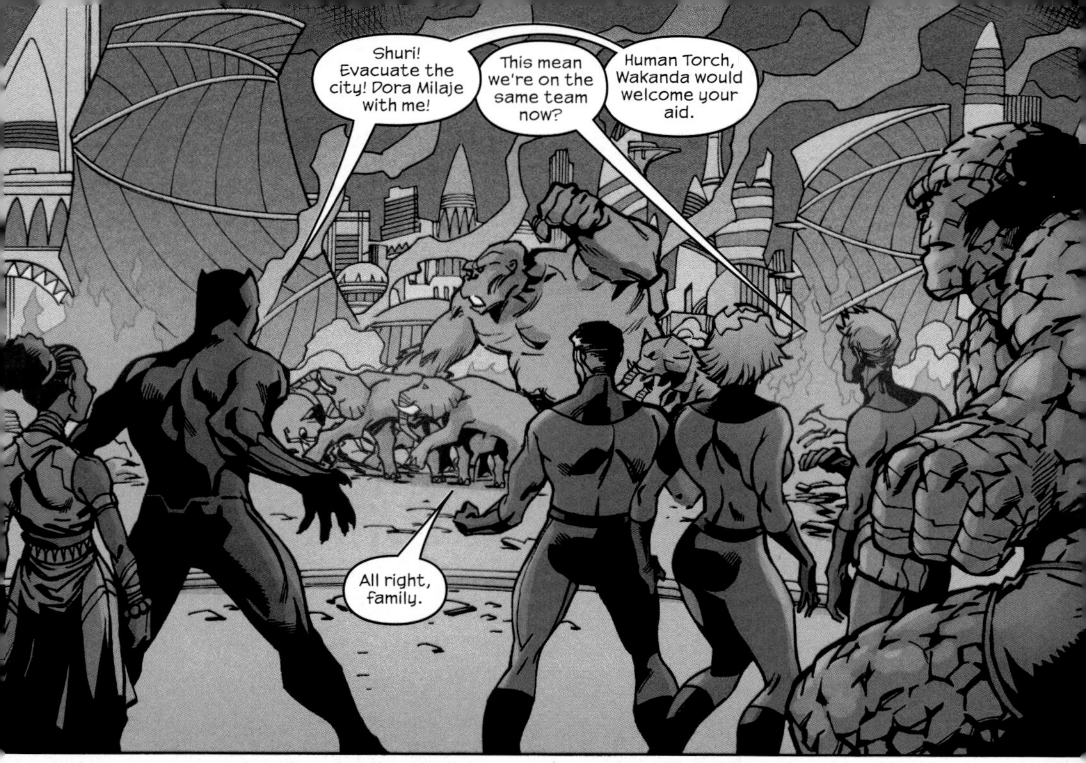
Shuri! Evacuate the city! Dora Milaje with me!
This mean we're on the same team now?
Human Torch, Wakanda would welcome your aid.
All right, family.

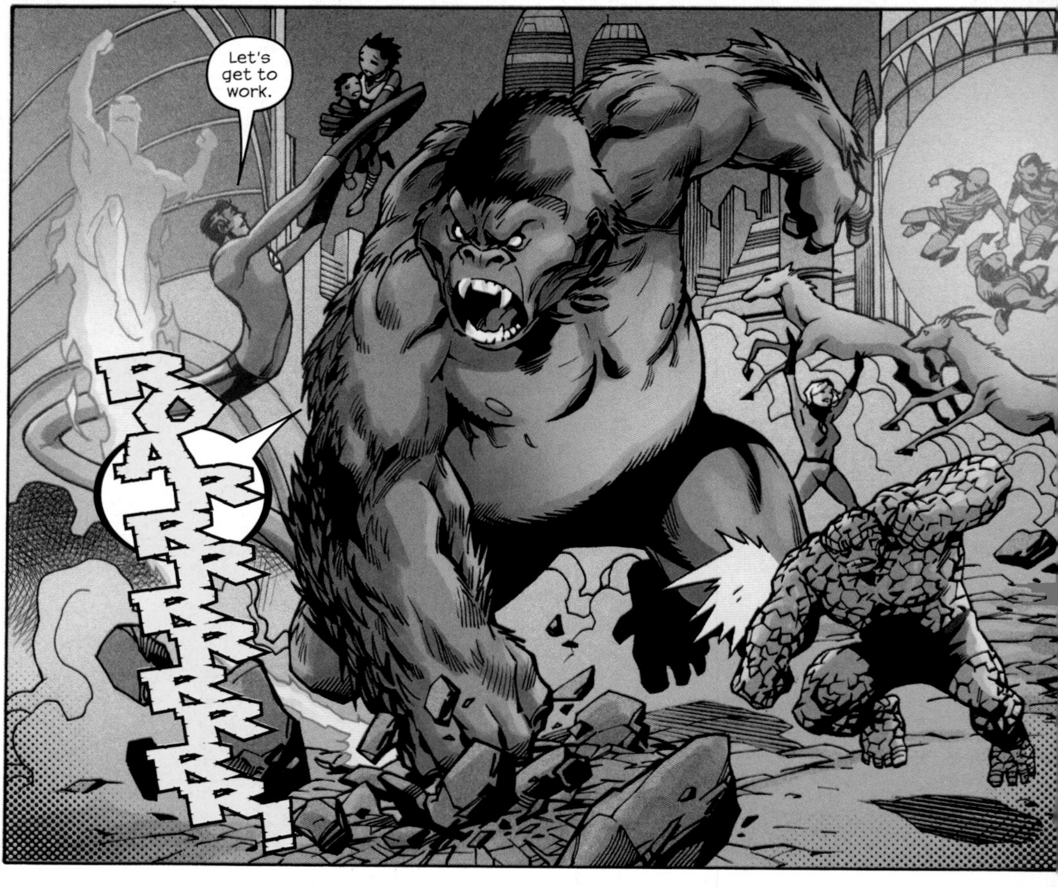
Let's get to work.
ROARRRRRR!

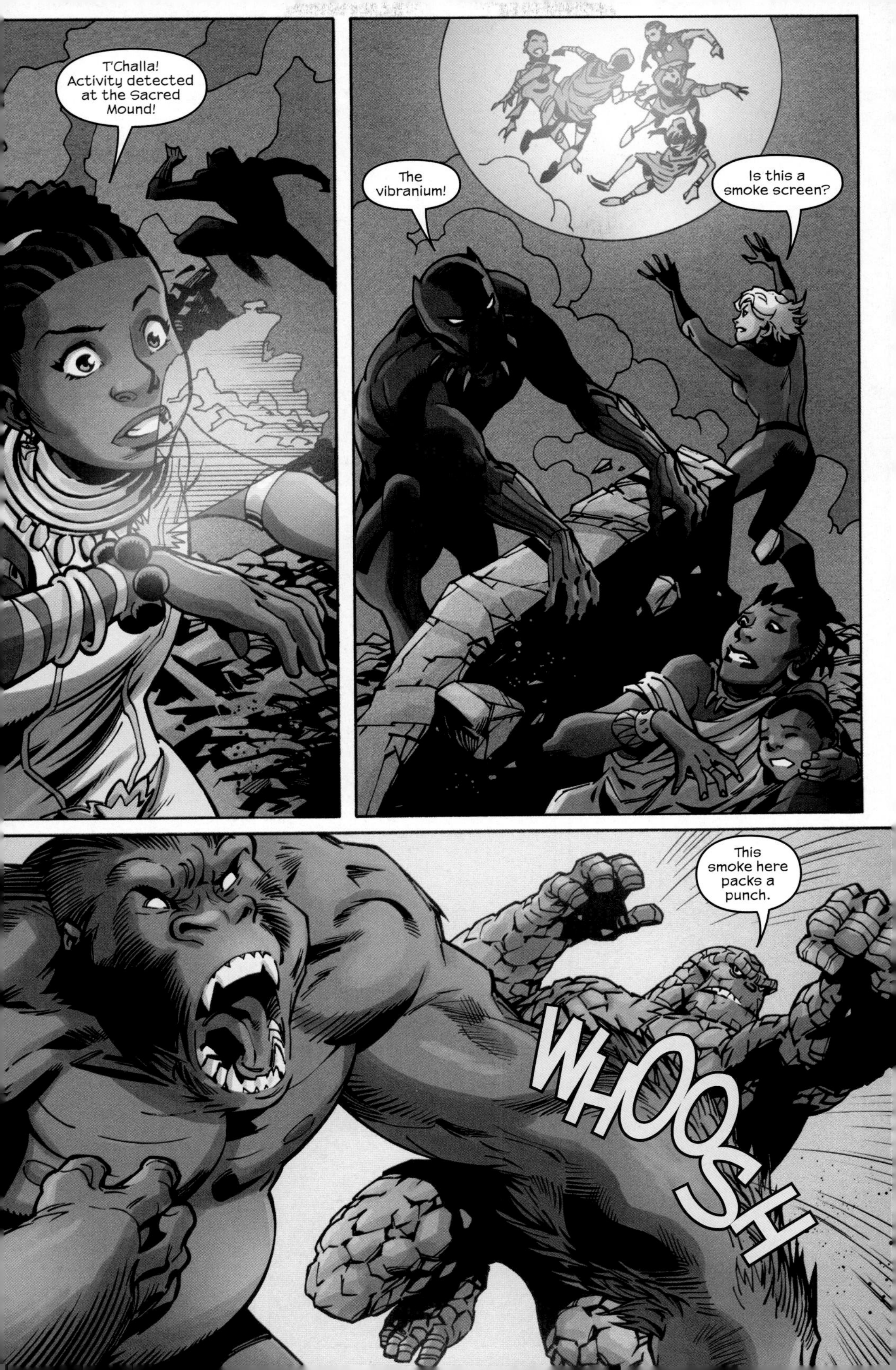

T'Challa! Activity detected at the Sacred Mound!
The vibranium!
Is this a smoke screen?
This smoke here packs a punch.
WHOOSH

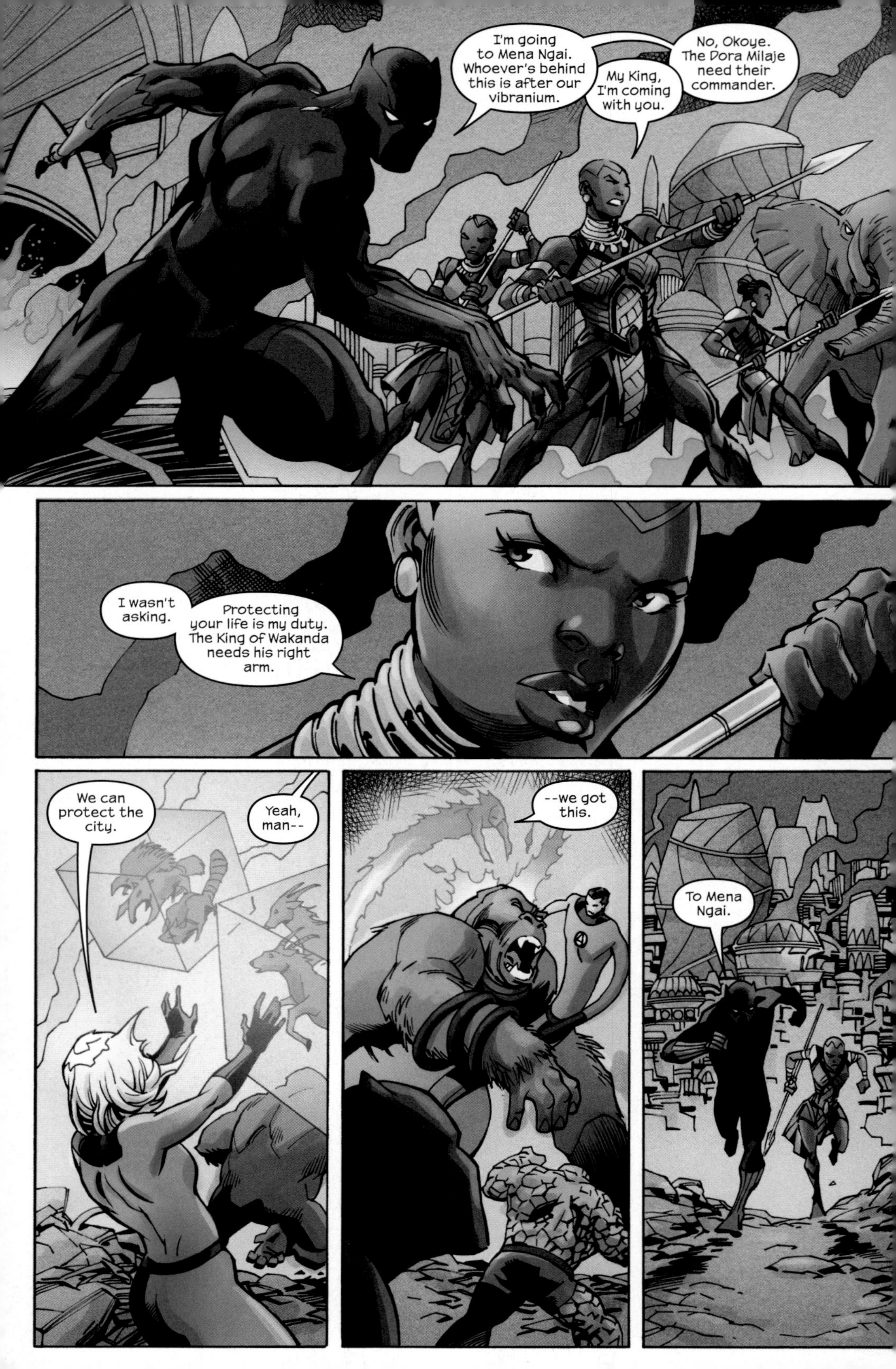
I'm going to Mena Ngai. Whoever's behind this is after our vibranium.
My King, I'm coming with you.
No, Okoye. The Dora Milaje need their commander.
I wasn't asking.
Protecting your life is my duty. The King of Wakanda needs his right arm.
We can protect the city.
Yeah, man--
--we got this.
To Mena Ngai.

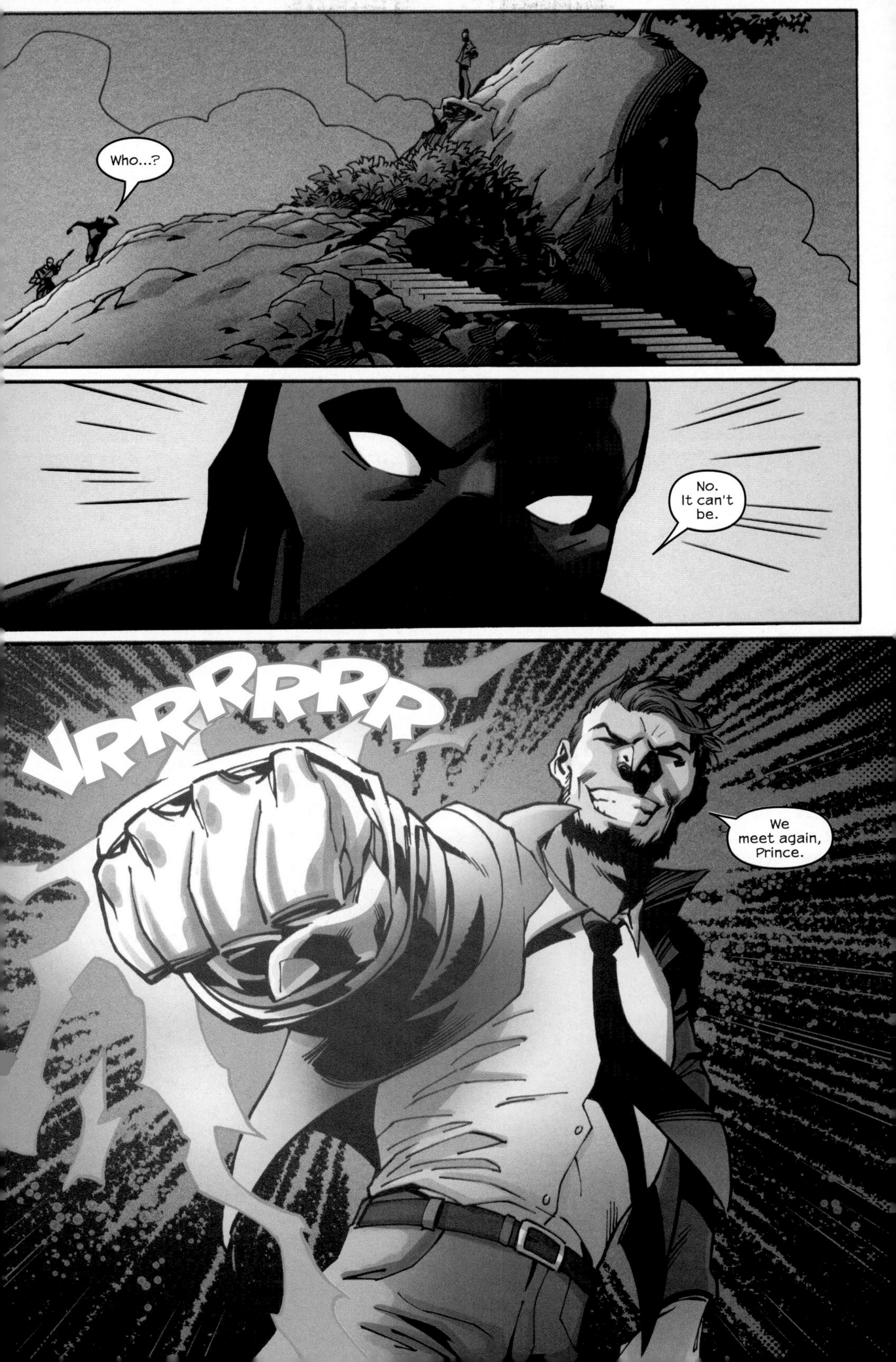
Who...?
No. It can't be.
VRRRRRR
We meet again, Prince.

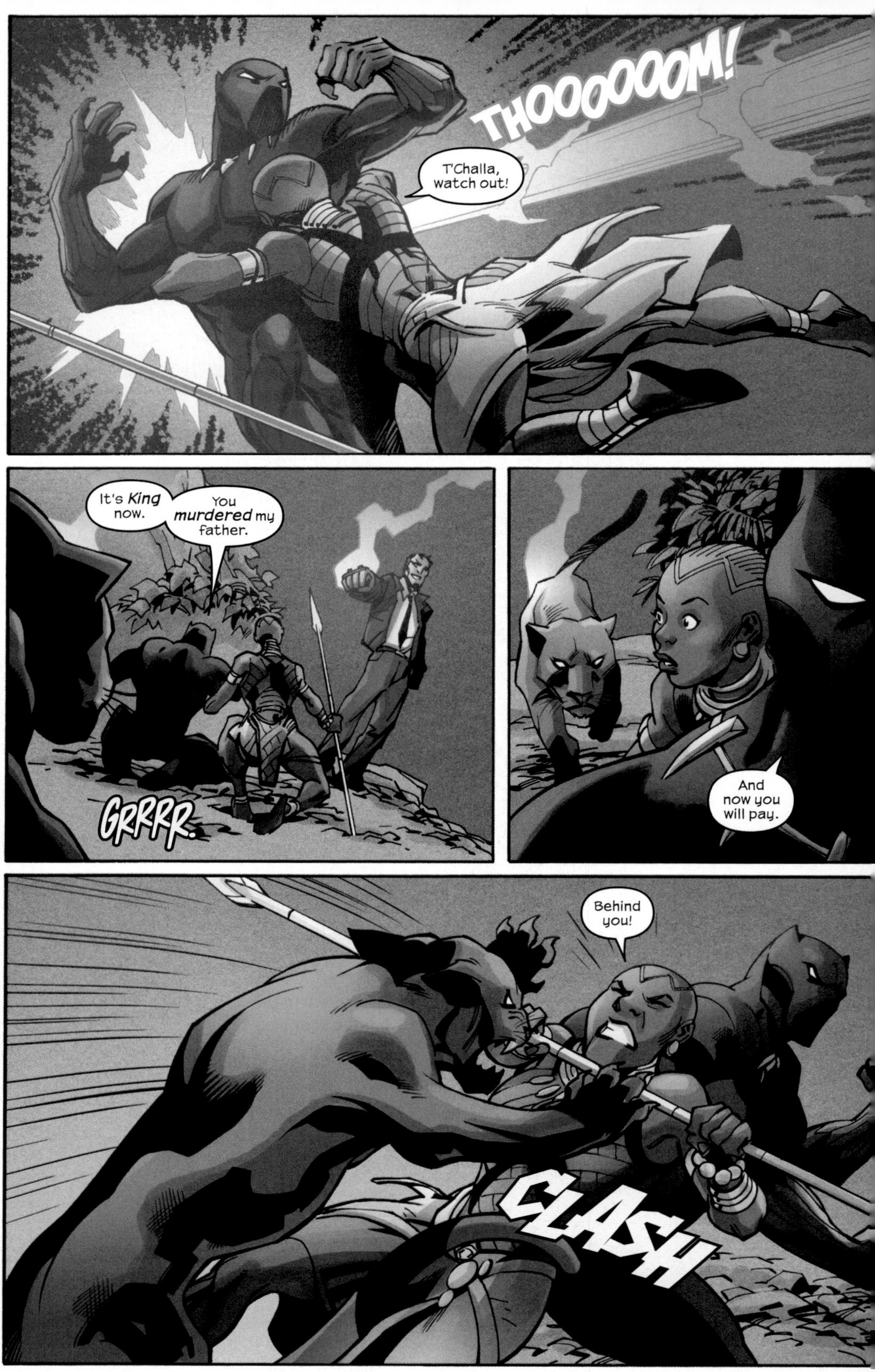
THOOOOOOM!
T'Challa, watch out!
It's King now.
You murdered my father.
GRRRR.
And now you will pay.
Behind you!
CLASH

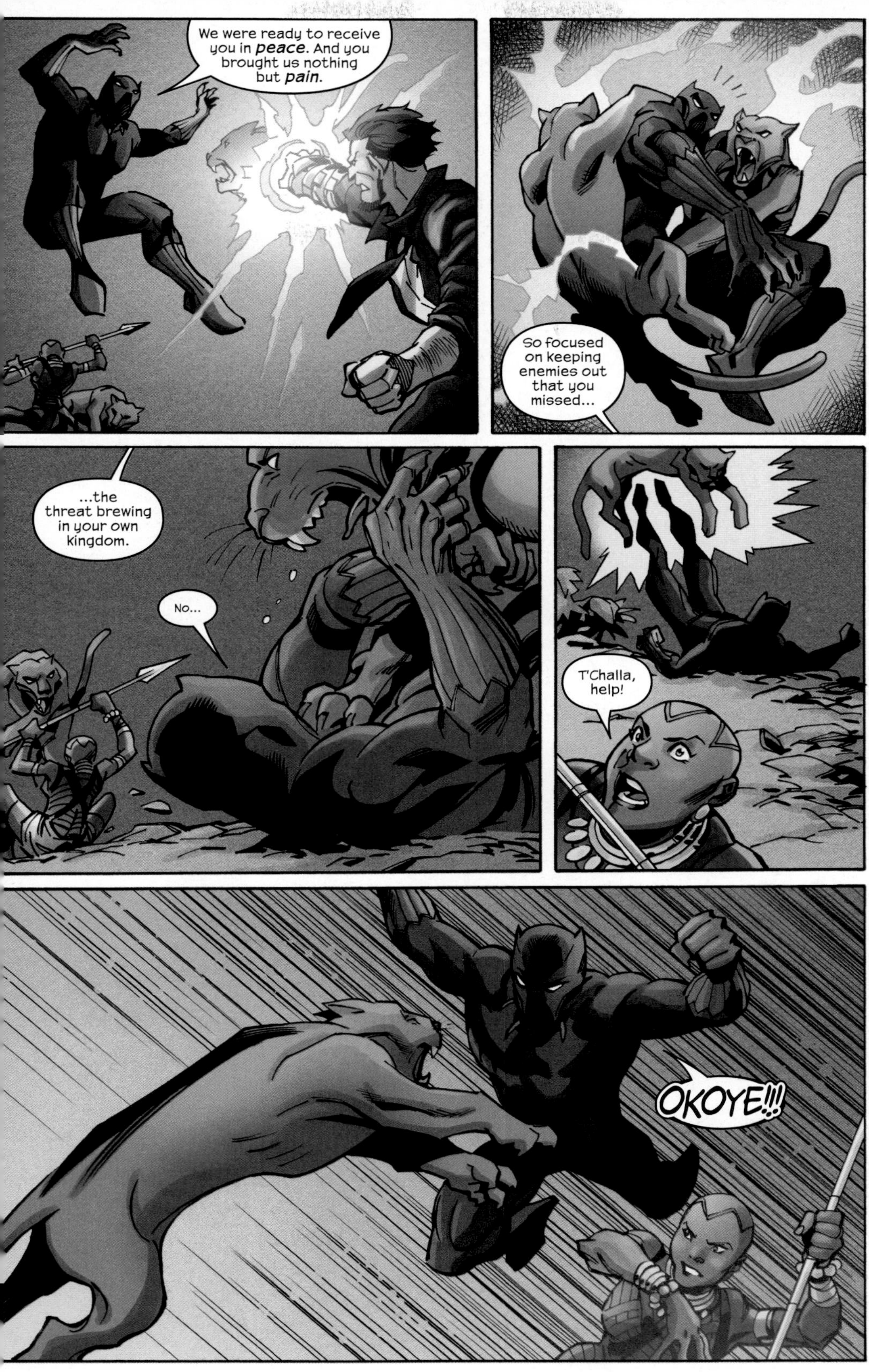
We were ready to receive you in *peace*. And you brought us nothing but *pain*.
So focused on keeping enemies out that you missed...
...the threat brewing in your own kingdom.
No...
T'Challa, help!
OKOYE!!!

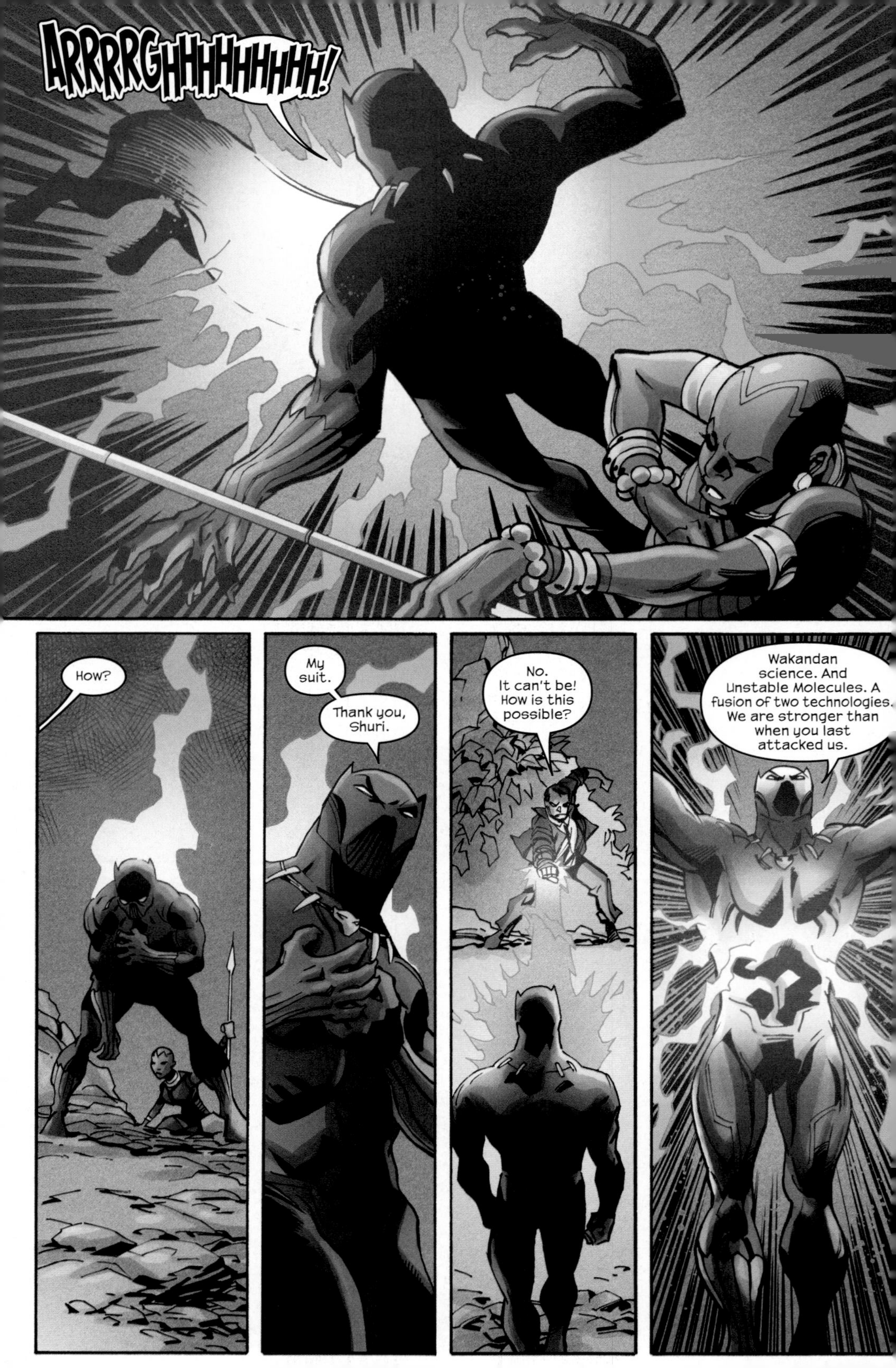
ARRRRGHHHHHHHHH!
How?
My suit.
Thank you, Shuri.
No. It can't be! How is this possible?
Wakandan science. And Unstable Molecules. A fusion of two technologies. We are stronger than when you last attacked us.

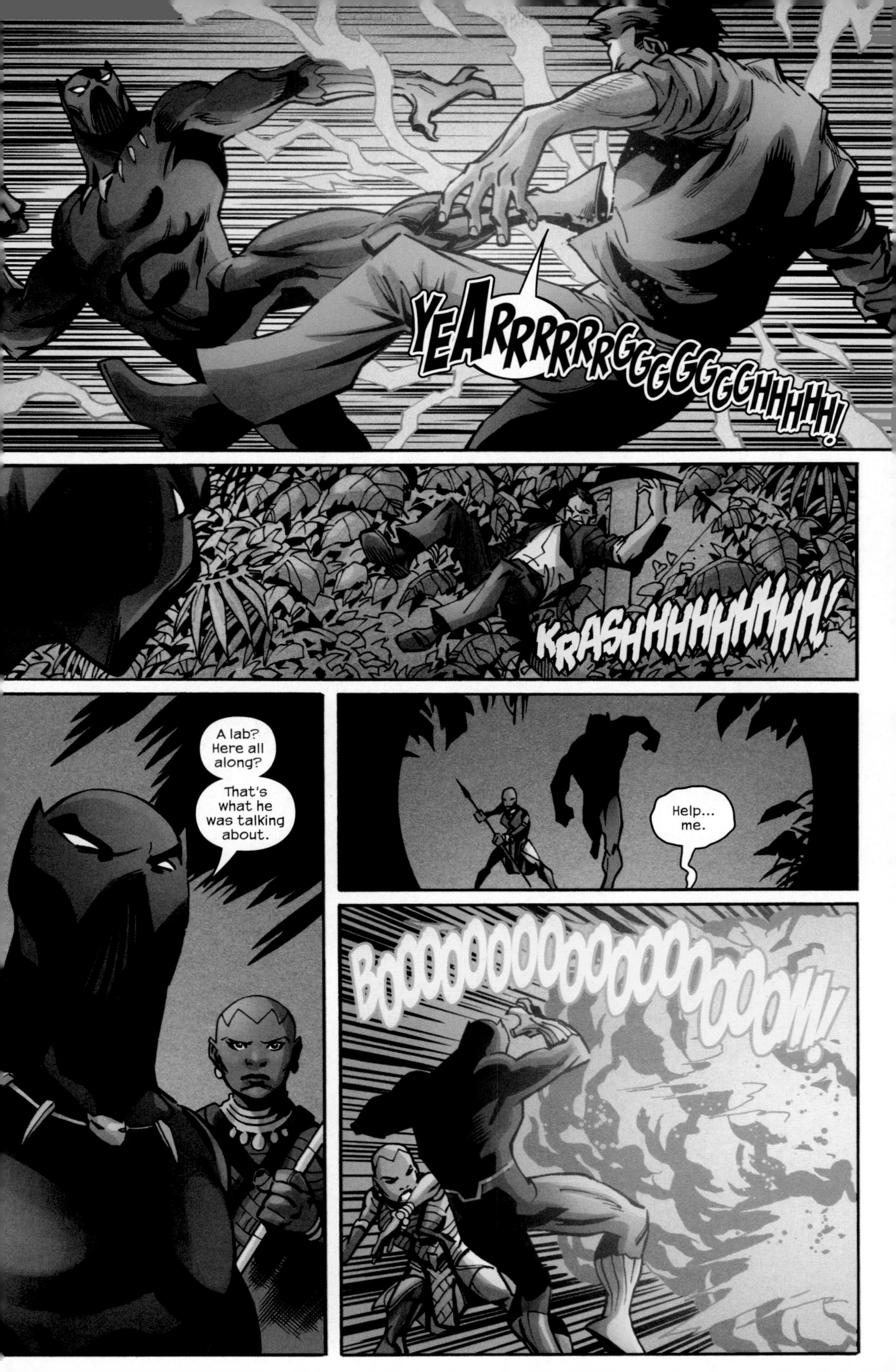
YEARRRRRRGGGGGGHHHHH!
KRASHHHHHHHHHH!
A lab? Here all along?
That's what he was talking about.
Help... me.
BOOOOOOOOOOOOOOOOM!

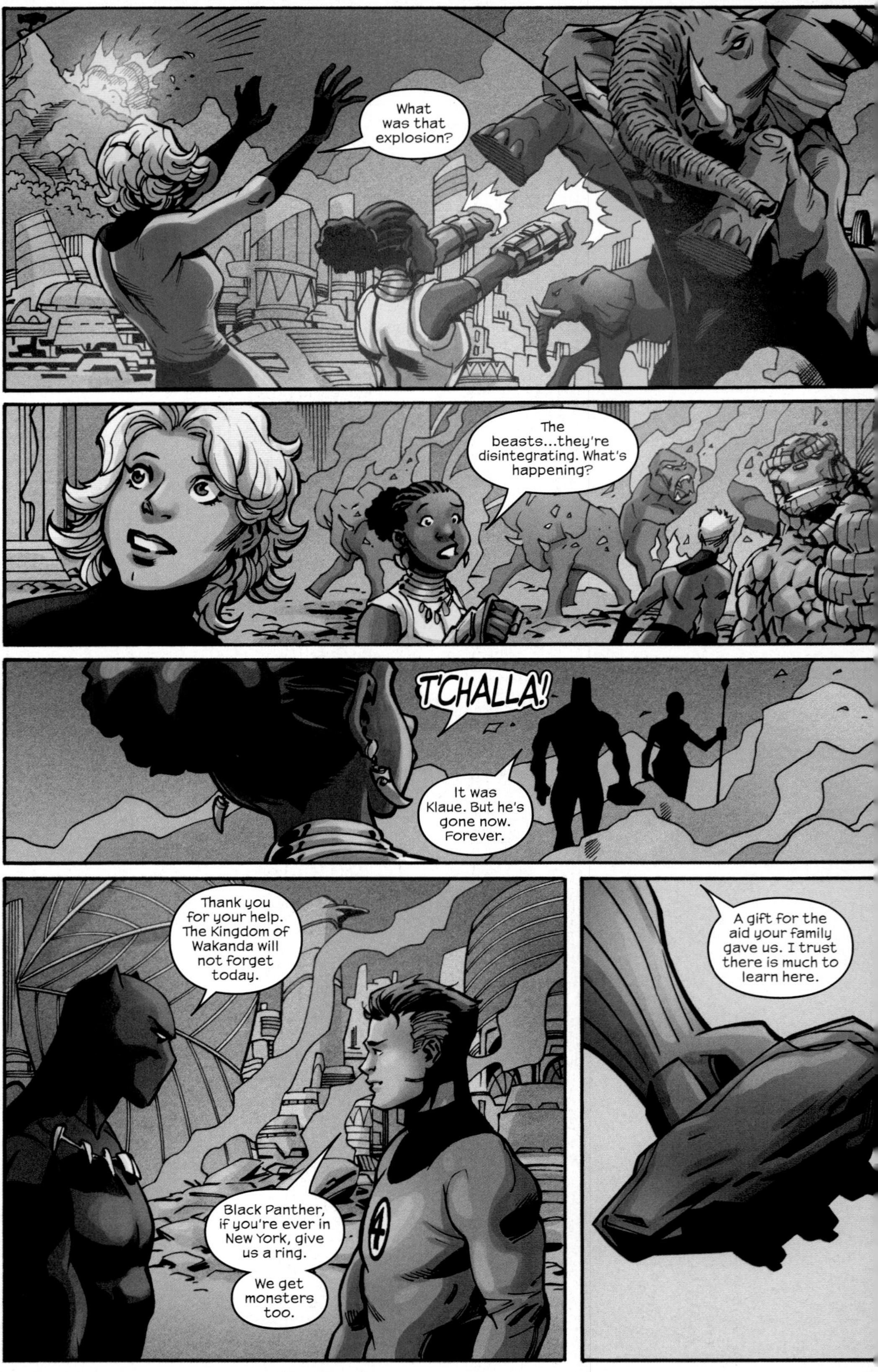
What was that explosion?
The beasts...they're disintegrating. What's happening?
T'CHALLA!
It was Klaue. But he's gone now. Forever.
Thank you for your help. The Kingdom of Wakanda will not forget today.
Black Panther, if you're ever in New York, give us a ring.
We get monsters too.
A gift for the aid your family gave us. I trust there is much to learn here.

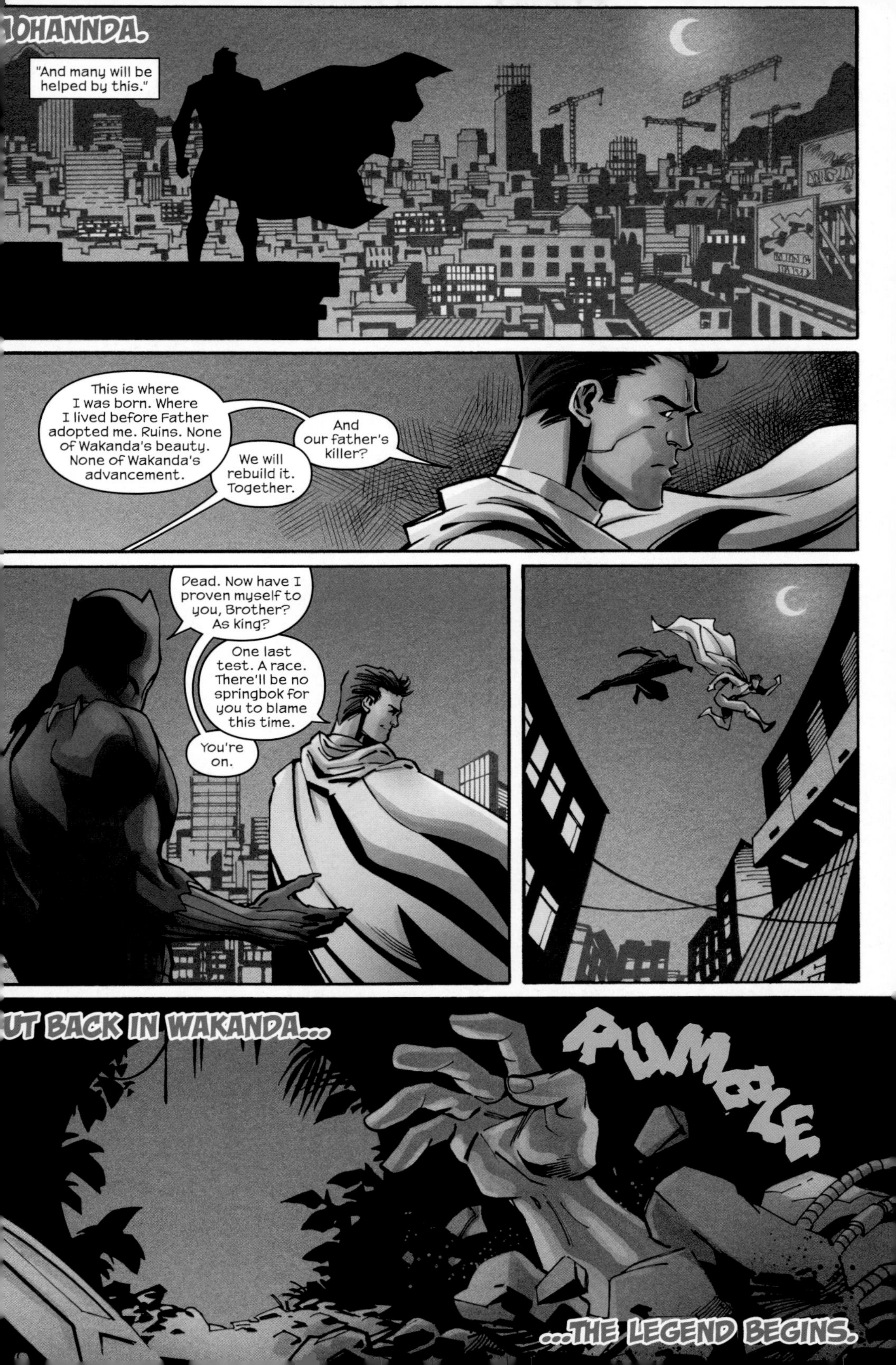

JOHANNDA.
"And many will be helped by this."
This is where I was born. Where I lived before Father adopted me. Ruins. None of Wakanda's beauty. None of Wakanda's advancement.
We will rebuild it. Together.
And our father's killer?
Dead. Now have I proven myself to you, Brother? As king?
One last test. A race. There'll be no springbok for you to blame this time.
You're on.
UT BACK IN WAKANDA...
RUMBLE
...THE LEGEND BEGINS.

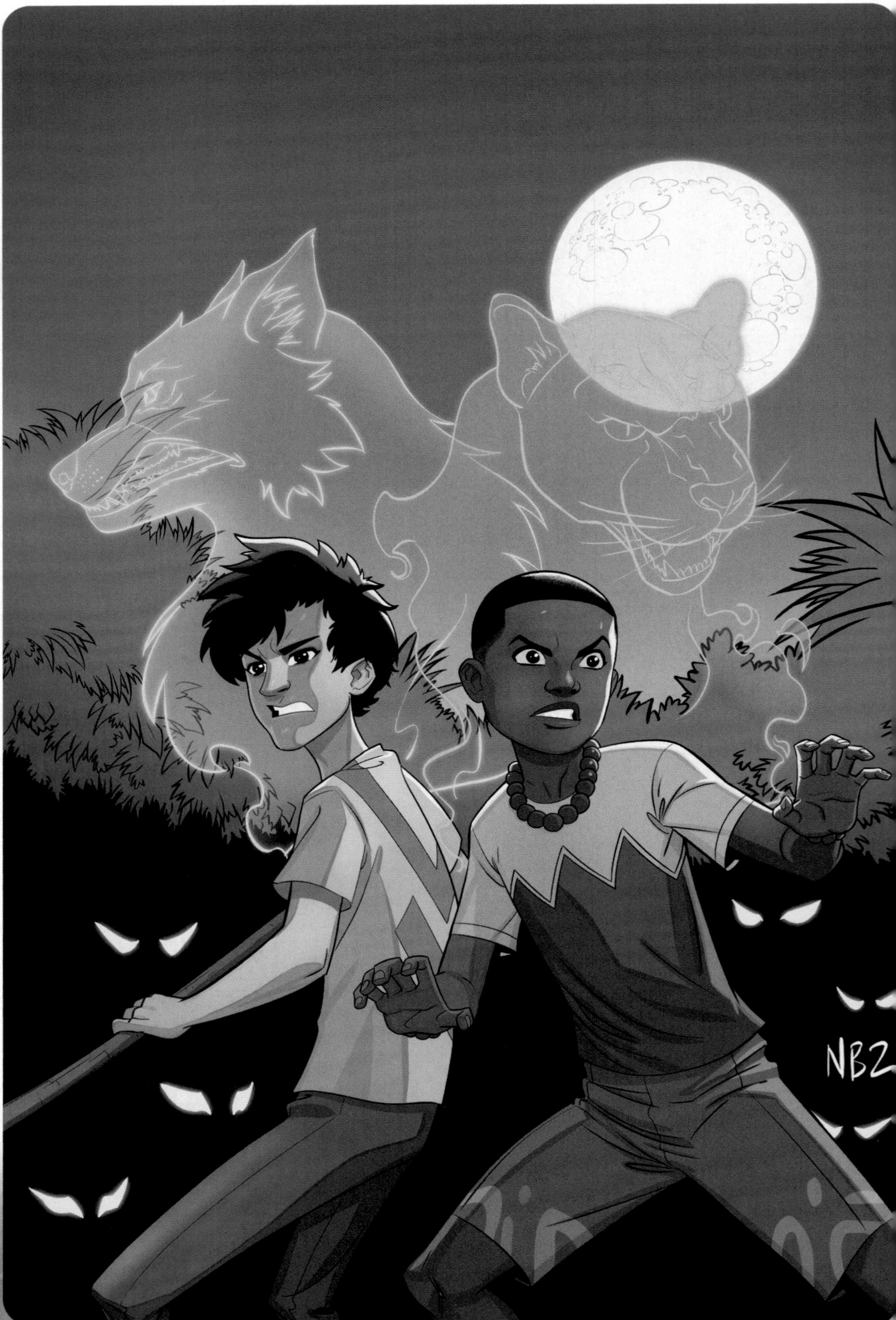
NB2

#1 VARIANT BY **NELSON BLAKE II**

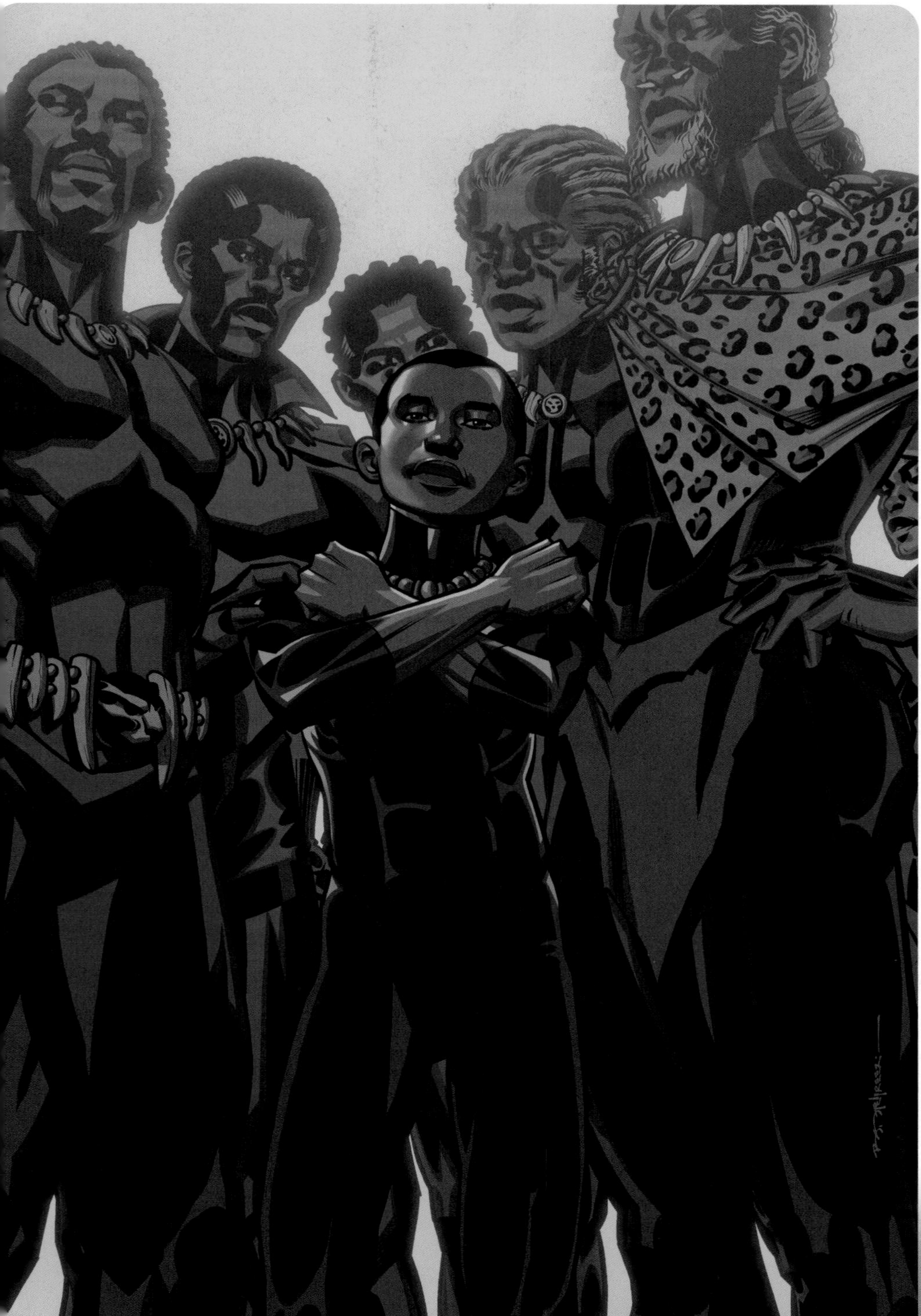

#1 VARIANT BY **BRIAN STELFREEZE**

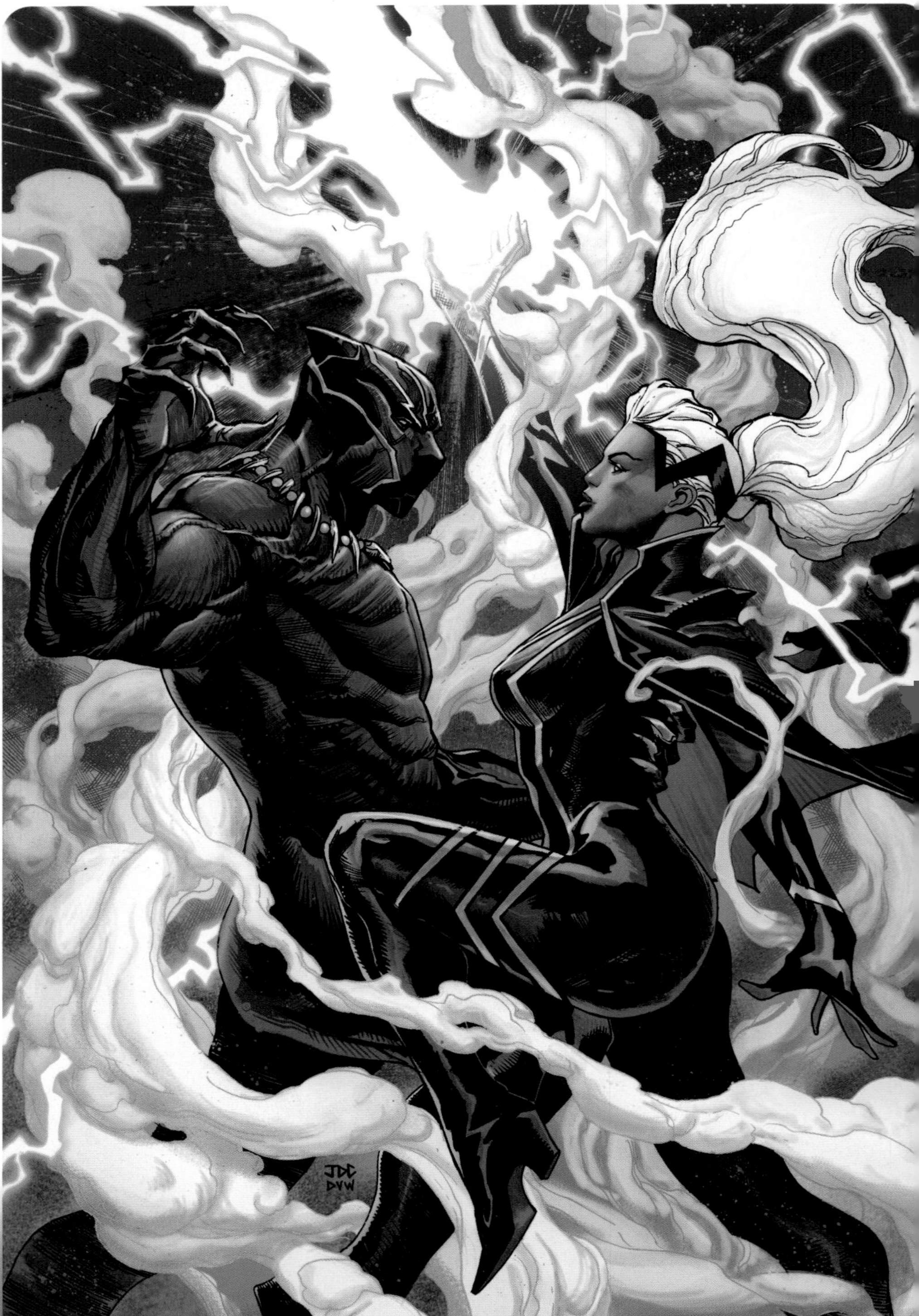

#2 VARIANT BY **JOSHUA CASSARA**

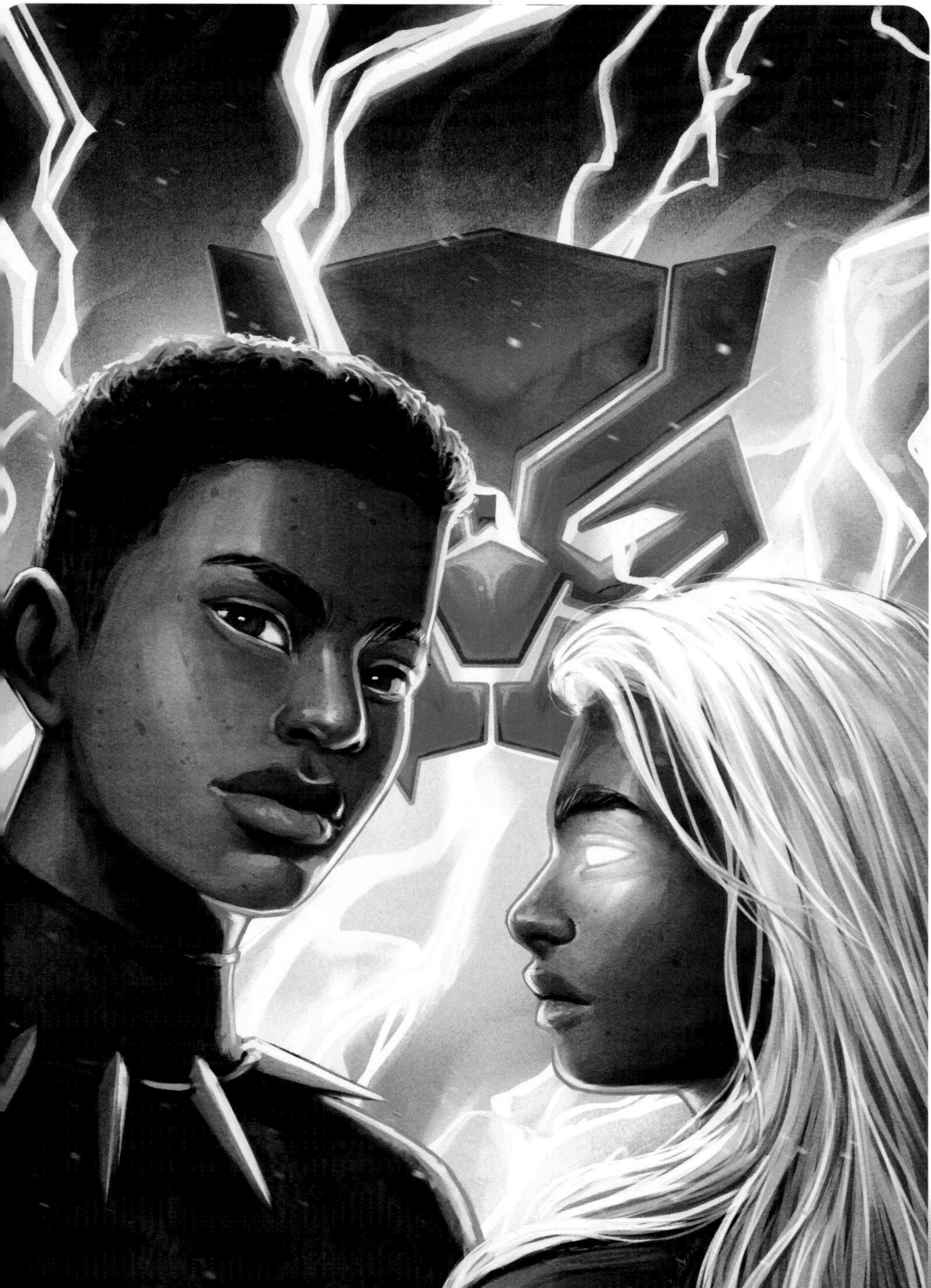

#2 VARIANT BY **EJIWA "EDGE" EBENEBE**

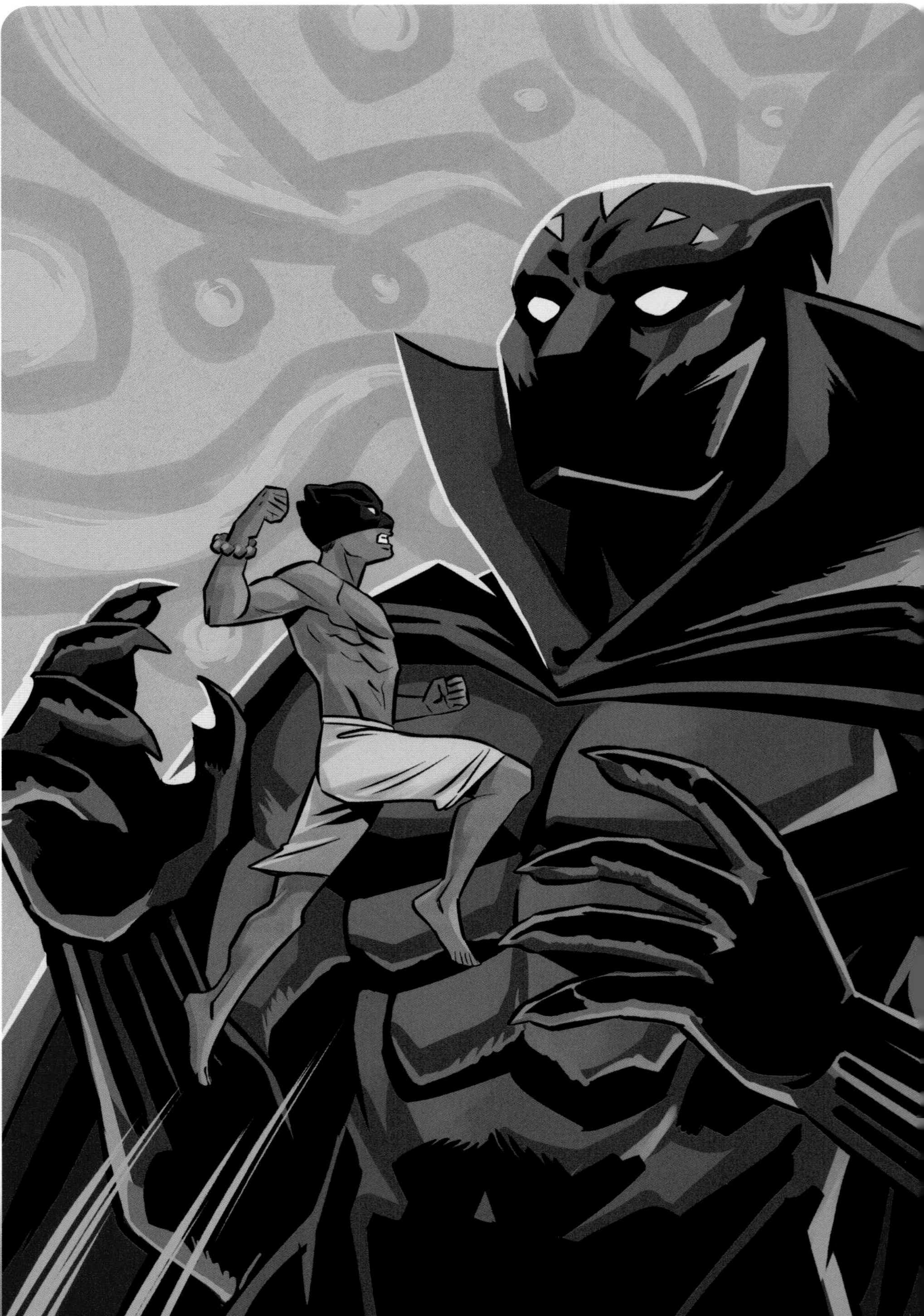

#3 VARIANT BY **NATACHA BUSTOS**

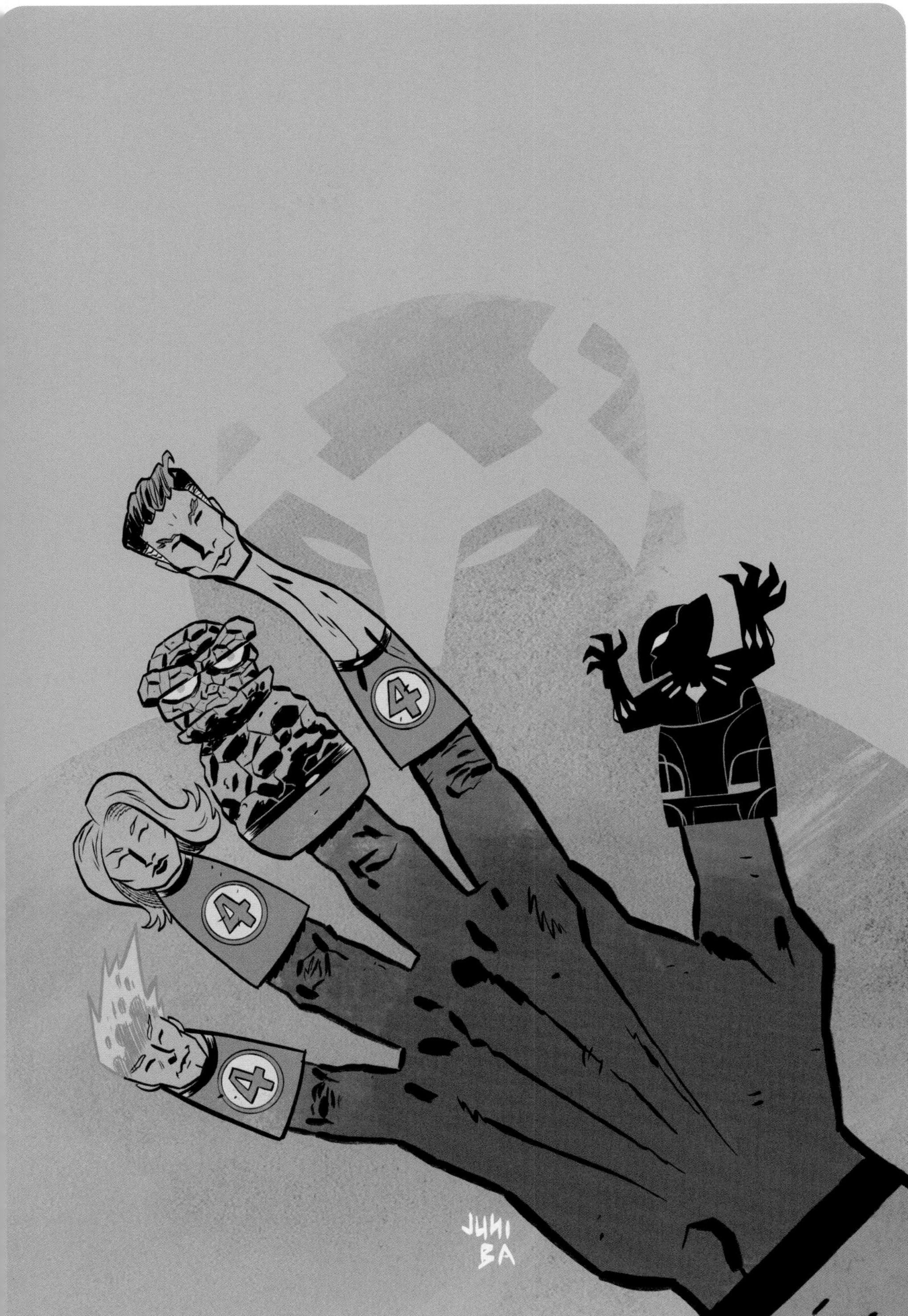

JUNI
BA

#3 VARIANT BY **JUNI BA**

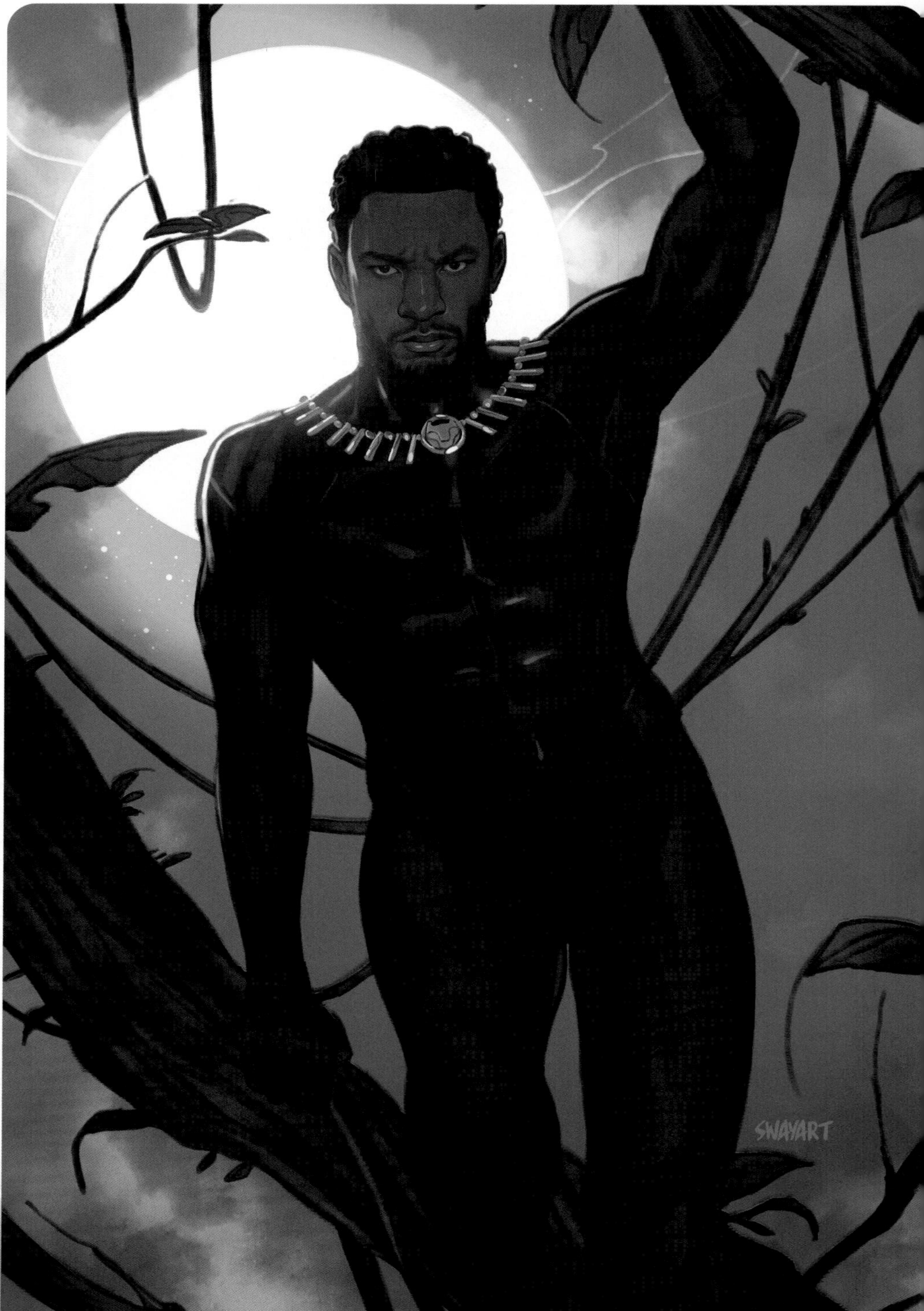
SWAYART

#4 BLACK HISTORY MONTH VARIANT BY **JOSHUA "SWAY" SWABY**

CHECK OUT A SNEAK PEEK OF

INTO THE
HEARTLANDS

A **BLACK PANTHER** GRAPHIC NOVEL

WRITTEN BY
ROSEANNE A. BROWN

ART BY
DIKA ARAÚJO & NATACHA BUSTOS

COLORS BY
CRIS PETER

LETTERS BY
VC's ARIANA MAHER

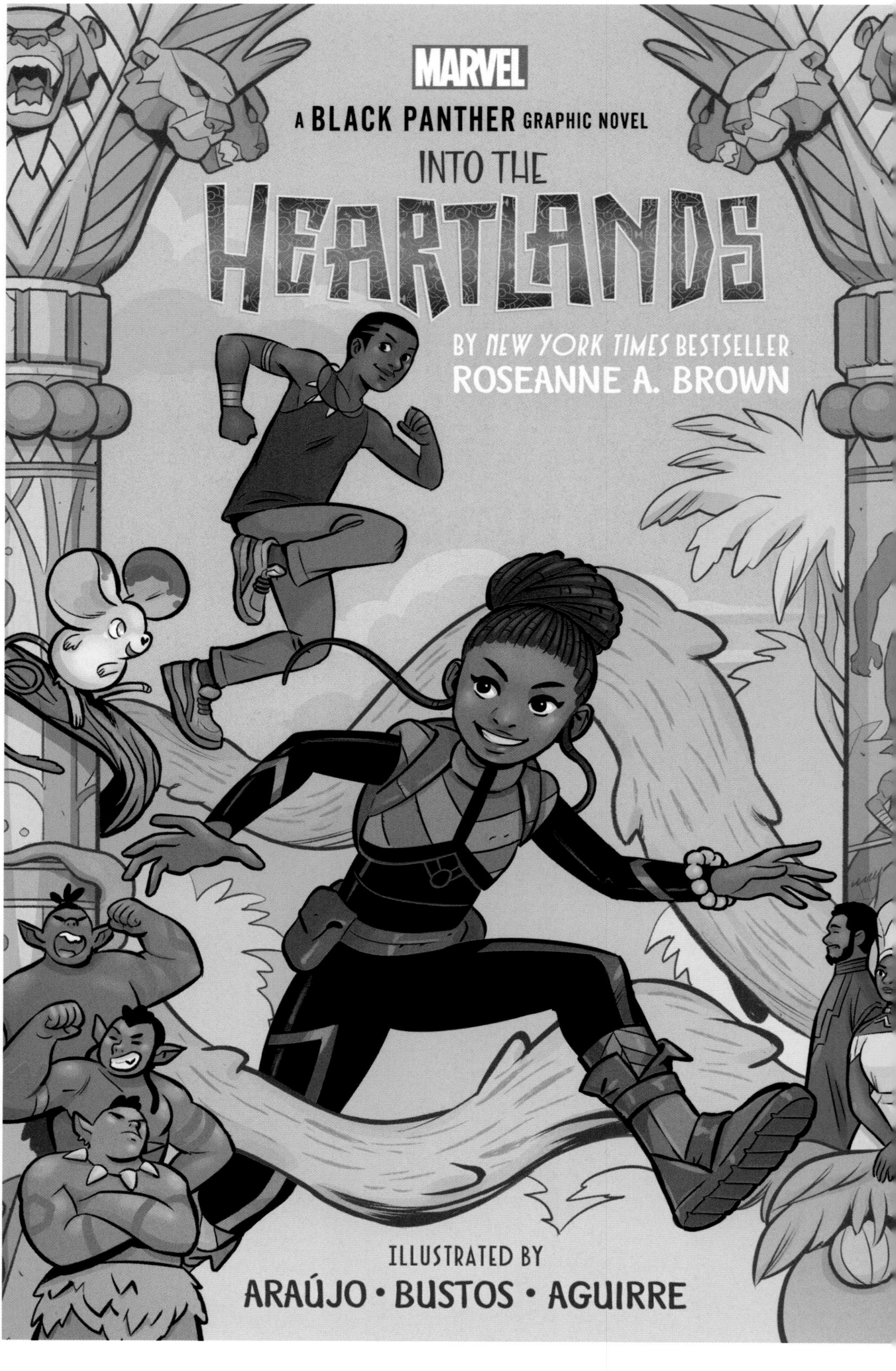
MARVEL
A BLACK PANTHER GRAPHIC NOVEL
INTO THE
HEARTLANDS
BY NEW YORK TIMES BESTSELLER
ROSEANNE A. BROWN
ILLUSTRATED BY
ARAÚJO • BUSTOS • AGUIRRE

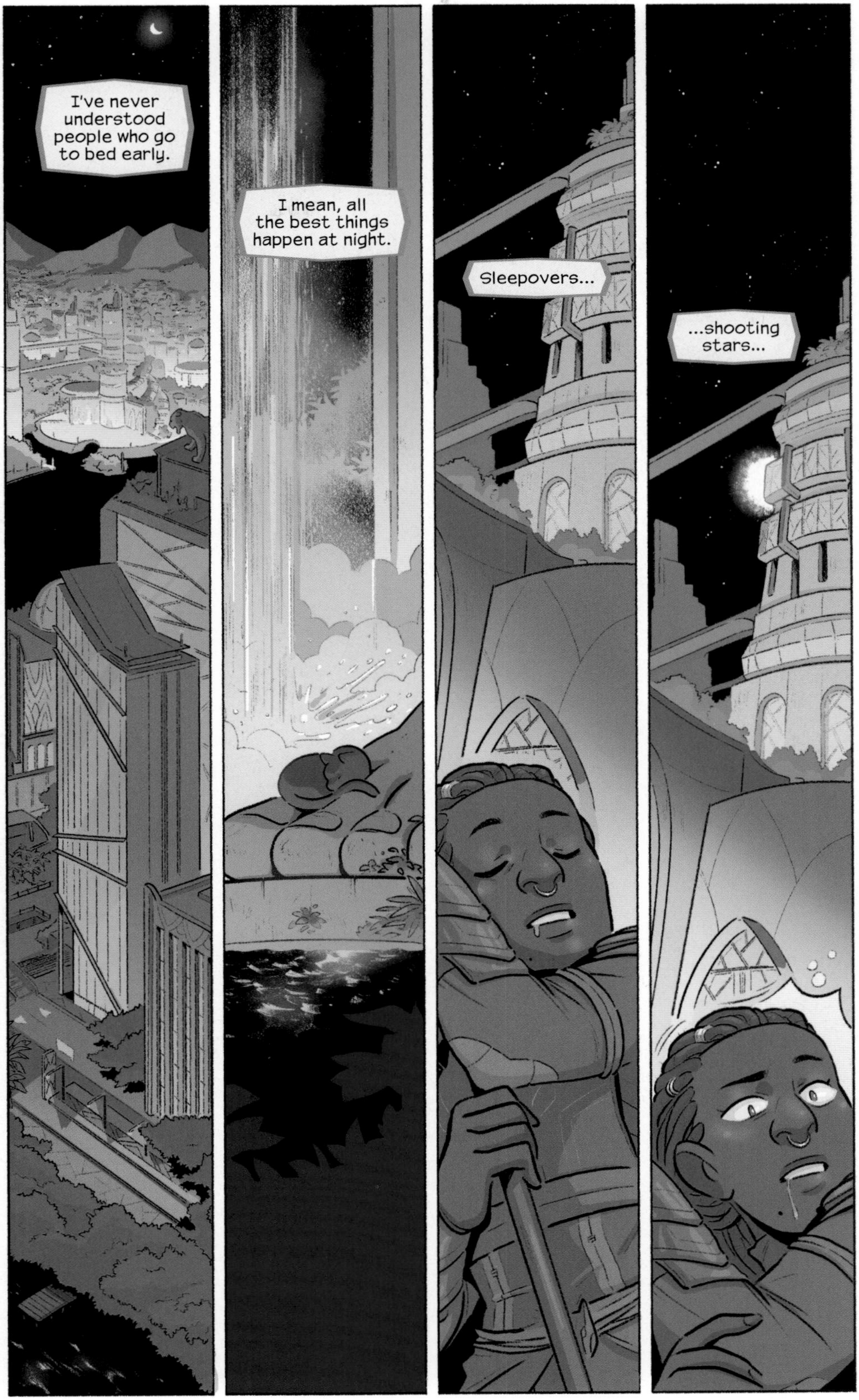
I've never understood people who go to bed early.
I mean, all the best things happen at night.
Sleepovers...
...shooting stars...

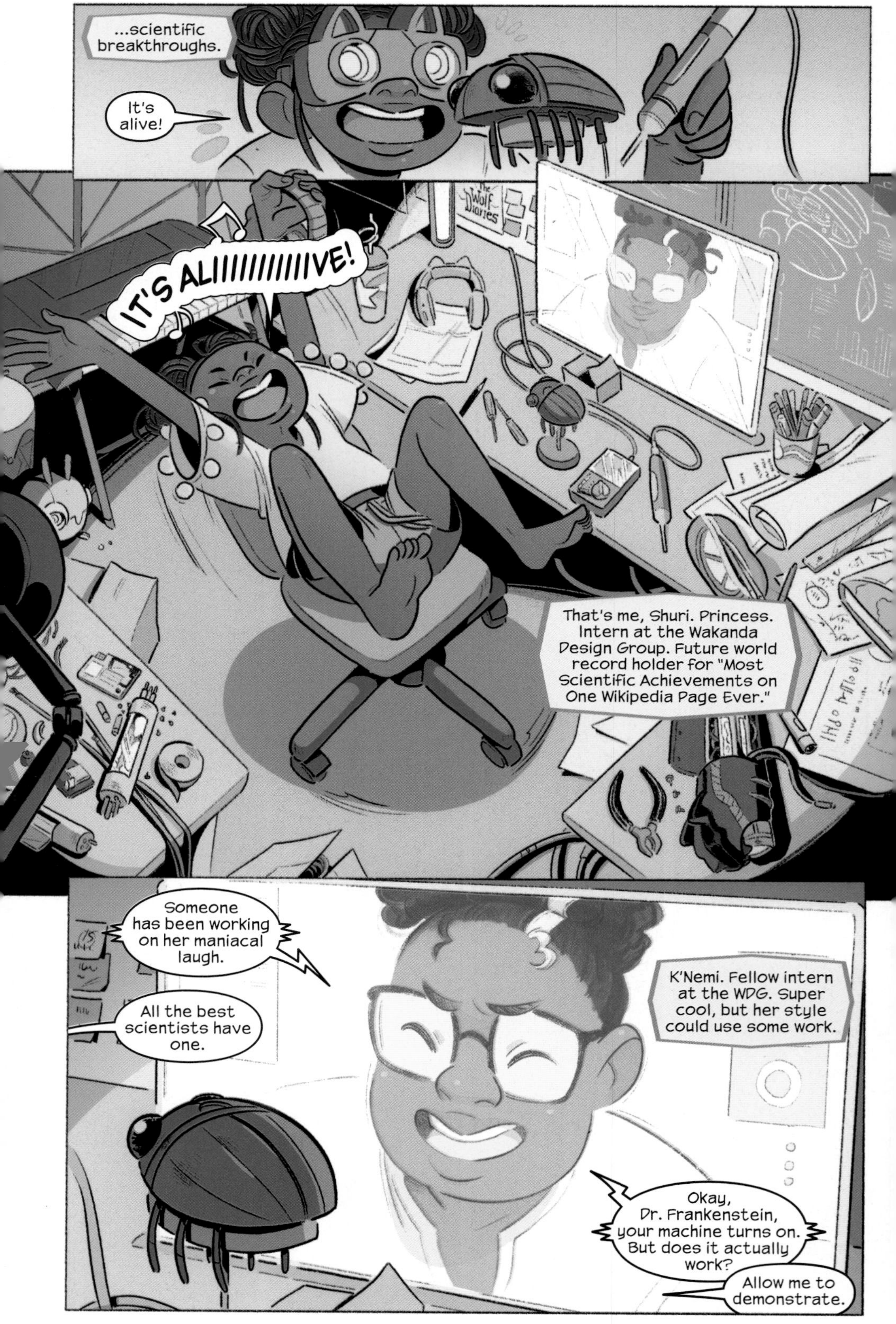
...scientific breakthroughs.
It's alive!
IT'S ALIIIIIIIIIIIIVE!
The Wolf Diaries
That's me, Shuri. Princess. Intern at the Wakanda Design Group. Future world record holder for "Most Scientific Achievements on One Wikipedia Page Ever."
Someone has been working on her maniacal laugh.
All the best scientists have one.
K'Nemi. Fellow intern at the WDG. Super cool, but her style could use some work.
Okay, Dr. Frankenstein, your machine turns on. But does it actually work?
Allow me to demonstrate.

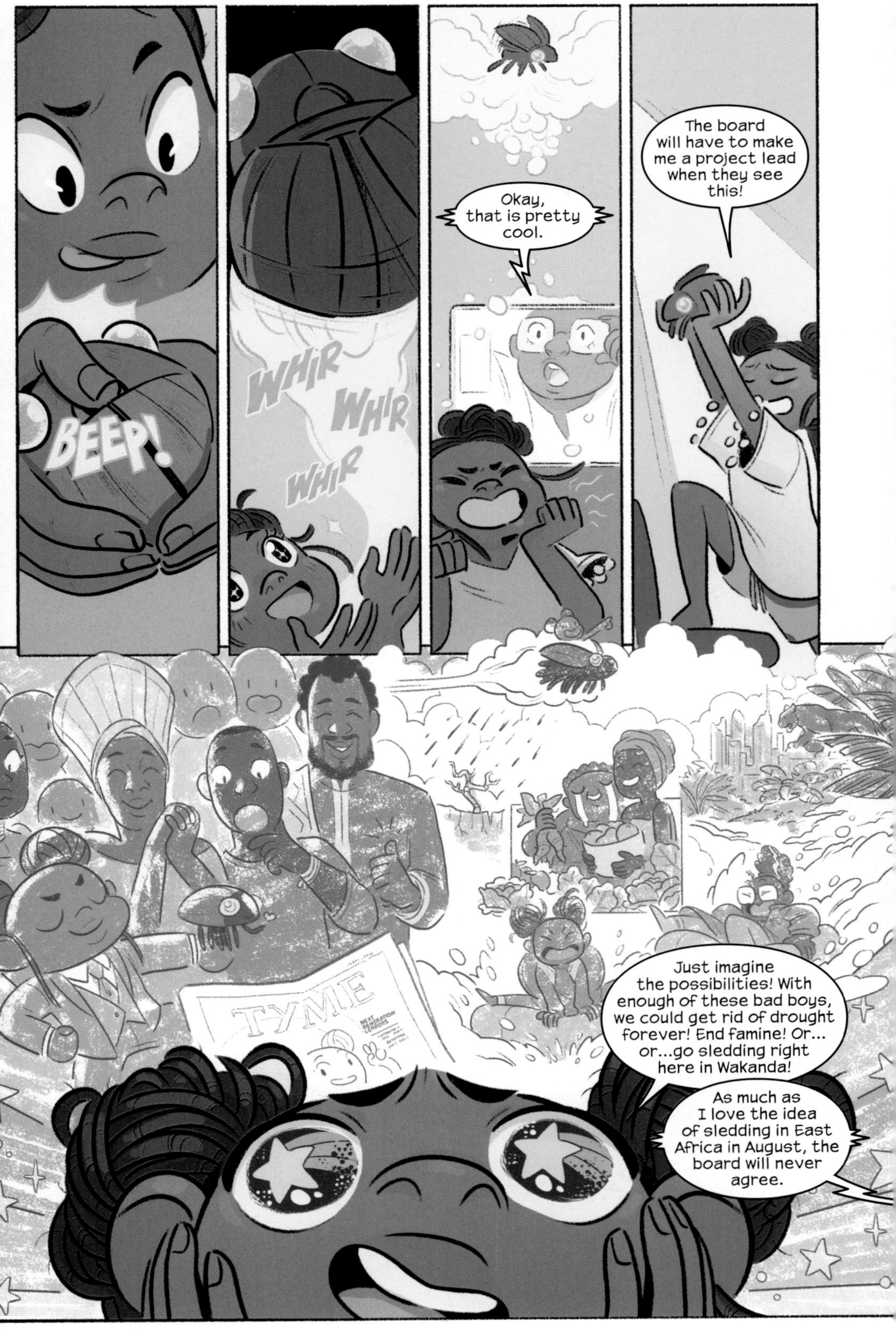
BEEP!
WHIR
WHIR
WHIR
Okay, that is pretty cool.
The board will have to make me a project lead when they see this!
TYME
NEXT GENERATION LEADERS
Just imagine the possibilities! With enough of these bad boys, we could get rid of drought forever! End famine! Or... or...go sledding right here in Wakanda!
As much as I love the idea of sledding in East Africa in August, the board will never agree.

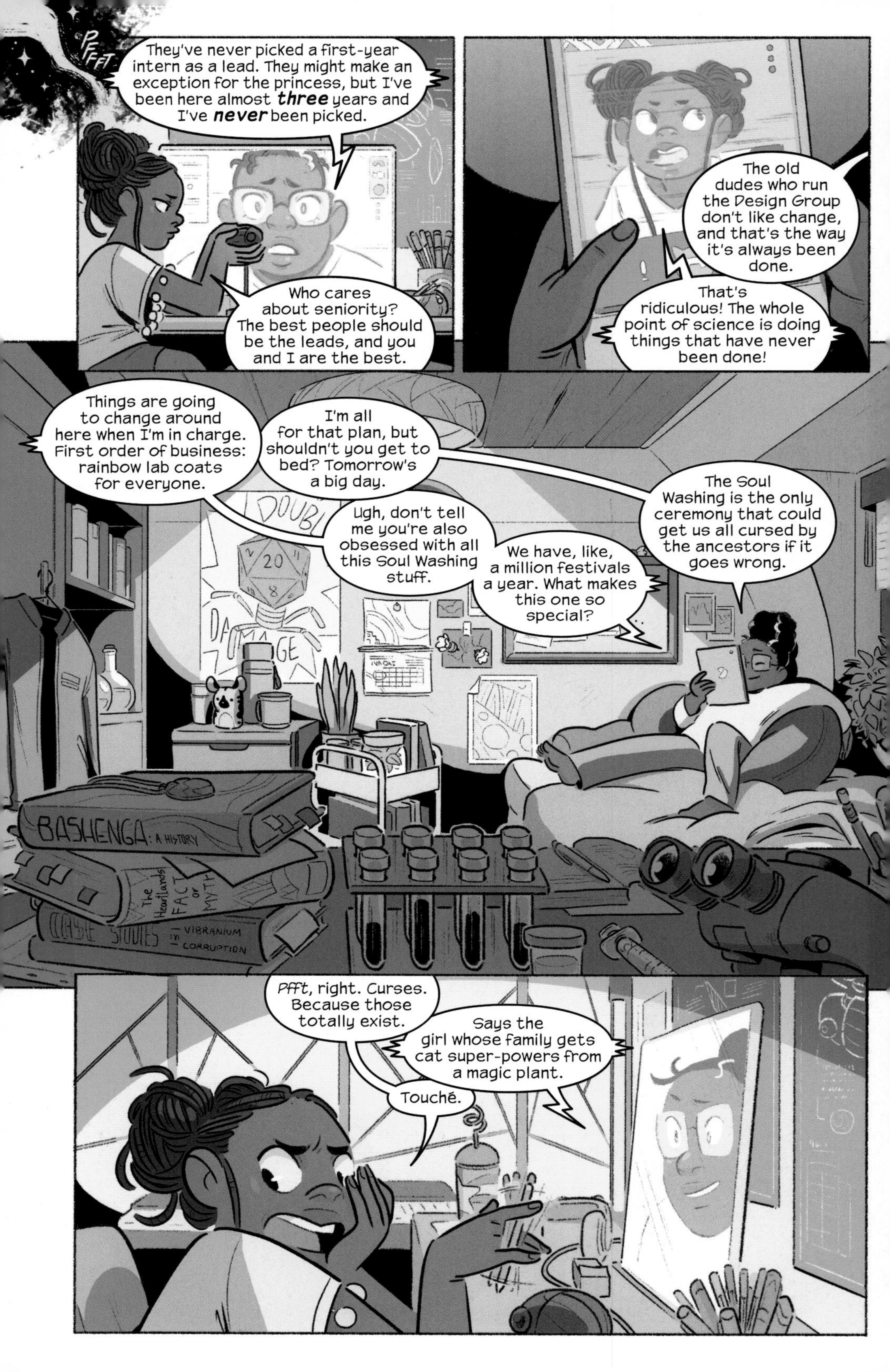
PFFFT
They've never picked a first-year intern as a lead. They might make an exception for the princess, but I've been here almost **three** years and I've **never** been picked.
Who cares about seniority? The best people should be the leads, and you and I are the best.
The old dudes who run the Design Group don't like change, and that's the way it's always been done.
That's ridiculous! The whole point of science is doing things that have never been done!
Things are going to change around here when I'm in charge. First order of business: rainbow lab coats for everyone.
I'm all for that plan, but shouldn't you get to bed? Tomorrow's a big day.
Ugh, don't tell me you're also obsessed with all this Soul Washing stuff.
We have, like, a million festivals a year. What makes this one so special?
The Soul Washing is the only ceremony that could get us all cursed by the ancestors if it goes wrong.
DOUBLE
DAMAGE
BASHENGA: A HISTORY
The Heartlands: FACT or MYTH
CASE STUDIES IN VIBRANIUM CORRUPTION
Pfft, right. Curses. Because those totally exist.
Says the girl whose family gets cat super-powers from a magic plant.
Touché.

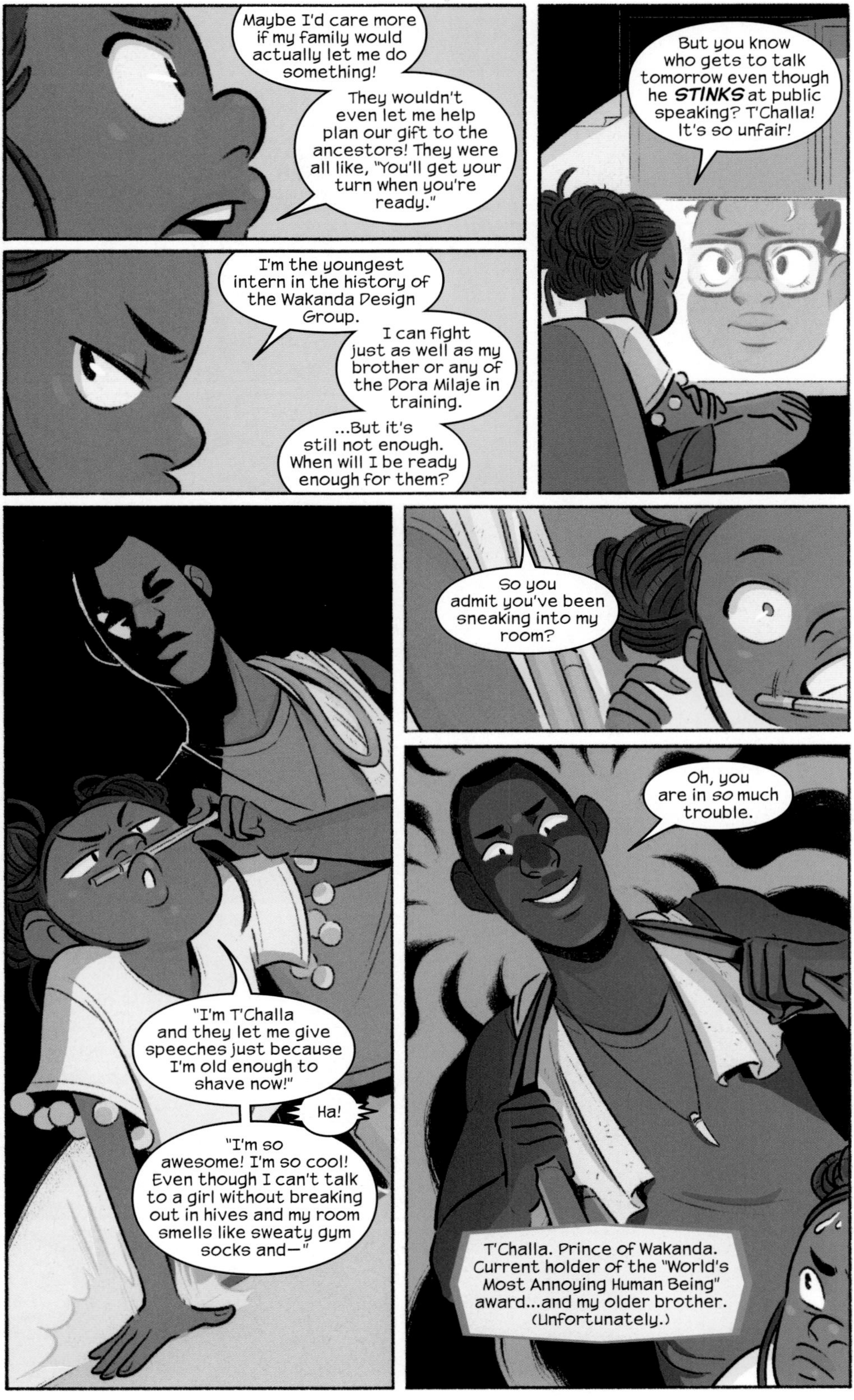
Maybe I'd care more if my family would actually let me do something!
They wouldn't even let me help plan our gift to the ancestors! They were all like, "You'll get your turn when you're ready."
But you know who gets to talk tomorrow even though he STINKS at public speaking? T'Challa! It's so unfair!
I'm the youngest intern in the history of the Wakanda Design Group.
I can fight just as well as my brother or any of the Dora Milaje in training.
...But it's still not enough. When will I be ready enough for them?
"I'm T'Challa and they let me give speeches just because I'm old enough to shave now!"
Ha!
"I'm so awesome! I'm so cool! Even though I can't talk to a girl without breaking out in hives and my room smells like sweaty gym socks and—"
So you admit you've been sneaking into my room?
Oh, you are in so much trouble.
T'Challa. Prince of Wakanda. Current holder of the "World's Most Annoying Human Being" award...and my older brother. (Unfortunately.)

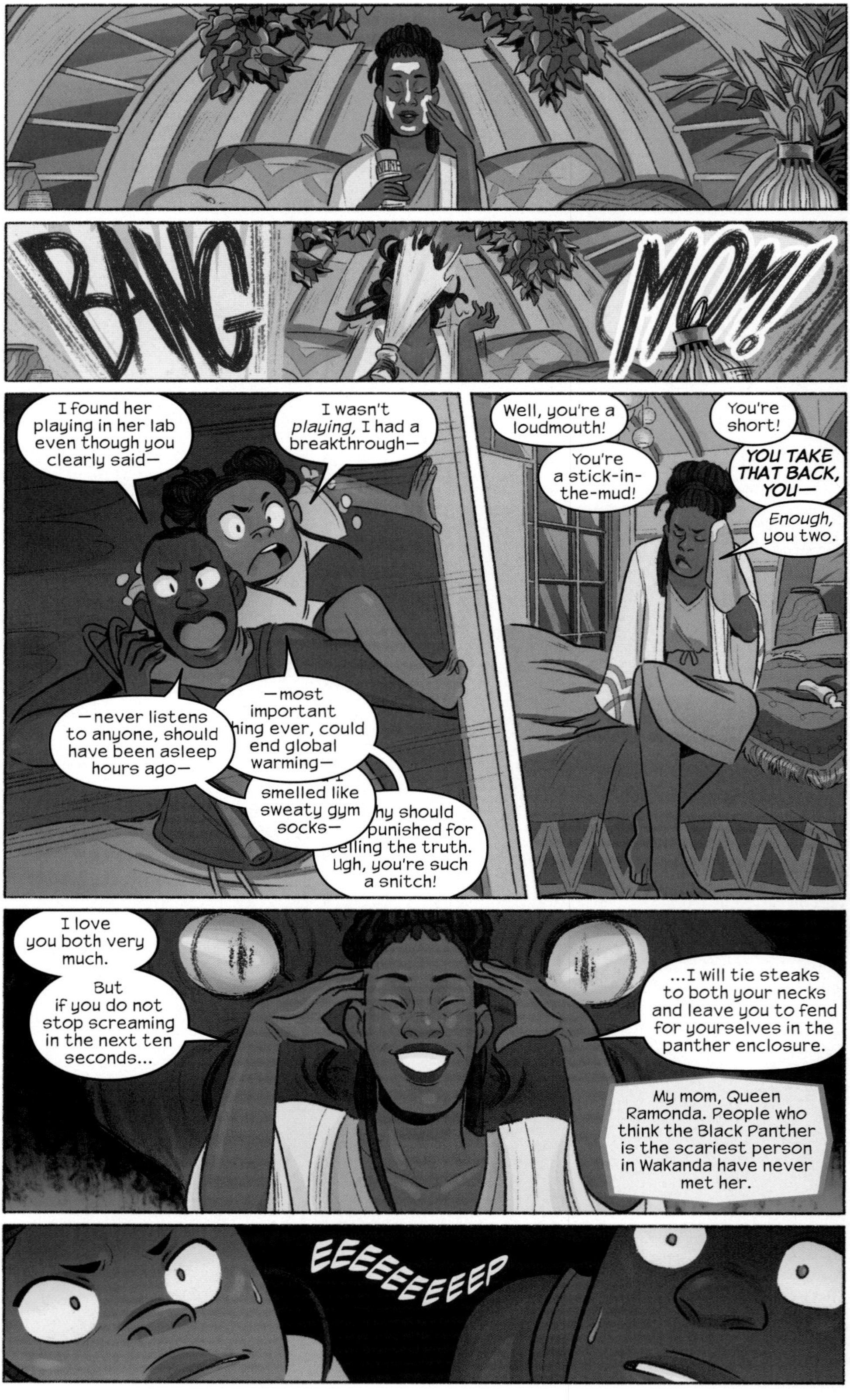
BANG
MOM!
I found her playing in her lab even though you clearly said—
I wasn't *playing,* I had a breakthrough—
—never listens to anyone, should have been asleep hours ago—
—most important hing ever, could end global warming—
smelled like sweaty gym socks—
hy should punished for elling the truth. Ugh, you're such a snitch!
Well, you're a loudmouth!
You're short!
You're a stick-in-the-mud!
YOU TAKE THAT BACK, YOU—
Enough, you two.
I love you both very much.
But if you do not stop screaming in the next ten seconds...
...I will tie steaks to both your necks and leave you to fend for yourselves in the panther enclosure.
My mom, Queen Ramonda. People who think the Black Panther is the scariest person in Wakanda have never met her.
EEEEEEEEEEP

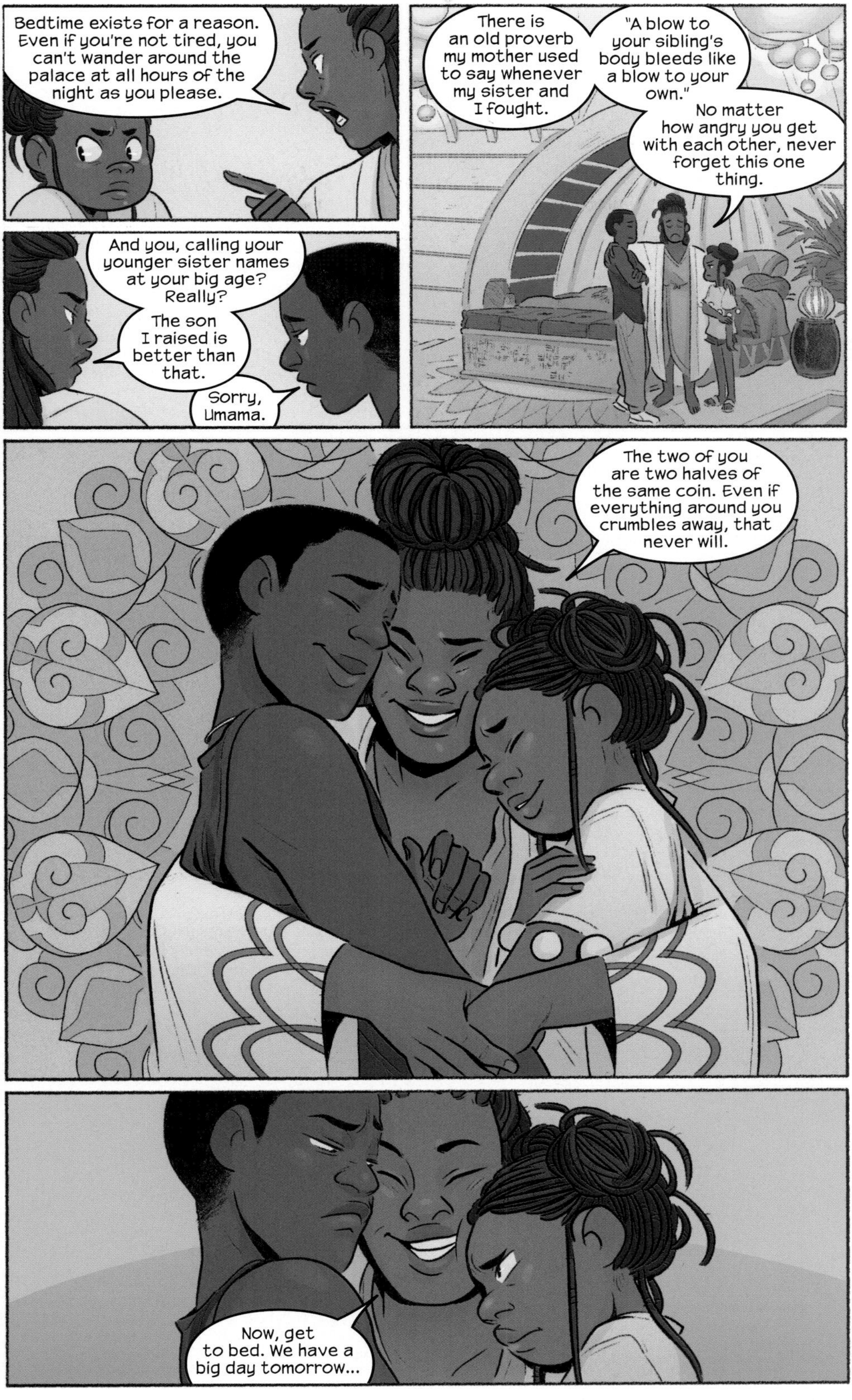
Bedtime exists for a reason. Even if you're not tired, you can't wander around the palace at all hours of the night as you please.
There is an old proverb my mother used to say whenever my sister and I fought.
"A blow to your sibling's body bleeds like a blow to your own."
No matter how angry you get with each other, never forget this one thing.
And you, calling your younger sister names at your big age? Really?
The son I raised is better than that.
Sorry, Umama.
The two of you are two halves of the same coin. Even if everything around you crumbles away, that never will.
Now, get to bed. We have a big day tomorrow...

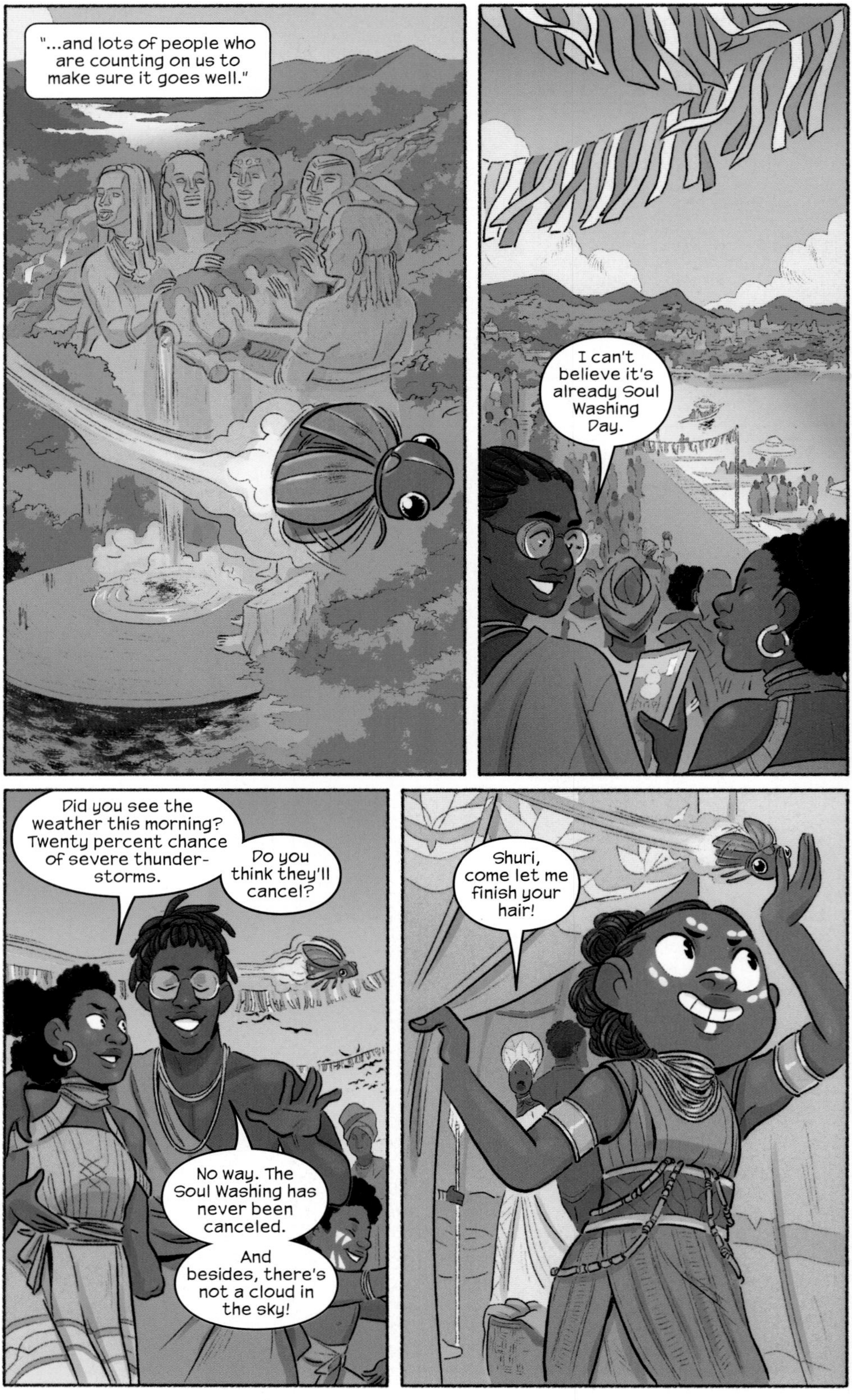
"...and lots of people who are counting on us to make sure it goes well."
I can't believe it's already Soul Washing Day.
Did you see the weather this morning? Twenty percent chance of severe thunder-storms.
Do you think they'll cancel?
No way. The Soul Washing has never been canceled.
And besides, there's not a cloud in the sky!
Shuri, come let me finish your hair!

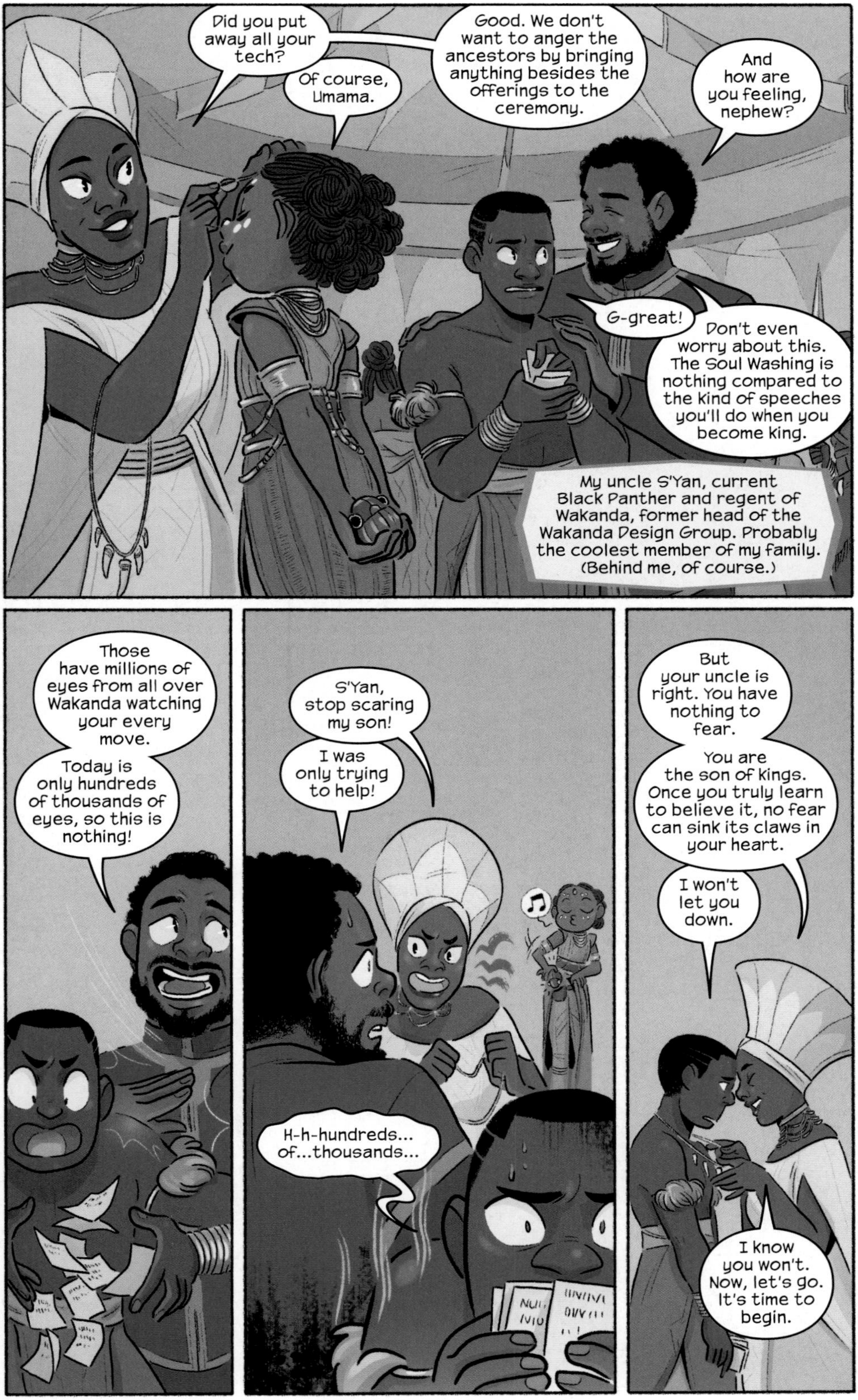
Did you put away all your tech?
Of course, Umama.
Good. We don't want to anger the ancestors by bringing anything besides the offerings to the ceremony.
And how are you feeling, nephew?
G-great!
Don't even worry about this. The Soul Washing is nothing compared to the kind of speeches you'll do when you become king.
My uncle S'Yan, current Black Panther and regent of Wakanda, former head of the Wakanda Design Group. Probably the coolest member of my family. (Behind me, of course.)
Those have millions of eyes from all over Wakanda watching your every move.
Today is only hundreds of thousands of eyes, so this is nothing!
S'Yan, stop scaring my son!
I was only trying to help!
H-h-hundreds... of...thousands...
But your uncle is right. You have nothing to fear.
You are the son of kings. Once you truly learn to believe it, no fear can sink its claws in your heart.
I won't let you down.
I know you won't. Now, let's go. It's time to begin.

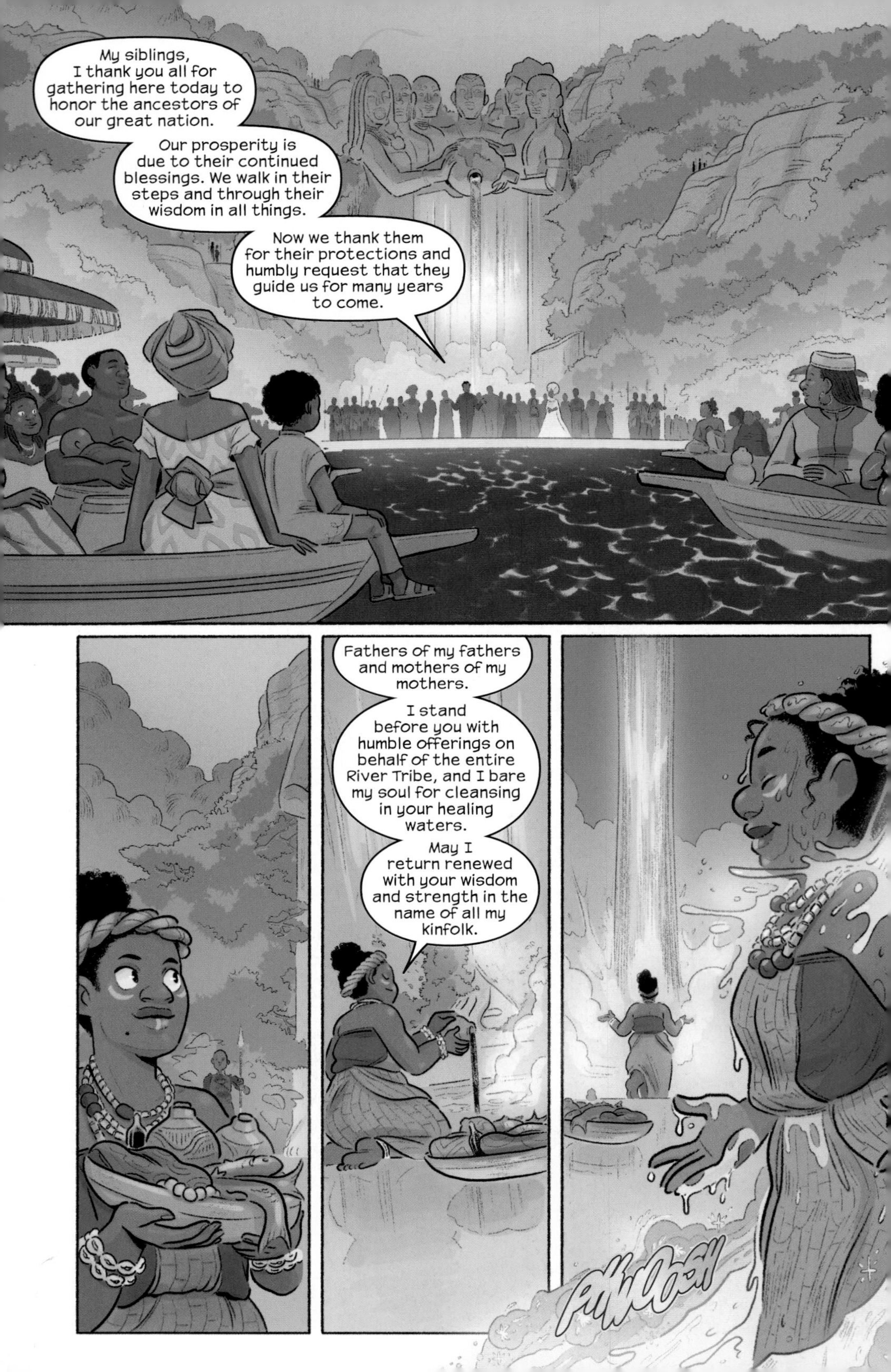

My siblings, I thank you all for gathering here today to honor the ancestors of our great nation.
Our prosperity is due to their continued blessings. We walk in their steps and through their wisdom in all things.
Now we thank them for their protections and humbly request that they guide us for many years to come.
Fathers of my fathers and mothers of my mothers.
I stand before you with humble offerings on behalf of the entire River Tribe, and I bare my soul for cleansing in your healing waters.
May I return renewed with your wisdom and strength in the name of all my kinfolk.

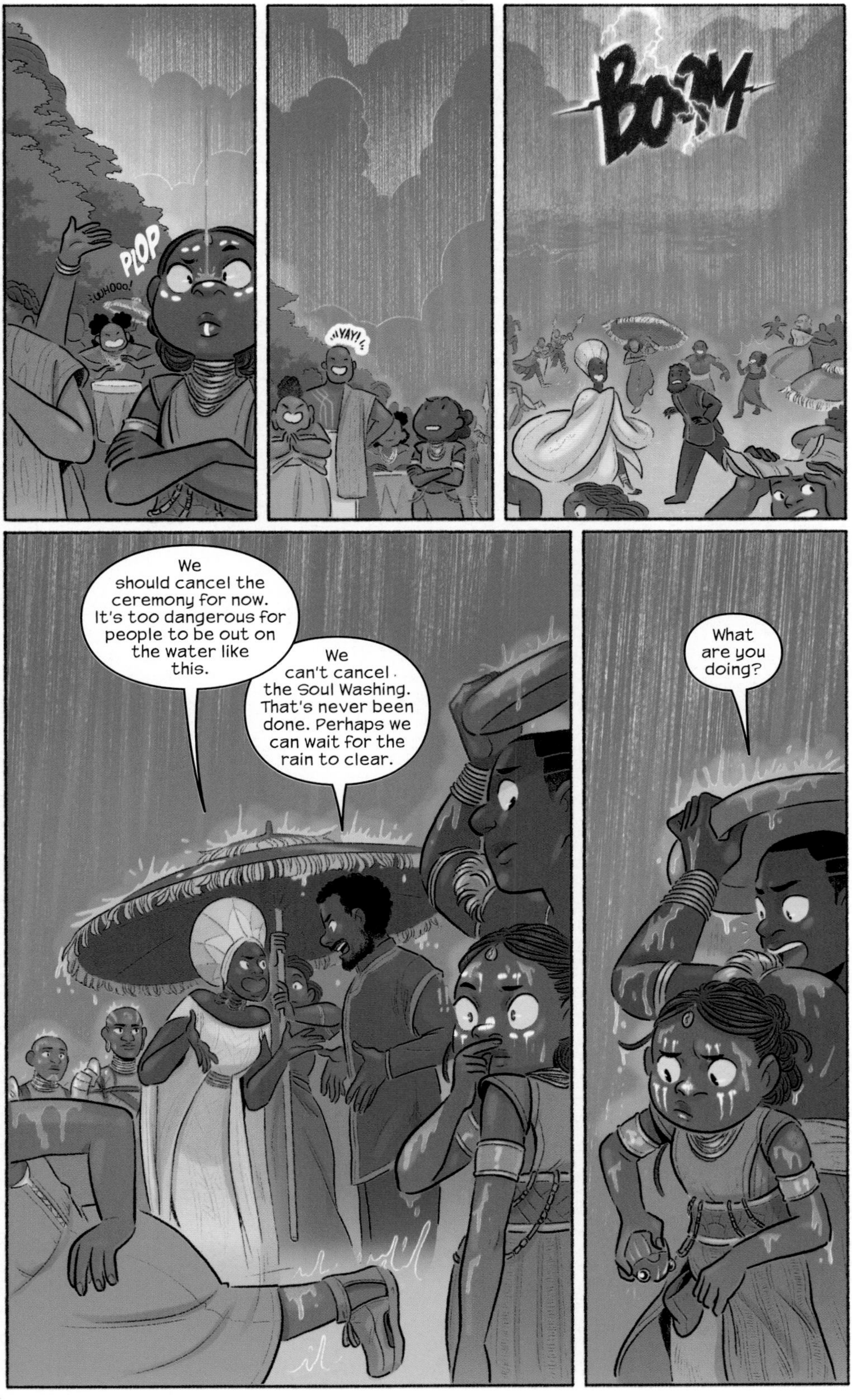
PLOP
WHOOO!
YAY!
BOOM
We should cancel the ceremony for now. It's too dangerous for people to be out on the water like this.
We can't cancel the Soul Washing. That's never been done. Perhaps we can wait for the rain to clear.
What are you doing?

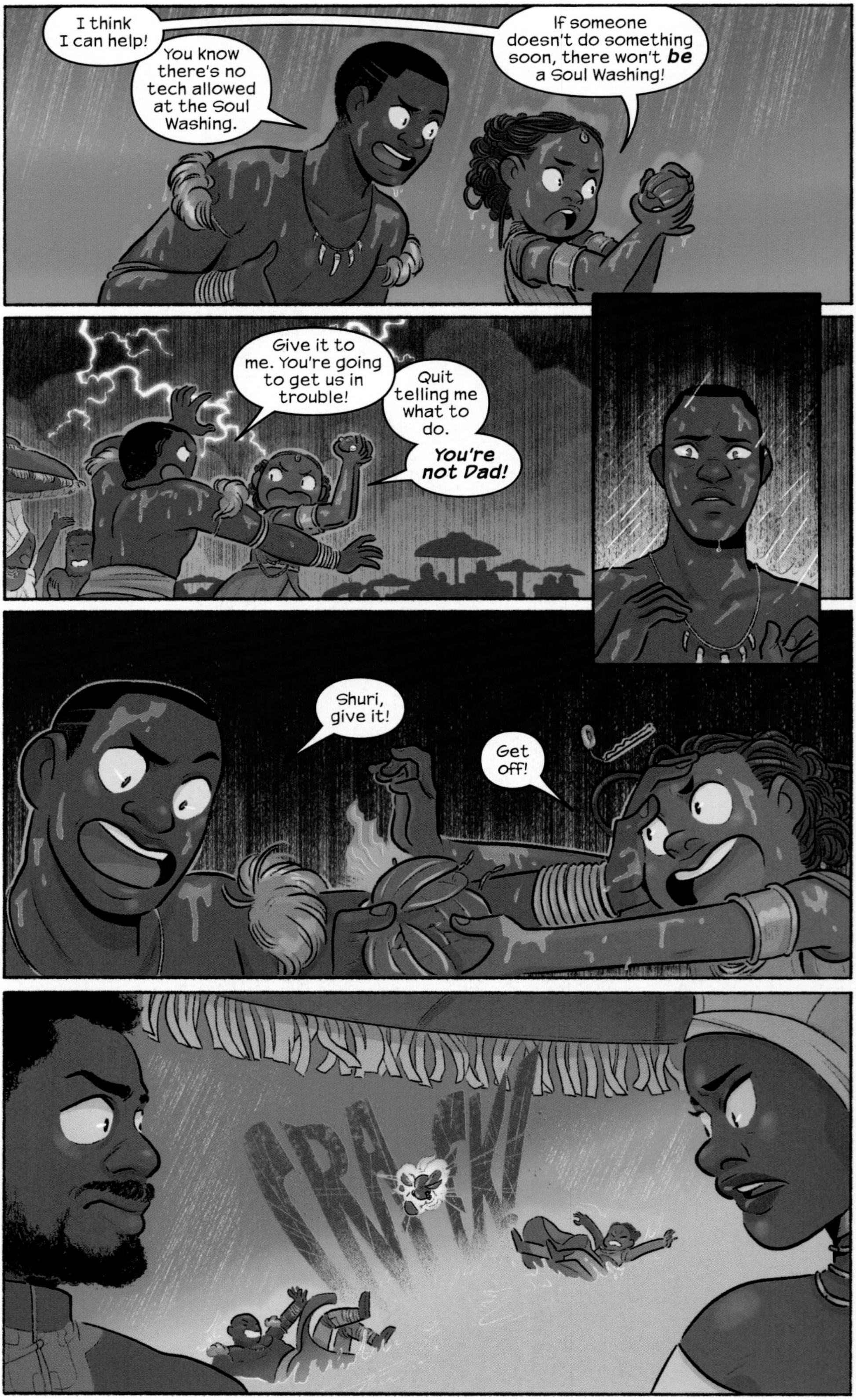
I think I can help!
You know there's no tech allowed at the Soul Washing.
If someone doesn't do something soon, there won't ***be*** a Soul Washing!
Give it to me. You're going to get us in trouble!
Quit telling me what to do.
You're not Dad!
Shuri, give it!
Get off!

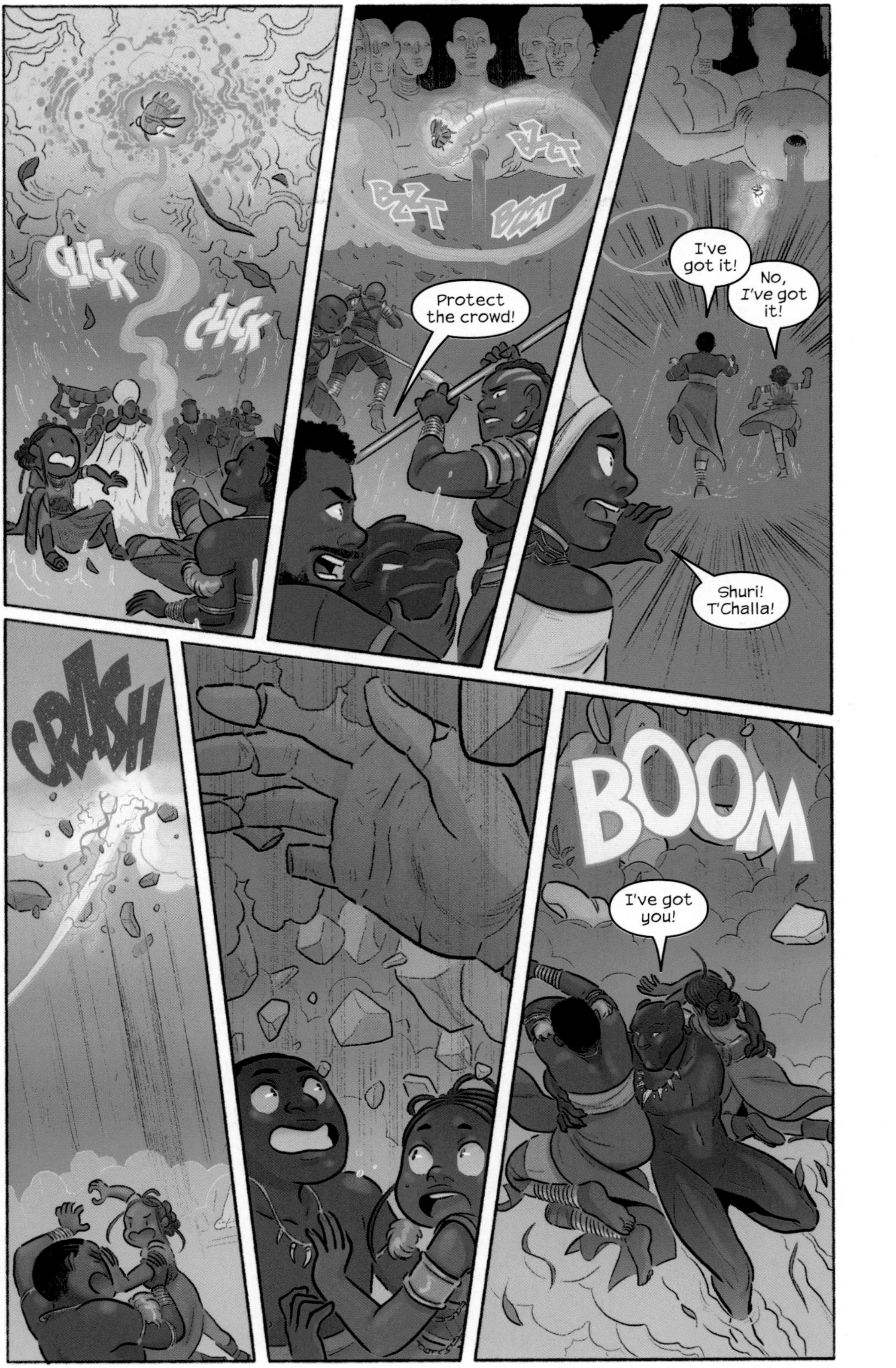
CLICK
CLICK
BZZT
BZZT
BZZT
Protect the crowd!
I've got it!
No, I've got it!
Shuri! T'Challa!
CRASH
BOOM
I've got you!

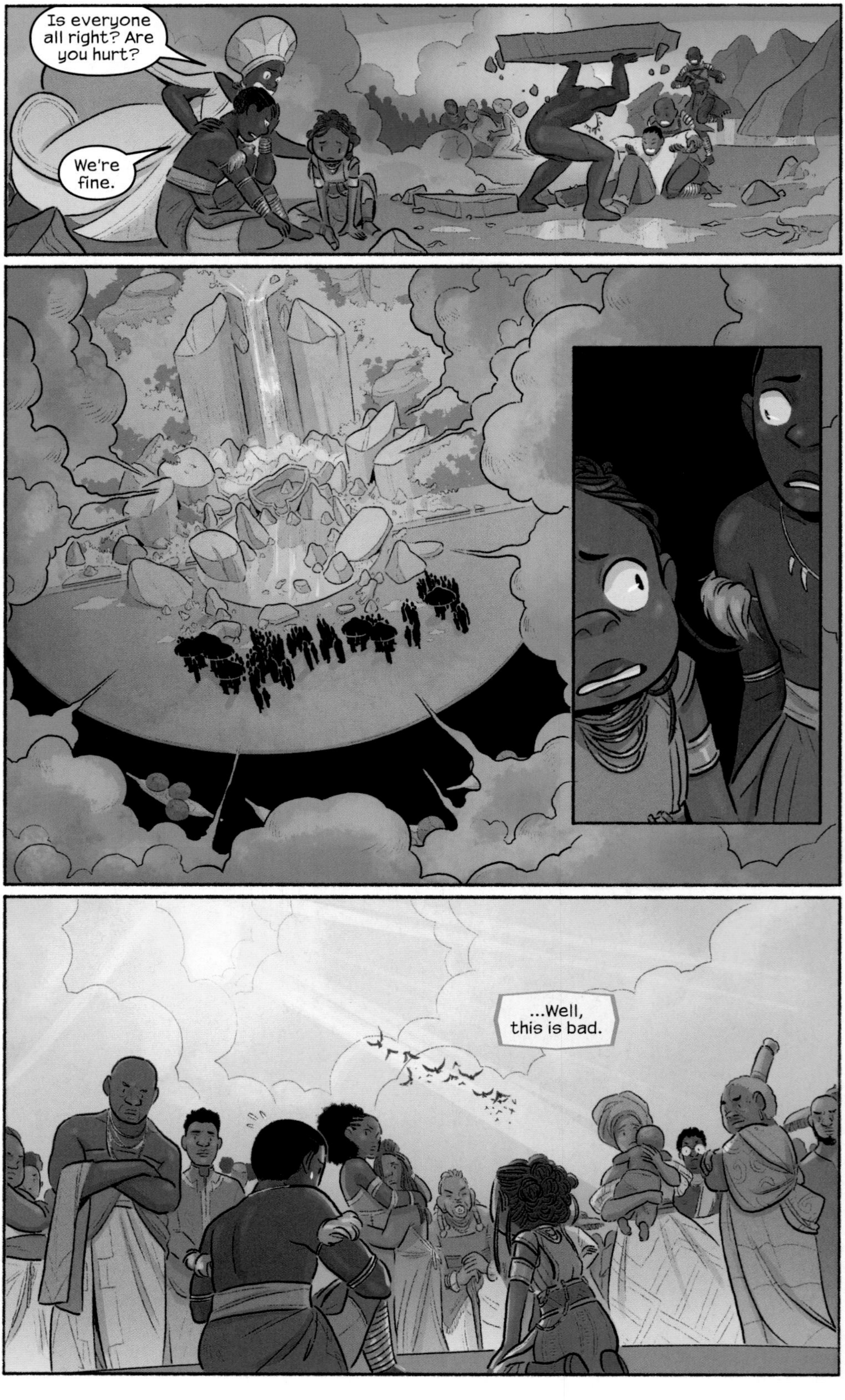
Is everyone all right? Are you hurt?
We're fine.
...Well, this is bad.

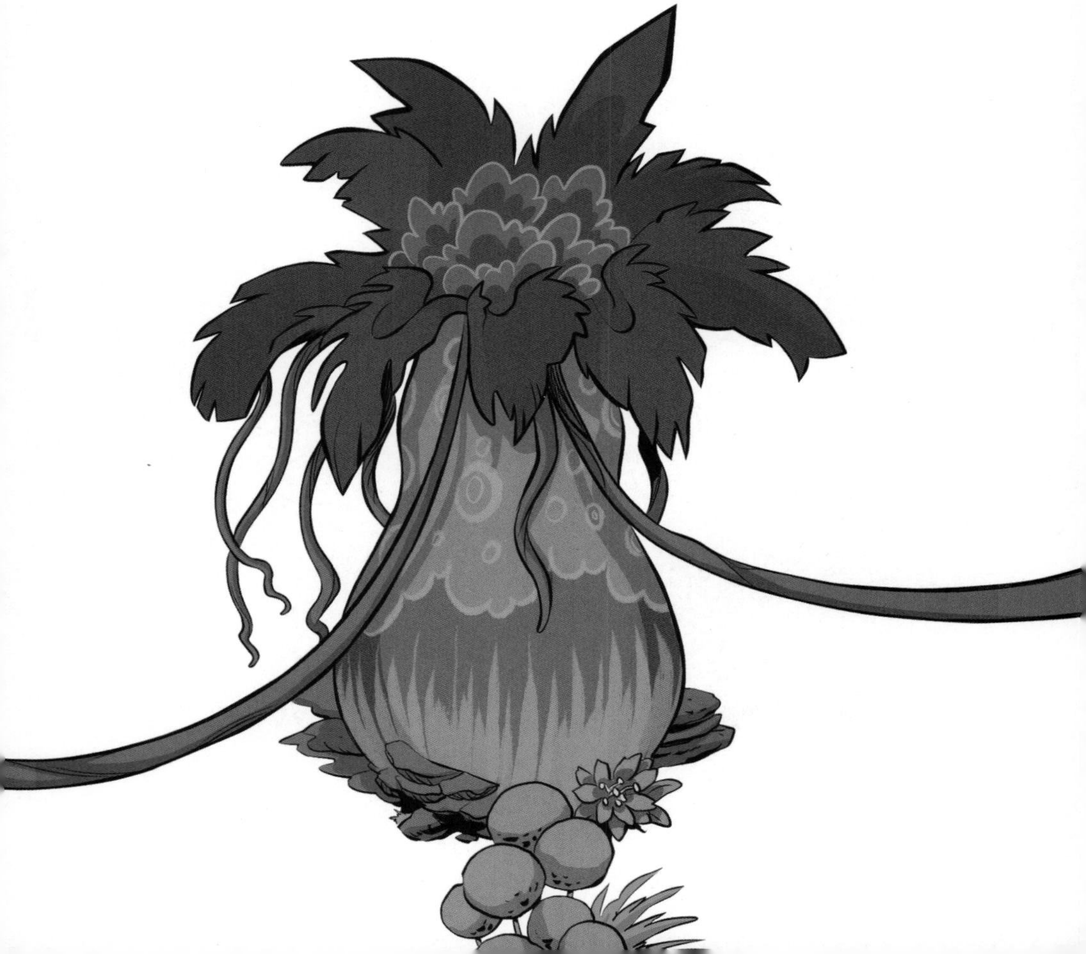

ROSEANNE A. BROWN was born in Kumasi, Ghana, and immigrated to the wild jungles of central Maryland as a child. She graduated from the University of Maryland with a bachelor's degree in journalism and was also a teaching assistant for the school's Jiménez-Porter Writers' House program. Her debut novel, *A Song of Wraiths and Ruin*, was an instant *New York Times* bestseller, a BuzzFeed Best YA Book of the Year, and a *Boston Globe* Best Book of the Year, among other accolades. Her middle-grade debut, *Serwa Boateng's Guide to Vampire Hunting*, will be out in Fall 2022 with Rick Riordan Presents.

DIKA ARAÚJO is a Brazilian comic artist and freelance illustrator based in Sâo Paulo. Her comic book work has appeared in several Brazilian indie anthologies, one of which (*Amor em Quadrinhos*) was nominated for an Angoulême International Comics Award in 2018. She has also worked as a character and prop designer, as well as a concept artist for Brazilian animated series, such as *Oswaldo* (Cartoon Network) and *Anittinha's Club* (Gloob).

NATACHA BUSTOS is a Spanish comic book artist who drew the story "Going Nowhere," written by Brandan Montclare, for DC/Vertigo's *Strange Sports Stories*. Bustos then made her Marvel Comics debut on Spider-Woman before reteaming with Montclare and cowriter Amy Reeder on the inaugural run of *Moon Girl and Devil Dinosaur*, winner of a Glyph Award for Best Female Character in 2016. In 2020, she drew the *Buffy the Vampire Slayer: Willow* miniseries (BOOM! Studios) and became part of Marvel's Stormbreakers artist program, dedicated to spotlighting the next generation of elite artists.

CLAUDIA AGUIRRE is a Mexican, Lesbian comic book artist and writer, cofounder of Boudika Comics, GLAAD Award Nominee, and Will Eisner Award nominee. Her comic works include: Marvel's *Voices*, *Lost on Planet Earth* (ComiXology Originals), *Hotel Dare* (BOOM! Studios), *Firebrand* (Legendary Comics), *Morning in America* (OniPress), and *Kim&Kim* (Black Mask Studios).

CHECK OUT A SNEAK PEEK OF

A BLACK PANTHER NOVEL

WRITTEN BY
NIC STONE

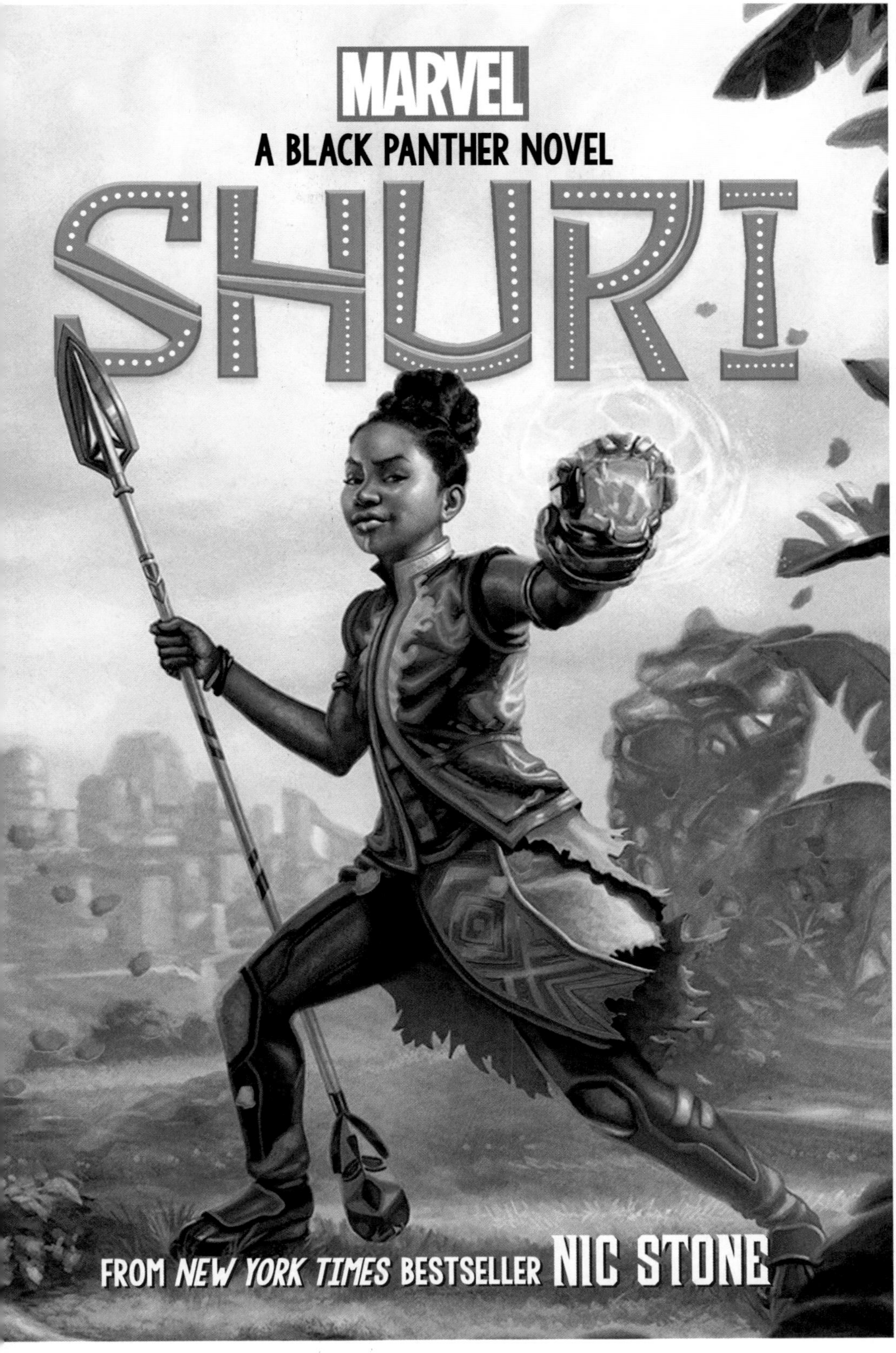
MARVEL
A BLACK PANTHER NOVEL
SHURI
FROM NEW YORK TIMES BESTSELLER NIC STONE

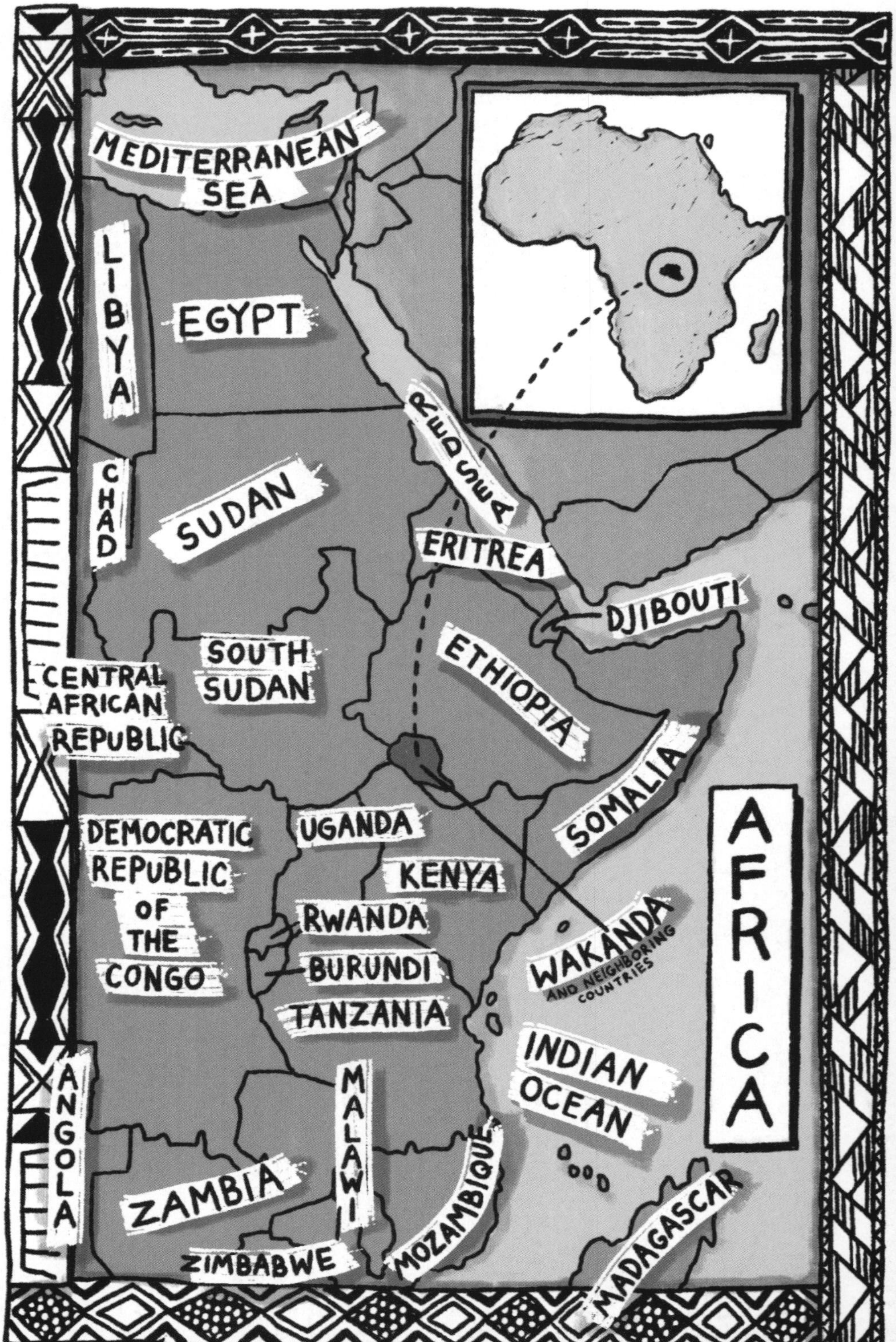
MEDITERRANEAN SEA
LIBYA
EGYPT
RED SEA
CHAD
SUDAN
ERITREA
DJIBOUTI
SOUTH SUDAN
ETHIOPIA
CENTRAL AFRICAN REPUBLIC
SOMALIA
AFRICA
DEMOCRATIC REPUBLIC OF THE CONGO
UGANDA
KENYA
RWANDA
BURUNDI
TANZANIA
WAKANDA
AND NEIGHBORING COUNTRIES
INDIAN OCEAN
ANGOLA
MALAWI
ZAMBIA
MOZAMBIQUE
ZIMBABWE
MADAGASCAR

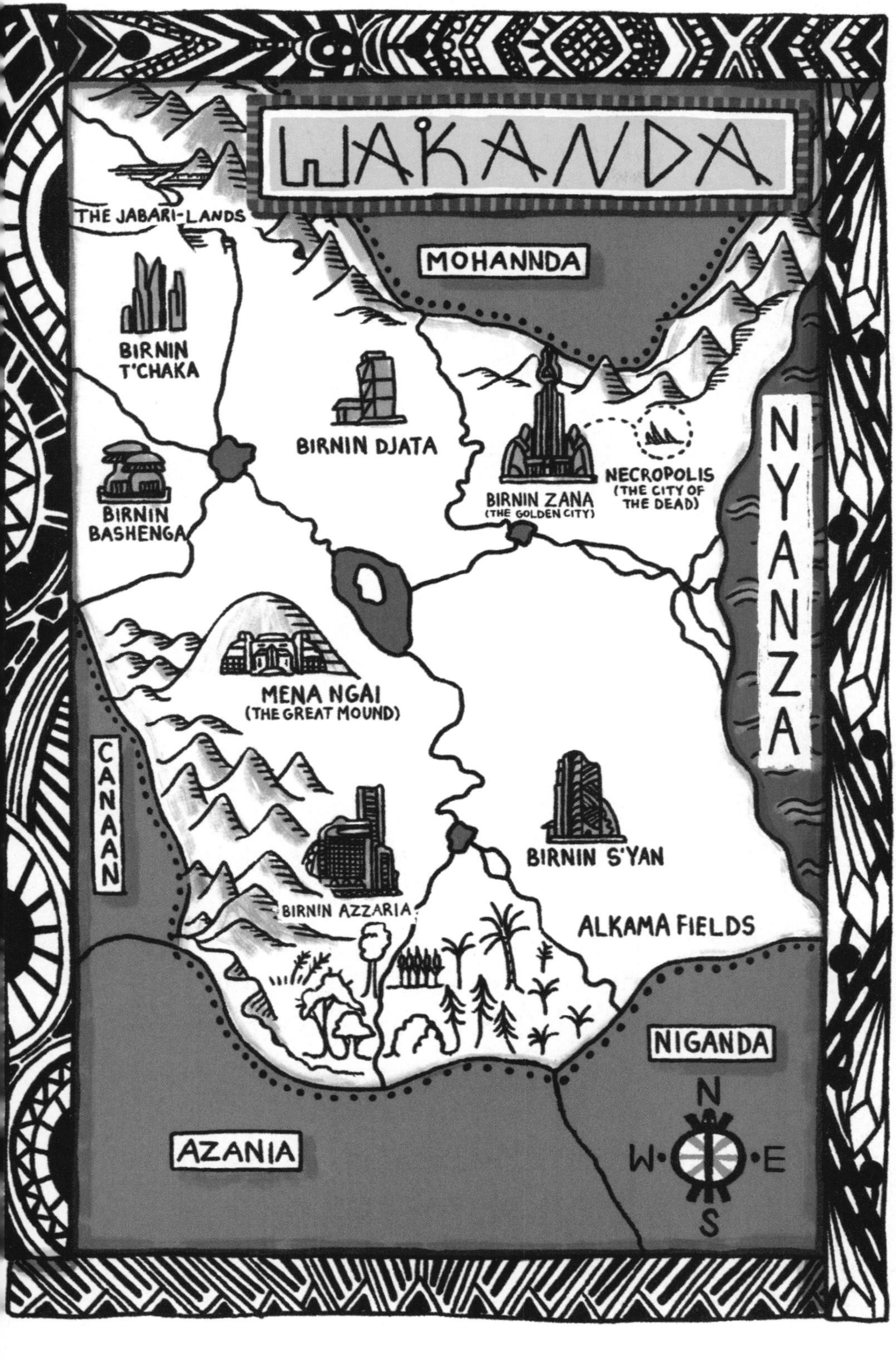
WAKANDA
THE JABARI-LANDS
MOHANNDA
BIRNIN T'CHAKA
BIRNIN DJATA
BIRNIN BASHENGA
BIRNIN ZANA (THE GOLDEN CITY)
NECROPOLIS (THE CITY OF THE DEAD)
NYANZA
MENA NGAI (THE GREAT MOUND)
CANAAN
BIRNIN S'YAN
BIRNIN AZZARIA
ALKAMA FIELDS
NIGANDA
AZANIA
N
W
E
S

PROLOGUE

She didn't know she'd have to fight.

"Who are you?" she asks, a feeble effort to keep him talking, though she has no idea what that will accomplish. Perhaps her trio of former Dogs of War will happen to turn the corner at just the right moment to come to her rescue . . .

◇◇◇

In fact, if you told her a *fight* would be waiting for her the first time she left Wakanda, she'd roll her dark eyes and wave you off like a conspiracy theory (which has no foundation in science).

"Who I am is of no consequence, Princess. The only thing that truly matters is what I plan to do . . ."

Not that she'd ever admit it aloud, but she's not even sure she *can* fight. Thanks to Mother, she hasn't truly trained in years. She was still a single digit in age the last time she made a fist.

"And what's that?" Shuri carefully, clandestinely shifts her feet into a fighting stance. Because she has a hunch about what his response will be.

Because fight she will.

"Well, to start, I intend to prevent your return to your beloved homeland."

For herself. Her life.

Her future.

For her people. For *their* future.

She will go out of her way. She will risk it all.

Her very existence.

The princess will *fight*.

For Wakanda.

And with that, his hand shoots out quick as a flash, reaching for Shuri's throat . . .

MISSION LOG

THERE IS SOMETHING FISHY GOING ON.
One week ago, my dear brother stormed my lab *begging* me to make him a new Panther Habit. "This one is too restrictive," he said, holding up the form-fitting catsuit he currently wears as our nation's ruler and protector, the Black Panther. "It hasn't been updated since Baba wore it. Can you *please* make me a new one? And fast?"

I could not have been more excited. I would never tell *him* because it would go right to his watermelon head, but I quite enjoy when T'Challa requests my assistance. Our father died when I was very young, but I think he'd be proud to see his only daughter doing her part to keep our nation safe and secure.

And anyway: The current habit *does* make T'Challa's butt look funny.

I scoured the markets for a . . . *stretchier* fabric. Something with an easy-to-manipulate molecular structure that would bond well with my favorite substance and our nation's most valuable resource: Vibranium. In theory, the correct composition will allow T'Challa to kick high and flip fast, but also absorb kinetic energy from any hits he takes, gather it in the palms of his gloves, and shoot it out as sonic blasts (*FWOOM FWOOM*) that will knock opponents right out of their shoes.

Except nothing is working. *Stretchier* apparently means thinner, and none of the existing fabrics I've tried can handle the optimal amount of Vibranium. I've managed to merge two of the trial fabrics into something new—and sufficiently stretchy—but even this hybrid material can only withstand 73 percent of the total volume of the magic metal in the previous habit. This is fine in terms of shock absorption and turning his hands into cannons, but the 17 percent decrease in bodily protection . . . well, I doubt big bro would be okay with punches and kicks hurting *more*.

My original idea was to distill the heart-shaped herb down to its strength-enhancing, speed-increasing, agility-augmenting essence, and infuse it into the fabric. That way, the longer the material is against T'Challa's skin and he's breathing through the mask, the more powerful and panther-like he would be.

However, the distillation process has proved more challenging than I anticipated.

In the first trial, I created a powder and then attempted to work it into the fabric by kneading. Seemed promising at first, but the moment I stretched it out, a puff of the powder filled the air. I inhaled it and . . . fainted. (Apparently those rumors about the herb taking out the unworthy are true. Bast forbid someone *not* of royal blood catches a whiff.

Also, the powder leaves a dusty film on the skin that makes one's skin appear in dire need of moisturization. And there's no way T'Challa would be okay with looking ashy once the suit retracts.)

In trial two, I tried a vapor. Which might've worked had I not put my head over the flask to check it and fainted again.

Trial three? A gel encased in patches as a suit lining. Thought I'd nailed it with this one . . . But then I tried to pull the piece of test fabric from my arm, and let me tell you: Band-Aid adhesive doesn't have a THING on Vibranium gel patches. *OUCH*.

Fourth and current trial *seemed* a step in the right direction: I lined the fabric with tiny liquid-filled bulbs that would break when hit, delivering small amounts of Heart-Shaped essence to the skin at the point of impact.

And it *does* work—I wrapped a piece around the midsection of a mannequin and gave it a good kick. The liquid *does* release at the point of impact, and *will* coat the skin (maybe even enhancing cell regeneration and creating a speed-healing effect that would prevent pain and bruising? Must test this later . . . In fact, there's a good bit I could test later. Which has me wondering if anyone has ever *studied* the herb before).

But it makes my entire lab reek of rotten fish.

And I just used my last herb bulb.

Frosting on the cake? I have a dead-line now. T'Challa just *appeared* in my lab in holographic form—perks of being able to override any and all security protocols, I suppose—to tell me that he needs the new habit by this Friday. That's five days hence.

Guessing he wants it for our ritual Challenge Day. Which would make sense. There's no telling who will come forward to face off against T'Challa for the throne and mantle of Black Panther, and though T'Challa is *virtually unbeatable*, as he likes to claim, an updated suit would certainly be to his advantage.

Come to think of it, our uncle S'Yan—who

stepped in to fill the role of Black Panther after Baba's death—was wearing the current habit when T'Challa challenged *him* four years ago.

And T'Challa obviously won.

No wonder he wants to be rid of the thing.

Back to the drawing board, I guess.

Wakanda forever.

Photo by Rachel Moron

NIC STONE is the *New York Times* bestselling author of the novels *Dear Martin* and *Odd One Out*. She was born and raised in a suburb of Atlanta, Georgia, and the only thing she loves more than an adventure is a good story about one. After graduating from Spelman College, she worked extensively in teen mentoring and lived in Israel for a few years before returning to the United States to write full-time. Having grown up with a wide range of cultures, religions, and backgrounds, she strives to bring diverse voices and stories into her work. Learn more at nicstone.info.

THERE'S MORE MARVEL TO EXPLORE!

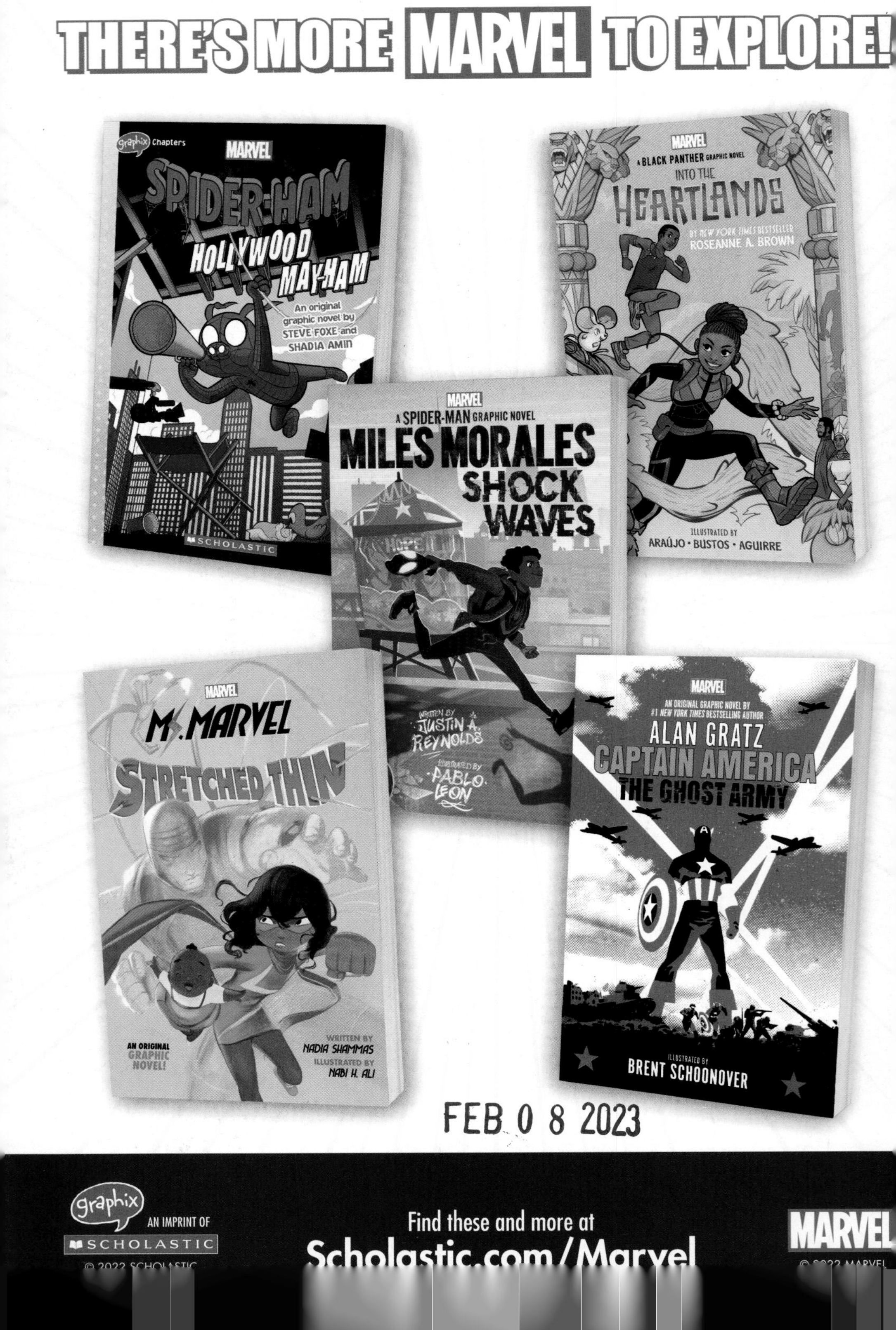
graphix Chapters
MARVEL
SPIDER-HAM
HOLLYWOOD MAY-HAM
An original graphic novel by STEVE FOXE and SHADIA AMIN
SCHOLASTIC
MARVEL
A BLACK PANTHER GRAPHIC NOVEL
INTO THE HEARTLANDS
BY NEW YORK TIMES BESTSELLER ROSEANNE A. BROWN
ILLUSTRATED BY
ARAÚJO • BUSTOS • AGUIRRE
MARVEL
A SPIDER-MAN GRAPHIC NOVEL
MILES MORALES
SHOCK WAVES
WRITTEN BY JUSTIN A. REYNOLDS
ILLUSTRATED BY PABLO LEON
MARVEL
MS. MARVEL
STRETCHED THIN
AN ORIGINAL GRAPHIC NOVEL!
WRITTEN BY NADIA SHAMMAS
ILLUSTRATED BY NABI H. ALI
MARVEL
AN ORIGINAL GRAPHIC NOVEL BY #1 NEW YORK TIMES BESTSELLING AUTHOR
ALAN GRATZ
CAPTAIN AMERICA
THE GHOST ARMY
ILLUSTRATED BY
BRENT SCHOONOVER

graphix AN IMPRINT OF SCHOLASTIC

Find these and more at
Scholastic.com/Marvel

MARVEL